KILLING GROUND

Douglas Reeman joined the Navy in 1941, where he was twice mentioned in dispatches. He did convoy duty in the Arctic and the North Sea, and later served in motor torpedo boats. As he says, 'I am always asked to account for the perennial appeal of the sea story, and its enduring interest for people of so many nationalities and cultures. It would seem that the eternal triangle of man, ship and ocean, particularly under the stress of war, produces the best qualities of courage and compassion, irrespective of the rights and wrongs of the conflict. The sea has no understanding of righteous or unjust causes. It is the common enemy respected by all who serve on it, ignored at their peril.'

Apart from the many novels he has written under his own name, he has also written more than twenty historical novels featuring Richard and Adam Bolitho, under the pseudonym of Alexander Kent.

KILLING GROUND
DOUGLAS REEMAN

arrow books

Published in the United Kingdom by Arrow Books in 2007

5 7 9 10 8 6 4

First published in the United Kingdom in 1991 by William Heinemann
First published in paperback in 1992 by Pan Books

Arrow Books
The Random House Group Limited
20 Vauxhall Bridge Road, London, SW1V 2SA

Addresses for companies within The Random House Group Limited can be
found at: www.randomhouse.co.uk/offices.htm

Random House Group Limited Reg. No. 954009

www.rbooks.co.uk

A CIP catalogue record for this book
is available from the British Library

The Random House Group Limited supports The Forest Stewardship
Council (FSC), the leading international forest certification organisation.
All our titles that are printed on Greenpeace approved FSC certified paper
carry the FSC logo. Our paper procurement policy can be found at:
www.rbooks.co.uk/environment

Mixed Sources
Product group from well-managed
forests and other controlled sources
www.fsc.org Cert no. TT-COC-2139
© 1996 Forest Stewardship Council

ISBN 9780099502333

Printed in the UK by CPI Cox & Wyman, Reading, RG1 8EX

**For my Kim —
together we found love**

Contents

Prologue

Dawn seemed slow to appear, reluctant, even, to lay bare the great ocean, which for once lacked its usual boisterous hostility. But there had been fog overnight which had finally dispersed, and the sea, which lifted and dipped in a powerful swell, was unbroken but for an occasional feather of spray. The sky was the colour of slate and only a feeble light betrayed the presence of another morning, touching the crests with a metallic sheen, but leaving the troughs in darkness like banks of molten black glass. Deserted, an empty treacherous place; but that was a lie. For, like jungle or desert, creatures moved here to seek cover from danger, to survive the ever-present hunters.

As the light tried to feel its way through the slow-moving clouds a few birds showed themselves, circling above the sea's face, or riding like broken garlands on the steep-sided troughs. To them the sea held no mystery, and they knew that the rugged coast of Ireland was barely a hundred miles away.

A deepwater fisherman, had there been one, or some wretched survivor on a raft or in a drifting lifeboat might have sensed it. The slight throbbing tremor beneath the waves — a sensation rather than a sound, which could make even a dying man start with terror. But there was no one, and forty metres beneath the surface the submarine moved slowly and warily as if to follow the line on the chart where her captain leaned on the table. His pale eyes were very still, his ears taking in every sound around him while he waited; the hunter again from the instant the alarm bells had ripped through the boat and brought him from a restless sleep to instant readiness.

He could feel his men watching him, as if he had actually turned to stare at them individually. Faces he had come to know under every possible condition, once so bright and eager but now blanched with the pallor of prison, their gestures the tired, jerky movements of old men. Like the boat, worn out with the weeks and months at sea. The stink of it: of diesel and cabbage water, of damp, dirty clothing which no longer defied the cold, of despair.

He glanced at the clock, resting his eyes in the dimmed orange glow. Two torpedoes only remained after that last attack on the convoy, which had almost ended in disaster. Some of his men would be thinking, *Why now? What does it matter? We are going home.* It was like hearing their combined voices pleading as one.

But it did matter. It had to. The hydrophone operator had reported a faint beat of engines. A large vessel, perhaps in difficulties. If it was anyone else he might have questioned it, disregarded it. But the seaman had been with him from the beginning in this command. He was never mistaken, and thousands of tons of shipping scattered the depths of the Western Ocean to vouch for his accuracy. The captain smiled but it remained hidden. The others were probably hating him for his skills now, when before they had blessed him for saving their lives. *The ears of the predator.*

He signalled to his engineer officer, who waited by his panel with its dials and tiny glowing lights, and without waiting for an acknowledgement made his way to the periscope well. Every step brought an ache to his bones. He felt stiff, dirty, above all exhausted. He thrust it from his thoughts as the air began to pound into the saddle tanks and the depth gauges came to life. What did he really feel? Perhaps nothing any more. The silent pictures in the periscope lens, explosions, burning ships and men – they no longer reached him.

To return to base was something different. There he might drink too much or forget too little.

He started as someone laughed. A young, careless sound. That was 'Moses', the nickname used in every U-Boat for the youngest member of the crew. The captain turned his eyes to the gauges as they steadied at fourteen metres. It was the boy's first voyage. Now his relief was pushing the nightmares into the darkness. He was lucky. For some reason the captain thought of his young brother, but saw him only as the round-faced student with his cap set at a jaunty angle, enjoying life, but sometimes being too serious, too outspoken about matters he did not understand. They had put him in the army despite his glasses and poor eyesight. Now he lay with two million others on the Eastern Front.

He tried not to grit his teeth. *I must not think about it.* For here, in the Atlantic, there was always danger; it waited like an assassin for the unwary, the one who forgot the need for vigilance just for a moment. He jerked his hand again and the forward periscope slid slowly from its well, while he crouched almost on his knees to follow it to the surface – his white cap, the symbol of a U-Boat commander, stained and greasy from a hundred encounters with deckhead pipes and unyielding metal, was pushed to the back of his head, although he never recalled doing it.

Slowly, so slowly now. The lens was nearing the surface, and he saw the first hint of grey. He tightened his grip on the twin handles as he had countless times, his mind quite steady, his heart beating normally. He could sense the unemployed men watching him still. But they were and must be like the boat itself – part of the weapon, an extension to his own eye and brain.

He licked his upper lip, feeling the stubble, and watched the sea's face begin to reveal itself. He switched the periscope to full power and turned it in a full circle before returning to the given bearing. *Empty.* No ships, no prowling flying-boats or bombers.

He blinked as the periscope misted over with spray, as if by doing so he would clear it. There was one patch of silver sunlight, which touched his eyes and made them the colour of the Atlantic.

And there it was. Drifting into the lens, then pausing in the crosswires as if snared in a web, while he followed the target and the details were fed into the machine behind him. The periscope dipped down again and he made himself stand upright, straddle-legged, his features impassive as he scraped his mind for any missing factor. A big merchantman, possibly a cargo-liner before the war; but why no escort? A ship that size – he glanced up as the lights blinked on to tell him that both torpedoes were ready to fire.

He almost laughed, but knew that if he did he might not be able to stop. A blind commander could not miss. What must they be thinking of?

The men closest to him saw his face and felt more at ease. *Get rid of those damned fish, then take us home.*

He gestured to the periscope operator and crouched down to take a final look. Nothing had moved. The range, bearing, even the feeble light were as before.

He gave his order and felt the periscope buck in his grip as first one, then the other remaining torpedo leaped from its tube.

Then he stared with chilled disbelief as a second ship appeared from beyond the barely moving target. The other vessel must have been lying hidden on the liner's opposite side, her engines momentarily stopped. Now with a bow-wave building up from her sharp stem like a huge moustache, she appeared to pivot around her consort's bows until she was pointing directly at the periscope. He had been too long in U-Boats not to recognise those rakish lines. She was a destroyer.

There was only one explosion. The torpedo struck the destroyer somewhere forward even as she completed her turn. The second one must have missed or run deep out of control. It was not the first time that had happened. A few of his men began to cheer as the explosion boomed against the hull, but the sound ended instantly as he swung towards them and ordered a crash dive.

He turned the periscope just briefly even as the water began to thunder into the tanks, then flung one arm to his face as if to protect it. Framed in the lens were a pair of racing propellers, as the bomber made her careful dive towards the shadow beneath the surface.

The U-Boat's captain was twenty-seven years old. On this bleak dawn he and his crew had just twelve seconds to live.

But this was the Western Ocean. The killing ground.

PART ONE

1942

I

No Reprieve

Any naval dockyard in the midst of a war was a confusing place for a stranger, and Rosyth, cringing to a blustery March wind, was no exception.

Every dock, basin and wharf seemed to be filled: ships being repaired, others so damaged by mine or bomb that they were only useful for their armament or fittings, all of which were in short supply.

Sub-Lieutenant Richard Ayres paused to stare down into one such basin at an elderly escort vessel, or what was left of it. She had once been a living ship, but now she was gutted down to and beyond the waterline. In the hard light Ayres could still see the blistered paintwork where men had once lived and hoped. From all the damage, it was a marvel anyone had still been alive to get her home.

Black shadows swayed and dipped over the battered hulk as gaunt cranes lifted pieces to be saved, and dropped the rest in rusty piles on the dockside. It was as if *they* were doing the destroying, he thought, like untidy prehistoric monsters with an abandoned carcass.

He turned up the collar of his blue raincoat and shivered in the biting wind which came down from the north-west to change the face of the Forth into a miniature sea of white horses.

A dismal place to many perhaps, but to Sub-Lieutenant Ayres, who was nineteen years old and about to join his first ship, as an officer anyway, it was like the culmination of a dream he had once not dared to hope for.

His only time at sea had been spent in a tired, over-worked patrol-vessel named *Sanderling*, for the compulsory three months all officer candidates had to complete before being handed over to HMS *King Alfred*. There, youthful hopefuls were expected to be turned into officers in a further crammed three months, before being dropped right into it and packed off to war. Except that the poor little *Sanderling*, with her solitary four-inch gun and a few anti-aircraft weapons, had been worked so hard she had spent much of Ayres's allotted time either having a boiler-clean or lying at a buoy, while harassed dock-yard men tried to find what had broken down this time.

Ayres shivered again. He had been two days getting here from the south of England. Trains that never arrived, another held up for hours in an air-raid – none of it helped.

He turned his back on the old ship and looked at the others looming from their moorings or peeping over the edge of a dock or wharf. Every kind, from powerful cruisers to the minesweeping trawlers which had once fished in these waters for herring and cod.

A coat of grey or dazzle-paint changed anything into a man-of-war; just as a building which had once been a swimming bath and pleasure centre in Hove had become a training depot where officers were manufactured overnight.

Boots grated on stone and he saw a tall chief petty officer in belt and gaiters pausing to stare at him as if unsure whether or not he should bother.

'Can I 'elp?' He cleared his throat and in those few seconds he took in all that there was to see. A brand-new cap and raincoat, the neat little suitcase; most of all, Ayres's pleasant open features. He added, 'Sir?'

Ayres produced his piece of paper. You never moved in the Navy without that. It had been almost the first lesson he had learned while he had been groping his way towards his goal.

'I'm joining the *Gladiator*, Chief.' He too was studying the other man. Old; probably retired when the war had erupted across Europe and their world had changed out of all recognition.

Gladiator. Just the name seemed to roll off his tongue like something familiar. Special.

The chief petty officer glanced at him again. 'You're Mr

Ayres, then. They was expectin' you yesterday.' It sounded like an accusation.

Ayres flushed, something he still did far too easily. 'Yes, but – she was supposed to be at Leith, and when I got there – '

The other man nodded. 'Leith is full. They moved your ship here as soon as 'er overhaul was done.' He made up his mind. 'I'll call 'er up and get a boat sent over. She's out there with another of 'er class.' He looked away. ''Bout the only two of 'em left now, I shouldn't wonder.'

As he walked towards a little hut Ayres had not noticed before, he relented and stood facing the new officer, his white webbing gaiters squeaking on his boots. Why should it matter to this young subbie anyway? Nice as pie at the moment. But a little bit of gold on the sleeve, even a wavy stripe, could change a man; and not for the better. He said, 'My son served in one, the *Glowworm*, durin' the Norwegian foul-up. They're fine ships – never mind me.'

Ayres stared at him. It was like feeling a cold hand on the shoulder. Everyone had heard of the *Glowworm*. She had gone down with her guns blazing, and even then she had managed to ram the German heavy cruiser *Hipper*. It was like one of the stories he had read as a boy. Destroyers, greyhounds of the ocean, 'eyes of the fleet' as they had always been romantically described.

He heard himself ask, 'Did he – I mean, your son – '

The chief petty officer glared at the sparking rivet gun which spluttered from the nearby cruiser like a maniac signal. 'No. He's down there with 'er.' Then he was gone.

Ayres picked up his case and walked over to stand by his other belongings, thinking about his new ship. A destroyer. He had been more afraid of getting sent to a big ship, or of going to a clapped-out veteran like *Sanderling*. All her officers had been regulars, and like the chief petty officer had probably been on the beach until they were needed to fill the growing gaps in men and ships. When he thought of *Glowworm* and her fate he was surprised and relieved that he still felt the same excitement.

It was almost noon by the time the destroyer's motor boat coughed alongside the jetty and her coxswain, a massive Scot in a shining oilskin, dashed up the stone stairs and began to gather up Ayres's luggage with a few quick comments.

'Mr Ayres?' He did not wait for an answer. 'They were expecting you forenoon yesterday, sir.'

'I know. I was sent to the wrong place.'

The boat's coxswain did not hear. 'The Cap'n don't like to be kept waitin', sir.' He waited for him to clamber down into the cockpit and yelled, 'Shove off, Nobby! I'm ready for ma tot!'

The bowman grinned and vanished beyond the canopy with the bowline and in seconds they were scudding across the lively white crests. Ayres looked astern and saw the elderly chief petty officer in his belt and gaiters watching him from the door of his little hut. Over the widening gap of frothing water he suddenly touched his cap in salute, and for some reason which Ayres was too young to understand, he was deeply moved. Ayres returned the salute and realised that it was the first mark of respect the old CPO had offered him.

That was something else you had to get used to. The sailors who went out of their way to throw up a salute, especially if you had your hands or arms full of things, and the others who would enter a shop if necessary to avoid it.

The coxswain studied him warily. 'First time in destroyers, sir?'

Ayres shaded his eyes to stare at the impressive spread of the Forth Bridge which dwarfed all the ships which lay near it, or passed beneath the great span of angled iron which linked up with Queensferry in the south. If ever a single achievement proclaimed how man had tamed this part of Scotland, this bridge must be it.

The Germans had tried to destroy it, without success; in fact it was the first target on the British mainland to be bombed by the unstoppable Luftwaffe. There had been indignation and anger at the ease with which it had been done. Ayres doubted if anyone would even comment if it happened today. Too many battles lost, too many men and ships gone forever.

He started as he realised what the coxswain had asked. 'In *destroyers*, yes.'

The coxswain nodded, and when Ayres looked away he winked to his bowman. Green as grass. Just like all the others.

But for the bitter wind and the spray which leaped occasionally over the little boat's stem, it was a perfect day, a far cry from the time when Ayres had joined the little *Sanderling* as she lay in a filthy basin at Chatham Dockyard. Nowhere to sling his hammock, and not much of a welcome from the seamen who were to be his messmates for so short a time. He knew he had been tested to the full. The lower deck's usual brutal humour, reserved for any would-be officer; the foul language and jokes which made him blush; taunts because of his 'posh accent'; contempt for an amateur – he took it all, and more.

Until that air attack on a ten-knot convoy up the East Coast. The scream of bombs and towering columns of spray and smoke. The old merchant ships keeping formation no matter what, with the minefield on one side of them and shallow water on the other. No room for manoeuvre, and if a ship was badly hit she was ordered to beach herself and keep the main channel open. There were mastheads a-plenty along that coast to show how many had been sunk in the process.

Ayres had been passing shells from the ready-use ammunition locker as fast as he could to the old four-inch gun while *Sanderling* and the mixed bag of escorts kept up a rapid fire on the diving bombers until the sky was pockmarked with shell-bursts, the filth of war.

A bomb had fallen too close to the ship's side and she had heeled over as the captain swung away from the explosion. Ayres had lost his footing and sprawled on the wet steel plates, his head striking a stanchion so hard that he almost lost consciousness.

A burly seaman, one of his worse tormentors on the messdeck, had leaped down to pull him from danger, and had shouted above the clatter of Oerlikons and the ceaseless beat of pom-poms, 'All right, Dick lad? One 'and fer th' King an' one fer yerself – just you remember that!' He had added awkwardly, 'See me at tot-time. That'll take your fuckin' 'eadache away!'

But that one act of kindness had changed everything for Ayres.

He caught his breath as he gripped the top of the canopy with both hands. There she was, lying at a buoy alongside her twin, her fresh dazzle-paint gleaming in the arctic sunshine so that she seemed to glow. She was exactly what Ayres had expected, had hoped for while he had studied the mysteries of gunnery and navigation, signals and square-bashing, all in a space of time which had gone by in a flash.

Gladiator, and he knew she was the nearest one by the pendant number *H-38* painted on below her forecastle, was every inch a destroyer, of the type built between the wars when the Royal Navy was paramount throughout the world, and the minds of planners still saw its role protecting the line-of-battle as in all other wars.

Dunkirk, Norway, Crete and the bloody campaigns in North Africa had changed all that.

'Our ship's over there, sir.'

'Yes.' It came out too sharply. 'Thank you.' But he did not want to share this meeting with anyone. He knew *Gladiator*'s statistics as well as his own. Three hundred and twenty-three feet long; built at Vickers-Armstrong at Barrow in 1936. Four four-point-seven guns; torpedo tubes; she even had radar in a sort of giant jam-pot above her business-like, open bridge. Two funnels gave her a rakish, dashing appearance – Ayres had got to know her silhouette at school, when *Gladiator* had been a part of the crack First Mediterranean Flotilla.

Ayres tried to look calm as the boat tore towards the accommodation ladder, where two sailors were already watching their rapid approach. Closer to it was possible to see the many dents and scars along her exposed side. What a story they could tell – coming alongside some stricken ship in convoy, possibly in pitch darkness, or taking shell splinters after an encounter with an enemy blockade-runner.

'Hook on, Nobby!' The boat churned to full astern and then idled to rest against the ladder despite the strong pull of the tide.

Men appeared to pick up Ayres's bags. Weathered, tired faces, people whom he would know, really know, given half a chance.

The coxswain grimaced. "Here comes Jimmy-th'-One, Nobby – watch out for flak!'

Ayres ran up the ladder and threw up a smart salute aft where a bright new ensign stood out stiffly from its staff between the ranks of depth-charges. A tall, unsmiling officer, his hands grasped behind his back, leaned over the guardrail and called, 'Wait for the mail-bag, Cox'n!'

The big man peered up at him from the pitching motor boat. 'Permission to draw ma tot, sir?'

'Later.' He turned to face Ayres like someone who had just dispensed with one pest and was about to deal with another.

'Ayres, right?'

'Come aboard to join, sir.'

Ayres felt the man run his eyes over him from cap to shoes. An impassive, strong face, dominated by a large beaked nose.

'You're adrift.'

'Adrift, sir?'

'The Commanding Officer will want to see you. Right away.'

'The Commanding Officer, sir?' He had only spoken to the little *Sanderling*'s captain once and that had probably been an accident.

The big nose trained round towards him like a gun. 'Do you always repeat everything said to you?' He glared at some seamen who were dragging a new coil of mooring wire across the quarterdeck and shouted, 'Watch that paintwork, you careless idiots!' He said in a controlled voice, 'My name is Marrack. I'm the first lieutenant around here.' Surprisingly he held out his hand and Ayres was further taken back by the two wavy stripes on his sleeve. A 'temporary gentleman', like himself.

Ayres smiled. 'Thank you, sir.'

'And don't call me sir, except in the line of duty.' He watched the men with the mooring wire and added, 'Number One will suffice.' He did not smile and Ayres guessed that, like the use of words, the smiles were strictly rationed. A strange man — what had Marrack done before the Navy, he wondered? In his late twenties at a guess, but he acted with the authority and experience of one much older.

As an afterthought Marrack said, 'You will share a cabin with our other sub. At the moment anyway. I shall give you a list of duties, watchkeeping and the like, within the hour. But now go and see the Old Man.' His tone sharpened as Ayres made to hurry off. 'Not that way! His quarters are down aft, in harbour, that is.' He glanced up at the box-like bridge. 'At sea he's always *there*.'

Then, without another glance, Marrack turned and strode along the iron deck towards the forecastle, pausing merely to glance up at the smoking galley funnel as if to sniff out the ingredients of the meal being served.

'This way, Mr Ayres.' A wiry petty officer steward was watching him from the door of the quartermaster's lobby beneath X-Gun. 'We was expectin' you yesterday.'

Ayres gave a tired grin. 'So I hear.' He saw that his bags had been taken from the deck. He stepped over a high coaming and entered the white-painted lobby with its stand of Lee-Enfield rifles and a leading seaman, who was obviously the chief quartermaster, reading a magazine which was spread over the deck log. He did not even glance up as Ayres followed the petty officer steward down a steep ladder.

The new smells rose to greet him. Fresh paint, oil, people.

He removed his raincoat and the steward took it and folded it expertly over his arm while running his eye critically over his new charge.

He said, 'I'm Vallance, sir. I'm in charge down aft, an' the Old Man is at the top of the list so to speak.' He saw Ayres smile. 'Sir?'

But Ayres shook his head 'Just a memory, um, Vallance.' He was still thinking of Vallance's description. *Down aft*. In *Sanderling* they had always referred to the officers as 'the pigs down aft'.

He paused and stared at the closed door with the small brass plate. *Captain*. Well, now he was one of the pigs!

Vallance watched his uncertainty. Ayres seemed like a nice young chap, as far as you could tell. He didn't even need a shave after two days on a bloody train. God, they'd be coming aboard in their prams if the war lasted much longer.

The bright new wavy stripe, the schoolboy haircut; Ayres's youth made Vallance suddenly depressed.

'A word, sir.' He watched, looking for any hint of arrogance. There was none. Encouraged by Ayres's obvious innocence, he added, 'Just be natural with the Old Man, sir. He don't like flannel, not from nobody, not even Captain (D).'

Ayres found himself nodding. Nothing was happening as they had told him it would. A chief petty officer who had at first not saluted him and then confided in him about his son lost at sea; a boat's coxswain who had asked him point-blank about his experience – even the First Lieutenant was not like those steely-eyed men in his magazine or in films about the war. And now Vallance was offering advice . . . or was he testing him to see if he was too weak to snap back at him?

But instinct made Ayres anxious, and he had to ask, 'What's he like?'

Vallance relaxed. A nice lad, not somebody to upset his wardroom.

'He's had a hard time, sir.' He looked above and around him. 'We've done some things between us – he's carried all of it. You can only handle so much . . . just be yerself, if you'll pardon the liberty.' He gave a slow grin. 'I'll save a nice bit of lunch for you.'

He watched Ayres's knuckles hesitate before rapping down on the door.

'Enter!'

Ayres turned to thank the steward but the passageway was quite empty. He swallowed hard and thrust open the door.

Unlike most wartime-built destroyers, *Gladiator*'s captain's quarters were almost spacious. They were situated right aft beneath the quarterdeck and divided into separate sleeping and day cabins. Even here there was a lingering tang of fresh paint, but the comfortable-looking armchairs and carpet still showed the wear and tear of too many Atlantic convoys when these same quarters had been used to accommodate survivors, wounded or otherwise, when the small sick-bay could no longer cope.

Beyond the bulkhead were the other officers' cabins, and of course, the wardroom. It was the one place they all met, to eat, to hold an occasional party, to wait to go on watch or for the hateful clang of alarm bells. Moving forward further still were the engine and boiler rooms, the ship's life-blood, which filled almost a third of the hull's capacity. Beyond them was the two-decked forecastle where the ship's company were crammed into their various messes, separated only by rate and department.

Seated at the desk in his day cabin, *Gladiator*'s commanding officer paused in writing a letter to look at the small old-fashioned coal fire which was kept burning in harbour. It made the place look lived in, or as the PO steward, Percy Vallance, would have it, 'more like 'ome'.

Lieutenant-Commander David Howard was twenty-seven years old, and, like his father and grandfather, had entered the Royal Navy as a young cadet. Nobody had ever discussed it; it had been the thing to do, taken for granted.

Apart from various training courses in larger warships, he

had spent most of his service in destroyers and could visualise nothing else. At the outbreak of war he had hastily taken command of an old V & W class destroyer from the Kaiser's war, and within no time had been involved in the first shattering defeat in France, and the bitterness of Dunkirk.

Now it seemed a million years ago, the war as different from those early days as Agincourt. Immediately after Dunkirk he was ordered to take his elderly V & W, *Winsby*, into the Battle of the Atlantic. He had been in the same fight ever since, and in command of *Gladiator* for eighteen months. That, too, felt like years.

He stood up suddenly, light-footed as a cat, and walked to one of the few pictures which hung in the day cabin: the place he could only dream about when he was at sea. His sea cabin on the bridge was little more than a steel cupboard with a narrow bunk and a telephone. When you hit the damp blankets, fully dressed if you had any sense left, you did not sleep; you just died. The place of escape, beyond the anxious eyes on the bridge; away from the heaving grey sea, the pathetic lines of rusty freighters and tankers following like sheep. He smiled bitterly. To the slaughter.

He reached out and straightened the picture of his first command. Relics from the Great War about which his father rarely spoke, but the V & Ws were excellent seaboats, and had a sort of jaunty confidence which more than made up for their outdated machinery and overcrowded quarters. Without them, this war might have been lost before it had really begun in earnest. *Winsby* had been a happy ship, although it was becoming harder to remember all the faces, most of whom had been regulars like himself.

He turned his head to glance through one of the polished scuttles towards the land, and considered how this ship rated now. Every time she entered harbour, for whatever reason, he lost more and more of his skilled hands. Officers too, for promotion or advanced courses to try and keep pace with the war's mounting ferocity. It took time to train new ones; and when you did they were taken too.

All ships were like that now. Bakers and postmen, clerks and errand-boys. Only half of the whole ship's company of one hundred and forty-five souls were old enough to draw their tot. It made you sweat when you found time to think about it.

He half-listened to the muted beat of a generator deep in the engine room and pictured the engineer officer, Lieutenant (E) Evan Price, who had been in this ship since before the outbreak of war. What would happen if they took *him*? The ship might fall apart. He smiled and groped for his pipe but it was still in the jacket slung carelessly on the back of a chair.

His was a young face, which might turn any woman's head; his dark unruly hair needed cutting badly, something else which Captain (D) would most certainly mention when next they met.

He stared hard at the glass scuttle, which was streaked with salt like frost, but saw only his reflection. Brown eyes, lines at the corners of his mouth, the haunted look which had not left his face since that last convoy from Newfoundland, and which this brief overhaul, at Leith and here, had failed to disperse.

Some captains would have gone straight ashore after a convoy like that. To hide in some hotel, to get drunk, to seek the company of some bored tart; anything. But here, in this little-used cabin, was his escape. Hot baths whenever he chose; eating alone; listening to music; pacing the cabin to go over it all again as if to punish himself in some way.

Forty ships had sailed from St John's on that terrible convoy. They had been attacked by a complete U-Boat pack when they had barely covered a third of the passage. When they had passed the Liverpool Bar there had been only thirteen left. He had seen it all before, but somehow that convoy had affected him more than anything. A big tanker, its cargo of high octane fuel so precious to this embattled country, had burned for three days, and her company with it. Another ship, loaded to the seams with armoured cars and tanks, had gone down in thirty seconds, her back broken by two torpedoes. It went on and on, as if there was no mercy left.

He walked back to the desk and patted his jacket for his pipe.

Muffled by the bulkhead the tannoy squawked, 'D'you hear there! Hands to dinner!' The quartermaster would add beneath his breath, 'Officers *to lunch*!'

He sat down again and began to fill his pipe, his eyes on the photograph of his father which he had given him when their world had fallen apart. Dressed in naval uniform, a young face with the same twinkle in his eyes. He had not wanted his son to have a recent picture. This had been taken before the famous Zeebrugge raid in 1918, when unknown to him the war had only seven months left to run its bloody course. He had lost an arm and an eye, and had been rejected by the service he had loved more than life itself. He still managed to joke about it. 'What about Nelson? *He* managed!' In angrier moments he had said, 'Anyway, I couldn't do much worse than the blockheads who're running things now!'

Howard held a match to his pipe and saw the smoke drifting up into the vents. His hand was quite steady, almost stiff, as if he was consciously holding it so, like his muscles when the alarms sounded; how would it be the next time?

He sighed. He had promised to join Spike Colvin, his fellow captain in their sister-ship *Ganymede* alongside, for a few drinks before the next orders arrived. Howard looked at his watch. They would soon know. Convoy escort. But surely not the Atlantic again, not yet . . . He stood up violently, angry with himself for admitting the weakness to himself.

He heard himself call, 'Enter!' and saw the door open to reveal an unfamiliar sub-lieutenant standing beyond the coaming.

'Come in – it's Ayres, isn't it?' He held out his hand. 'Might have had to sail without you.'

Ayres shifted his new cap from one fist to the other. 'I went to Leith, you see – '

Howard pointed to a comfortable chair. 'Take a pew, Sub. Drink?'

Ayres sat down, completely baffled by this unusual welcome. Howard was not a bit what he had anticipated. He seemed very relaxed, and far more youthful than expected.

'Perhaps a gin, sir. I'm not much of – '

Howard opened the cupboard and poured two glasses of gin. The new subbie was no drinker then. The Atlantic would change that.

'I've put you down to share your watches with the navigator. He's RNR, a good officer, so I expect I shall be losing him too very soon. Number One will fix you up with your action and defence stations, etc – have you met him yet?'

Ayres recalled the big nose, the faint air of disapproval. The first lieutenant behaved more like a regular, straight-laced officer than the captain, who, Ayres observed, was wearing an old jumper over his shirt, and a pair of grey flannel trousers. Ayres looked at the jacket on the nearby chair, the tarnished gold two-and-a-half stripes. His mind fastened on the small blue and white ribbon on the jacket's breast. The DSC. In destroyers you didn't get that for nothing.

'You've joined the ship during a bit of upheaval, Sub.' Howard leaned back in his chair and allowed the pipesmoke to curl above him. He saw Ayres hold back a choking cough as he swallowed some of the gin, and tried to contain his disappointment. His other sub-lieutenant had joined the ship just before the refit, transferred from Light Coastal Forces after his motor gunboat had been shelled and sunk off the Hook of Holland. A withdrawn, tense young man who seemed to regard the transfer as some kind of stigma. Even the gunnery officer, an RNVR lieutenant, had only been in *Gladiator* for four months, and the new midshipman, a youth with a permanent round-eyed look of wonderment, had arrived when they had been in Leith. He continued, 'A third of the company are pretty new – a lot of them came on board just before the last convoy.' His voice seemed to linger over the word. Burning ships, men being swept past and swallowed by the racing screws, their cries lost in the thunder of depth charges. *Don't stop. Don't look back. Close the ranks.* The convoy commodore's signals never ceased. Howard wondered what that fine old man had been thinking when his own ship had been torpedoed and left astern to die.

Ayres felt the gin burning his empty stomach. What had happened on that convoy, he wondered? He glanced round the cabin, so still, apart from an occasional movement when another ship churned past. It seemed so wrong to put a beautiful destroyer like *Gladiator* on escort work. His gaze fastened on the ship's crest, which hung above the desk. An uplifted, stabbing sword gripped by an armoured fist, the motto *Manu Forti* painted below it. Ayres had struggled through enough Latin at school to know it meant *With a Strong Hand*. Right for the destroyer, but not for the deadly boredom of convoy work.

Howard saw it clearly on the young officer's open features and said, 'In this ship we have no passengers, Sub. I'm telling you that right now so you can use every opportunity to learn from the more experienced members of the team. Pilot, with whom you'll be sharing watches, the First Lieutenant, and men like the cox'n, Bob Sweeney, and Mr Pym the Gunner (T) – they're all old destroyer hands who can teach you more in a dog-watch than six months in a classroom. If you have any problems, put them to Number One. He may seem a bit severe, but he was a barrister before he volunteered.' He forced a smile. He was getting nowhere. What did they teach them at the training depot? To die bravely? To be a bomb-happy survivor like the other subbie? 'He's a marvel with defaulters!' He put down his pipe and glanced at his empty glass. 'You'll feel new and awkward to begin with – everyone does. But remember this. You wear an officer's uniform now, and to all the other new hands you are just that. Someone to turn to, to hate if you like – but sometimes you have to come down on people like a ton of bricks. It's not enough to be popular.'

Ayres nodded. 'I wanted to be in destroyers, sir.'

Howard almost relented, but said, 'Keenness and courage go with the job – I have to take that for granted. But endurance and survival are what count in the end. Otherwise we are going to lose this war. Do you understand?'

Ayres swallowed hard. Nobody had ever said things like that to him. *Lose?* He felt confused, even betrayed, by the captain's blunt manner.

Howard watched his words hitting home. There might be no time later on. There never was.

He added, 'For the first time since the balloon went up, the enemy are sinking more ships than we can build.' He paused, counting seconds, trying not to remember Ayres's predecessor, his pathetic eagerness when he had stood on this same stained carpet. 'And the enemy are also building more submarines than we can sink, at present anyway. It is a brutal equation, but there it is.'

There was a shout from the deck above, the chugging vibration of a boat coming alongside. Marrack would deal with it. He could manage just about anything now.

Ayres said in a small voice, 'I'll not let you down, sir.'

'I hear you were in the *Sanderling*?'

'Yes, sir.'

Howard looked at him, his eyes in shadow from the hard

sunlight. 'You'll find out anyway, later on when their lordships feel moved to announce it. She was sunk last night. A mine.'

Ayres was on his feet without realising it, the faces swimming back like pictures in his mind. The sailor who had helped him after the air attack. The elderly captain on his open bridge, an unlit pipe always in his mouth.

'Any survivors, sir?'

Howard shook his head. 'She was apparently in pretty poor shape. No match for a mine.' He stood up and added angrily, 'It's murder, nothing less.'

He held out his hand, 'Sorry, Sub. But this is the only place I'm allowed to let off steam.' He grasped Ayres's hand. 'If you get really rattled, talk to me if you like.'

There was a tap at the door and the first lieutenant peered into the cabin, his sharp eyes flitting between them.

'I thought you should know, sir. The guardboat has just delivered the pouch.' He stepped over the coaming, his neat, shining hair almost touching the deckhead. 'Otherwise I'd not have troubled you.' He laid the worn leather pouch on the deck and studied it thoughtfully. 'Our orders.'

The door closed and Howard realised that the sub-lieutenant had gone. He sat down heavily and said, 'You'd better assemble the wardroom at stand-easy this afternoon.'

Marrack waited, watching Howard opening the packet and breaking the seal. He added, 'Just us, sir. Our chums alongside haven't drawn a ticket this time.' He saw the captain's hands hesitate on the open packet. *He doesn't want to know. He's like the rest of us.*

To break the spell he asked casually, 'What do you think of Ayres, sir?'

Howard looked at his hands. Still steady enough. 'He'll shape up, with a bit of help.'

He drew the papers into the light and felt his mouth go suddenly dry.

Marrack remarked, 'I hope they give us a rest from the Atlantic.'

Howard did not answer directly but stood up again, moving to a scuttle. There was cloud about. It came suddenly here.

He answered slowly, 'No, not the Western Ocean, Number One.'

He turned away from the mocking glass and faced him. Afterwards Marrack remembered his dark eyes as being quite still, like a man already dead. 'It's North Russia, I'm afraid.'

Marrack said, 'I see. Dicey.'

Howard wanted to cry out or laugh. *Dicey*. The understatement for all time.

Marrack had his hand on the door clip. 'When, sir?'

'Last mail ashore tomorrow forenoon. We get under weigh at thirteen-hundred. I'll tell you the rest when I've read through this lot.'

As the tall lieutenant turned to leave Howard said, 'Thanks, Number One. If I ever murder the admiral, which I may well do, I'd certainly like to have you on my side.'

Marrack shrugged. 'It's a living.' He almost smiled. 'Like this one.' Then he was gone.

Howard opened the cupboard and rummaged about for something stronger than gin.

He could already sense the change around him. It was not merely leaving these quarters and returning to the bridge, the stage of battle. Not this time. Secret orders or not, the whole ship knew, or soon would. It was the Navy's way. Like a family.

He swallowed some neat brandy and thought of Ayres. What a way to begin.

Petty Officer Vallance entered the cabin and began to lay the table for his captain's lunch.

He only looked up once from his plates and cutlery.

He said, 'We'll need all our warm gear then, sir?'

The rest was over.

2

Open Boat

Lieutenant Gordon Treherne, Royal Naval Reserve, *Gladiator*'s navigating officer, wiped his binoculars with a piece of tissue and slung them inside his duffle coat. Beneath the well-used coat he wore a sheepskin-lined jacket and a heavy roll-necked sweater which had once been white. But even without the layers of clothing Treherne made an imposing figure, one that would not have been out of place facing the Armada, or the French at Trafalgar. Beneath his blue, folded balaclava his hair was as black as his beard, his eyes, with deep crowsfeet on either side, as blue as any ocean. He licked his lips and tasted the raw salt and tugged the towel tighter around his neck. He had taken over the forenoon watch only minutes earlier, and the towel was already sodden.

He glanced around the swaying upper bridge, open to the elements, a place so familiar at any time of the day or night that he would instantly notice if anything was wrong or different. Lookouts, equally muffled against the cold, their glasses moving to cover their allotted arcs; the yeoman of signals, always an early bird, crouched with two of his young assistants, stabbing the air with a gloved hand to emphasise this or that as the steel deck rolled drunkenly as if to hurl them all down. A glance over one bridge wing, and he saw the nearest Oerlikon gunner standing by his weapon, trying to stamp his booted feet quietly so as not to annoy anyone. Treherne's own new assistant, Sub-Lieutenant Ayres, was bending over the chart table, his legs straddled while he peered at their course and checked the pencilled figures beneath the shaded light.

Treherne smiled grimly. Eight-ten a.m., another forenoon watch, and the sea was only just beginning to show itself. Great sliding banks of grey glass patterned with salt and angry, breaking crests. It had been like that ever since *Gladiator* had left the shelter of the land to head north-west leaving the Orkneys abeam in the darkness and pressing on for the Shetlands. And on, and on, all three-and-a-half days of it in this savage, turbulent ocean. It might have been barely bearable but for their two small consorts, Flower Class corvettes, *Cynara* and *Physalis*, which, like their numberless sisters, had been flung together to fight in that separate conflict becoming known as the Battle of the Atlantic. Tiny single-screwed warships which were said to roll on a heavy dew. So *Gladiator* had had to reduce speed to the corvettes' most comfortable cruising rate of eleven knots. Destroyers were designed for the cut and dash of attacking with torpedoes, and retiring under a smoke-screen. But their role now seemed only to get convoys home and away again, and to kill the hated U-Boats whenever they had the chance. As for the convoys, the only rule concerned the speed. *It shall be that of the slowest ship in it.* So it was often the case that new, fast freighters had to crawl along with some ancient, dragging tramp-steamer which looked like something from the Great War, and probably was.

The two corvettes were placed out on either beam, smashing their way over the same impressive waves as *Gladiator*. With a quarter sea and a wind to make your gums ache, there would not be much to choose between them, Treherne thought.

Ayres approached him where he stood in his heavy leather sea-boots, one arm around a stanchion near a gyro-repeater. The sub-lieutenant seemed to rise up and then drop away as if in some weird dance, and when he eventually found a handhold he sounded breathless.

Treherne regarded him thoughtfully. Was he learning anything? He had asked him on their first watch together if he had had any maritime experience other than his seatime in *Sanderling*. Ayres had screwed up his face as if to conjure up something useful but had replied lamely, 'I was in the sea-scouts, sir.'

Treherne had made a joke of it, if only to take his mind off the ship which hit a mine in the North Sea.

But it was no joke really. At thirty-three Treherne was the

oldest officer in the ship, apart from Evan Price, the chief, and Pym the Gunner (T), but there was nobody in the whole Navy as old as *him*. He wondered what the grumpy gunner thought of Ayres; they shared duties on the quarterdeck when entering or leaving harbour. The veteran and the innocent amateur. Treherne was a Cornishman, a professional seaman to his fingertips, who had spent his pre-war time in the merchant service, in one of the clean, fast banana ships which ran regularly from the sunny Windward Islands to Liverpool and Cardiff. *Gladiator* was often in Liverpool, the nerve centre of Western Approaches. It always reminded him of those faroff, impossible days: peaceful trips with only a handful of passengers to irritate you.

Ayres gasped, 'We shall be sighting Iceland today.' He hesitated and would have flushed but for the bitter spray. 'Er, Pilot.'

Treherne grinned and showed his strong teeth. 'Sure will, Sub. All lava-dust and people who hate our guts.'

'But I thought they were on our side.'

Treherne studied him sadly. So naïve. 'We occupied the place, otherwise the krauts would have got there first. It's not much of a prize, but it does have one of the biggest airstrips in the world – something which appealed to the Germans quite a lot. Anyone who holds Iceland commands the convoy routes to North Russia.'

He leaned over a voicepipe and snapped, 'Watch her head, quartermaster!'

'Sorry, sir.' The voice echoed tinnily from the wheelhouse beneath their feet. 'Steady on three-three-zero, sir.'

Treherne's eyes crinkled as they followed the ticking gyro-repeater. To himself he murmured, 'You too, mate!' Because he knew what the quartermaster was thinking.

Ayres wiped his wet face and blinked through the glass screen. The waves were enormous, but not too dangerous, or so Treherne had explained. When they broke across the maindeck he had known the bridge to be cut off completely from the wardroom; there was no way forward or aft along the iron deck except out in the open, and even lifelines couldn't save a man under those conditions. It had meant that the captain and the luckless officer-of-the-watch had been isolated, and forced to stand watch-and-watch until the sea moderated, and praying all the while that they would not be called to action stations.

'Is it pretty safe now, sir?'

Treherne looked at the captain who was sitting on his tall chair, which in turn was bolted to the deck. He was lying with his head on his arms below the screen, his body pitching with the violent movement, his duffle coat and hood black with spray and flying spindrift. 'Safe?' He considered it. 'With two corvettes in company and all our combined Asdic going, we should be. Mind you,' he looked astern, past the wildly shaking signal halliards and the funnel smoke which seemed to point directly abeam, level with the surging wavecrests, 'when we got close to the Rosegarden I did have a twinge or two.'

He saw the utter bewilderment. 'The Germans call that three hundred-mile stretch of the sea between Iceland and the Faeroes the Rosegarden. In the early part of the war every U-Boat, surface warships too, had to creep through that strip. We put down deep-level mines to make the U-Boats stay on the surface or at periscope depth so the RAF could have a go at 'em, but they still managed, in spite of that.' He added with unusual bitterness, 'Now the Germans don't have to bother going through the Rosegarden, unless *Tirpitz* comes out looking for trouble. When France chucked in the towel and our other allies went down like a pack of cards, they presented Mister Hitler with an unbroken coastline all the way from Norway's North Cape down to the Bay of Biscay.' He saw it in his mind's eye like a chart. 'That's about two-and-a-half thousand miles. Makes it nice and easy for them, eh?'

Someone groaned, 'Daylight, at long last!'

Ayres was thinking about his rare encounters with the destroyer's second sub-lieutenant, Lionel Bizley. He was only a few months older than Ayres but seemed like a veteran by comparison. They shared the same cabin because the new addition to the wardroom at Leith had been Surgeon-Lieutenant Jocelyn Lawford, a doctor so young that he must have only just completed his time in medical school. Prior to that, like many smaller warships, *Gladiator* had had to be content with a PO sickberth attendant. Had they any choice, most of the company would have preferred it to remain that way.

And yet Ayres had barely spoken a dozen words to his cabin-mate and they had met only when passing one another to go on or off watch, or to exercise action stations. His experience must have scarred him deeply, Ayres thought; and felt a certain respect.

The yeoman of signals snatched up his telescope, which he preferred to any binoculars, and stared across the grey water as a light blinked through the drifting spray like a bright diamond.

'From *Cynara*, sir. *Good morning.*'

Treherne smiled. Things were moving again. Somehow he had known Ayres had been preparing to ask him about the convoy, or worse, what the North Russian run was like. 'I'll call the captain.'

'No need, Pilot.' Howard levered himself from the tall chair and banged his boots on the wet, wooden gratings. 'God, I'm stiff. Any char about?'

A boatswain's mate spoke into a voicepipe and called, 'Told the galley, sir.'

Several of the tired-looking faces responded with grins. Tea from the galley would at least be hot when it got here. From the wardroom it would be full of salt-water by the time a steward had negotiated the deck and the unprotected ladders to the bridge.

Howard crossed to the chart table and rested his elbows on the stained paper.

About forty miles to go. He recalled their expressions in the wardroom when he had told them. A convoy to Russia. The new ones looking at the others for explanation or hope. Number One grim-faced; the chief, Price, probably thinking about the extra stress on his engines; Arthur Pym working his thin mouth in and out as he often did when he was troubled. Only Treherne had been his usual unperturbed self.

Howard straightened up even as a young seaman in a streaming oilskin tumbled into the bridge with a steaming fanny of tea. Dirty enamel mugs were produced as if by magic, and Ayres found time to notice that the char-wallah was the young sailor called Nobby, the motor boat's bowman.

Despite his misgivings, Ayres told himself he was finding his way. Faces had names, or some of them did; Pym the old Gunner

(T) hated his guts; the first lieutenant no longer noticed him at all.

He heard the captain say, 'Call up *Physalis*, Yeoman. Tell her to take station on *Cynara* as ordered for entering harbour.' He swallowed the sickly, sweet tea and said, '*Good morning* indeed! All right for some!' More grins, as he knew there might be.

Howard stared abeam and thought he could see the other corvette as the lights blinked over the water.

He saw Treherne explaining something to Ayres. Like a rock. A corvette could be Treherne's for the asking. He had earned his own command. The true professional.

He loosened the clinging towel around his throat. A good, hot wash – no shave, just a wash in the reeling sea cabin abaft the bridge. Another dream.

He said, 'Warn all the lookouts. We may sight a local patrol or some fisherman selling his catch to a U-Boat.' That was not so flippant as it sounded. To Treherne he added, 'Begin the turn to the next leg in thirty minutes. I shall – '

'Radar . . . bridge!'

Petty Officer Tommy Tucker, the yeoman, pushed one of his young signalmen to one side and exclaimed, '*Shit!*'

Howard stooped over the voicepipe. 'Bridge. This is the Captain.'

The man hesitated, probably wondering if he were doing the right thing. 'I'm getting an echo. Very faint, dead ahead – about two miles.' When Howard said nothing he continued, 'May be a throwback from the shore. I – '

Howard was thinking rapidly, his eyes on the red button by his hand. 'McNiven, isn't it?' A face took shape in his mind. 'Keep watching. I'm looking at my radar-repeater now.' He winced as water ran off the canvas hood above the repeater and explored his neck like ice. 'I'm just getting a confused picture.' It was hardly surprising in this heavy sea, with the land mass of Iceland comparatively close.

McNiven said, 'Echo is stationary, sir. Very small.' He was a good operator, second only to his leading-hand.

Treherne asked, 'Shall I call up the corvettes, sir?'

Howard shook his head, still thinking. McNiven could see it, therefore it was not just a throwback. It was on the surface. Afloat but unmoving.

He bent over the voicepipe again. 'Any change?' McNiven came back instantly, 'None, sir.'

Howard said, 'Not a U-Boat. Too close to land to surface to charge batteries.' He saw them listening and realised he had spoken aloud. 'They've got seven hundred fathoms to play with around here.'

Another voice intruded from the wheelhouse. 'Cox'n on the helm, sir.'

'Very good.' Howard looked at Treherne and smiled. How did the old hands like Bob Sweeney the coxswain always know? Like the yeoman of signals, they never seemed to need the alarm bells.

Treherne asked, 'Fishing boat?'

'Not sure. But this is the time to be certain, eh?' Howard knew Treherne understood. How many ships had been sunk when lookouts had been thinking only of getting into a safe harbour, dry clothes, food which was not flung off the plate in a force nine gale? *Out of nowhere.*

He pressed the red button and heard the alarm shrill through the hull, the staccato reports on voicepipes and handsets as the men dashed to their action stations.

The first lieutenant joined Howard. 'Ship at action stations, sir. Trouble?'

'I'm not certain. Radar has reported a faint echo at three-three-zero. Unmoving, so not a conning-tower.'

Marrack squinted his eyes at the wet haze. 'Can't see a damned thing.'

'Radar – bridge!'

'Bridge.'

'I think it's a boat, sir. It just turned round. Drifting.' He sounded almost apologetic.

'You did well, McNiven.' He looked at the others. 'There's a northerly current just there, right, Pilot?'

'Yes, sir.' His bearded face was expressionless.

'Fall out action stations, resume defence stations.' Howard heard the feet thudding gratefully down ladders and along the deck. 'We'd better take a look. Maintain course and speed, Pilot. I don't want to shake the guts out of her in this sea.'

By the time Ayres had reached the bridge again from his action station which was by Y-gun right aft, the sea had brightened still further, and although the waves were too high to allow an horizon you could feel the depth and latent power. To starboard there was the hint of land, a purple shadow which looked like a fallen cloud.

'Object in the water, sir! Dead ahead!'

'Slow ahead together.' Howard climbed on to the forward gratings and levelled his glasses. He felt his stomach contract. 'Dead' was right. 'Warn the chief bosun's mate!'

'He's already there, sir.'

'He would be.' Knocker White, another one who was always ready.

He turned and saw Ayres standing by a signal locker, the hood fallen from his head as he stared at the boat drifting down the ship's side until it was snared by the chief boatswain's mate's grapnel. How far had they been journeying? What ship, and how long had it taken? Scarecrows. Torn, tattered faces, some eyeless, others fallen across the motionless oars. In the stern-sheets a hunched figure with a cap down over his face, two faded stripes on the sodden jacket.

Howard called, 'Stop, together.' He saw the new doctor hurry to the guardrail, then pause as if he had been paralyzed by what he saw.

Marrack snapped, 'There should be an officer down there, sir.'

Ayres tore his eyes from the horrific lifeboat, and knew Marrack meant him.

'I – I'll go, sir!'

Howard looked at him. 'Stay with the Buffer and his men. If you feel faint or sick, keep out of sight.' He added gently, 'But Number One is right. You've got to show them.'

Ayres almost fell as he lowered himself down the first ladders, past a grim-faced Oerlikon gunner and then to the maindeck itself. A few off-watch onlookers stood at the break of the fo'c'sle; others leaned out from their defence stations, sharing the moment.

Petty Officer Knocker White climbed from the boat and saw Ayres staring at him. Good lad, he thought, surprised that he should be there. He heard someone retching helplessly. It was the new doctor. God help us if we runs into the fucking *Tirpitz*, he thought savagely.

'I got the details, sir.' He pulled something leather from his oilskin; it was covered in mildew. He held it out for Ayres to see and said quietly, 'Poor bugger was 'anging on to the picture of 'is girl, sir. Probably the last thing 'e ever saw.' He waved up to the bridge and barked, 'Cast 'er off, Jim!'

The deck began to tremble again and white froth surged away from the great propellers. The boat seemed to hesitate against the side, as if reluctant to leave now that they had reached help.

Ayres asked huskily, 'What will become –'

The Buffer eyed him for a few moments while he watched the forlorn boat rocking as it passed over the destroyer's churning wake.

'The skipper'll signal for an RML as it's so close inshore. They can deal with them things better than us.'

Ayres stared until his eyes were raw, oblivious to the biting air, everything but the lifeboat and its ragged occupants. It was as if he still expected to see the officer at the helm wake up and stare after them, to curse them, maybe, for leaving them.

He said aloud, 'I'll never forget.' He shook his head so that his schoolboy haircut ruffled in the wind. '*Never!*'

White, 'the buffer' as he was known in all ships, said, 'At the end o' the forenoon, sir, drop into our mess. 'Ave a tot with some of the *real* sailors.' He strode away to muster his men again, unable to watch Ayres's gratitude.

When he reached the bridge again to continue his watch Ayres saw the navigating officer studying him.

'All right, Sub?'

Howard turned in his chair. 'You did well, Sub. It gets easier in time. It has to, you see?'

Ayres moved to a corner of the bridge and tried to make himself small. He kept seeing them. Who had been the last one left alive? The girl in the photograph; did she know, did anybody at home realise just what it was like?

By the time the watch had run its course they were turning around the last headland with the bay opening up; beyond that lay a great fjord with snow and high ground beyond it.

'Hands to stations for entering harbour. Starboard watch fall in, first part forrard, second part aft!' The orders seemed endless. Lights winked and flashed from all directions and the yeoman was kept busy replying with his hand-lamp.

'Signal from ACIC, sir. *Anchor off Videy Island*.'

Howard looked at Treherne and saw him grimace. That meant that the other anchorage was already filled. *The convoy.* 'Bring her round, Pilot.' He looked down at the forecastle and saw Marrack at the head of his men, the chief stoker groping around the starboard capstan, his breath like steam in the cold air. In England they would be hoping for a good spring in a matter of a few weeks, to give an illusion that the war was not too bad. Howard glanced aft and at the men around him. Spring would be a long time coming up here, with plenty of ice at the end of the journey. He saw Ayres's pale face, a youthful determination which had been lacking before. Thinking of that lifeboat still, probably the closest he had been to the war so far. He lowered his eye to the compass and took a quick fix on the brightly painted marker. 'Dead slow, together.'

'Coming on now, sir.' Treherne sounded calm, completely absorbed as usual.

'Stop engines! Slow astern together!'

Ayres trained some glasses on the nearest anchored warship. A big Tribal Class destroyer. He read her name on the plate by her quartermaster's lobby: *Beothuck.* Canadian, then. He felt himself shiver like that morning in Rosyth. *Just days ago.* It was not possible.

He turned, startled, as the anchor splashed down and the cable started to rumble out across the bottom.

Howard gave him a quick smile. 'You tell the wheelhouse, Sub. Ring off main engines.'

The vibrations ceased instantly and he heard the coxswain's surprised acknowledgement.

Treherne touched his arm as the watchkeepers began to relax and step down from their stations.

'Go and get that tot, Sub, the one that old rascal Knocker White offered you.' He saw the sudden embarrassment and added, 'You earned it back there. It's their way of telling you.'

Howard unslung his binoculars and wondered about a bath before he was summoned to some senior officer.

'I'll need the motor boat, Pilot. About an hour.'

The yeoman called, 'Signal, sir. *Captain to report to ACHQ when convenient.*'

'Acknowledge.' He ran his fingers through his hair. 'About an hour,' he repeated. Then he clattered down the ladder and made his way aft. Another landfall. Soon, another departure.

The tannoy came to life. 'D'you hear there! Men under punishment to muster!'

Howard paused at the entrance of the watertight door and looked along the destroyer's deck. *My ship.* In just the time it took to walk from the last bridge ladder to here, men had died and were still dying. But routine and duty ruled their lives nonetheless.

Other things stood out in his mind. Ayres had come through his first lesson, the new doctor had failed. The other sub-lieutenant, Bizley, was driving himself round the bend, or so Marrack had told him. That had to be dealt with promptly before it endangered some or all of them. Nobody else could handle it. Midshipman Esmonde had rushed on deck when the drifting lifeboat had bumped alongside, and had fainted. He might get over it. If there was only more time.

His day cabin door opened even as he raised his hand and he saw Petty Officer Vallance beaming at him. A fire was already flickering in the grate.

'Nice bath, sir, an' a clean shirt ready, special for the admiral, like!' Vallance saw and recognised the fatigue which the others rarely shared. The Old Man had got them here. He would go on doing it. Till it was all bloody well over.

Gladiator took the strain on her cable and swung to the swirling current. But Vallance knew it was their young captain who carried all of them.

The place chosen for the operational briefing was within the perimeter fence of Area Combined HQ where the Navy had joined with the Royal Air Force to control the destiny of every allied vessel. It was a grand name for a scattered collection of Nissen huts, all of which were dominated by a giant radio mast. Howard, with Treherne sitting beside him, looked around at the other naval officers who sat like pupils on rows of hard wooden chairs.

Howard guessed that this hut, larger than all the others, was normally used as a cinema for the many servicemen who were incarcerated on this inhospitable island. But the screen was folded up to the roof, and had been replaced by a long trestle table which faced the audience.

It had been four days since *Gladiator* had arrived at Reykjavik, and apart from moving alongside a fleet oiler to replenish the tanks, nothing much had happened. *Ganymede*, their sistership, had arrived to join them, delayed in Scotland only to collect and accompany two more corvettes. There were about twenty commanding officers and their navigators present, he thought, maybe more. It was to be that important.

Ganymede's captain, Lieutenant-Commander 'Spike' Colvin, nudged him with his elbow. 'Some of our chaps look as if they've just left school!'

Howard nodded, but through and beneath the unmoving fog of pipe and cigarette smoke he saw a few of the more experienced faces, the interwoven gold lace of the RNR, like Treherne, and several regulars like himself and Colvin. The majority were Wavy Navy, hostilities only; the new blood.

Howard wondered how they would all stand up to another run to Murmansk. Fifteen hundred miles as the crow flies, but far longer with all the detours thrown in. One of the worst sea areas in the world, even without the enemy.

The door opened and the little procession trooped to the table while the assembled officers got to their feet with much scraping of chairs. Rear-Admiral Henry Giffard took his place in the centre, ranked on either hand by his team of 'experts' and one naval commander whom Howard had already met. He was the captain of HMCS *Beothuck*, the big Tribal destroyer, who was to be the senior officer of the escort. A good choice it seemed, as he had done several of these trips before. He was a powerfully-built man with impassive features. One who would have no time for fools.

The rear-admiral was a complete contrast. Old for his rank, his chest brightened by a full rectangle of decorations most of which Howard did not recognise, he looked rather like a modern Pickwick. He was bald but for two white wings of hair, and he looked polished and scrubbed. When he put on a pair of small, gold-rimmed spectacles he *was* Pickwick.

He looked at them over the glasses and said dryly, 'Gentlemen, you may smoke.' He glanced pointedly at the drifting pall and added, 'If you must.'

Colvin grunted and immediately fished out a tin of duty-free cigarettes. Eventually everyone settled down and the navigating officers had their pads and pencils ready to hand.

The rear-admiral cleared his throat. 'Before I hand you over to the Met officers and my operations commander I should like to put you all in the picture. I shall of course be attending the convoy conference to address the ships' masters, but there are certain things they need not be told, yet, anyway.' Again that slow search of their faces. 'Our allies, the Russians, are having a very bad time of it. Too many retreats, terrible losses in men and materials, and more especially aircraft. The Luftwaffe dominates the whole front, and the Russians do not have the means to keep pace with the enemy.' He added with a certain irony, 'It has rather a familiar ring about it, don't you think?'

Howard thought of the way Britain's fortunes had suffered. Even in North Africa where there had been so many victories, the newsreels full of Italian soldiers surrendering to the Eighth Army, the situation was critical. One man ruled the Western Desert: Rommel, with his famous Afrika Korps. He was heading even now for Egypt, beyond which lay Suez, India, total victory. And nothing but the battered and demoralised Eighth Army could prevent it.

He recalled his own harsh summary, which he had offered Ayres. But he was no different from all the others who had not experienced the odds of battle. They wanted to close their ears or listen to Vera Lynn.

The admiral was saying, 'This will be a fast convoy. Almost all the ships are new – each will be loaded with essential weapons and aircraft, and tanks.'

Howard saw the Canadian escort commander look down at the table and sigh. He would know better than most what the admiral was hinting at. Their destination, Murmansk, as bleak as it was dangerous, had only one really functional crane, and that was capable of lifting just eleven tons at a time; far less than a tank. It meant more time lost and fretting over delays while they offloaded them on to any available slipway or jetty, using a solitary lifting vessel.

It was never made any easier by the thinly disguised hostility and suspicion with which the Russians behaved. Even the anchorage was far too deep for the tired escorts, and their allies persistently refused to allow any of them into the relative security of the Russian naval base at Polynaroe.

The men who manned the ships were more than bitter about this treatment, after all the risks they had taken to get there. Even then they still had to reach home again along the same dangerous highway. The convoys were beyond Allied air cover for the worst part of the passage, and the Germans used their Norwegian bases to full and deadly advantage.

Rear-Admiral Giffard dabbed his mouth with his handkerchief and Colvin whispered, 'Just had a bloody good lunch, I'll wager!'

Giffard removed his glasses and said, 'Unfortunately I have to tell you that intelligence reports suggest that the Germans may attempt a surface attack by cruisers which are said to be lying at Tromsø. There is a ring of steel around the place and even the Norwegian underground has stayed silent. There will be a covering force from the Home Fleet, a match for any such cruisers.'

Howard waited. Why was he hesitating, drawing it out?

Giffard replaced his glasses as if to afford protection. 'It is also rumoured that *Tirpitz* may make a sortie this time.'

If he had shouted some terrible obscenity the little admiral could not have had a greater effect.

Colvin said quietly, 'Jesus Christ, that battlewaggon could swallow this convoy and never notice it.'

Around the room officers were glancing at one another, seeking out familiar faces, starkly aware, not of their numbers, but of their complete vulnerability.

Howard felt Treherne stiffen beside him. Remembering *Tirpitz*'s giant sister-ship *Bismarck* which had escaped through these very same waters. Not before she had destroyed *Hood*, the darling of many a peacetime review and Britain's greatest warship, and sent a brand-new battleship, *Prince of Wales*, in full retreat from her great guns. The ill-fated *Prince of Wales* had shared *Hood*'s fate at the hands of the Japanese just seven months later.

They had sunk the German giant eventually, but it had taken most of the Home Fleet to find and destroy her.

While *Tirpitz* remained in her Norwegian lair the battleships and cruisers of the Home Fleet were tied down at Scapa Flow, just in case she came out.

Would the German Navy risk such an important battle-group on one convoy? Even as he asked himself the question Howard knew the answer. They would want to destroy *any* convoy that might help the Russians recover when the ice and snow released their ruthless grip on the Eastern Front. When the thaw came to those hundreds of miles of contested ground, Hitler would order his armies to attempt that which Napoleon had failed to do.

With Russia beaten into submission and slavery the enemy would double its efforts elsewhere. North Africa, and then – he thought of his father's little house in Hampshire, the pleasant garden from which you could see the old windmill on the top of Portsdown Hill on a clear summer's day. No amount of courage and sacrifice would stop them coming there, too.

He realised that the RAF Met officer was droning on about wind and snow flurries, about the fact that the ice-edge was still holding firm, later than usual, so that the convoy would have to sail closer to the German bases than had been hoped. Even around the approaches to the Kola Inlet and Murmansk there would be similar hazards although the port was selected in the first place because it was ice-free all the year round. It was also chosen because of the direct railway connection with Leningrad and the Baltic.

The Ops Officer was last, his hands in his reefer pockets, thumbs hooked over the sides.

He ended by saying, 'The convoy will not disperse, gentlemen.' He looked at their intent faces. 'It goes through. No matter what.'

To Howard as he turned up his coat collar and stepped over the dirty snow to find the jeep that had carried him here, those final words sounded like a covenant, a perfect epitaph.

3

From a View to a Kill

'Forenoon watch closed up at defence stations, sir!'

Lieutenant Neil Finlay nodded and trained his glasses on the nearest merchantman again. 'Very well.'

Finlay was a Scot and proud of the fact, and also of the knowledge that he was the first RNVR officer to be put in charge of gunnery in this hard-worked destroyer. Because his captain was a regular he was all the more determined to make no mistakes. If anyone else made any in the gunnery department, Finlay had left no doubts as to what he would do about it.

It had taken three days to marshal the convoy into their allotted positions and move out of Reykjavik, then north and into the Denmark Strait. Apart from a few minor collisions with drifting patches of ice they had managed without incident. Now, with the sea rising and falling in a deep swell, they were in open water: the Arctic Ocean. There were thirty merchant ships in the convoy, arranged in five columns, with the commodore's vessel, a fine-looking cargo liner named *Lord Martineau*, leading the centre column. To protect them on the long haul to North Russia were six destroyers, eight corvettes, two Asdic trawlers and a tug. In the centre of the convoy was a converted Dutch ferry named *Tromp II*, described in the orders as an anti-aircraft ship. She was manned by naval ratings and her deck appeared to be crammed with short-range weapons, pom-poms and Oerlikons, while right aft by her stylish bridge she mounted two twelve-pounders. Lieutenant Finlay moved his glasses towards the other odd-looking vessel at the rear of the centre column, one he had heard Ayres asking about as soon as the convoy had got under way.

Another converted merchantman, her upperworks had been cut away but for her bridge and spindly funnel, while the upper deck was dominated by a long catapult. A Hurricane fighter stood all alone on the catapult, like some huge seabird which had landed there for a brief respite from its flight.

The first lieutenant's comment had been typically curt and scathing. 'Fighter catapult ship. If the convoy is sighted by a German recce plane they fire off the catapult and our gallant pilot shoots the German down before he can home the U-Boats onto our position.'

Marrack had met Ayres's unspoken questions with, 'After *that* he bales out, and we pick him up.'

Finlay smiled grimly. They were well north of the Arctic Circle. If the flier had to ditch he wouldn't last much longer than twelve seconds.

Tucker, the yeoman of signals, raised his telescope, his lips moving soundlessly. 'Signal from commodore, sir. *Mersey Belle is losing way. Investigate.*'

Howard stood up and gripped his chair while the signal lamp clattered an acknowledgement.

The ship in question was at the rear of the port column. She had already been told off by the escort commander for making too much smoke. Now what?

Howard shaded his eyes to study the great array of ships. Five columns of vital equipment, every hold packed with weapons, medical supplies and vehicles. Most of them carried deck cargo as well, crates and crates of aircraft destined to fill the critical gaps in Stalin's air force. The other five destroyers were out of sight, steaming in a widespread arrowhead formation ahead of the convoy. The corvettes were divided on either beam, their sturdy little silhouettes lifting and diving in the huge swell like lively whales.

Gladiator was two miles astern of the convoy, 'Tail-end Charlie', ready to do anything required by the commodore, or go for any U-Boat which might try to catch up with the ships on the surface. It was unlikely in daylight, for no submarine could outpace the convoy submerged.

'Half ahead together.'

In the wheelhouse Treherne was checking something with his yeoman, which was why Finlay had relieved him for a few moments. Finlay had lost no time in summoning their other sub-lieutenant and Esmonde the midshipman to the bridge to press home the main points of his fire-control system.

As the revolutions mounted Howard glanced at the trio of young officers below the compass platform. The two subbies, side-by-side but somehow totally apart, and Esmonde swaying jerkily with the uncompromising rolls and swoops, his features the colour of parchment.

'One-one-seven revs replied, sir!'

Howard raised his glasses again. The sky was very cloudy, with small patches of shark-blue here and there. No sign of snow as promised. No sign of anything for that matter. Even the far-off Admiralty had refrained from making signals. A covering force from the Home Fleet was somewhere to the north-west; there was supposed to be an escort carrier with it. Howard looked at the fighter catapult ship. At the moment that was all the air-cover they could expect once they had reached the limit of shore-based aircraft to the north-east of Jan Mayen Island, that lonely outpost at the very extremes of the ice-edge.

It was too calm. Bad weather was the best ally so close to enemy airfields and the deep fjords where the big surface ships were said to be hiding. Maybe the Met officer would still be proved right. If not . . .

'Slow ahead.' Howard walked to the side of the bridge and switched on the loud-hailer.

'*Mersey Belle*! Make more revs! *You're falling astern*!' He waited, tapping his leather sea-boot impatiently until two heads appeared on the freighter's high bridge. It was shining like glass, he thought. So, probably, was *Gladiator* as the freezing spray drifted over her. Marrack would have to get his people to work on the forecastle. A destroyer was not built to take a build-up of ice on the upper deck; too much top-hamper had been known to capsize an escort in heavy seas.

'Hello, *Gladiator*!' He had a Geordie accent you could cut with scissors. 'It's a spot o' shaft trouble. I'll have to slow down some more while my chief is working on it!'

Howard said, 'Signal the commodore, Guns.' He moved his glasses along the freighter's hull. The sea was lifting right up to her wash-ports one moment, then falling away to reveal her waterline. Deep-laden, like the rest. She had armoured cars on the upper deck; there were even crates of aircraft lashed across her hold covers. Not much chance if the cargo shifted, he thought. He often marvelled at how they stood it. They were, after all, civilians, but they bore the full fury of the enemy's attacks by sea and air. Howard had known merchant ships to pick up survivors only to be torpedoed themselves, then sometimes a second roar of destruction with the survivors crowding into other ships And yet they always seemed to go back. This convoy's commodore, for instance, had been sunk twice already, and he was here again in the thick of it.

Finlay called, 'From commodore, sir. *The convoy will reduce speed to ten knots.*'

The yeoman lowered his lamp and said, 'Fast convoy, did someone say? A bloody snail could do better!'

Howard heard him. It was unusual for Tommy Tucker to show his feelings. *Edgy.* We're all getting like that.

He said over his shoulder, 'Take her round and resume position. Warn the messdecks first. She'll show her keel when we turn in this sea!'

A boatswain's mate switched on the speaker and touched his lower lip gingerly with his frozen silver call.

'D'you hear there! Stand by for a ninety degree turn to starboard!'

Ayres could picture it as he remembered the old *Sanderling*. Men seizing cups and food, others putting half-written letters away to prevent them from getting lost under-foot. It was strange, he thought. When he was in the little patrol vessel he had been desperate to leave her and go to the training establishment. Now, he could not get her out of his mind.

His silent companion, Bizley, gripped a safety rail and braced himself. He wanted to shut it all out. Be anywhere but surrounded by others he did not know, nor want to.

He was finding it harder instead of easier to sleep whenever he was off watch. It was always there, the vivid flashes of cannon-fire across the black water, sparks flying as the balls of red tracer had cracked over the hull. Men had fallen, some blinded by wood splinters from the deck, or hammered down by the E-Boat's rapid and deadly accuracy.

His commanding officer, a young lieutenant like Finlay, had fallen in the bridge, bleeding badly, one of his hands missing. In the dreams there was no fire, but he had known that the forward messdeck was ablaze when he had . . . He tried to accept it, to deal with it without lying to himself. There was nothing he could have done. The skipper would have died anyway. He chilled as he saw him again, reaching out with his remaining hand. Pleading with him without speaking. Two others had been trapped below when a machine-gun mounting had fallen across the hatch. They had been screaming still when Bizley had inflated his lifejacket and hurled himself outboard where two of the surviving seamen had been struggling with the Carley float. They had stared at him, their eyes white in the darkness, but they had shoved off without protest when he had yelled at them.

The motor gunboat had been carrying a full rack of depth-charges, and someone had failed to set them to safe when the hull had eventually raised its stern and dived from view. At fifty feet the charges had ignited and the sinking hull with dead and wounded still trapped inside had been blown into a thousand pieces.

That was last year. It seemed like yesterday. They had transferred him to general duties before sending him here, to *Gladiator*.

It was over. Finished with. Who could know now? The only other survivors barely remembered what had happened; they had been too busy trying to launch the float and escape.

'Stand by!'

Howard gripped the chair again. 'Starboard fifteen!'

'Fifteen of starboard wheel on, sir!'

Round and further still until they were dangling from any handhold they could find, skidding on steel and cursing, while the starboard Oerlikon gunner was heard to sing out, 'Any more for the Skylark?'

Gladiator asserted herself like the thoroughbred she was, lifting her sharp stem towards the clouds like the short sword on her crest. Water spurted from her hawsepipes as she plunged down again, surging around A-gun and bursting over the bridge in a miniature tidal wave.

They headed back to their allotted position before repeating the turn all over again.

Howard climbed on to his chair and watched the spread of ships as they appeared to slide back and forth across the salt-streaked screen.

Finlay said, 'You can cut along, Sub — you too, Snotty.' He turned to Ayres. 'Bring her back on course, Sub.' He saw the genuine pleasure on Ayres's face. *That one couldn't hide anything if he tried.* He heard the others clattering down the bridge ladder. The midshipman was no better or worse than he had once been himself in his first ship. But Bizley — he was something else. He wondered if the Old Man had noticed. While Ayres was like a kid let loose in a toyshop, Bizley seemed to resent any sort of advice or instruction. As a sub-lieutenant he had probably been a big noise in his MGB, maybe even the Number One. Here, he was just another green subbie.

He was surprised that Marrack had not already come down on him like a ton of bricks. They shared the same watch after all. Perhaps he was sorry for him after losing his boat in the North Sea. Finlay smiled wryly. It was hard to imagine the first lieutenant being sorry for anyone.

Treherne appeared on the bridge and grinned. There was ice-rime on his beard.

'Thanks, Guns. I'll take over again.' He glanced across to the voicepipes as Ayres acknowledged the helmsman's report. 'Been a good boy, has he?'

Finlay nodded. 'He's got the makings, Pilot. Not too sure about —'

'*Aircraft, sir! Dead astern!* Angle of sight three-five! Moving right to left!'

Howard swung his glasses over the screen even as he slid from the chair. The signalman who had called out lowered his own glasses and exclaimed, 'It *was* there, sir!'

Howard continued with a slow sweep, rising and settling again with the ship. Only low cloud, with a sparse break where the aircraft had supposedly been. He looked at the signalman; just a boy, but he had already proved there was nothing wrong with his vision.

'Large or small?'

The youth, his cheeks and throat rubbed almost raw by his cold wet clothing, stared back at him, very aware that he was speaking to his captain.

'Large, sir. I'm certain it was.'

Treherne suggested, 'Could have been one of the big Yank planes from Iceland.' The signalman nodded, heartened that they actually believed him. 'Four engines. Flying just there through the clouds.'

The yeoman of signals said dourly, 'You'd better be right, my son!'

Howard walked to the chart table. 'Inform the commodore. *Aircraft sighted*, possible course and bearing.' A small voice seemed to ask, *theirs or ours?* It was the margin of life or death up here.

The yeoman reported, 'From commodore, sir. *Convoy will alter course in succession to zero-three-zero. Follow father.*'

Treherne chuckled, 'He sounds a lively old bugger!'

Howard saw fresh tea coming to the bridge and was glad of the interruption. The commodore was right about one thing. It was pointless to fly off their one and only Hurricane. It would never find the other aircraft in this cloud, and what if it turned out to be a Yank, or an RAF long-range anti-submarine patrol? It would mean a plane wasted with possibly a dead pilot as well. But the alteration of course was not good. It would add to the overall distance, and the destroyers, which used more fuel than any other ships in the convoy, would have to take on oil from the fleet tanker *Black Watch* earlier rather than later while the weather held.

Howard took the steaming mug and said, 'Warn all the lookouts. Double vigilance. It will do no harm anyway.'

He wiped the compass repeater with his sleeve and felt the ice cling to it. *The convoy will not disperse.* It was as if the man had spoken to him from Iceland. But if they had to fight, how long would it take the heavy ships of the Home Fleet to reach them?

He sipped the scalding tea and watched the ant-like figures through the glasses balanced easily in his right hand. They were working around the Hurricane. Making sure it would still fly if required.

He recalled the tough humour in the desperate days of the Battle of Britain. Join the Navy and see the world. Join the Air Force and see the next.

The watches changed, the bitter air was tinged with the smell of the galley. On the darkening sea the ships sailed on until in the deepening shadows the columns appeared to join like some gigantic Roman phalanx on the march.

A guessing game, so that Howard could picture the markers and flags on the operation boards in Iceland and the Admiralty, and presumably in Kiel, too.

When darkness had finally closed over the sea, Howard left the bridge and climbed stiffly down to his sea cabin. It had become a sort of ritual. A quick wash with warm soapy water, and a clean dry towel to wrap round his neck. PO Vallance thought of everything. He tried not to look at the untidy bunk. If he even just sat on it he would be finished. He looked at himself in a mirror and tried to comb the salt out of his unruly hair.

The telephone on the bulkhead scattered his thoughts.

'Captain?' He wondered if the petty officer telegraphist, 'Pots' Hyslop, could hear his heart beating down the line.

'From Admiralty, sir. *Immediate. There are said to be five U-Boats to the east of your position.*'

Howard nodded. 'I'm going up.'

The others were waiting for him and he was glad they could not see his face.

'Well, now we know, Number One. It was *not* one of ours!'

In the private, enclosed world of the chart table Howard and Treherne were leaning side-by-side while they stared at countless calculations, bearings and the pencilled line of their course. Behind them on the open bridge Howard could hear the other watchkeepers moving occasionally to restore circulation or to break the tension.

He picked up the brass dividers and moved them along the chart while he listened with half an ear to the ship, to the pattern of sound and movements. The dreary, repetitive ping of the Asdic, the squeak of B-gun as it was trained from bow to bow. Although every weapon was supposed to be safe from freezing, the special oil they used had been known to fail on rare occasions. Howard made a quick calculation on the pad and glanced at the misty, revolving picture in the radar-repeater. Like a faint beam of light as it passed across the invisible convoy, the unwavering shapes of the columns, the fainter blips of the corvettes' close escort on either beam.

It was unnerving, he thought. Another day with nothing untoward to report. Maybe the U-Boat warning had been misunderstood by the coding staff at the Admiralty, or perhaps they were off after some other convoy.

The sea was calmer, with a long procession of low swells which lifted the ships with surprising ease before rolling on with nothing between them and the Norwegian coastline. Some of the destroyers had even managed to top up their bunkers from the fleet oiler, a nervous moment for any captain with his ship restricted by the hoses and lines.

He said, 'The motion is easier, Pilot.'

Treherne rubbed his eyes; they felt sore from the bitter air and from peering for the sight of the nearest ships in case there was a collision. On the previous night, one freighter had lost contact with the next ahead and had increased speed to such an extent that it had almost run the other vessel down. Somebody had sounded off his siren, either to warn the rest or from sheer fury at the culprit's carelessness, and had immediately been given a bottle by the commodore. As Marrack had remarked, 'The enemy don't need *his* bloody siren to find their way!'

Treherne replied, 'Ice, sir. There's ice about.'

'I think you're right.' He heard someone laugh; it sounded so out of place – like a lost soul, he thought. He was surprised anyone still could crack a joke with each dragging hour tearing at the nerves.

He could picture his men, huddled and crouched around the ship. Only half the company were closed up at their stations, but Howard had cleared the lower deck so that gun crews and damage control parties, stokers and fire sections could be close to hand if the balloon went up. Marrack was going round the ship for much of the time, keeping an eye on things, making certain that the men on watch were alert. Ready.

'We'll be up to Jan Mayen Island tomorrow, Pilot. The commodore will have to alter course if he wants to avoid the ice.'

Howard felt him start as something boomed against the hull. He said, 'If we remain on this course the pieces will get bigger than that one!'

Treherne grinned, his teeth very white in the faint glow. 'Lucky it wasn't a mine!'

In the privacy of the chart table, Howard seized the opportunity to say, 'Pilot, tell me about Ayres. Why did you swap him around with the other subbie?'

Marrack had already told him of the new arrangement but he wanted to hear it from the big, bearded navigator.

Treherne said, 'He's learned a lot in the past few days, sir. Bizley, on the other hand, has done some close-action, and I thought he would be better off with the after-guns and depth-charges. Ayres will do more good up here with me, I think, sir – anyway, that's what I told Number One.' He gave what might have been a shrug. 'So he changed the duties. I hope that was all right?'

Howard nodded. 'Good thinking.' He had always approved of his officers using their own initiative in such matters. It showed they understood, that they cared.

Bizley on the other hand had seen action in Light Coastal Forces, and according to his report he had behaved well when his boat had gone down. He had taken charge of the remaining survivors and had got them clear before the depth-charges went up. That sort of behaviour took plenty of nerve and guts. The report even hinted that Bizley might be recommended for a decoration.

They switched off the little light and backed out from under the protective canvas hood, shutting and opening their eyes to accustom them once more to the darkness.

Marrack had arrived on the bridge and said, 'Full readiness, sir. All watertight doors closed and checked.' The ship rolled steeply and an enamel mug jangled on the deck like Bow Bells. Ayres heard the yeoman of signals using some choice language to the man who had dropped it and recalled how he used to blush because of it. He saw Treherne speaking with the captain. He smiled to himself; 'The Old Man', as they called him, even though he was still in his twenties. He and the first lieutenant must be the same age, but Marrack looked much older. At that very second the two officers, who had been merely black shapes like the others around him, seemed to flare up like molten copper. Ayres exclaimed, '*Oh my God!*' He stared with disbelief at the expanding fireball which lit up the ships in the convoy like models on an uneven table. It took just the blink of an eye, and yet to Ayres it felt like an eternity before the shockwave of the explosion rolled across the heaving water and thundered against *Gladiator*'s steel flanks as if she, herself, had been hit.

Alarm bells jangled insanely and from every voicepipe the chatter of hoarse voices filled the bridge.

Howard could hear the men around him, their breathing strained and heavy, like people who had been running. In the flickering glare he saw their faces, grim, or shocked by the suddenness of disaster.

Treherne called from the radar-repeater, 'Two of the wing escorts are standing away, sir.'

Howard said nothing, picturing the corvettes, veterans of this kind of warfare, as clearly as if they were visible. Another explosion rebounded against the hull and for a moment he thought a second torpedo had found its mark. But it was aboard the stricken ship, and he could see the glow of fires beyond her bridge.

It was unlikely that the corvettes would make any contact, he thought. A U-Boat, probably sailing alone, had surfaced to chase after the convoy and had fired a torpedo, maybe more, at extreme range. The German captain was making off now, still on the surface, to call up his consorts to share the spoils.

Ayres pulled himself from a voicepipe and shouted, 'From W/T, sir, commodore has ordered *increase speed to fourteen knots.*'

The yeoman said harshly, 'No need to slow down any more. That was the poor old *Mersey Belle* that copped it!'

A blunt shadow passed between them and the spreading flames: *Bruiser*, the big salvage tug, known by most of the sailors as the Undertaker. She would assess the ship's damage, then either take her in tow or lift off the crew.

Ayres said, 'From commodore, sir. *Investigate but do not remain with Mersey Belle.*'

'Acknowledge.' Howard rubbed his chin, feeling the bristles. 'Too many damned signals.' He watched the flames intently. 'I've a feeling about this one, Pilot. Pass the word to damage control. Number One can rig scrambling nets as soon as he likes.' The flames were blazing higher than the freighter's derricks. Something really powerful must have been set alight by the explosion.

'Sea boat, sir?' Treherne's eyes were glowing like coals in the reflected inferno. He felt it badly. Most of the ex-merchant service officers were like that. Seeing a ship dying. Not a man-of-war, going down with guns blazing or trying to ram an enemy cruiser like the poor little *Glowworm*, but ships that worked for a living, in the Depression and in times of peace. Without them England would not, could not, survive. Howard felt the pain jar up his arm as he banged his fist on the unyielding steel. *And we are not protecting them. Not because we don't try, but because the enemy are better at it.*

He saw a shaded torch on the maindeck, men already moving to free the scrambling nets.

Treherne repeated dully, 'No sea boat then, sir?'

Howard raised his glasses and watched the other ship. Her shape had lengthened so she must have lost power on her engines and was drifting beam-on in the swell.

'Negative.' He realised how sharply it had come out. 'I'll not risk men more than necessary.'

'Escort commander reports no contacts, sir!'

Howard thought of the pencilled lines on the grubby chart where so many had leaned on it in the night watches.

'From Admiralty, sir. *Immediate. There are now six U-Boats in your vicinity.*'

The boatswain's mate muttered, 'Roll on death, let's 'ave a good rest!'

Howard watched narrowly as sparks burst up from the helpless freighter, and her funnel seemed to crumple like paper before pitching overboard in a great splash.

They were trying to lower a boat while the tug stood by, her screws beating up the water as she manoeuvred astern to keep station on the *Mersey Belle*. A ragged sheet of flame seemed to burst straight up through the deck where the tiny figures were trying to free the lifeboat's falls of ice. They were like dried leaves caught suddenly in a wind and tossed into the fire. Not men any more, who had loved and hated with the rest of them, but little burning flakes; nothing.

The yeoman said, 'From *Bruiser*, sir. *Mersey Belle has aircraft fuel on board.*'

Howard heard the brief click of his lamp and watched the tug's screws beat the sea into a mounting froth as she swung heavily away from the flames. So that was it. He felt his fingers gripping the binoculars so tightly that his fingers became numb even through his thick gloves. There had been no mention of that in the convoy report. A last minute decision perhaps, just to fill another space.

He felt his mouth go dry as a vivid red eye opened suddenly in the other ship's side to spread across the undulating water and set the sea itself ablaze.

'Port ten.' He did not recall moving to the voicepipes. He was just there. Where he belonged. *No matter what.* Those words again.

'Midships.' He heard the coxswain's thick voice, pictured the tense faces in the shuttered wheelhouse. The telegraphsmen, Treherne's yeoman with the plot-table and its moving lights, Midshipman Esmonde who was in charge of it and the charts it might need. Faces like carved masks, picked out by reflected flames through the steel shutters.

'*Steady.*'

'Steady, sir. Course three-five-zero.' Howard lifted the glasses from his chest and said, 'Very easy, Cox'n. Like the last time, remember?'

He heard him sigh. 'Not likely to forget, sir.'

Howard strode to the side of the bridge and sought out Marrack's oilskinned figure by the guardrail.

'Number One!' He saw him peer up. 'This will have to be fast!'

Ayres wanted to throw the glasses aside but could not move. Half to himself he whispered, 'They're trying to swim clear!' It was as if he was there, right amongst them. The shining faces in the water, the bulky lifejackets dragging them back, the desperate terror of their thrashing arms as they made frantically for the slow-moving destroyer.

Treherne wiped his mouth with the back of his glove. *Gladiator* would stand out clearly in the flames; she was barely making headway through the water. At any second a torpedo might find her. He controlled his sudden anxiety with a physical effort. But he could hear one of the seamen repeating over and over again like a prayer, 'Let's get out of it, for Christ's sake. *Leave them!*'

Howard asked sharply, 'Where's the doctor?'

A signalman called, 'Sick bay, I think, sir!'

'I want him. Here and now.'

He lowered his head to the voicepipe, his lungs filled with the stench. They could not get any closer. At any second she might blow up, engulf *Gladiator* in her own pyre.

'Dead slow, Cox'n.' He heard Ayres give a quick sob as the fire overtook two of the swimmers. He imagined he could hear their terrible screams. More explosions ripped through the freighter from her keel to upper deck. All the crates were alight, and some of the armoured cars had torn free of their lashings and were hanging drunkenly through the bulwarks, or burning with everything else.

'You wanted me, sir?'

Howard did not turn his head from the dying ship. 'Yes, Doc.' It was amazing how calm he sounded. Perhaps it had got to him at last, and he really was going crazy. 'I want you to be there with your team when those sailors are pulled aboard. They will be frozen, shocked and close to dying.' He let his words sink in. 'There won't be too many of them this time.'

The doctor's face shone in the fires, his lips parted as he took in each part of the scene which seemed to be drawing closer by the minute. Howard heard him going down the ladder, his feet dragging. *Another second and I would have shaken the fear out of him.* He stiffened, craning forward.

'*All stop!*'

He hurried to the bridge wing again, and felt a lookout move aside for him. The first gasping figures had reached the scrambling nets while others reached out to catch the lines being thrown to them.

Some fell back retching and crying out as their hands, already black with their own ship's leaking oil, let the ropes slip through their grasp. Howard tightened his jaw as he saw some of Marrack's men clambering down the nets to help them, bowlines already made into heaving lines to pull them to safety. A few seemed to give up, and floated along the destroyer's side. Frozen to death even within yards of rescue.

Howard could feel the heat of the fires now on his face, saw steam rising from the lookout's duffel coat. *Oh God, just a few more minutes.*

One man was holding on to the nets but seemed reluctant to climb aboard. He was peering back towards his drifting ship but he was not looking at her. Above the roar of flames Howard heard him calling to someone who was still out there swimming,

swimming. Then a terrible scream came from the sea of fire and the man on the nets completed his climb to the hands reaching out to help him. The scream had been his answer.

Marrack looked up at the bridge and waved his hands. *No more.* Or if there were, they were already doomed.

'Slow ahead together. Port fifteen.' He felt desperately tired. Like a sickness. A despair.

A dull explosion rolled towards them and more blazing fuel gushed from the ship's hull and crept up and down across the swell to the place where *Gladiator* had been.

'Half ahead together.'

The yeoman said, 'From commodore, sir. *Resume station.*'

Howard took off his worn, sea-going cap and shook his hair to the wind. The heat was fading already, the icy cold regaining its grip.

'Take her round, Pilot. Revs for twenty knots.'

He turned to watch as the *Mersey Belle* began to heel over, armoured vehicles splashing alongside, only so much rubbish now. There were two figures right up in the vessel's stern. *Don't let them suffer like that.*

He offered a silent prayer as some of the flames vanished and he heard the grating crash of metal as the ship began to break up, the stern half diving first in a great welter of steam and bubbles, the two lonely figures still there to the end. A last great explosion rocked the destroyer's sleek hull and then the sea was empty once more.

At first light they rejoined the convoy, and as the visibility improved Howard saw that the formation was as before. As if *Mersey Belle* had never been. He said, 'Fall out action stations. Get some hot food into the people. It may be the last for some time.'

Treherne asked quietly, 'And what about you, sir?'

Howard gave him a curious glance. 'Me? I'd like the biggest Horse's Neck in the whole bloody world, but I'll make do with some fresh kye if you can arrange it.'

Treherne glanced at Lieutenant Finlay who was climbing down from his fire control position, and gave a brief wink.

Just for an instant back there he had been worried. But Howard was OK. He thought of the men, dying in the water. *He had to be.*

4

Ice and Fire

Gladiator's small chart-room was situated abaft the wheelhouse and opposite Howard's sea cabin. The only light came from the chart table where everything was clearer to read and understand than the cramped ready-use hutch on the upper bridge.

Howard and his three lieutenants stood around it now, sharing the illusion of warmth after the biting cold of the open bridge.

Howard watched Treherne adjusting the course to another alteration from the commodore, oblivious to the condensation which fell like heavy drops of rain from the deckhead. Marrack and Finlay the gunnery officer waited in silence while they contemplated their own possible fate.

It was past noon, and the pace of the convoy had dropped to nine knots as more and more ice-floes cruised slowly down their ranks. The heavy tug *Bruiser* had steamed to the head of the convoy, ready to assist if one of the deep-laden ships got into difficulty, or to smash her way through with her tough, ocean-going hull.

The survivors from the *Mersey Belle* were aft in the ward-room. There had been only seven, but one had died an hour ago from his burns and other injuries.

Howard had accepted the news in silence. It was terrible what war could do to your judgment, he thought. *To me.* In those early days, learning the job, he would have been grateful, proud even, to have snatched just six men from the jaws of death. But experience made him ask questions now. Were a handful of survivors worth risking this ship? She had been stopped, outlined against the blazing fuel, an easy target for any U-Boat had there been one. They *had* to be worth it. *Otherwise we are as bad as the men who struck them down without mercy.* Every U-Boat commander knew that his weapon could be the vital one to win the war. Up here, in these bleak wastes, submarines and bombers alike were ordered to go for the main targets, merchantmen and aircraft carriers.

As one senior escort commander had told Howard, 'When the U-Boats start going for *us*, you'll know we're winning!'

He heard boots scraping on the deck overhead and wondered what Sub-Lieutenant Bizley thought about being on watch alone while Finlay was down here. He must have done it many times in his racy motor gunboat. But this was quite different. A powerful destroyer, a company of one hundred and forty-five to consider, and signals which might burst upon him from any direction: the commodore, the senior escort, or the distant Admiralty.

Howard still felt guilty at leaving the upper bridge even in the face of exhaustion. In the event of an attack, one more ladder to the centre of his 'stage' might make all the difference.

Treherne straightened his back, wincing. 'There it is, sir. We know that the ice-edge is still to the south-east of Jan Mayen Island. The convoy has to make a turn very soon or get scattered amongst the floes.'

Howard rubbed his chin, and tried to sip from his mug. It was empty, although he could not recall drinking the glutinous pusser's kye so beloved by sailors.

'At best we shall have to alter course to east-north-east, which will take us up to the final big change below Bear Island.'

Treherne grinned. 'Run like rabbits all the way for the Kola Inlet and our Russian "chums" – I don't think!'

There had been no more U-Boat reports, but they were out there somewhere. It was like fighting something unreal and unreachable, Howard thought. *Perhaps they know something we don't?*

He glanced at Marrack's impassive features. 'What d'you think, Number One?'

'*I think*,' he cupped his hands around the calculations on the chart, 'they're trying to herd the convoy as close to the ice as possible. In the summer we could have sailed further north, around Bear Island, but not now.'

Howard nodded, seeing the slow-moving columns going on and on like that drifting lifeboat and its tattered crew.

'I agree. The Germans probably know the Home Fleet has a shadowing force at sea big enough to cope with *Tirpitz*, if she is reported on the move. Then there will be our cruisers – *they* wouldn't risk an encounter with that big bastard, and in any case they would have been ordered not to proceed beyond longitude twenty-five east.' He smiled dryly. 'Just where we'll need them most, of course!'

Marrack grimaced. 'They seem more intent on keeping the battleships intact than using them for this job.' He spoke with all the intolerance and contempt shown by destroyer and small-ship men for the ponderous goliaths of the Navy.

The door opened slightly and Morgan, the navigator's yeoman, peered in at them. 'Fog warning, sir.' He glanced at his charts as if to check that nobody had put a dirty mug on them. 'Cox'n said it's quite usual so near to the ice.'

Treherne patted his arm. 'That ancient mariner would say anything!'

Howard snatched up the chart-room handset in one movement.

'Captain!'

'Bridge, sir.' Bizley sounded very calm. 'General signal from commodore. *Reduce distances to avoid losing contact.* To us, sir: *Remain on station and maintain contact by radar.*'

'Very good. I'll come up.' He looked at his lieutenants as he put down the handset. 'We've got the fuel, and even without air-cover after today, we may have one ally after all – fog. We could just shake 'em off our backs for a bit longer.'

He tightened the towel around his neck and fastened his coat once again.

Finlay bustled away to resume his watch, while Howard paused by the wheelhouse door and glanced inside. It was almost hot in there, and he saw the men on watch stiffen, then relax again when they realised this was not an official visit.

The coxswain, Bob Sweeney, one of *Gladiator*'s only two chief petty officers, was standing near the plot table, red-faced and comfortable-looking as he chatted with one of the tele-graphsmen. Sweeney should have been below, off watch. Maybe his instinct was warning him again.

Howard nodded. 'All right, Swain?'

Sweeney shrugged. 'Fog's goin' to be a proper pea-souper, sir.' He had a pronounced London accent and had been raised in Stepney in the East End before joining up at the age of fourteen. He had seen it all, and had been due for retirement exactly two days before the Germans had bombed Warsaw. The coxswain was the core of any small ship. He handled defaulters, attended to problems of leave and welfare when one of the lads' wives was having it off with the milkman while he was at sea. But in this ship there were not too many wives to worry about. For the vital task of entering and leaving harbour, going alongside another vessel, or at action stations, the coxswain was always there – at the wheel. It was good to know when all hell broke loose.

The man now on the wheel was the chief quartermaster, 'Bully' Bishop, a dark-featured leading seaman who was nick-named for his savage temper when he was drunk ashore, which was often. How he had managed to retain the hook on his sleeve was a miracle, for he had lost all his good conduct badges along the way.

He said, 'I was in a fog once, sir.' His eyes never left the ticking gyro-repeater. 'Worse than this – '

The cox'n eyed him scornfully. 'That's right, Bully, you swing the lamp! The worst fog you bin in is when the shore patrols carry you on board!'

Howard heard them chuckling as he faced the cold again and climbed into the upper bridge.

He walked aft and peered towards the quarterdeck. But it was already lost in the slow-moving white mist, as if she had lost her stern completely. He made his way to his chair again and felt the cold air driving away the brief reprieve in the chart-room.

He said to the bridge at large, 'Good lookout all around.' He stared through the glass screen and watched the stem blunting itself in the bank of fog. 'Might hit some straggler up the arse otherwise.'

Their faces cracked into grins. They seemed to trust him, even the new hands. *I must never lose my trust in them.*

It was eerie, but far better than being up ahead with all those ships around you. Any collision at sea was bad enough. Up here it was a nightmare. Ice thudded and grated against the hull, and he found time to pity the little corvettes. They would take it badly, especially as they had just one screw to drive and wriggle them amongst the ice.

It would be dark soon. There was hardly any real daylight, and yet in the summer it would be reversed so that enemy aircraft could have a field-day.

Sub-Lieutenant Bizley trained his binoculars over the screen and watched his breath falling away to join the fog. He had been in Channel fogs often enough, but on this comparatively high bridge you felt as if the ship had lost contact with the sea, that only the thick mist was moving. He stiffened as Midshipman Esmonde moved across to join him. He was always understudying someone, he thought impatiently. More like a soft, stupid girl than a budding naval officer.

Esmonde asked timidly, 'Will this fog make much difference?'

Bizley recalled his disgust when the youth had fainted at the sight of the eyeless creatures in the lifeboat. Ayres had been close to that too. Now they seemed to think he was some kind of bloody hero.

'Why? Scared, are you?'

Esmonde seemed to cower. 'I'm not frightened. Not any more.'

The roar of an explosion seemed to come at the ship from several directions at once. The nearness of the ice and drifting banks of fog made a mockery of the frantic reports which echoed from every side.

Howard jabbed the button. '*Action stations!*'

He gripped the arms of his chair as the fog ahead of the bows seemed to change colour, to writhe as if some maniac painter had decided to change the substance of his canvas. Orange one second, deep scarlet the next.

Voices ebbed and flowed around him as his men ran to their stations, hearts pounding, throats suddenly like dust.

'Ship at action stations, sir.'

'Warn the Cox'n, Pilot. Be ready for an instant change of

course and speed.' He held out his hand and touched Marrack's wet sleeve. 'Stay here for the present, Number One.' He heard Treherne speaking into the voicepipe, knowing that the coxswain would be ready for anything. But you had no room for chance.

Marrack polished his binoculars. 'Think that one may drift down on us, sir?'

'Not sure yet.' Howard tried to hear something else. There was more flickering light, but no further explosions. 'Strange. I thought it was a double bang.'

Marrack raised his glasses. 'I heard that. But too close together for torpedoes, unless there's another sub out there.'

'Signal from commodore on R/T, sir. *Retain course and speed. Do not lose contact.*'

Treherne muttered, 'Some hopes!'

Howard shifted uneasily in his chair. Another long-range, unlucky shot. There was always the chance of a hit, especially if they were using the much talked-about homing torpedo.

God, those poor devils would stand little chance of being saved. He found himself wondering where the gap would be when the fog cleared and left them naked again.

'Radar – Bridge!'

'*Bridge!*'

Marrack held his ear to the voicepipe while his eyes flickered in the savage glow of fires.

He said quietly, 'Radar reports a strong echo at one-four-zero, three miles.'

Treherne exclaimed, 'Why the hell didn't he see it before?' But nobody answered.

Howard stood up as if he was afraid of disturbing something evil. Then he lowered his mouth to the voicepipe. 'Captain speaking. Who's that?'

'Whiting, sir.'

Howard spoke slowly to give himself time. Leading Seaman Whiting was the senior operator. A good man, who had been decorated for courage under fire at Dunkirk.

'What d'you think?'

The man took a deep breath. 'No doubt in my mind, submarine on the surface. Stopped for some reason.'

Howard turned to Marrack. 'Go and give them some support,

Number One. It may be a false alarm, a wreck or a piece of one, but if so we should have detected it earlier when we altered course.'

He watched as Marrack hurried away. *It had to be.* Chasing the convoy while surfaced, then firing off a torpedo for fear of losing the chance in the fog. He said aloud, 'It's *got* to be!'

'Gunnery officer, sir!'

Howard found the voicepipe and spoke into it closely to exclude all the others. 'Yes?'

Finlay sounded as if he was right beside him instead of up there in his fire-control position.

'I had a thought, sir. There was a *double* explosion.' He sounded very crisp, as if he were lecturing trainees on the parade ground at Whale Island. It was always hard to see Finlay as a junior librarian, which was what he had once been.

'I heard it.'

'I think the Jerry fired two fish but one exploded prematurely. Maybe it was touched off by a drifting floe.'

Howard stared at the voicepipe, almost invisible now as the darkness closed over them again. The fire was still burning. Another dying ship; as if all the rest had been swallowed up.

He walked to his chair and said, 'Make by W/T to commodore. *There is a U-Boat on the surface three miles to the south-east of my position.*'

Treherne said in a fierce whisper, 'Suppose he orders us to stay put?'

Howard thought suddenly of his father, and it gave him a strange sense of comfort. 'Remember Nelson!'

The yeoman finished scribbling in his pad. 'Any more, sir?'

Howard looked up towards the sky and tried not to listen to the groan of metal as a ship began to break up.

'*Am engaging. Ends.*'

'Hard a-starboard! Full ahead together! Stand by all guns and depth-charges.' He heard the jingle of telegraphs and pictured the wheelhouse suddenly stirred into activity.

'Hard a-starboard, sir!'

'Steady! *Meet her!* Steer one-four-zero!'

He turned and looked over his shoulder as a shadow dashed up to the yard. Even in the early darkness the yeoman would not overlook that. The black pendant. *Am attacking!*

Sub-Lieutenant Lionel Bizley clung to a safety rail beneath X-gun's blast screen and stared astern at the mounting banks of *Gladiator*'s wake. As the revolutions mounted the ship appeared to bury her narrow stern deeper and deeper until the glistening deck was awash. It was a strange, sickening motion as the destroyer rose and plunged over each successive bank of swell, as if she were in her true element. The hull shook and trembled, the excitement of a wild animal going for the kill.

Leading Seaman Fernie, a great bear-like figure made even more bulky by the oilskin he wore over his other clothing, lurched across the deck to join him. He had been checking the depth-charges, making sure that the settings were correct. Fernie was also the captain of the quarterdeck, and knew every wire, shackle and rivet even in pitch darkness.

He shouted above the din, 'The bugger'll dive soon, sir!'

Bizley looked at him, thinking of his motor gunboat at times like these. *Gladiator* must be doing close on thirty knots despite the troughs and glittering patches of ice dashing past in the darkness. There was no other comparison but speed, and the wild excitement which churned at your insides like madness.

'The U-Boat might be waiting for *us* — have you thought of that?'

He did not hear Fernie's answer, nor did he care. In the little MGB there had just been him and the skipper and a dozen men. Here, he had to wait for the order, chase up anyone who was slow off the mark.

The crouching figure with the headset wedged beneath his hood yelled, 'Load with semi-armour-piercing! X- and Y-guns train to Green four-five!'

Bizley watched the two four-point-seven guns swinging round almost to their full extent even as the breeches opened and clicked shut like rifle bolts.

The communications rating called, 'Sub still on the surface, sir! We will alter course and engage to starboard!'

Bizley thought, Well, that's bloody obvious, surely? He snapped, 'Tell the gunlayers to check their sights while there's still time!'

Fernie watched him in the gloom, his eyes raw with salt. This young officer was a hard one to know. He grinned to himself. If you *wanted* to know him. He seemed to know what he was doing, but might prove to be a real bastard when he thought he had the weight. Not like poor Mr Ayres. A nice chap, but handling seasoned hands amidst a mass of mooring wires when entering or leaving harbour was not his cup of tea. Especially with the old Gunner (T) fucking and blinding all the while.

Bizley stared at the depth-charges right aft and recalled exactly when his MGB's pattern had exploded. If he hadn't ordered the float to be paddled away they would have gone up with them. It had become much clearer with each passing day and he could sense a sort of wary respect from some of the ship's company. What would have been the point of dying? The boat had been done for. The skipper would never have made it anyway.

Even *Gladiator*'s captain, a straight-ringed regular who would have seen any flaw in his personal report, seemed impressed, especially at the idea that a decoration might be considered.

He thought of his father and mother, what they would say when he next saw them. His father was a local bank manager, at the same branch where Bizley himself would have ended up but for the war. Paying out cash to people who looked down on him, who were not fit to clean his shoes.

A telephone handset buzzed in its metal box like a trapped insect and Bizley tore it out and covered his other ear with one hand.

'Quarterdeck!'

It was the first lieutenant. A man with no emotion, Bizley thought. The one person who had made him uneasy by asking, 'Surely *somebody* ought to have set the depth-charges to safe when your boat bought it?' Not two officers sharing tea and a momentary break from watchkeeping. More like being in the dock, or how he imagined a court martial would be.

'The U-Boat is diving. Stand by to engage!'

Somewhere a thousand miles away a gong tinkled and instantly B-gun, which was immediately below the bridge, shot back on its springs, the jarring crash of the explosion making some of the new ratings squeak with alarm.

Fernie barked, 'Easy lads, that'll be a starshell, you'll see!' He glared at Bizley's back. *He* should have told them, not leave everything to others.

The bursting starshell made the seascape starkly beautiful,

with patches of drifting fog breaking around the destroyer's headlong charge, while the hard glare transformed the swell into moving banks of searing whiteness. Bizley felt the deck tilting over, and saw the sea clawing over the side as the wheel and rudder went over.

He tried to hold his glasses steady while he clung to the safety rail with his spare hand. Just for a brief moment he held it in the powerful lens, before spray dashed over him and soaked him from head to foot.

He didn't know what he had expected. He had seen submarines alongside in Portsmouth, had even been over one when he was at school. Shining and purposeful within, and somehow placid-looking from the dockside, like basking whales.

What he had just witnessed had been something so incredibly evil he had been shocked by his sudden fear. He had even seen the tell-tale burst of spray as she had vented her tanks and begun to dive.

'Target bears Green four-oh! Range oh-one-two. Moving left to right!'

The slender guns moved in unison and then settled.

'Independent – commence!'

'*Fire!*'

Bizley gritted his teeth as both of the after-guns fired together, the shells tearing towards the starboard bow where he had briefly glimpsed the enemy. She would be submerged now, damaged or not.

Again the guns roared out while from the bridge and pom-pom mounting the arching balls of livid red tracer floated away towards the U-Boat's last position.

Bizley thought wildly that it would only take a few cannon shells to destroy the periscopes and she would come floundering to the surface. With something like a great sight of disappointment the revolutions began to fall away as the captain conned his ship at a more manageable speed in pursuit. Radar would give over to Asdic, the searching echo beneath the sea, like the stick of a blind man in a great empty room.

Bizley heard the breech-blocks snapping shut again.

'X- and Y-guns ready, sir!'

Surely at this range the German captain could not get away? He must have imagined that the convoy's escorts had closed in to protect the other ships. He stared at his crew of depth-charge handlers. '*You*, get ready to fire!' It was somehow characteristic of Bizley that he never bothered to learn the names of anybody but key ratings, or, of course, trouble makers.

He could picture the U-Boat – the *thing* – diving steeply, her commander using every skill to shake off his pursuer, the eerie ping of the Asdic against his hull.

Once the bridge have got a perfect position it will be left to me. Some new methods of firing depth-charges were coming off the blue prints, but for the most part these were the only ones in service.

A pattern over the stern, rolled off like great dustbins, while two other sets were fired abeam even as another pattern was rolled over the stern. In theory and the classroom, the explosions should make one great diamond-shaped design which ought to surround the target and sink it or force it to the surface.

A sudden explosion rolled across the water. Another ship torpedoed? Or the last one blowing up?

Bizley knew each charge took its time to reach the set depth. Even now . . . He swung round. '*What?*'

Fernie held out the handset and replied just as sharply, 'Gunnery Officer, sir.'

He snatched it. 'Bizley, sir.'

Over the line Finlay's Edinburgh accent was even stronger. 'Keep your team on the jump, Sub. If the U-Boat comes up, I need to know wherever it is, right?'

Bizley handed the big leading-hand the instrument and said, half to himself, 'I'm not a bloody child!'

Fernie patted one of his men on the arm. 'Could have fooled me, mate!' He gestured to the throwers. 'I give it about half a minute.'

The men peered at one another, their faces and scarves covered with frozen rime.

'Done, Hookey! Gulpers at tot-time!'

The communications rating shouted, '*Continuous echo, sir!*'

'*Fire!*'

Bizley ran to the guardrails and saw the port depth-charge flying lazily away, then it lost itself in a welter of spray. He knew without looking that a full pattern had rolled off the stern, and found he was trying to moisten the roof of his mouth, which felt like old leather. He stared as if mesmerised as a great column of spray shot from the sea astern, and the crack of explosions seemed to shake the ship from truck to keel, as if *Gladiator* and not the enemy was being torn apart.

Fernie called hoarsely, 'Come on, lads! Reload the throwers, *chop, chop!*'

Bizley shouted, 'Taken over, have you?'

The big leading-hand seized a stanchion for support as the deck tilted steeply once more. The ship had lost contact. The Old Man was going for another search.

He took time to confront Bizley's fury and thought of the pleasure it would give to poke him right in his stupid, arrogant puss.

But he was a good leading seaman, and was hoping for a chance to rate petty officer. They at least had space to stretch their legs.

He retorted, 'We're going in for another attack, *sir*. If we make a pass over the target with nothing to drop on 'em, it won't be *me* what gets a bottle from the Old Man!'

Bizley swung away. 'Don't be impertinent! I'll be watching you!'

The breechworker of Y-gun whispered sarcastically, 'Don't think 'e likes you, 'Ookey.'

The deck swayed upright again and men peered at one another, breathless with all the heaving at tackles and struggling with the unwieldy charges.

'Ready, sir!'

'In contact, sir!' The man in the headset crouched like an athlete and tried not to think of the target as a form of warship, which contained men, Germans, who wanted to kill all of them.

Minutes dragged by while the ship appeared to weave her own pattern through the sea, as if she and not her company was trying to sniff out her enemy.

'*Continuous echo, sir!*'

'*Fire!*'

Someone broke free from the huddled group of figures by Y-gun's open shield and ran to the guardrail.

'*We must have got it!*' His voice was almost breaking. 'She *can't* have got away!'

Fernie seized his arm as the great columns of water cascaded down and were soon swallowed up astern in *Gladiator's* frothing wake.

'Hold your noise, Croft!' He shook him and felt the complete lack of resistance. Just a kid; he had only been aboard since Leith. What a way to begin. He glanced at Bizley's intent shape and hissed, 'Don't let *him* see you! Get back to your station!'

Bizley shouted, 'Next pattern!' He peered astern until his mind throbbed. But no slime-covered hull or bursting air-bubbles appeared. He glared angrily as one of his men fell sprawling while the deck lurched over in another violent turn.

Perhaps the submarine had been sunk after all. He had seen on the charts that there were places where the depth was as much as two thousand fathoms. Even now, the enemy could be falling like a leaf in that perpetual darkness until the hull was crushed like a tin can, and their lives with it.

'Lost contact, sir.'

Bizley heard someone say wearily, 'Gulpers, then?'

But all he could see was the shadow in the depths.

'Steady on zero-seven-zero, sir.'

Howard peered down at the faintly glowing compass repeater. Every bone in his body seemed to be protesting at once, and he felt that if he stared into the darkness and thinning mist much longer he would go blind. He heard the regular ping of the Asdic and thought it was louder than usual. Mocking him as he took his ship this way and that in a careful search. The area was becoming larger every time. The U-Boat could be miles away right now, or licking its wounds in readiness for another attack.

Howard realised that he had thought nothing about the convoy since he had seen the surfaced submarine, so black and stark in the drifting flare. He had heard the machine-gunners and pom-pom crews cursing and shouting as they poured tracer at the target even as she had begun to dive.

The wildness of battle after all the frustration of convoy duty, seeing their helpless charges marked down time and time again.

Howard lowered his head and felt his neck crack. 'Alter course ten degrees to starboard.'

Sweeney's muffled voice came back; a man of endless patience.

'Steady on zero-eight-zero, sir.'

He heard Treherne's clothing scrape over the chart table as he recorded this latest change of direction.

What does he think? That I'm obsessed, unable to concentrate on anything else? It was probably what they all thought.

A shadow moved from the bank of voicepipes and he heard Ayres say, 'The first lieutenant reports, *lost contact*, sir.'

'Tell him we're not giving up!'

Treherne straightened his back and hoped he had not forgotten to put some newly sharpened pencils in his coat. He had heard Ayres's careful message and Howard's abrasive retort.

He means *he's* not giving up. The thought troubled and impressed him.

Treherne started as Howard remarked, 'You know, Pilot, we've been fighting bloody U-Boats for two and a half years now.'

Treherne relaxed slightly. 'God, is that all it is?'

Howard shrugged his shoulders more deeply into his coat. 'And that was the first one I've ever laid eyes on.'

To himself he added bitterly, *And I lost it. Any moment now and we shall be recalled to the convoy. What was the point of . . .*

It was Marrack again, using the bridge speaker to save time.

'In contact, sir! Bearing one-five-oh, moving slowly right to left!'

Howard slid from his chair. 'The crafty bastard! He's crossing our stern, making a run for it!

'Hard a-starboard! Steady, steer one-five-oh!' He turned to Treherne even as the wheel went hard over. 'Warn Bizley!'

Again they tore through the uneasy water and dropped another full pattern of charges. *Gladiator* was doubling back on her tracks as the last towering columns fell back into the sea.

'Slow ahead together!'

A boatswain's mate called, 'Signal from commodore, sir. *Rejoin without delay.*'

There was a far-off explosion. Yet another victim? Or the unknown ship that had blown up in the fog?

Howard swung round. 'What the hell are those men doing?' They were cheering, the voices ragged and partly lost in the sounds of the sea and the great thrashing screws.

Treherne ran to the side and seized the screen with his gloved hands. 'Oil, sir!' He cocked his head and sniffed like a hunting-dog. '*You got him!*'

Howard stared at him blankly as his mind explored the pattern. 'Perhaps – we'll probably never know. Releasing oil is an old trick of theirs.'

'No contact, sir!'

The boatswain's mate coughed nervously. 'W/T office is waitin', sir!'

'Yes.' He thought about climbing into his chair but the effort was too much. 'Reply. *Am rejoining convoy. One U-Boat possibly sunk.*'

He heard Treherne rapping out the change of course and speed to the wheelhouse and said, 'We can't claim a kill, but it will give the others some comfort.'

The U-Boat might still slip away, he thought. But it was already damaged, and would have a hard time of it to reach port in Norway.

Hitting back, instead of taking it all the time.

It was what it was all about. He found that he was in his tall unsheltered chair again.

Treherne said, 'I'll get some hot drinks laid on for the gun crews and watchkeepers.' He turned away, shaking his head. The captain was fast asleep.

5

Bright Face of Danger

'Afternoon watch closed up at defence stations, sir.'

Lieutenant Finlay nodded. 'Very good.'

The new watchkeepers moved restlessly, or glanced at one another as if to reassure themselves.

The yeoman pointed over the screen and said to his youngest signalman, 'Just you watch the commodore's ship, see?' He saw the instant anxiety on the youth's face and added abruptly, 'I'm goin' to th' mess for some mungie – my guts are pleadin' for grub!' He touched his arm. 'Call if you need me.'

Howard was moving along the port gratings, lifting his binoculars every so often, watching the convoy, his ship, and the faces around him. They had found the convoy in the early dawn, with the promised snow-flurries outlining the bridge and gun mountings like pieces of a giant cake.

He raised the glasses and studied the distant columns of ships, partly lost in the irregular flurries of snow. He had noticed the change in the pattern on the radar as soon as they had caught up. Two more ships gone; one, hit by the torpedo, had burst into flames and after losing steerage way had somehow collided with the American tanker *John L. Morgan*. It must have been an agonising decision for the commodore, to steam on and leave the entangled vessels blazing together in a single pyre until that last explosion they had heard when hunting the submarine. What a hideous way to die. One corvette had boldly attempted a rescue and pulled seventeen survivors from the blazing sea. It was not many for two such large ships.

Someone handed him a mug of hot, sweet tea; so much sugar you could almost stand a spoon in it.

He leaned over the littered chart table and massaged his tired eyes until they focussed properly.

What had happened to the U-Boats? Was it possible, after all, that the one which had been damaged and then driven deep by *Gladiator*'s onslaught of depth-charges had been the only one close enough to shadow the convoy, and home others onto the precious targets?

He tried to think like the U-Boat's commander but found, not for the first time, that he could not. But he *might*, he just might have tossed caution aside when the fog had drifted protectively over the plodding columns of merchantmen, more afraid of missing the chance of a shot at them than of anything else.

It was like the scales of justice, he thought vaguely. You added the pros and measured the cons against them.

The commodore had decided to make his own judgement and altered course east-south-east sooner than expected. It would cut a day off their final passage, and if the U-Boats were elsewhere, there might still be a few odds in their favour.

He straightened his back and looked at the sky, knowing the young signalman was watching him despite the yeoman's advice.

A strange day. The sky was full of low cloud and the snow still swirled over the bridge, making the nearest ships difficult to recognise. That was good. Beyond the clouds he could see lighter, brighter patches, as if the sun might try to break through. He smiled grimly. That was bad.

What a barren place. It was impossible to see it set against all the other war fronts. Here, they were totally isolated and alone. Going on and on, with nothing gained by previous Russian convoys to offer even a hint of encouragement.

He wondered how his father was making out in the little house in Hampshire. Even if he owned a car, the petrol ration would have been denied him. There were the local village shops, of course, but if he had swallowed his pride he could have visited one of the several naval establishments. There was one situated quite near, well outside the tempting target of Portsmouth, where he would surely have been offered some extra rations. No, he was not the type.

Howard's mother had died immediately after the Great War

from the devastating 'flu epidemic which had followed the Armistice. He could remember little more than a shadow of her now. His brother, Robert, three years his senior, had often tried to describe her to him; instead she had become even more of a stranger.

Robert was an acting-commander now, on a course in Portland before being offered one of the new escorts, as second-in-command of a whole group. He would likely have found a billet nearby for his wife Lilian. That would mean the Guvnor, as they called their father, was all on his own. *Unless* . . . There had been another woman after their mother had died; maybe more than one. It was like entering the Navy in this family, he thought; you never really questioned it.

In his mind he could see him now. So different from here. Spring over Portsdown Hill and in the many villages lying off the Portsmouth Road which sailors had used for centuries.

The Guvnor had lost himself in his garden, digging for victory, so that he was almost self-supporting. What he did not need he shared with his old chum, Mister Mills. Howard could never recall his being called by any other name. An army veteran from that other terrible war, who nearly caused a riot in their quiet village by running the engine of his little van on Armistice Day while everyone else stood in respectful silence, heads bared, faces sad.

When someone had accused him of insulting the dead, Mister Mills, not a big man, had seized him by his lapels and had retorted hotly, 'What d'*you* know, eh? An' what do all those po-faced hypocrites know? You bloody well tell me that!'

He had served in Flanders, the Menin Gate, the lot. He knew well enough. They made a strange but companionable pair, Howard thought.

A voicepipe muttered tinnily and Sub-Lieutenant Bizley snapped, 'Forebridge?'

Howard paused with an unfilled pipe half drawn from his duffel coat pocket. It was amazing how the past few days had changed Bizley in some way. Tougher, more confident, and yet . . .

Bizley faced him, his face and eyebrows wet with dissolving snow.

'W/T, sir. From Admiralty, *Most Immediate*. *A large enemy surface unit has left Tromsø, heading West.*'

Howard returned to the chart and remarked, 'Not many other ways they could go, I'd have thought.' It gave him precious seconds to think, to escape their eyes as they listened to Bizley's clipped voice.

'When? Does it say?'

He pictured the other escort skippers like himself, the big Canadian in his Tribal Class *Beothuck*, Spike Colvin in their sister-ship *Ganymede*, all studying their charts, measuring the distances, weighing the chances.

Bizley returned from the voicepipe. 'Not known, sir.'

Howard stared at the jagged outline of Norway's north-west coast. The big warships had often used the Tromsø anchorage, *Scharnhorst* and *Hipper*, even the biggest of them all, *Bismarck*. It made good sense because of the heavily defended airfield there.

Perhaps this was the moment the Home Fleet had been anticipating, and their own heavy units were already smashing through the Arctic waters to seek out the enemy, cut them off from their base.

Over his shoulder he said, 'Call Pilot to the bridge, Sub.'

What men had braved capture and torture to provide this piece of intelligence? But where free people were oppressed, there would always be the brave few to outshine the collaborators and the black-marketeers.

'Sir?' Treherne's heavy boots thudded across the bridge while he brushed some biscuit crumbs from his beard. He listened to Howard's news and said, 'I think we've slipped past the U-Boats, sir. The one we put down – ' he grinned at Howard's frown, 'but can't "claim" must have been the only boat close enough to matter.' His grin vanished. 'As to this signal of joy from the Admiralty – well, we were sort of expecting it.'

Howard shrugged. Treherne was never afraid to speak his mind, to admit if he was wrong. Marrack was an excellent first lieutenant, but you could never imagine him admitting being wrong about anything.

'The Russians are supposed to be sending additional support for the last part of the trip.' He saw the scepticism in Treherne's eyes and added, 'But we have to be prepared to crack it on alone. We're in range of enemy aircraft all the rest of the way now, and tomorrow the Home Fleet will begin to withdraw.'

Treherne grimaced. 'Poor old Jack. Pull up the ladder, as usual!' He saw a shaft of hard sunlight lance off the gyro-compass and looked at the sky. 'All we have going for us is that we've lost them. So far.'

Howard stared ahead towards the elegant *Lord Martineau*, but the commodore's ship was still invisible.

Aloud he said slowly, 'The Boss knows a thing or two. But being blown up makes you careful.'

Treherne eyed him wryly. 'Also, sir, despite the RNR handle, he's still a merchant navy man at heart!'

The yeoman climbed onto the bridge and banged his gloved hands together. He studied the young signalman and said angrily, 'What did I *tell* you afore I went for some grub, Rosie?'

Howard turned aside to look at him and saw the youth staring over the screen, just as the starboard lookout reached the end of his own sector.

Ordinary Signalman Rosie Lee was almost incapable of speech, let alone the words of identification he had learned since he had completed his training. He pointed blindly and gasped, '*There!*' He swung round and looked at his captain and repeated, 'There, sir!'

Howard realised that it was the same signalman who had reported that other aircraft, the one that had directed the U-Boats. Even as he thought about it the starboard lookout swivelled his powerful glasses on their mounting and shouted, '*Aircraft*, sir! Bearing Green eight-oh, angle of sight three-oh, movin' right to left!'

Every man squinted into the patch of hard light where the reflected sky gave the sea its only pretence of warmth.

Howard found it as it flew, so very slowly; or so it appeared on a parallel track, like some huge disinterested bird.

He said, 'Signal the commodore.' Howard kept his words to a minimum so there would be no hint of despair. They had got this far, and had lost only three of their charges. *Until now.*

Disinterested this aircraft was not. He had watched them so many times circling a convoy in the Atlantic, close enough to see everything, but keeping out of range of the guns while homing the U-Boat pack onto their victims. It was a Focke-Wulf

Condor, that great four-engined long-range reconnaissance bomber that had made history at sea between plane and submarine.

'From commodore, sir. *Increase to fourteen knots. Stand by for alteration of course.*'

They all turned as a sudden throaty roar thundered across the water like a marauding aircraft. It was the solitary Hurricane perched on its catapult, smoke darting around it while men cowered away, their reason and purpose lost in distance.

Howard said, 'The commodore's sending him in pursuit, for God's sake.' He looked away in case the others saw his sudden anger. This was not the Atlantic, and the Focke-Wulfe was within easy reach of its airfield and support.

Treherne observed mildly, 'He might catch the bastard, sir.'

Howard knew that Marrack and Ayres had come to the bridge but he was alone in his thoughts as he said, 'Tell W/T to make this request at once to the commodore. From *Gladiator*. *Request you withhold aircraft until –* '

He turned on his heels as the Hurricane roared along the catapult, dipped momentarily towards the eager water, and then climbed rapidly towards the clouds.

'Belay that!' Howard watched the fighter getting smaller and smaller until it was lost in another flurry of light snow.

The commodore wouldn't have listened anyway. A young man he had never met, and he had just seen him thrown away. 'For bloody nothing!' He realised that he had spoken the last thought aloud and added, 'Prepare the sea-boat, Number One. It'll be too dark to see anything soon.' He stared at the patch of bright sky, now so treacherous and empty.

Treherne asked quietly, 'Shall I sound off action stations, sir?'

'No, I shouldn't think so. They're in no hurry now. They've got all the time in the world.'

A boatswain's mate called, 'Sea-boat lowering party standing by, sir. The first lieutenant and th' Buffer are in charge.'

They all looked at the clouds and Howard heard the far-off tapping sound of machine guns. Like woodpeckers on a summer's afternoon.

Treherne watched him. 'He could stand a chance, sir?'

'Perhaps.' So Treherne was thinking of the pilot, and not his hopeless mission. He looked at the young signalman and tried to smile but his mouth felt rigid. 'Good work, Lee.' If only he would stop staring; his eyes seemed to fill his face.

There was no sound of a distant explosion or the great four-engined bomber dropping through the clouds. It was as if neither plane had ever been. Only the empty catapult made it a lie.

The Hurricane when it reappeared raised a cheer from some of the boat-handling party who waited by the whaler's falls while the crew in their oilskins and lifejackets prepared to be dropped into the water alongside. The cheer died instantly as the Hurricane dipped and then fought its way up again, the engine coughing and roaring out suddenly with fresh hope, as if the plane and not a man were dying.

The pilot managed to turn towards the slow-moving destroyer; it was usually Tail-end Charlie they were told to make for. Perhaps he could even see the men at the falls, the whaler already swung out above the sea, finding hope, praying.

There was a chorus of shouts as the plane staggered suddenly, then seemed to tilt right over on to one wingtip before hitting the water. It exploded in a livid fireball while fragments showered all around it. Then there was just the drifting smoke. Then nothing.

Howard said, 'Secure the sea-boat. Increase revolutions to resume station, Pilot.' He hung on to the rail beneath the screen and was as close to vomiting as he could remember.

He heard his orders being passed, the increased tremble of the bridge and fittings around and below him.

When he spoke his voice was calm again. Too calm. 'Make to commodore, *Aircraft lost. Pilot killed.*' He wanted to scream it out loud, as if the commodore and all those others might hear. Instead he climbed into his chair and held it all back. He could even offer a smile of sorts. Perhaps the cynical Mister Mills had been right after all.

'From commodore, sir. *Alter course in succession. Steer one-four-zero degrees.*'

By the compass platform Treherne filled an extra pipe with pusser's tobacco and watched the quiet preparations around him. *Gladiator* was at action stations and had been since the first hint of daylight. He saw Ayres at the voicepipe which connected him with Midshipman Esmonde and Morgan, his navigator's yeoman. They would be watching the plot-table, ready to change to a different scale of chart. To perform miracles up here if the whole bridge party was wiped out.

The captain was standing by his chair, his pipe well alight, the wind burning it away in minutes. He looked less tired now, Treherne thought. It was something he had never got used to with Howard. The prospect of action, set against the chance of surviving the day; his reactions were never what Treherne expected.

He often wondered if the captain had a girl somewhere. If so, he kept her safely stowed away. Treherne thought of his own wife, Carol, who had just walked out of his life after two years of marriage. He didn't understand that either; she was, after all, a sailor's daughter. He smiled to himself. Maybe that was the reason. Maybe she wanted something more in her life than hello and goodbye.

Treherne had been born and raised in the little port of Fowey. He had always wanted to go to sea, even as a nipper. It was in his blood; almost every family around that busy harbour had a sailor in its midst. It seemed natural, expected, perhaps that he should choose one of the local china-clay steamers for his first step. But he soon lost his heart to the deep-water ships, and the lure of the Caribbean had taken him all the way.

When his ship, packed to the deck seams with bananas, had crossed and recrossed the great Western Ocean, he had never thought that those same waters might one day be a terrible enemy, not only to him and his companions, but the one real, unbeatable menace to his country.

He felt the deck lift and slide as *Gladiator* came round on the new course and he heard Howard speaking with the coxswain in the wheelhouse. *The team*. Boots on a ladder and the welcome clatter of mugs as they waited for the promised hot tea in its dented fanny.

Here and there a light flickered in the convoy or there was a stammer of static from the W/T office voicepipe.

The commodore was getting jumpy. Rounding up his flock while one of the wing escorts entered the convoy and steamed fussily up the ranks of heavily laden ships. Demanding more speed and less smoke, telling one of the masters to watch his course, another to acknowledge signals and not just take it as read.

It was funny if you thought about it. Treherne was a highly-skilled navigating officer like so many RNR people who had once served in peaceful ships. He knew the dangers and the stupidity of some masters who preferred to go their own way, but he still resented the manner in which they were chased around by the Navy. They were, after all, civilians; they were also well aware that they were themselves the main targets. Bomb, torpedo, or the impartial mine – they faced it all, and still went back for more.

He realised that Howard had joined him, his pipesmoke thinning as he took another long puff. I must be getting shagged out, Treherne thought. I didn't even see him move.

Howard eyed him thoughtfully. 'Any views, Pilot?'

Treherne grinned and felt his skin crinkle where he had once got frost-bite in the North Atlantic. One of the reasons he had grown a full set.

'I think it'll be today, sir.'

Howard glanced at the men around him. Hands reached out for mugs to be filled, but the lookouts never took their eyes from their various sectors.

'I agree. No more signals about the German ship out of Tromsø. No bloody news of anything!' He seemed to make up his mind. 'You know what I think? They're going to come at us from the air.'

They both looked up at the fast-moving wisps of cloud. The sky would be properly blue when the day finally opened up. No cover.

The young signalman Rosie Lee stared up with them, as if to see something terrible there. But he heard Treherne chuckle and saw him hand his tobacco pouch to the captain. It was all right after all.

'God, look at the sun!'

Howard turned and saw the two funnels slowly light up like burnished copper as the first rays spilled from the horizon. It was as if the light were being poured across it, molten metal over a dam.

Faces became personalities again, the muzzles and barrels of the anti-aircraft guns shone as the sunlight played over the glistening ice and the huddled figures of their crews.

Treherne glanced at the White Ensign as it flapped out stiffly from the gaff. Their sea-going one, torn and shredded by a hundred gales. It could not last much longer. The yeoman of signals had a system. The best ensigns were used only in harbour, and for covering the dead awaiting burial. After that they took their chances aloft.

A boatswain's mate by the voicepipes called sharply, 'From commodore, sir! *Aircraft sighted at Red four-five. Four miles.*' He was squinting with concentration as he pressed his ear to the pipe. '*Believed to be Focke-Wulf Condor again.*'

Treherne thought of the exploding Hurricane. 'Cheeky bastard!'

But Howard's mind was exploring another route. The commodore was using his radio more than usual to save time. *Because he knows.* There was no hiding-place now.

He heard the crump-crump-crump of gunfire, far away beyond the head of the convoy. That would be the RCN's *Beothuck*; she mounted eight four-point-sevens in twin turrets. Most destroyers like *Gladiator* mounted only four. There was virtually no chance of hitting the German reconnaissance bomber, but the escort commander would let fly just to break the tension. The anger and frustration of seeing the big aircraft flying lazily around the convoy, just out of useful range, close enough to count the ships then radio back a full report. Loosing off a few shells was better than nothing.

He heard signalman Lee murmur, 'I'll bet it's the same one I saw!' He made it sound suddenly personal.

A voice yelled, 'There it goes, Green four-five, angle of sight two-five!' Right across the path of the convoy. But the sun was so harsh and bright that the aircraft only showed occasionally, like a sliver of glass or bright metal.

Howard lowered his binoculars, his eyes stinging. They would have a perfect view from up there, he thought. He tried to remember all the lectures he had endured on aircraft recognition. How many were there in a Condor's crew? It was eight. Probably sitting in the sunlight, sipping *erzatz* coffee while they speculated on their chances of getting back to base in time for lunch.

A party of men scampered down the starboard side, one with a big Red Cross satchel bouncing on his hip. Another part of the ship's intricate pattern, like the damage control party which would be waiting to douse fires, shore up bulkheads, patch holes while their messmates fought the guns. The six survivors would be doing their best, although one was so badly burned that he could scarcely move. Prosser, the sick berth attendant, had given him some bandages to unpack in case they were needed. It was very likely the same in the other ships which had managed to snatch up some survivors. To sit and do nothing, in pain or not, was worse than being occupied; work kept you from thinking the ship that had saved you might be the next one to catch it.

Sub-Lieutenant Ayres lowered his glasses and wiped his eyes with a glove. His breath poured through the blue and red scarf around his neck and mouth so that it looked like steam. Little gems of ice clung to the scarf as his breath froze on it.

He had seen the slow-moving aircraft, now a mere speck above the hard horizon. 'The bright face of danger.' He said it without emotion, his tone almost matter-of-fact.

Treherne looked at him searchingly. He guessed the scarf was part of the earlier Ayres. The schoolboy.

'What was that, Sub?'

Ayres gave a little shrug. 'Something I had to learn once.'

Howard moved to the forepart of the bridge. He knew what the big, bearded navigator was thinking. Ayres could easily give up right now. There was no fear any more. You only felt fear when you retained some hope of survival.

'From commodore, sir! *Aircraft approaching from Green one-five* – ' The rest was lost in the din of commands and the crisp Scottish voice of Finlay in his control position.

Howard looked at his bridge team. 'We shall close the convoy to offer anti-aircraft support. Revs for twenty-five knots, Pilot.'

He felt his ship begin to quiver as Lieutenant (E) Evan Price, the son of a Swansea collier, opened the throttles on his thirty-four thousand shaft horsepower like a man raising weir gates on a flooded river.

'Aircraft, sir! Bearing Green three-oh, angle of sight two-oh!'

Finlay's voice, calm and unhurried over the bridge speaker: 'Twenty-plus bandits! All guns stand by!'

Howard stood high on the forward gratings and watched A- and B-guns swinging onto their targets. The snick of metal, a man's quick, nervous cough like one in church before the sermon.

Finlay again. '*Barrage!*' He was speaking to one of his men but had left the speaker switch down. 'Ju 88's. Coming low. Feeling their way.'

Howard lifted his glasses. By excluding all the other ships it felt as if *Gladiator* was completely alone. He stared at the two arrowheads of aircraft. The sky was full of them, or appeared to be.

'From commodore, sir. *Open fire at will.*'

A seaman gave a tight laugh. 'Who's Will, then?'

'Barrage – *Commence!*'

Howard let the glasses fall to his chest and took a deep breath. *Here they come.* He heard the staccato crash of guns over the convoy, and as Finlay passed his order the bridge shook to the instant response from the main armament.

Howard saw the convoy spreading out on either bow, as if *Gladiator* would charge unchecked into its midst.

But he heard Treherne passing his orders, the bow-wave easing slightly. Below the bridge he heard the next shells clanging into the breeches. 'Gunlayer – target!' Then, 'Trainer – target!'

'*Shoot!*'

The sky was already pockmarked with drifting balls of smoke, as if it were indelibly stained and would never regain its colour.

Howard looked at the solid lines of merchantmen, their grey and dazzle-painted escorts weaving around them, automatic and close-range weapons blazing their challenge.

He said quietly, 'No, we are not alone.'

The leading aircraft thundered overhead, their wings reflecting the cones of tracer around them as they screamed towards the ships.

Then came the first bombs.

Chief Petty Officer Bob Sweeney, *Gladiator*'s coxswain, eased the wheel carefully as the wheelhouse shook and rattled to the crash of gunfire. Despite the steel shutters across the ports and windows the air was already filled with acrid smoke from the bridge Oerlikons as they kept up their harsh rattle, pausing only briefly for the loading number to slam on a fresh magazine.

On either side of Sweeney's thickset figure the telegraphs were manned by Bully Bishop, the chief quartermaster, and an able seaman named Melvin. A messenger crouched by the voicepipes while Midshipman Esmonde and the navigator's yeoman wedged themselves in a corner behind the vibrating plot-table.

Sweeney listened to the voices from the upper bridge, a shout from one of the lookouts followed instantly by more rapid fire from the main armament as well as other ships nearby.

He growled, 'Easy, lads. 'Ere they come!'

He concentrated on the ticking gyro-repeater and tried not to think of the bombers as they streaked towards the convoy. When *Gladiator* had been released from the Atlantic run to carry out a much-needed overhaul, Sweeney had gone home on leave. It was more of a formality than any sort of comfort. He no longer *had* a home, and his patient, long-suffering wife was buried in one of the East End's big communal graves.

It had been an eerie experience even for him, and he had seen just about everything from the Spanish Civil War to Dunkirk, from the Western Ocean to North Cape.

The worst part had been that he had not known where he was. The streets where he had grown to boyhood before joining the Andrew, where most of his relations had lived, worked, or been on the fiddle, had simply ceased to exist. A desert of flattened and burned bricks, the roads only marked by their broken kerb stones.

A sympathetic ARP warden had pointed out the place where his house had been. There was not even any wallpaper to show him its exact position.

'Hard a-starboard!'

'Hard a-starboard, sir!' The wheel seemed to spin in his meaty hands. 'Thirty of starboard wheel on!'

Boots skidded on the metal plates as the deck tilted hard over and Esmonde almost fell headlong, his face like a sheet.

'*Midships!*' Sweeney ground his teeth together as the bombs screamed overhead. The Old Man sounded cool enough. Just as bloody well. He added, 'Revolutions one-one-zero!'

The chain of dull explosions seemed to lift Sweeney off his

feet, and he sensed that some of the bombs must have found their targets.

Bully Bishop exclaimed harshly, 'Why th' hell don't we go faster, 'Swain?'

Sweeney nodded warningly at the bell-mouthed voicepipe. 'Keep yer voice down! Wot's got into you then? 'Ad a bellyful already?'

Esmonde touched the navigator's yeoman's arm and felt him jump.

'Why don't we?'

Morgan eyed him wearily. ''Cause we've got to stick with the merchantmen!'

Sweeney heard the captain again. 'Steady on one-seven-zero.'

Someone whispered, 'Oh God, here they come again!'

Sweeney ignored him and listened to the muted beat of engines. Ju 88's, Guns had said. Twin-engined and heavily armed. They were no strangers to Sweeney. Again that insane scream of bombs, and over it all a mad cheer from one of the voicepipes. '*Got the bastard!*'

The explosion must have been almost alongside. Morgan jerked open a shutter in time to see a huge aircraft wing complete with black cross as it disappeared past the bridge.

Sweeney snapped, 'Shut that, Morgan! Don't want a splinter in me guts!'

How long it lasted he had no idea; he never once took his eyes from the compass to consult the wheelhouse clock. Smoke eddied around them until caught and dispersed by the fans, and their aching bodies were spotted with deckhead paint like snow.

'*Full ahead together!*'

Sweeney hid his relief as the telegraphs sent their message to the engineroom. Christ, he thought, the chief and his mob would be feeling it down there. You would never hear a bomb or see a torpedo until the side caved in and you were scalded to death.

The revolutions mounted and Sweeney tried to picture what was happening. A gong rattled sharply through the din of engines and gunfire, and for a moment he thought he had gone deaf.

'Cease firing!'

They stared at one another in disbelief. Morgan said thickly, 'Near thing.'

'Revolutions seven-zero.' Just as promptly the speed began to drop away. Howard must be standing right by the voicepipe, Sweeney thought.

'Sea-boat's crew, Pilot! Doctor to the bridge at the double!' Then he said, 'Cox'n up here, please.'

Sweeney automatically made to wipe the paint flakes from his cap and duffel coat. 'Take over, Bully.'

After the trapped confinement of the wheelhouse the sky seemed unnaturally bright through a great undulating pall of smoke.

Sweeney climbed the ladder, past the starboard Oerlikon where the crew were re-loading and checking over the firing mechanism, their eyes wild and glaring.

Sweeney had seen pictures of similar faces in his father's old books about the Western Front. Faces driven beyond hope, even despair, with only the madness left; the need to kill.

Sweeney stepped through the bridge gate and stared at the scene ahead of the ship with stunned dismay.

The convoy was scattered into uneven straggling lines, and the oil-covered swell was covered with the flotsam of battle. Broken lifeboats and packing-cases, bodies and men still, unbelievably, alive as they foundered towards the destroyer moving amongst them. Sweeney kept his face hard and expressionless as he saw the others: pieces of men, no longer human, just things.

He touched his cap. 'Sir?'

Howard swung towards him, seeing him for the first time. 'I'd like you to take over aft, 'Swain. Sort the wounded out in the wardroom.' He tried to smile but it did not reach his eyes. 'You know what to do.'

Sweeney shaded his face to study a dark shape in the far distance. The keel of an upturned freighter. There were men there too, some standing on the stricken hull. Sailors were often like that. Unwilling to quit their ship even at the end.

Howard said, 'You did well, 'Swain.' He lowered his eyes and stared at his sleeve. 'We lost seven merchantmen.'

Sweeney watched him gravely. A third of the convoy wiped out since they had left Iceland. God alone knew how many blokes had gone with them. He asked, 'Did we get any of *them*, sir?'

Howard stood motionless and stared at the drifting smoke. 'Two, and a probable.' He faced the coxswain. 'Pretty good deal for Jerry, I'd have thought?'

Marrack clattered onto the bridge, his nose probing around. 'Sea-boat ready for lowering, sir.'

His expression asked, *Is it wise?* But one look at Howard's despair gave him his answer.

Petty Officer Tucker levelled his telescope above the gently shivering screen.

'From commodore, sir!'

Treherne said heavily, 'I thought they'd done for him too.' He sounded dazed by it, sickened at the simplicity of slaughter.

Tucker continued relentlessly, '*Am abandoning ship.*'

Howard raised his glasses and found the elegant *Lord Martineau* drifting bows-on in a bank of smoke. There were flames too. She had been straddled several times by bombs, and with her massive cargo of tanks and armoured vehicles she would go suddenly when the time came.

'*Beothuck* is standing by to take off survivors.'

Howard saw the foremast and derricks topple over the side, the noise lost in the distance. *Eight then.* In what? An attack which had lasted only two hours.

He crossed to the other side and peered down at the deck where the whaler was already swinging above the sea, its crew grim-faced; hating it, not wanting to be left by their own ship.

'Lower away!' Marrack was standing on a washdeck locker, hands on hips, his nose trained towards the men at the boat's falls.

Howard said, 'Dead slow.'

'Vast lowering! Out pins!' Marrack watched as the oily swell rose evenly below the whaler's keel. '*Slip!*' The slender hull hit the water and with the helm lashed over was guided away from the destroyer's side by the long boatrope from the forecastle.

Howard forgot them and looked at the scattered convoy. Here and there a lamp stammered amongst the smoke, and the big tug was somehow managing to take a freighter in tow. The damaged vessel's bows were so deep in the water that her screw was lifted cleanly above the surface.

He watched the commodore's ship give another shudder, her stern sinking even as he watched. The strange hull of *Tromp II*, the makeshift anti-aircraft vessel, steamed slowly across his vision. But for her, the Germans could have wiped out the whole convoy. No bother at all. By the time she had passed, the commodore's ship was almost gone, obscene bubbles bursting around her as her heavy cargo began to break free and complete her destruction.

Treherne said, 'Escort commander has ordered the corvettes to carry out another sweep, sir, while the rescue goes on.'

'Good decision, Pilot, and a brave man to make it.' He said it with the bitterness which held him like a vice. All this way, and for nothing. It was a game where one player held all the aces. The Home Fleet support group had stayed well clear because of the U-Boat reports, and had retained their carrier for their own protection. The large enemy surface ship had failed to appear, and it was unlikely she would now that the Kola Inlet was so near. She was probably back in harbour. Another ruse, then?

'Stop engines!' He heard the Buffer's rough voice bellowing at his men at the scrambling nets and bowlines.

The gasping, anonymous faces in the sea alongside, soaked in oil, bloody and nearly done for.

I should be too used to it to care. But I do care. He found he was gripping the cold steel so hard that his fingers cracked.

Treherne said, 'Have another fill of mine, sir?' He was holding out his tobacco pouch, concerned. 'I'll join you in that first Horse's Neck when we get back, sir. If I may?'

Howard took the pouch but did not speak. Treherne knew he could not. Dare not.

Ayres moved silently to his side and whispered, 'I've never seen anything so terrible!'

Treherne made certain Howard was out of earshot and noticed that he had not managed to fill his pipe.

'Well, my lad, Winston Churchill has promised our wonderful allies, the Russians, that we shall push a convoy through to Murmansk every three weeks.' He turned his gaze from Howard's stooped shoulders. 'Can you imagine anything so bloody crazy, Sub? Like the Germans trying to send a convoy up the Thames Estuary!' He spat it out. '*The bloody bastards!*' But Ayres did not really understand who he meant.

The whaler was picking its way through the drifting wreckage, the carnage. They were still doing it when a Russian unit of six destroyers and a tug came to join them for the rest of the way.

'Tea, sir?'

Howard turned in his chair and took the chipped mug with great care.

The Russian senior officer and *Beothuck*'s captain were exchanging signals, while the convoy gathered its strength and tried to take up its positions again.

'Ready to proceed, sir!' Marrack was calm, as usual. 'We should be in port by dawn.'

But Howard was listening to the port Oerlikon gunner, who was squatting below his mounting and banging his gloved hands together in time with a quiet lament, which he recognised was sung to the tune of 'What a Friend We Have in Jesus.'

> When this bloody war is over
> Oh how happy I shall be,
> But we're here today and gone tomorrow,
> So let's get back to bloody sea . . .

6

When Do You Leave?

The great stretch of the natural harbour was the colour of dirty pewter, so that the craggy hills and fjords seemed without life or movement. Narvik, once a busy Norwegian port, was partly hidden in mist, and there was no horizon to separate land from sky.

The apparent lifelessness of the place was an illusion. Even as another snow-flurry blotted out some of the small houses above the harbour, a fighter roared out of the shadows, her engine shaking the hills and cutting a sharp passage across the sea's face.

The submarine moved slowly, her powerful diesels throbbing as if, like a wounded beast, she was returning to her lair to recover. There was barely any wash, and the men who stood on her casing, muffled to the eyes in their heavy clothing, watched the approach of land, some probably regarding it as some kind of miracle.

When the small minesweeper pushed abeam and tooted to them, nobody moved or returned the waves of welcome and admiration.

There were no such gestures from some nearby fishing-boats, for this was an occupied country where it was wiser not to display any feelings at all. A big launch detached itself from the powdery snow and surged to meet the incoming U-Boat, a lamp already stabbing through the gloom, so that the long, shark-like outline turned slightly to starboard as if on an invisible towrope.

At the rear of the conning-tower, on the 'bandstand', a flag had suddenly appeared, scarlet with black cross and swastika to match the ones on the launch and minesweeper.

By the periscope standard the submarine's commander turned his head to stare up at it, sharing the moment with the rest of his men. There would be other eyes watching from the land, he thought. Spies, terrorists, who would be quick to send word by their forbidden radios to London, to report their presence. Their survival.

With a kind of defiance the German threw off his weather-proof hood and jammed his white-topped cap on to his untidy hair. The white cap, the mark of a U-Boat commander.

They might even see the extent of the damage, he thought. He touched the side of the bridge, the buckled plating, the holes punched through it by cannon fire while they had gone into a steep dive. One man had been hit by splinters and had died a few moments after they had gone under. If the enemy's attacks had continued the sailor's corpse, with some more fuel, could have been sent to the surface. That might have convinced them.

Kapitänleutnant Manfred Kleiber had been in submarines for most of his naval service. He was now twenty-six years old, and until that last attack had never really considered the real possibility of being killed himself. It happened to others, for theirs was a dangerous trade.

But this time things had gone wrong; and he still searched his mind, trying to discover if he had failed in some way.

They had sailed from Kiel after a short refit to make their way north around the Faeroes, through the *Rosegarten* and then down to a new base on the French coast near Lorient. A change from these bitter seas, with only cold stares and hostility to greet a U-Boat's return. But he had received orders redirecting him to find and shadow the convoy. To keep pace with it, he had had to surface, and had been very aware of the dangers afforded by the ice and what it could do.

He had known the vents to freeze solid in Arctic waters, so that a U-Boat was unable to dive and would lie surfaced until an enemy flying-boat or bomber found her.

They had fired at extreme range, knowing it was the only chance to slow down the convoy, to fight for time to home other U-Boats to the area. Now he knew differently: that the other boats had been sent after the heavy British war ships to the north-west.

He had taken his boat into a dive, barely knowing if the damage from the torpedo which had exploded prematurely was fatal; realising only that he had done his best, and had managed to send one more precious supply ship to the bottom.

Even as he had reached up to pull the upper hatch behind him, and the tracer had shone so vividly in the dying seaman's blood, he had seen the destroyer ploughing over the sea towards him as if all else was excluded and it was a personal fight to the death.

When the hydroplanes had finally responded and the water had thundered into the saddle-tanks, Kleiber had retained that picture starkly in his mind. And later, while he had used every trick and skill which had managed to keep him and his men alive, he had recalled the destroyer's number as it shone in the bright tracers like the dead man's blood. *H-38*. He had looked it up in his soiled and well-used copy of *Weyers Kriegs-Flotten*: his bible. So now he had one up on the enemy which had so nearly sent them down into the crushing depths for the last time. HMS *Gladiator*.

But for the damage caused by the explosion Kleiber knew he would have had another attempt to find the convoy. And H-38.

Boots grated on the casing and he saw the seamen gathering up the mooring wires, kicking them free of ice.

Kleiber glanced around the narrowing anchorage. They could not stop here. It would be back to Kiel again to put matters right. By the time they eventually reached their French base it would be summer. They said there was fresh butter, wine and good food a-plenty in France. Women too probably, to get his men into more trouble.

He thought of his home in Hamburg. They would all ask, 'Home again? When do you leave?' Maybe it was like that in all navies.

He thought of the thunder and crack of depth-charges. He had grown to accept them, although he had heard that the enemy were acquiring better anti-submarine weapons.

But time was running out for the British. They did not have enough escorts, and could not provide air cover for the convoys where it was most needed. Whereas Germany was building more submarines, faster and bigger than ever before. It was a race which could only have one ending. The Americans could not offer much help; they were too enmeshed in the Pacific, fighting the Japanese and seeing the enemy drawing closer and closer to a homeland which had never known the destruction of war.

The Russians were falling back and the convoys to Murmansk must soon stop. Even the British, desperate, with their backs to the wall, would have to admit defeat there, just as their army was being defeated in the Western Desert. He paused in his private evaluation and passed a few brief orders down to the control room. The first heaving-line snaked through the thinning snow and soon had a wire eye bent on to it.

Kleiber saw the caps and greatcoats of senior officers waiting to come aboard. To hear his part of the game they played at HQ with their flags and coloured counters.

The diesels puffed out choking fumes and shuddered into silence.

Kleiber straightened his oil-stained cap and climbed down to the casing-deck.

'*Besatzung stillgestanden!*'

He saluted his men on the fore-casing, and only then did he turn to meet the visitors.

Respect had to be earned from these men. It did not come only with the white cap.

Lieutenant-Commander David Howard switched off the remaining light in his day cabin and felt his way to one of the scuttles. It took physical effort to unscrew the deadlight and then open the scuttle; weeks and weeks of being tightly secured had seen to that.

He held his face to the air and took several long, deep breaths. It was all so unreal, like the day cabin, or part of a nightmare, the strangle-grip which almost stopped his breathing when the alarm bells screamed out in the night, or when Howard had awakened in his bridge chair, the sky bright from some burning merchantman.

The only light here was a fine edge of deep gold around a solitary cloud, and soon that would be gone as night gave an even denser darkness to the Firth of Clyde.

After the bitter days and nights on the upper bridge the air here felt almost balmy. He strained his eyes as if to see the sprawling town of Greenock beyond the dockyard, but it was sealed-off as tightly as any cupboard. Here and there a boat chugged through the darkness, showing itself occasionally with a bow-wave, or some shaded light as it approached a mooring buoy. After so many weeks of endless duty, *Gladiator* had been sent back to Britain in this, the middle of June.

But not before she had completed another convoy to Murmansk and several hazardous anti-submarine sweeps to clear the way for a second, homeward bound.

He still thought of that convoy which had been the first for many of his company, when they had been attacked by aircraft. There had been one final victim before the ships were taken into the port for unloading. The freighter *Empire Viceroy* which had been under tow with her stern high out of the water had gone down quite suddenly within sight of land. So the losses had risen to twelve, nearly half the total number when you considered that the fighter catapult vessel, and the converted anti-aircraft ship *Tromp II* had been counted amongst the thirty to be escorted from Iceland. It was ironic that none of the escorts had lost a man.

Reluctantly, Howard sealed the scuttle again and switched on all the lights. Even this place felt different, he thought. Damp, unlived-in; that was nothing new, but he could sense another change in the whole ship, as if there was surprise and not just relief at being here.

When he had opened the scuttle he had heard music blaring out from the messdecks and W/T office, the buzz of voices through the bulkhead where Marrack would soon assemble the officers and Howard would be invited to join them in what was theoretically their own, private mess.

He stared at the desk, the neat piles of papers and requests he had spent most of the day scrutinising and signing so that Ireland, the petty officer writer, could parcel them up to be collected by the guardboat.

Breakages, losses, reports on machinery and supplies, ammunition and fuel. He had to deal with it, stand in a queue with all the other commanding officers.

He glanced at the cupboard where he kept his personal stock of brandy but decided against it. Not yet anyway.

He crossed to the mirror inside his sleeping cabin and touched his face with his fingers. The first real shave he had had for weeks.

He thought suddenly of his ship's company, and smiled. They would care little for the neat piles of forms and documents. First priority was mail from home. Second, leave.

He watched his eyes as he smiled. Like a stranger. The lines around his mouth, the deep shadows beneath his eyes seemed to smooth out. He was twenty-seven. He had been feeling as old as time. Howard looked at the neat bed which Vallance or a messman would turn down for him. Another rare harbour ritual.

Would it work this time? He stared around with sudden anxiety. His quarters, usually so spacious, seemed to have shrunk so that he felt restrained. He knew it was because of the convoys, where his quarters had been the sea and the sky with only cat-naps in his hutch of a sea cabin to confine him.

He winced as he touched his face again – his freshly shaved skin felt raw and tender. Perhaps Treherne and some of the others had the right idea in growing beards. He thought of young Ayres. They said he did not shave at all yet.

A few familiar faces would be gone when *Gladiator* was committed to her next task. New ones to know and trust, or to have them trust him.

There was a tap at the door and Marrack stepped over the coaming, his cap beneath his elbow. He looked fresh and sleek; 'polished' might describe him best, Howard thought. He had come through it all very well, and had shown little concern for the hatred he had roused by his constant efforts to keep everyone on top line.

Marrack glanced past him at the cabin, like a detective looking for clues. 'All ready, sir.' He gave a brief smile. 'Bar's open.'

With a start Howard realised it was another rarity to see all his wardroom together at once. The place was welcoming and comfortable, with the foul-weather covers removed from the red leather chairs and club fender. All the usual wardroom clutter, pictures of the King and Queen on either side of the ship's crest, a rack of revolvers behind a locked glass door, an empty letter-rack, and beyond the barely swaying curtain which divided it from the dining section, the table, properly laid out, instead of the mugs and slopping dishes which had been common enough in the Arctic. Those officers who had been seated got to their feet, and Howard nodded to them. Another sea-change, he thought. Gilt buttons and ties, instead of filthy sweaters and scuffed boots.

A ship at rest.

Petty Officer Vallance held out a glass to him on a tray. It was filled almost to the top and he guessed it was a Horse's Neck.

Treherne spoke as he raised his own glass. 'The first one — remember, sir?'

Howard drank slowly, although he did not recall what Treherne meant.

'Relax, gentlemen.' He perched on the club fender as Vallance and a messman refilled glasses and made notes at the little bar counter to make certain no officer conveniently forgot his mess account.

Howard said, 'I'll tell you what's happening — what *I* know, that is.'

That brought a few grins, except from old Arthur Pym the Gunner (T). In the deckhead lights his bald pate shone like a marker buoy, and his tight-lipped mouth was set in the usual sour disapproval. He looked ancient, and beside Ayres he could have been a grandfather.

Howard continued, 'The Asdic and radar boffins are coming aboard as soon as we move alongside tomorrow forenoon, then there's a boiler clean.' He glanced at the Chief, unrecognisable without his white boiler-suit and grease-smudged cap. 'So be ready for the signal.'

It was a miracle how Evan Price and his engineroom crew had kept the shafts spinning in all seas under every kind of pressure. This morning, when they had made fast to a buoy, Price had come to the bridge to stare at the land, drinking it in.

When Howard tried to thank him for his efforts Price had shrugged and had offered his lop-sided grin, something originally caused by a loose wrench when he had first gone to sea, and said, 'I must be mad, sir. My dad was a miner, see? I worked to *better* myself, no down the pit for me, I said!'

Together they had watched the gulls swooping over the masts, sharing their momentary freedom. Then Price had said, 'Look at me now — I spend more time creeping about in the darkness than my Dad ever did!'

Howard saw Vallance taking his empty glass away to refill it. He had barely noticed drinking it. *The old wardroom devil.*

'We've got a list for the dockyard maties to lose themselves in for about . . .' He felt them tense and added, 'Three weeks. So there'll be leave for the port watch and the first part of starboard watch. Number One and the cox'n are already working on it.' He met their various gazes. 'We had the usual signals from Welfare, I'm afraid. Two homes bombed — one, Stoker Marshall, lost his whole family. Such cases get preference, of course.'

He looked at the crest; it enabled him to turn away from their eyes. What a bloody awful thing to happen. One of Evan Price's men. A stoker who had been aboard for over a year. To go through hell, half-expecting death to come bursting into the racing machinery, then to get back and be told about his family.

And for what? He remembered the smouldering anger of the Canadian escort commander who had come aboard in Murmansk. The commodore had died of wounds shortly after making his last signal and *Beothuck*'s captain had assumed overall charge. He had been ashore to discuss berthing and fuelling for the escorts, and the Russians had barely been interested. When he had told them something of the losses, the sacrifice in men and ships, one had merely commented, 'Then, Captain, you should send more ships!'

The Russians had refused to allow them into their base at Polynaroe, but Howard had been expecting that. Worse, they had not permitted the landing of some of the badly wounded and disabled survivors.

And it was still going on, exactly as they had left it. One convoy, which had been reduced to three-and-a-half knots by a gale-force head-wind, had been attacked by aircraft and destroyers from Norway because some of the escorts had been running out of fuel and were detached to head for the Faeroes to top up their bunkers. A third of that convoy had been scattered and sunk.

You should send more ships.

He tore his mind from the shrieking bombs and the stricken freighters lurching out of line, sinking or on fire.

'This is confidential. After taking on new equipment and some replacements for our company, we shall join a newly-formed escort-group for a working-up period, yet to be decided. Questions?'

Finlay asked, 'Back to the Atlantic after that, sir?' So casually put, like a man asking about the cricket score.

Howard smiled. Finlay, perhaps more than anyone, had actually thrived on their discomfort in the Arctic. It was the first time his department had been able to fire on and actually hit a U-Boat, and the overall gunnery against aircraft had been faultless. He was losing his gunner's mate, who was going for warrant rank ashore, and one of his ordnance mechanics too.

He replied, 'I believe that may be so.' In minutes it would be all over the ship. A spot of leave, then back to the bloody Atlantic. Sugar and poison. He shook his head as Vallance made to refill his glass. Then he said quietly, 'I don't have to drum it into you,' his glance fell on the pink-faced midshipman, 'any of you, after what you have just seen and done. If anyone asks you what you're doing, tell them simply this: you are achieving impossibilities because each and every one of you has become a veteran, *just by being there!*'

Marrack said, 'Thank you, sir. I can speak for the wardroom as a whole, I think.'

Treherne grinned through his beard. 'You will anyway, Number One!'

Marrack frowned slightly. A witness had distracted his brief. 'We all appreciate what you have done, sir.' There was a murmur of approval, even from old Pym. 'We've lost a lot of good ships, but we saved quite a lot too. For myself, I'm proud to be a part of it.'

Nobody laughed at Marrack's remark, and for him it had been an outburst, Howard thought. The tall lieutenant meant every word of it.

Howard moved through them to the door where Petty Officer White, the Buffer, was waiting to do Rounds.

Howard hesitated, then turned away from his own quarters and ran lightly up the ladder to the lobby where Leading Seaman Bishop was leaning over the quartermaster's desk.

Howard could feel Bishop staring after him as he stepped out onto the deck, the breeze of the firth greeting him like an old friend. Had he been thinking that it was hopeless, wasted – marking time while awaiting the inevitable? The thought seemed to shake him bodily. All the parades and the training in peacetime, regattas and girls in low-cut dresses at wardroom parties in the Med. He had since been made to re-learn *everything*, no less completely than men like Marrack and Bizley. What he had been taught in those far-off days had proved utterly useless. Was that how his father's war had been, why Mister Mills had lost control of his feelings on that and probably other Armistice Days?

The shock seemed to steady him in some way. How could he have failed to see that the men who served *Gladiator*, and all those unknown ones who faced death and fear each time they put to sea, were too precious to waste, to be tossed away for nothing?

He remembered the Oerlikon gunner's little ditty. *Here today and gone tomorrow* ... He gripped the guardrail and stared at the invisible town. '*Well, not if I can bloody well help it!*'

Vallance, who had padded quietly after him from the wardroom, paused and nodded to himself. The Old Man was letting off steam. Thank God for that. I've served a few, he thought, but I'll see the war out with this one.

Back in the wardroom again Vallance realised that Sub-Lieutenant Bizley was still slumped in his chair, some neat gin splashed over his trousers. The others were already sitting around the table, and there was a rare excitement at the prospect of the meal.

'Wake up, sir!' Vallance stepped back as Bizley stared at him, his eyes red-rimmed while he recovered his bearings.

'*What?*' He had been deep in thought when the gin had taken charge. Dreaming of the proposed decoration, what his parents and friends would say. He lurched to his feet, but not before Vallance had made sure he had scribbled his name on a bar-chit.

At the table old Pym was saying, ''Course, in them days we didn't 'ave no big searchlights, y'see?'

Finlay peered doubtfully at the soup. 'I expect *you* had oil lamps, eh?'

Treherne reached for the bread, two helpings of it, brought

aboard fresh that afternoon from Greenock. He held it to his nose and sighed. *Real bread.*

He saw Pym's watery eyes glaring at the gunnery officer and said easily, 'Go on, T, tell us about Jutland again, when you were in the old *Iron Duke* with Jellicoe.'

Pym regarded him suspiciously and then squinted at the deckhead. 'Well, as I may 'ave told you before, Lord Jellicoe was standin' right beside me when the Jerries opened fire . . .'

Vallance watched him and rubbed his hands while the messmen bustled around the table.

Normal again. Just one big happy family.

The naval van pulled up with a jerk after dodging a mobile crane and a whole squad of marching sailors. The driver called, 'Here she is, Sunshine, the *Gladiator.*'

After a momentary hesitation, the driver, a tough-looking leading seaman from the Railway Transport Office, climbed down to help his last passenger lift his gear from the back. Afterwards he wondered why he had done it; he could not recall helping anyone before.

The young seaman dragged his kitbag and hammock to the side of the jetty and stared slowly along the moored destroyer from bow to stern. She was a powerful-looking ship with fine, rakish lines, very like the ones he had studied in his magazine at school. She appeared to be littered with loose gear, while wires and pipes snaked in all directions and overalled figures groped over them, adding to the confusion with their tools and paint pots.

The driver stood beside him, arms folded, and said, 'She was on the Ruski convoy run 'til recently. In the thick of it.'

He glanced at the youth and wondered. Slightly built, with wide eyes and skin like a young girl. God, he thought, he only looks about thirteen. In fact, Ordinary Seaman Andrew Milvain was eighteen, just, but certainly did not look it. In his best uniform, the jean collar still the dark colour it was issued, unlike the Jacks who scrubbed and dhobied them until they were as pale as the sky. Everything was brand new, straight off the production belt. He thought he knew what the driver was thinking, but he had become used to that.

A seaman in belt and gaiters, a heavy pistol hanging at his hip, walked to the guardrails and called, 'One for us, Hookey?'

The man nodded and said to Milvain, 'Off you go, your new home then.'

The youth picked up his bag and small attaché case and the gangway sentry came down the brow to carry his hammock.

The driver made to get into the van and looked back. There was something very compelling about the new seaman. So serious; dedicated, whatever that meant.

The sentry waited for the duty quartermaster to make an appearance and said, 'New hand come aboard to join, Bob.'

They both looked him up and down and the quartermaster asked, 'Where from?'

'Royal Naval Barracks, Chatham.' He had a quiet voice which was almost lost in the din of hammering and squealing tackles.

The quartermaster took his draft chit and studied it. 'Before that?'

'HMS *Ganges*, the training establishment where . . .'

The two seamen grinned. 'Oh, we know where *that* is, right enough.'

The sentry added, 'Where they make mothers' boys into old salts in three months, eh?'

The quartermaster glanced forward. 'I'll tell the Cox'n. You carry the load 'til I get back.'

The sentry grimaced. 'The chiefs and PO's are givin' the gunner's mate a sendoff. I'll bet there's enough booze there to float this ruddy ship!'

The other man nodded. 'I'm sort of bankin' on it!'

The sentry watched a Wren riding her bicycle along the jetty, her skirt blowing halfway up her thigh.

He called after them, 'Don't let Mister snotty-nose Bizley catch you!' Then he stared after the Wren. Rather be on her than on the middle watch, he thought.

Laird, the duty quartermaster, led the way through and around many obstacles. 'Half the lads are already on leave. I'm afraid you've come at a bad time.'

Milvain asked politely, 'That officer – Bizley, wasn't it?'

Laird heard the laughter and clinking glasses from the chief and petty officers' mess and licked his lips. He dragged his mind back to the question. 'Oh, don't worry about *him*. He's fairly

new to the ship, a real little shit, but nothing we can't handle.'
He turned to see the youth blush. 'Why?'

'My brother had an officer of that name. In Coastal Forces.'

A note of warning sounded in Laird's mind. 'Your brother —
the skipper, was he?' He saw the sudden lift of the youth's chin,
a brightness in his eyes. *Had*, he thought. He said casually,
'What do they call you, then?'

Milvain thought of his mother sobbing over him at the
railway station, the other sailors watching curiously while they
waited for their various transport.

He replied, 'Andy, usually.'

Laird said, 'Well, Andy, I'm sorry I put my foot in it. It
happens. You'll see soon enough.'

The coxswain, massive and sweating, appeared in the doorway and beamed, 'What are all we, then?'

The quartermaster handed him the draft chit. God, he
thought, the coxswain reeked of rum. The whole mess did. He
said abruptly, 'His brother was Mister Bizley's skipper.'

The coxswain looked at the new arrival, Laird's remark
slowly penetrating the fog of the sendoff for the gunner's mate.

'*Ganges* boy, eh?'

'Yes, sir.'

'Not "sir" 'ere, my son. Cox'n will do very nicely.'

It was all coming back. Bizley's bravery when his motor
gunboat had gone down, his efforts to rescue the survivors.
Maybe even a medal . . .

'First ship?' He nodded slowly, picturing the various messes,
the leading hands who ruled them like barons. 'I'll stick you in
Nine Mess. Bruce Fernie is the boss there.' He stared down at
him. Officer material most likely, he thought. *Ah well*. All eyes
and innocence. Bet he had to watch out for his virginity at the
bloody *Ganges*.

He belched. 'I'll make out a card for you. Just wait 'ere, my
son.' He scowled at the quartermaster, '*You* can 'ave a wet, if
that's what you're after!'

Milvain stood by the door and watched the petty officers
laughing and drinking, as if they hadn't a care in the world. He
looked around him, seeing the scars beneath the new paint.
Russian convoys. He shivered and thought suddenly of his dead
brother. He might have been proud of him.

A youngish-looking man in a raincoat, and without any sort of cap, ran up one ladder and paused to glance at him as he moved his attaché case out of the way. 'Just joined?'

Milvain nodded and remembered what the burly coxswain had told him. 'Yes, Petty Officer. From Chatham.'

'Welcome aboard.'

The coxswain reappeared with a card for the new rating, then froze as he saw the youth chatting away.

He said awkwardly, ''Ere's yer card.'

Silence fell in the mess as the newcomer went inside. Milvain heard him say, 'Just one then, I'm catching a train south as soon as I can.'

Milvain asked quietly, 'What does *he* do – er, Cox'n?'

Sweeney breathed out heavily. 'That was the captain, my son. Gawd, wot are things comin' to in this regiment!'

He watched Milvain climb down the ladder, looking around, trying to find himself in his new world. A grin spread slowly across his battered face. Wait till I tell the others about this. *What does he do?* But it was also a side to the commanding officer he had not seen before.

Back in the crowded mess he saw the Old Man chatting with the departing gunner's mate. Should he tell him about Milvain's brother? He decided against it. Wait and see, that was best.

Howard looked across at him. 'They're getting younger, 'Swain.'

From one corner of his eye Sweeney saw the duty quartermaster slip out of the other door in case the Old Man should see him here.

He nodded heavily, 'You're off 'ome then, sir?'

Howard studied him gravely, wondering how Sweeney would manage. There must be hundreds like him, thousands, like Stoker Marshall. Nothing left, and nothing to look forward to. He glanced at the mess clock. 'I'm off then.' He thought of Hampshire. The Guvnor's garden. It would be good to see him again. But the ship seemed to hold him. Howard shook himself and said, 'I've left a phone number in case . . .' He walked from the mess and went aft to retrieve his cap from the lobby. Time to go.

The quartermaster was just about to tell the sentry all about the party when Sub-Lieutenant Bizley strode aft, his cap at the rakish angle he seemed to favour.

'Somebody came aboard just now!' It was a statement. 'I should have been told. I'm OOD in case you'd forgotten!' He jabbed a finger at the sentry and snapped, 'Tighten your pistol belt, man! I'll not have you making this ship look sloppy, so don't you forget that, either!'

The QM hastily intervened for his friend's sake. 'It was another replacement, sir. Name of Milvain.' He watched him warily, like a cat weighing up a dangerous hound. He had not anticipated Bizley's reaction.

'What name?' He felt his mind reeling. It couldn't be. Even in the Navy it was too much of a coincidence.

Sure of his ground now, the quartermaster said, 'Your last CO was his brother.'

They both stared after Bizley as he hurried away. He was almost running.

'Well, well, well, what tin of worms have *I* discovered, then?'

They grinned at one another like conspirators, while the gangway sentry gave up his attempt to tighten the offending belt.

The Buffer appeared by the after torpedo tubes and lurched towards them, his face flushed from the sendoff in his mess. 'Where's the officer of the day?'

The quartermaster replied innocently, 'Not sure, Buffer.'

'*Jesus!* The skipper's goin' over the side at any minute!'

At that moment Bizley made an appearance, but Knocker White was too full of rum to notice the corresponding smell of gin from the duty officer.

Howard came up, still wearing his plain, unmarked raincoat, and stood to look along the littered deck, wondering what Marrack would have to say about it.

He carried just a small grip; he would change into some old clothing when he reached home. The heaviest things in it were tins of duty-free cigarettes for the Guvnor. He could not manage a pipe with only one hand.

The three figures at the brow froze to attention, and the quartermaster moistened his silver call with his tongue even as a taxi came to a halt on the jetty.

Aloud Howard said, 'Take good care of her.' Then with his

fingers to his cap in salute he hurried down the brow, the twitter of the call still hanging in the dusty air.

Only once did he look back and upwards to the high, open bridge where he had stood for so many hours and days.

It was behind him now. But it would never leave him.

7

I Saw Him Go

The passenger seat of the small army fifteen hundred-weight lorry felt like iron but Howard barely noticed it as he stared out at the rich green countryside. Beside him a young lance-corporal, from Yorkshire by the sound of it, seemed eager to get as much speed as he could from the much-used vehicle.

Howard had not realised just how tired he was after the lengthy journey from Scotland. On the final leg of the trip from Waterloo he had fallen into a deep sleep and had been awakened by a porter tapping his knee to tell him that the train had reached the end of the line. It had been Portsmouth Harbour station which had been so much a part of his life even from childhood: the old wooden platform, through which you could see the water underfoot at high-tide, and the imposing masts and yards of Nelson's old flagship *Victory* rising above the dockyard wall outside the station. He could recall walking through the yard shortly after the start of 1941, when there had been a devastating air-raid on the city and anchorage. The continuous attack had lasted all night, and when a smoky dawn had laid bare the terrible destruction it had seemed a miracle that anything had survived. Over three thousand people were made homeless and famous buildings like the Guildhall and the George Inn were laid in ruins. Hundreds were killed and injured in that single raid, but the thing so engraved on Howard's mind was seeing the *Victory*'s fat black and buff hull unscathed amidst devastation, with shattered vessels all around her.

Today he had been standing frustrated by a deserted taxi rank when the lance-corporal had offered him a lift. He had barely stopped talking since they had joined the Portsmouth Road and headed inland towards the village where Howard's father lived.

It had been over a year since Howard had been here on leave and he was still trying to come to terms with the undertones of war which had changed almost everything. Hotels, once so popular with holidaymakers visiting Southsea and the Isle of Wight, were now billets and stores for the military. There were checkpoints everywhere, barbed-wire barriers and protective banks of sandbags around some of the buildings. More sinister, he thought, were the little newspaper stalls and tourist information huts with their faded posters and shuttered windows. He had supposed they were shut 'for the duration' until he had seen them close to, when his driver had been forced to slow down by a column of tanks crossing the road.

The huts were fake. Underneath their disguises they were solid concrete blockhouses from which machine-guns could cover the road with cross-fire. They were even here in the countryside, painted with camouflage or disguised as farm out-buildings. Like the tall poles poised in the fields to prevent aircraft or gliders from landing, they were a true reminder of the ever-present danger and threat of invasion, as was the fact that the nearest enemy airfield was less than ninety miles from this pleasant stretch of deserted road.

Howard thought of the grim newspaper headlines, the so-called strategic withdrawals in North Africa. What a familiar ring they had. *Would* the enemy ever come here?

He glanced at his companion, the crumpled khaki battledress, the youthful intentness on his face as he roared around a shallow bend and braked hard to avoid a marching squad of soldiers. A pleasant, homely youth, the sort you saw on the newsreels giving a hopeful thumbs-up before some disaster or other. What would he and his friends make of the battle-hardened Panzers and Wehrmacht, he wondered.

'Where are you from?'

He darted him a quick glance. 'Bradford, sir – can't you tell?' He grinned broadly. 'Th' Riviera of the North!'

'How long have you been in the Army?'

The grin remained. 'Ah, sir, I can't tell thee that! Careless talk, you know!'

Howard smiled and thought of the one telephone call he had

made to the ship. Marrack distant and self-assured, enjoying total power. 'Nothing to bother about, sir. Just chaos, that's all. If you don't bolt everything down it vanishes. Poor old Gunner (T) even lost his spare dentures!'

Howard leaned forward and said, 'Here it is, coming up on the left.' His mouth had gone quite dry, as if he was afraid of what he might find.

The lance-corporal looked doubtfully at the narrow lane which led off the main road. 'Tight squeeze, sir!'

'This will do fine.' He glanced at two figures in battledress similar to the driver's. Until they turned round. Each had a large coloured disc or diamond stitched to his clothing. 'Who are they, for God's sake?'

The driver watched him curiously. 'Eye-ties, sir. Prisoners of war left over from the desert, when we were chasing *them* for a change!' He took it for granted, and Howard was now the stranger here.

He explained, 'The trusted ones work on the land, y'see, sir. Big shortage of proper farmhands. They're even after our lasses if they get half a chance. One of our lads found his missus in bed with one when he popped home unexpected!'

Howard tried to come to grips with it. 'What happened?'

The huge grin reappeared like the Cheshire Cat's. 'The Eye-tie's in hospital, our bloke is in th' glasshouse! Worth it though, I'll bet!'

Howard groped for his bag and heard the tins rattle together. He pulled out one of them and handed it to the soldier. 'Duty-frees. Thanks for the lift.' He climbed down and walked into the lane, knowing that the unknown soldier was still staring after him. It seemed an age before the lorry's engine revved up again and left the lane in silence.

He stopped suddenly and stared at the house. Exactly as he had remembered it; cherished it. Seventeenth century – well, some of it anyway, but all of it very old. As a child he had frightened himself in his bed when the wind had moaned around its eaves, picturing the press-gangs marching through the night, or some felon hanging from the gibbet which had given its name to the hill outside the village.

The two POW's were inside the garden discussing things with his father. Of course, he spoke fluent Italian; or had once.

Another picture formed in Howard's mind like an old photograph, he and his brother on holiday in Venice, his father in a white suit and panama hat. The locals had admired the Englishman with the one eye and single arm. *Capitano*, they had called him. Howard felt the bitterness again. But the Italians had been their allies in the war which had done that to his father.

At the moment the Guvnor looked up, his eye squinting in the bright sunshine. He hurried towards him, his arm outstretched. 'Good to see you, David!' He hugged him warmly. 'So *bloody* good!'

Howard looked across at the two Italians. 'What are they doing here?'

'Helping *me*, of course.' He sounded surprised. Like the lance-corporal. 'But never mind that, my boy, come inside and tell me all about it.' The bright gaze moved over him, missing nothing. The strain, the tightness around the mouth. The youth which had gone forever.

He seemed to notice a bicycle beside the front door for the first time. 'Almost forgot. Something quite extraordinary has happened today. Better come in and be introduced.'

It seemed fresh and cool after the lorry and the dust. The furniture was a bit more battered, the pictures on the walls not as straight as they might be. But the living room with its oak beams, and fresh flowers in the great fireplace where they had sat as children with their dreams, were as welcoming as ever.

Howard realised with a start that there was a young woman beside a window, her features lost in shadow behind the sun's probing rays.

She came to meet him and held out her hand. He thought about it afterwards. She had met him halfway. On equal terms. 'I'm very sorry to do this to you, Commander Howard. I didn't know it was your first day home.'

He released her hand and watched her as she turned towards his father. Younger than he had first thought; in her early twenties, with short brown hair, and eyes which might be green if he could see them properly. She was dressed in an old tweed hacking jacket and corduroy trousers. A green headscarf which she must have been wearing on the road lay across the sofa. He also noticed the RAF brooch, like a pilot's wings, on one lapel, and that she wore a wedding ring.

The Guvnor murmured, 'I'll lay on some tea, unless – ' He fixed Howard with his eye. 'Something stronger perhaps?'

Howard felt lost. 'Stronger for me.' He faced the girl again. 'What about you?'

She smiled, but only briefly. 'I shouldn't be here. No – I think I *will* have a drink.' She looked at his father. 'A sherry perhaps?'

What could she want? How could she possibly know when he was due here? He thought of the soldier's quip about careless talk. Somebody must be doing quite a bit of that.

He waited for her to sit on the sofa, then pulled out his pipe and pouch. Like those times on the bridge. Faced with the unanswerable question. Needing the time to fashion his observations. She looked up at him and in the cooler light he saw the tiredness in her eyes. Someone who had been and still was under pressure. She was very withdrawn, wanting only to accomplish her mission and leave.

She took the glass from his father and Howard saw that her hand shook slightly. It made her apparent composure a lie.

His father stared at him. 'I've got to tell the chaps what I want digging.' He did not wink, but he might easily have done so. 'I'll leave you to some privacy.' Then he was gone and they heard the excited chatter of Italian from the garden.

'A lovely man.' She sipped her sherry. 'You see, I thought my letter had gone astray, or that you might not wish to see me.'

He frowned. 'What letter?'

She took a deep breath. 'I'm Celia Kirke. My home is over in Chichester.'

'And you cycled all this way?'

'Hardly. I borrowed the bike from an oppo in Pompey.' She watched him as he crossed to the table where his father kept letters ready for forwarding to his two sons. No wonder he had kept this one. It was stamped with some official-looking numbers and dates, and had been signed for.

She said abruptly, 'I'll tell you, now that you're here.' She sounded less confident. Troubled. 'I was in the Wrens.' She stared at her glass. 'I was stationed at HMS *Daedalus*, the naval air station at Lee-on-Solent. Where I first met Jamie.'

Howard nodded. It explained her familiarity with things naval; her casual use of Pompey, slang for Portsmouth.

She was gripping the stem of her glass with both hands, and a lock of hair fell across her forehead unheeded.

She said in the same contained voice, 'He was a squadron-leader in the RAF. He was attached to the Fleet Air Arm as an instructor.' Her chin lifted as if with pride. 'He had been a fighter pilot in the Battle of Britain.'

Howard sat down opposite her and wished the sun was not so strong in his eyes. So her husband, Jamie, was dead. *Bought it*, as they said in all three services. Casually uttered to keep up the pretence and hold back the fear you might be the next one.

She looked at him with sudden despair. 'I'm not making any sense, am I?'

Howard stared at his unlit pipe. 'Where exactly do I come in, Mrs Kirke?'

'My husband was a fine pilot; everyone looked up to him, until – ' She hesitated. 'They told him he was grounded for good, that he would stay as an instructor, but not in the air.'

'He must have hated that.'

She did not hear him. 'Then there was this signal. Asking for volunteers. Pilots, anyone who could stay airborne and was mad enough to do it.'

'How old was your husband?'

She eyed him steadily. 'Thirty-one. Older than most. Flying was his *life*. Perhaps I didn't realise it before – ' She broke off and gave a small shrug. 'Catapult aircraft merchant ships, CAM for short.' She saw his instant response and added, 'Yes, Jamie was the Hurricane pilot aboard the CAM ship on your convoy to Russia.'

Howard stared at her. 'How did you discover all this?'

'Jamie's mechanic came to see me afterwards . . .'

The picture thrust into his mind. The Hurricane rising and dipping, pouring smoke as it headed towards them. *Tail-end Charlie.*

She said, 'He explained that it was your ship Jamie was making for – you know, how they're taught to do. I just wanted to see you, to find out.' She wiped her cheek with her knuckles as if angry that she might break down. 'You see, we'd had a row. The last time we were together.' She spoke faster now. 'I didn't want it to end like that.'

Howard moved across and sat beside her without looking at

her. He could feel her tension, her sudden guard as if she expected him . . . 'Yes, I saw him go, Mrs Kirke. He was trying to reach us, although I think he must have been dead already when the plane hit the sea.' Then he did turn his head to look at her. 'I'm very sorry, but there's little more I can tell you. The Hurricane blew up. There was nothing.'

'Thank you. I had to speak to the man who might have saved him, had there been a chance.' She gazed at him for several seconds. 'Now I've met you, I know there *was* no chance for him.'

The Guvnor entered with a tray of plates but she stood up and shook her head. 'No, I must go now. But thank you.' She faced Howard again. 'Both of you.'

He followed her out of the house and waited while she put some clips around her corduroy trousers. Even the old and shabby clothing could not hide her attraction – perhaps it too was another sort of defence. He wondered what that last argument had been about.

She began to push the bicycle towards the gate. The two POW's were careful to avert their eyes but were probably watching all the same.

'What will you do now?'

She glanced at the clear sky. Looking, remembering, perhaps, when it had been filled with criss-crossing vapour trails, and schoolboys had shot each other down until luck deserted them. Like Jamie's.

'I shall go back in the Wrens.' There was no sort of doubt there, but Howard had seen her resistance almost break in the quiet, cool room. It was another side to the war. He had written to the parents of men who had been lost at sea, killed in action. He had even attended a couple of funerals because there had been nobody else. But this seemed more personal because he had shared it, and because of some unknown RAF mechanic he was a part of it.

'Perhaps we shall meet again some time?'

She looked at him. Her eyes *were* green, keeping him at a distance.

'Well, you know the Navy. Maybe we will.' She mounted the bicycle and tightened the headscarf under her chin.

She added, 'Take care of yourself, Commander Howard.'

He was taken aback by the old-fashioned way she said it. More like a mother speaking to her son than a young girl.

He called after her, 'If ever you need . . .' But she was already out of earshot.

The Guvnor had joined him in the sunlight and said quietly, 'Poor kid. She thinks she killed him, you see.'

Howard stared at him. 'He didn't stand a chance!'

'I've known men go like that. A letter, a rumour maybe, and you see death on his face. Mister Mills will tell you. It was the same in the trenches.' He put his arm round him and added, 'Try to forget it. I want to hear all about *Gladiator* and the bloody Russians!'

But that night as Howard lay in his old bed and listened to the vague drone of aircraft, 'theirs' or 'ours', he did not know, he found that he could not forget it, or the girl with the green eyes.

Gordon Treherne lay back sleepily on the disordered bed and tried to guess the time. He heard her humming in the other room and felt the returning need running through him like a fever in the Gulf. She had drawn the blackout screens across the windows. He ran his fingers through his hair and sighed deeply. So they had been *at it* for most of the day, and within an hour of his arrival at her flat.

Outside the room it was quiet, the town of Birkenhead bracing itself for another sneak air-raid. The shipyards were still, all work stopped until the new day. So many fine vessels had gone from here, he thought. He had served in a couple of them.

She came back into the bedroom, a tartan blanket wrapped around her nakedness. Her name was Joyce, and Treherne had met her shortly after the outbreak of war, over the water in Liverpool where she had been working in a pub to make a few extra bob. She was married, and her husband was now serving somewhere in the Royal Army Service Corps.

His eyes narrowed as he thought of the first time he had made love to her. Lust, need; there had been no thought of permanence then. Perhaps it had been the savage scar on her back after her husband had beaten her up, as he had apparently done quite a lot.

She stopped by the bed and put down a tray with some beer and sandwiches on it.

She smiled. 'Only spam, I'm afraid, Gordon. You must eat as well, you know!'

She gasped as he dragged her down and flung the blanket to the floor. 'You're lovely, Joyce!' He squeezed her breasts and pulled her closer, feeling the urge rising to match hers.

She had beautiful breasts and a body to match. She must have been quite lovely as a bride, he thought wistfully.

All at once he was above her, kissing her, while she moved her body against his.

When it was over they lay entwined, exhausted by their hunger for each other. He stroked her back and made her shiver when he touched the scar. 'If that bastard ever bothers you again . . .' He never used her husband's name, as if it was something foul. 'I'll take him apart.'

She nodded, like a child, then touched his beard. 'I'll never go back to him. I'll manage. I have before.'

'*We'll* manage, right, Joyce?' He did not know how, but somehow wanted it to be so.

She said, 'I've got a good job now, making duffel coats for the Navy!'

Treherne grinned at her. A real sailor's girl. God alone knew how it might end, but he knew that he wanted her for himself. She was not at all like his Carol, nor any of the brief affairs he had entertained in the Caribbean or various ports where they had dropped their cargoes of bananas. Joyce was different, and she was fun to be with.

They both jumped as the telephone jangled beside the bed. She made to pick it up but Treherne said, 'If it's that bastard, pass it to me! I'll tell him a few home-truths!' She watched his smouldering anger with quiet admiration. Gordon could make mincemeat of her old man. But she handed it to him anyway and whispered, 'It's for you.' It sounded like a question.

Treherne bit his lip. 'Had to leave a number, love.'

She retrieved her blanket and hurried towards the little kitchen. When she came back she found him sitting on the edge of the bed, his hands locked together, his face set in deep thought.

He looked at her, then held out his arms to her. 'I've got to go back, Joyce. That was the skipper.' He glanced at the telephone as if he could not believe it. 'Thought he was on leave.'

She clung to him and pressed her face against his chest. 'But it's not right, Gordon! You've only just got here!' She was crying now, her eyes red with tears. 'I wanted to have such a nice time with you . . .' She could not go on.

Treherne stroked her back and murmured into her hair, 'I'll make it up to you, love.' He was trying to remember exactly what Howard had said. It had been a bad line, too.

Then he said quietly, 'He wants me to take over as Number One, for the moment anyway.' She stared up at him, not understanding. He added gently, 'Second-in-command, that means.'

She wiped her face and eyes with one corner of the sheet. 'Second-in-command! Of a destroyer!' Her momentary pride vanished as she said in a small voice, 'You won't want me any more. Mixing with all those posh officers.'

Treherne grinned as he pictured the *Gladiator*'s wardroom, the old Gunner (T) minus his teeth, snoring in a corner after too many gins. 'Pusser' Finlay, and dear old Taffy Price, the chief.

He replied, 'You're my girl, Joyce. Next time I come I'll get you a ring.'

She stared at him with disbelief. 'But I'm still married!'

'I don't care. You belong to me, see? I want everyone to know it!' He let out a sigh. '*Posh* officers indeed!'

She looked at him searchingly. 'When do you have to go?'

'Tomorrow, love. I'll be back, probably sooner than you think.'

She looked at the blackout screen. 'Liverpool again?'

He nodded. 'Something like that.'

She moved against him and they lay down together. Too exhausted to make love, too sad to talk about the future.

When the first shipyard hooter sounded the start of another day, they had still barely slept.

Lieutenant Graham Marrack remained quite still, his face expressionless while he watched Howard standing by an open scuttle, the sunshine on his face.

Howard said, 'I don't see what all the fuss is about, Number

One. Of course you must accept it. God, man, a command of your own – it's what any officer would give his right arm for!'

Marrack replied stubbornly, 'I'm very aware of the honour, sir. But there will be lots of people in the queue without my jumping the gun.'

Howard turned aside as a rivet gun shattered the silence like an ack-ack fusillade. He did not know what angered him more. Losing the best first lieutenant he had ever known, regular *or* reservist, or Marrack's pigheaded attitude about accepting command.

'Look.' Howard faced him. 'This bloody war will last for years. If we win, there'll still be the Far East waiting, after that probably Russia, the way they're going on. But win or lose, the Navy must have good, experienced commanding officers. You've seen the green kids we're getting, willing to die, and that's what they usually do before they can learn anything!'

There was no movement in the little pantry and he could imagine Petty Officer Vallance with his ear pressed to the hatch, reaping a harvest of gossip for the chief and PO's mess.

'And anyway, if their lordships offer you this appointment it is not a *request*, Number One!'

Marrack frowned. '*Gladiator* will be going back to Western Approaches after this. Nobody has said so, but we both know it.'

Howard nodded and waited without comment.

Marrack finished his summing-up. 'You carried the lot of us last time. If I've learned anything, it's come from you, not out of books. You tell me that the Navy needs experienced commanding officers.' He eyed him calmly. 'And skippers need good subordinates.'

Howard smiled. 'Remember that when you take command, eh?'

As if to a signal they both shook hands as Marrack said, 'Of *course* I wanted it, sir. But not like this. I'd thought to stay in *Gladiator* for a while longer.'

Howard looked at the appointment lying on his desk. They must have worded it much the same in Nelson's day, he thought.

He said, '*Tacitus*. Flower Class corvette. She's in Western Approaches too.'

Marrack nodded slowly, watching him as if he wanted to forget nothing.

'We've seen her many times in the Atlantic.'

Marrack moved to the door. 'I've a few things to do, sir, before I leave.' He hesitated. 'Who will you get, I wonder?'

'Not another bloody lawyer, that's for sure!'

He saw the tall lieutenant give his private smile before he closed the door behind him.

Howard thought suddenly of his father, his obvious disappointment when he had cut short his visit after a call from Marrack. He could see him exactly as he had left him by the garden wall, his tousled white hair, the single, busy hand which could do almost anything. Like an extension of his eye and brain. *I shall give him a ring later on.* It seemed unfair that the Guvnor had grown so old.

That evening, when the ship was blacked-out alongside the jetty, Howard telephoned Treherne in Birkenhead.

He thought of it later. Treherne's surprise, which matched Marrack's stubbornness, so that they each had to be convinced in different ways.

He went on deck and looked at the tall cranes stark against the pale stars, and thought of the woman who had answered the telephone. Treherne was a dark horse. Full of surprises.

The gangway sentry stiffened in the darkness and Howard said, 'All quiet, Laker?'

'As a boneyard, sir!' The man grinned at him, pleased that the Old Man remembered his name.

Howard strolled along the iron deck beneath the whaler's davits, and thought about Treherne.

It was the first time that he could recall being so envious.

The red-faced coxswain stood massively to one side of the table and bawled, 'Quick march! 'Alt! Off cap!' He did not need to consult his clipboard. 'Leading Seaman Bishop, sir! Drunk an' disorderly!'

Lieutenant Finlay stared at the chief quartermaster across the little desk, his eyes hostile.

'Will you never learn, Bishop?'

The man met his gaze with equal animosity. 'Nuthin' to say, sir.'

The gunnery officer, who was OOD, glanced at the coxswain. 'Well?'

Sweeney tilted his cap against the sunshine. 'Brought aboard by the shore patrol, sir. That was after bein' thrown out of the *Coach an' 'orses*, and then the wet canteen, sir.'

Finlay glanced at his watch. 'You're a fool, Bishop — your own worst enemy.' When there was no response he snapped, 'Stand over for first lieutenant's report!'

'On cap, right turn, double march!'

'Next!'

Sub-Lieutenant Bizley waited impatiently by the lobby door. He hated being made to understudy Finlay's duties, or anyone else's for that matter. In the motor gunboat he had been first lieutenant, gunnery officer and watchkeeper, and anything else that was thrown his way.

The tannoy squeaked into life. 'Stand easy!'

'That's the lot, sir.' Sweeney folded his list of defaulters. He did not sympathise with Bully Bishop, nevertheless he had seen some of the officers pissed enough in the wardroom. Probably not the gunnery officer, he thought. 'Pusser' Finlay was sharper than any regular he had known. He never bent the rules for anyone. Unlike Treherne. He gave a grin. Even Jimmy-the-One had been known to offer a second chance. Bishop would dip his hook for certain this time.

Finlay looked along the deck. There was less disorder and mess now, fewer power-leads, and only a handful of boiler-suited dockyard maties grouped around the new gun mounting amidships, a multiple-barrelled pom-pom. To hell with dockyard rules, he thought. *They* don't have to fire the bloody things.

'I'm going to look over this job, Sub. Take over for me, and let me know when the captain comes back. He's in the dock office, so watch out.'

Bizley looked sulkily at the coxswain. 'I'll see you at up spirits.' He was about to move away when he noticed the young ordinary seaman coming aft, bent almost double under a parcel of heaving-lines. He had seen Milvain several times, working ship with the part-of-watch still on board, and knew that the young seaman had been studying him too. He made up his mind. There would be too many people about when the hands turned-to again.

'Here, Milvain, put that lot down a moment. It's standeasy anyway.'

The youth looked at him shyly, and Bizley felt a chill run through him in spite of the sunshine.

'Sir?'

Bizley cleared his throat. God, he thought, I can *see* his brother in him. 'Just wanted to say how sorry I was about your brother.' If only he would stop staring. 'I was going to visit your family, but I was in a bad way myself.'

The youth nodded. 'They understood, sir. It must have been terribly dangerous, what you did. I read all about it in the newspaper.'

Bizley's eyes blinked. 'Newspaper? I didn't see that!'

Milvain plunged his hand inside his overalls and withdrew his paybook and wallet. He opened it carefully and took out the cutting, which had obviously been studied many times. 'Here, sir.'

Bizley stared at the article which had Milvain's brother's photograph, and one of himself he did not know existed. Probably obtained from the gunnery school when he had done a course there.

It was all there; words like 'courage' and 'unselfish behaviour, above the line of duty,' stood out like banners on a cinema.

Milvain offered, 'Keep it if you like, sir. I've another one at home.'

Bizley could barely think straight. In a way it was all true, so why should he feel guilty? He saw Milvain fumbling with his paybook and another photograph as he made to close it. To cover his excitement he asked, 'Who's that, may I ask? Bit young for a pretty girl like *her*, I'd have thought?'

The seaman held it out to him. 'It's my sister, sir. Sarah.'

Bizley held it to the sunlight. The same look as the youth who was staring at him with something like awe. '*Very* nice.'

'Wait until I tell her, sir. She was dying to meet you, to thank you for what you tried to do for Gregory.'

Bizley had had little or no success with girls. He knew that the Milvain family was very unlike his own, that the head of it was a major-general.

The tannoy again. 'Out pipes! Hands carry on with your work!'

Bizley nodded. 'Perhaps I *shall* be able to pay them a visit when I get some proper leave. It will be easier to tell them now there's been some time since . . .' He broke off as Finlay came striding aft to the bow.

The lieutenant exclaimed angrily, 'I *told* you to warn me, Sub!'

The captain was at the foot of the brow, a pipe in his mouth which he removed only to salute the quarterdeck as he came aboard.

Howard sensed the tension between them but decided to ignore it. It had been agreed that Treherne should take over as first lieutenant, for the moment anyway. There was no available replacement in any case, so he would have to go over the watch-bill with Treherne when he arrived.

'Ask Number One to join me in my cabin, will you, Guns?' He could tell from Finlay's curiosity that Marrack had said nothing to anybody. He was playing it close to his chest. As usual.

He would tell the wardroom when Treherne was present; the others who were on leave would get the news later.

He looked at the bright sky. It was hard to believe that the ice and bitter weather had existed. That the convoys had ever been. He thought of the exploding Hurricane, and his father's simple explanation. 'She thinks she killed him.' Surely that was impossible?

He saw Marrack strolling towards him. 'It's on, Number One.'

Marrack smiled. 'Sun's over the yardarm, sir. Will you join me in a gin?'

Finlay glared after them and said, 'Don't do that again, Sub, *ever*! Or I'll have your guts for a necktie!'

If Bizley had retained any reservations about what he had done, Finlay's anger had dispelled them.

Just you wait, you Scottish bastard! You'll soon change your tune!

It was such a warm evening that the Guvnor could not bear to go indoors. He was on his knees, his hand digging into the soft earth like a grubby crab searching for food, while the garden around him was alive with bees and other insects, and a blackbird began a late bath in the dish he kept for them.

He would stay out as long as possible, watching the late sunshine; there was always a chance that someone would pause at the wall for a chat. Once inside the house the loneliness always tightened its grip.

Perhaps it would be another quiet night. The area had been lucky recently, as if the enemy was staying his hand while he concentrated on London and the north-east.

He thought of his two sons, especially of David, who had gone back to his ship to face more problems. The refit was taking longer than expected. It would be the end of July by the time they went back to sea. He gave a satisfied grunt and pulled a fine bunch of radishes out into the sunshine.

'Not bad at all!' He slapped them on his patched gardening trousers, then laid them in a basket with some crisp-looking lettuces he had also cut that afternoon.

When Mister Mills dropped in for a glass of something they would share them and pass the time together.

He got painfully to his feet and felt a tiny insect fly into his eye. He blinked it away and dabbed his eye with his handkerchief. It was an ever-present fear. That the other eye would go bad on him.

He heard the muffled roar of engines from the main road, voices raised in song. As regular as clockwork, he thought. The mobile anti-aircraft batteries taking up their positions for the night. He smiled grimly. Typical, Mister Mills would say. The old horse and stable-door policy.

The Guvnor opened his tin of duty-frees and lit one with great care. As he watched the smoke rising straight up by the greenhouse, he thought about his own war. That day at Zeebrugge.

He looked up as more wheels grated along the pot-holed lane. Some soldiers who had taken the wrong turning. It happened often enough. He walked slowly towards the gate and then stopped with surprise. A khaki Humber staff car was parked outside, almost filling the lane. A sailor sat behind the wheel and for a moment the Guvnor could not get his breath. He felt suddenly angry with himself. Getting senile. If anything was wrong they wouldn't send a bloody great staff car. It would be a telegram, like all the others which had been delivered around here over the months.

Anyway, sailors lost their way too.

He got a second surprise when a Wren officer stepped from the rear of the car and adjusted her tricorn hat over her eyes against the low sunlight. She wore two pale blue stripes on her sleeve – a second officer, then. She was slim and neat in her uniform, and it was only when she walked uncertainly towards him that he remembered. The shabby hacking jacket, the old corduroys; like another person entirely.

She paused by the gate and said, 'I'm sorry to do this to you again, Commander Howard.' She reached out impulsively and touched his arm.

He stared at her, sensing her nearness, her freshness and youth, so that he felt old and dirty by comparison.

'Please come in, my dear. I'm afraid it's in a bit of a mess!'

A voice called after her from the car. 'Don't be too long, Celia, we're late as it is!'

The Guvnor strained his eye but the car was in deep shadow so that he could not see the man, except that he too was in uniform.

'Ten minutes, Daddy!'

She walked with him up the path and took off her hat to shake out her short curls.

The Guvnor said, 'How can I help you? I'm afraid . . .' He smiled. 'There, now *I'm* apologising again too!'

She turned and faced him in the same direct manner she had used with David. 'I hope you like dogs.' She hurried on, 'Some friends of mine were bombed-out. The dog escaped. I would take her, but I'm back in the "regiment", as you can see.' She looked at him and added quietly, 'They were both killed. My friends, I mean.'

He saw her lip quiver and guessed they had been close.

He said awkwardly, 'Well, fetch her over, my dear. A dog would be nice company. I get a bit fed up discussing Venice with my two POW's!'

She called, 'Let her go, please, Tom!'

The door opened and then the gate, as a plump Labrador padded curiously up the path.

She stooped down and ruffled her ears. 'She's called Lucy.

She's not young, but she's such a dear. She'll eat you penniless if she gets the chance!' She hugged the animal and said, 'You can take care of each other. I'll come and see you one day!' When she stood up there were tears in her eyes.

He said gruffly, 'Be certain you do.' He walked with her to the gate and was astonished to see that the dog was already lying on the mat by the front door.

'See? She feels at home already!'

The girl replaced her hat, then leaned over and kissed him on the cheek. She said, 'Goodbye, again.' Then she was in the car without another glance at the yellow Labrador, who was snapping at flies by the mat. But not before the Guvnor had seen the gold lace on her father's sleeve. A rear-admiral, no less.

He watched as the big car reversed carefully, to the main road before turning across it towards Portsmouth.

Aloud he said, 'Don't keep punishing yourself, my girl. It's the bloody war, not you.'

He walked back to the gate and stared at his new companion. 'Well, now. That was a turn up for the book, eh?'

8

Convoy

David Howard returned the salutes of the dock sentries and presented his identity card to an armed policeman. Around him the place seemed to be teeming with sailors, naval and merchant alike, and although it had only just stopped raining there was an air of scruffy defiance which appeared to be Liverpool's stock in trade.

Howard slowed his pace as he approached Gladstone Dock, where *Gladiator* lay with many other Atlantic escorts. He had just left the imposing presence of the new Captain (D), a tall, powerful man with the battered features of someone who had been well-known on the rugby field in the impossible days of peace. Even the flotilla-leader had changed while *Gladiator* had been fighting to stay afloat on the North Russian 'run', as it was discreetly called in the press. Captain Ernle Vickers DSO, DSC, Royal Navy, had as his own command the *Kinsale*, one of the famous K's which had been almost the only new destroyers available when the war had begun. Like Mountbatten's *Kelly*, which with some of her consorts had been bombed and sunk near Crete in the spring of last year. Raked bows, with a single funnel instead of the usual pair, and an impressive armament, she would make any recruit's heart beat faster, Howard thought. Like her captain, whose record he knew very well; he was exactly what they needed when things looked so bad in the Western Ocean.

All the captains had been there to meet the great man, and Howard was relieved to discover that Spike Colvin's *Ganymede* and another of their old team, *Garnet*, were still with the flotilla.

She was commanded by an impish two-and-a-half named Tom Woodhouse whom Howard had known for years. They had done the long gunnery course at Whale Island together as sub-lieutenants, and the instructors in that fearsome place had more than met their match with Woodhouse and all his practical jokes.

Most of the other ships had been less lucky and had been sunk in the first two years of conflict. Their names, the places where they had gone down, read like a brutal record of the country's lost campaigns. *Gipsy*, mined off Harwich just two months after the declaration of war. *Glowworm* dying bravely off Norway, *Grenade* and *Grafton* bombed and sunk at Dunkirk, and *Grenville* lost in the North Sea, all in 1940; the list seemed endless.

Captain Vickers had presented his own summing-up of events and the current measures, which it was hoped would cut down the appalling loss of tonnage in the Atlantic convoys. 'The enemy are already moving more submarines from the Norwegian and Baltic bases down to the Biscay coastline. Large surface units too, but at least the Air Force should be able to keep an eye on them after what happened in March.'

Howard recalled it well. While they had been riding out storms in the Arctic, dodging bombs and torpedoes while trying to protect their convoys, there had come one of those bright moments which flare up in all campaigns. A touch of hope, like the sun after a northerly gale. An ancient destroyer named *Campbeltown*, one of those transferred from the US Navy almost at the end of their useful life, had been expended like one giant, floating bomb when she had rammed the lock gates at St Nazaire and blown them to pieces. It had been the only dock on Hitler's impregnable West Wall which was large enough to hold and repair the battle-cruisers, or even the mighty *Tirpitz* if she ever left her Norwegian lair.

Destroyer men always felt different from anyone else. That one incident had convinced them.

Vickers had continued in his thick, resonant voice, 'We shall use new tactics too. To meet their wolf-packs of U-Boats we shall increase the use and deployment of small killer-groups. To this end the yards are now producing newer and faster frigates, solely designed to find and destroy U-Boats. If we can get these vessels to sea, and release other destroyers and corvettes from elsewhere, and *if* we can cling on until that time.' He had given an eloquent shrug. 'I will not dwell on the consequences of the *if nots*, gentlemen. You know them as well as anyone.'

Howard had found a quiet moment to explain to him about Treherne, and his new standing as first lieutenant.

Vickers had nodded, his mind already grappling with some other problem. 'I shall see what I can do. Good navigators are at a premium just now. But so are efficient escorts. I'll try and get you fixed up with an extra hand as soon as I can.' A pretty Wren had entered at that moment to present Vickers with a clip of new signals, and he had left.

Howard had pondered on the girl called Celia Kirke a good deal while his ship sorted herself out from the Greenock refit.

While his father had told him about his new companion, Lucy, he had thought about her even more. What had prompted her to do it after she had left so abruptly? There were so many things he wanted to know about her, even though he knew he was being ridiculous. An escape, then? Perhaps; but it stayed with him nonetheless.

The Guvnor had told him that the girl had been returning to Portsmouth, but when he had found occasion to speak with that naval base on the telephone and had asked casually about her, the Wren on the end of the line had replied sharply, 'No second officers of *that* name here!'

Perhaps she had put it about that she wanted to speak with no one who might remind her of her husband's terrible death.

No wonder she had been so confident about returning to the WRNS; her father held flag-rank and could probably pull all the strings for her. But with the way the war was going it seemed unlikely she would have any difficulty in getting back to the world she understood.

Howard was pleased about the Labrador. His father had spoken of little else. Just what the doctor ordered.

The thought brought a frown to his face. He had hoped to get rid of Surgeon-Lieutenant Jocelyn Lawford, but doctors, like good Scotch, were apparently very thin on the ground. If Lawford was confronted with another convoy like the last one *Gladiator* had brought across the Atlantic, he would be utterly useless.

He paused and saw his ship waiting for him, her dazzle-paint shining faintly in the smoky sunshine.

If ever he was ordered into Portsmouth . . . He felt his lips move in a smile. *Pompey*. He would try and find her himself. It would probably mean the brush-off, he thought. Everyone would be after her once they knew what had happened.

He strode down the brow and touched his cap to the quarterdeck where the gangway staff and Sub-Lieutenant Ayres stood at attention.

'Hello, Sub, got you on duty already? Good leave?'

Ayres stared away, seeing nothing. 'My brother's missing, sir. In the desert.'

Howard watched his despair. 'I'm sorry.' How stupidly inadequate it sounded. Like all the other times. *I saw him go.* 'It's not definite, is it?'

Ayres shook his head wretchedly while the quartermaster and gangway sentry tried to melt away. 'Not yet, sir.'

He touched his arm impetuously. 'Keep your chin up. Come and talk if you feel like it.'

Treherne appeared in the lobby door and saluted. 'Orders have arrived, sir.' They fell in step and Treherne added quietly, 'I'm keeping the kid busy. Take his mind off it.'

They reached the door marked *Captain* and found Petty Officer Vallance hovering by his pantry.

Howard tossed his cap on to a chair and sat down at his desk where Ireland the PO writer had lined up his papers in order of importance.

He said, 'Drinks, if you please, Vallance.' His eyes skimmed the neatly worded signal and pictured one of the Wrens typing it, watched over perhaps by someone like the girl with green eyes.

'Day after tomorrow, Number One.' He glanced at him. 'It's confirmed, by the way. The Boss just told me he would do what he could to keep you with me, until – '

Treherne grinned. 'We can discuss *that* later on, sir. Thanks a lot!'

He was thinking of Joyce, her supple body taking him, holding him.

Howard turned over another sheet. 'Send for Sub-Lieutenant

Bizley.' He waited for Treherne to speak on the bulkhead telephone and then said calmly, 'He's getting a gong after all.'

Treherne tried to look pleased, although he could not bring himself to like Bizley. He replied, 'There'll be no holding him now!'

There was a tap at the door and Bizley entered the day cabin, his features filled with curiosity, or was it something else? Like guilt?

'It's just been put in orders, Sub. You are being awarded the Distinguished Service Cross at their lordships' convenience. Suit you?'

But Bizley seemed unable to speak or take it in. His eyes moved instead to the solitary blue and white ribbon on Howard's reefer.

Howard smiled. ' "Like yours", were you going to say?'

Bizley stammered, 'T-thank you very much, sir! I never expected . . .'

Treherne looked at his empty glass. *Not much you didn't, you little twit!*

'More good news.' Howard ignored Treherne's expression. 'You are to be made acting-lieutenant on the first of the month. So you can put up your second stripe any time after that. You'll get all the bumf about it after we've done our next convoy.'

Bizley did not even hear him. He muttered something which made little sense and then found himself on the mat outside the cabin door.

He had done it. It was even better than he had dared to dream. He stared wildly at the single stripe on his sleeve. *Lieutenant Lionel Bizley.* It even sounded right, and he wondered dazedly if the King would make the award personally. He thought of Finlay and the others, and found himself laughing but making no sound. He was on his way.

The wardroom steward, PO Vallance, watched him around the curtain that hung across the pantry entrance. There would be no more peace down aft after this, he thought gloomily. Bizley was a proper little toe-rag, and would be a bloody sight worse now.

Two days later as *Gladiator*'s narrow hull throbbed steadily to the deeper beat of her main engines, Howard sat at the same desk and thought of the sea cabin on the bridge where he would have to snatch his catnaps whenever possible. There was still a lot to do, and there should have been more time for the flotilla, or escort group as it was now termed, to work together. But Vickers had made his thoughts clear to each commanding officer. 'There *is* no more time. So let's get out there and beat the hell out of them!'

Treherne entered the cabin and waited for Howard to look up. 'Special sea dutymen closed up, sir. Postman's gone ashore with the last mail.' He hesitated. 'One man absent, sir.'

'Stoker Marshall?' He saw him nod. The rating who had lost all of his family in an air raid. Where was he? What would he be doing?

Treherne spoke for him. 'He should be here, with *us*, sir. A lot of the men have lost relatives.' He added harshly, 'My God, it seems as if the civvies get all the casualties in this war!'

Did he mean the people who crouched in their primitive air raid shelters, Howard wondered. Or was he still thinking about the merchant seamen?

He asked, 'What about young Ayres?'

'He's heard nothing more, sir.' He glanced up as a mooring wire was dragged noisily over the deck. 'Bit of a breeze across the dock. We may have to use the back spring to work her clear.'

More quivering from Evan Price's engine rooms. The beast stirring herself, getting ready to face her old enemy. At least they were in better weather this time.

Howard stood up and began the routine of patting his pockets for the things he would need. He wore a comfortable grey roll-necked sweater he had bought in Reykjavik, his oldest reefer and battered sea-going cap with a paint-stain on the peak. Binoculars, fresh towel. He glanced at himself in the mirror. Hardly what they might expect at Dartmouth or Greenwich.

'Fifteen minutes then, Number One.'

Treherne smiled through his beard. 'The old firm, sir.'

Howard nodded, remembering.

And so once more HMS *Gladiator* went back to war.

For many of *Gladiator*'s ship's company the days that followed their leaving Liverpool were more of a strain than if they had faced immediate action. Day in, day out, with a convoy of some forty vessels of every type and size, the escorts swept ahead and abeam of them seeking the telltale 'ping' of Asdic to betray a submarine, or, if half the rumours were true, a whole pack of them.

But apart from exercising action stations and testing guns, the hands worked watch-and-watch, four hours on, four off, a kind of stumbling sleepwalk in which they ate the greasy meals brought down to the messes, catching a few moments of rest where they could. Sometimes they slept on the steel decks where cursing watchkeepers stepped over them in the darkness, or faced a torrent of abuse from the ones who were forced to sleep by the vertical ladders which linked the messdecks to the world above.

Lashed hammocks stood like monks in their nettings in each crowded mess, not to be used in case they jammed a hatchway, or were needed as lifesaving floats if the ship bought it.

It was a dawdling convoy, the speed of which was that of the slowest vessel in it, in this case a Greek freighter that looked as if she had dropped out of a picture book from the Great War.

The old sweats were not surprised at this or much else either. Every kind of hull was needed, and those which should have been scrapped years ago were ploughing the Atlantic with all the rest. Long tankers in ballast which with luck would be almost awash on the return trip, every bunker filled to the brim with fuel, the life-blood of any war-machine.

Ships which had come from the Clyde and the Solway Firth, from Liverpool Bay and Londonderry to join in this great array of salt-smeared and rusty silhouettes, around which the escorts plunged and harried like terriers. The merchantmen were more used to it, while for the lean destroyers the slow passage was hard to take, and for the new hands it was an introduction to the Atlantic roll and the seasickness which went with it. The slow lift of the bows, so that the ship seemed to hang motionless while the sea surged against one side, before giving that terrible corkscrew plunge down again, hurling water high over the bridge and sheltering gun crews.

Many a meal went flying, or untouched; personal possessions clattered about the messdecks in a mixture of spilled tea and vomit.

This, then, was the world Ordinary Seaman Andrew Milvain

shared with the old hands — old to him anyway — and those like himself who had joined straight from the spit-and-polish of a naval training establishment.

Apart from the usual quips about his very youthful appearance and what the seamen called his 'posh' accent, he was accepted far more easily than he had expected. His quiet dedication and almost fanatical efforts to learn all he could, even when he was laid low with seasickness, won him both respect and curiosity.

As the forenoon watch was relieved on this particular day Milvain climbed down the ladder to join his new companions in the mess. Nine Mess was little more than a scrubbed wooden table, which was covered in oilcloth for the main meal of the day. There were benches to sit on, and the curved side of the mess was lined with cushion-covered lockers, above which the lucky ones stowed their cap-boxes and other personal items on shelves.

Leading Seaman Bruce Fernie, 'killick' of the mess, sat on one of the lockers reading an old newspaper while the meal was passed down from the deck above by the duty cooks. He glanced up and said wearily, 'All out of bloody tins again! I'll bet them buggers in the barracks do better!'

The plates were passed along the table where fiddles were fitted to restrain them when the ship rolled, which was often.

Fernie watched the boy tucking in busily, as if he had not eaten for a year. Tinned potatoes, tinned sausages, tinned carrots, with some kind of plum duff and watery custard to follow. 'Don't they feed you at 'ome?'

Milvain gave his shy smile. He was thinking of the letter he had written to his mother before the ship had sailed from Liverpool. *His first ship*. What she was like, and a piece about these very same men. Rough and tough for the most part, but always ready with grudging praise when he did something properly. He wrote of the captain, but left out the piece about mistaking him for a petty officer. He still blushed about it. But mostly he had told them about Sub-Lieutenant Bizley, the talk about the medal he was going to receive. They would like that. He often thought about his dead brother; he had been something like the captain in a way. A face full of experience, a match for any occasion from taking over the bridge to facing Bully Bishop across the defaulters' table, where he had indeed dipped his hook as Leading Seaman Fernie had prophesied.

He felt his stomach heave as the deck lifted again. If only the sea were visible. But the scuttles had the deadlights screwed tightly shut. That was hardly surprising as the mess was the closest one to the bows, directly below the main messdeck which ran the full length of the forecastle. They had pulled his leg about that too. He glanced at the deck between the messes. They had told him that some of the main fuel tanks were under there. Some joker had said, 'You won't feel a bloody thing, Wings. Straight up to the pearly gates!'

It was a Sunday, and as bridge-messenger Milvain had been kept busy with tea or kye for the watchkeepers, up and down the steep ladders, gauging the moment so as not to be drenched by an incoming sea, or flung bodily to an unyielding deck. He made up little sketches in his mind as he bustled about and tried to keep out of everybody's way.

The captain, hatless, his hair thick with spray as he chatted to the yeoman of signals, an unlit pipe between his teeth. The officer-of-the-watch, in this case Lieutenant Finlay, as he passed his helm and revolutions orders, or shouted over the loud-hailer at one of the merchantmen as they thrashed abeam.

On the bridge there was always a sense of purpose, whereas elsewhere the ship seemed to exist on rumour. The latest buzz had been about Bizley and his medal . . . Milvain could not fathom it out. Nobody seemed to like him. Even the bear-like leading seaman with his newspaper, usually a tolerant man, had remarked, 'That's all I need, a bloody 'ero! That sod will get your arse shot off and still expect a salute!'

Milvain was astonished and overwhelmed by the sea itself. It was like nothing he had seen, even in the cinema. This summer's morning when the watch had changed, and the weary lookouts and gun crews had scattered to their messes, the ocean had seemed all-powerful and fierce. Dark, dark waves and troughs broken only here and there by fans of spray, the whole lifting and falling, it seemed level with the bridge itself. When the sun found its way across the horizon he had felt no warmth, just salt hardening on his cheeks and lips. Then the sea would change, the colour a shark-blue which rolled along the columns of merchant ships with disdain, as if merely to display its latent power. He could not imagine it in a full gale as one of the boatswain's mates had described it.

Fernie had interrupted scornfully. 'That's right, Bill, swing the bloody lamp, will you?' To Milvain he added, 'Bill talks so soddin' much you'd think he was vaccinated with a gramaphone needle!'

At first Milvain had flushed at some of the language he had heard, the embellished experiences some had had on runs ashore, but not now; not too much anyway. It was like the sea and the danger. It was there all the time. Something you had to accept.

One by one the men of Nine Mess found corners to lie or crouch into, their lifejackets worn loosely and uninflated. Just in case.

As it was Sunday, there was a make-and-mend for the afternoon. Then on watch again for the first dog at four o'clock. Order, routine, and, many said, boredom. But not Milvain.

He watched as the big leading hand opened his ditty box and produced some intricate ropework, turk's heads which he had fashioned into handsome handles for a chest he kept somewhere. Milvain was fascinated by it. Fernie's hands, like the man, were huge, scarred by his work as captain of the quarterdeck and in charge of the depth-charges there, and yet he could produce delicate mats of twine, and carving from old packing cases which would put a joiner to shame.

Fernie looked at him thoughtfully. 'You don't mind talking about it, do you, laddie?'

Milvain flinched. He knew now what *it* meant. 'No. Not really.'

Fernie peered down at his ropework. 'I lost one of my brothers at Dunkirk.' So casually said. 'I still miss him, strangely enough.' Again that steady stare. 'We never really got on, y'see, not close like we should 'ave bin. I think about that sometimes.'

Milvain stared at him. He had never imagined that this huge man could be moved by anything.

The fingers tugged at the rope. '*Sod it!* It's not right!' Then he said, 'I wouldn't 'ave too much to do with Mister Bizley, if I was you. I know 'is kind. In this ship I've seen 'em all.' He darted a glance at the opposite mess which was made up mostly of telegraphists, signalmen and supply assistants. A few snores from there, but nobody moved.

'But – but – the medal, Hookey? He's getting the same one as the captain's!'

Fernie grinned at his outraged voice. 'Bits of tin. This ship was awarded some gongs after one trip, and the lads 'ad to draw names from an 'at.' He stifled a laugh. 'A leadin' cook we 'ad then drew a medal, an' *he* was drunk and still ashore on the day of the action!' It amused him greatly. 'The Old Man, that's different. 'E earned it, 'e does every time 'e gets us back 'ome in one piece, in my book!' He changed tack and asked abruptly, 'Did anyone see Subbie Bizley when it 'appened?' He saw the sudden brightness in Milvain's eyes and said, 'Forget it, son. It's just that I don't see 'im as a ruddy 'ero!'

Milvain was still thinking about it when he went on deck and climbed to the bridge for the first dog watch. As he passed the chart-room which opened off the wheelhouse he heard the murmur of orders and acknowledgements as the watchkeepers handed over to their reliefs. It never failed to excite him. The shining brass telegraphs and wheel, and the gyro-repeater ticking this way and that, as the quartermaster, a very subdued Able Seaman Bishop, brought the ship on to a new course.

'Want a look?' It was Morgan, the navigator's yeoman. He led the way into the chart-room and explained the ship's track, speed and estimated time of arrival. There had been plenty of buzzes about that too, but now Milvain actually knew their destination. Halifax. *Canada*. His heart thudded. He had never been further than Bournemouth or Ramsgate until he had joined the Navy.

Morgan saw that he was impressed and added loftily, 'I'll try and get you transferred here if you like. With Jimmy-the-One doing two jobs at once it's more than enough for me. Besides,' he added accusingly, 'you're hoping to be an officer, right?'

'Well, yes. I thought that you . . .'

Morgan grinned. 'I failed.'

Milvain digested the information. 'When we reach Canada, I mean what . . .'

Morgan looked at the gently vibrating chart. 'Big convoy. Heard the Old Man discussing it with Jimmy.'

'What about this one?'

'Safe now.' He lowered his voice. 'W/T had a signal last night. A homebound convoy was clobbered to the south of us. Sounded like a butcher's shop.' He bit his lip as if the casual dismissal was no longer a protection. 'It's the full convoys the krauts are after, not the likes of this one.' He stared at him, but Milvain thought he did not see him. 'The PO telegraphist was saying there were *thirty* U-Boats in the attack! Can you believe it? That's more than the bloody escorts!'

Sub-Lieutenant Ayres entered the chart-room and picked up some brass dividers.

Morgan guided Milvain to the door. 'You heard about his brother?'

Milvain shook his head although he guessed what was coming.

'He was in North Africa.' He drew one finger across his throat. 'Rest in peace!'

Milvain went down to the steaming galley to collect another fanny of tea. He was learning quite a lot.

Milvain was on the bridge for the morning watch when daylight uncovered the craggy shoreline in the far distance, and shortly afterwards they were joined by two Canadian destroyers and a dozen corvettes fussing around to divide and re-route the convoy, which had arrived without the loss of a man or a ship.

He was pouring the last of the tea for a boatswain's mate by the voicepipes, while lights clattered and winked in greeting from the Canadian warships. He heard the captain say, 'Local leave only tonight, Number One, whichever watch is due. But we go alongside the oiler first.'

Milvain heard Lieutenant Treherne say, 'God, look at that lot!'

He peered over the salt-splashed glass screen and saw a mass of deep-laden ships anchored in lines, and without asking, knew it was part of the next convoy. Their convoy.

Treherne raised his binoculars and added flatly, 'Lambs to the slaughter.'

Howard said, 'I'll take over the con, Number One. We'll go alongside, starboard side-to, if I can find the bloody thing!'

They both laughed and Milvain felt the cold fingers around his heart relax their grip. He tried to cheer himself up at the prospect of a run ashore in Halifax. A foreign country.

Across the bridge Howard was watching him. He said, 'Take it off your back, Milvain. This isn't *Boys' Own Paper*, this is the *real* Navy. You know what they say, don't you?'

Milvain nodded. 'If you can't take a joke, you shouldn't have joined, sir!'

Howard grinned. 'So be it. Off you go for another brew of sergeant-major's tea, eh?'

Treherne paused at the bridge gate, one leg hanging in space. 'You just made his day, sir.'

Howard stared past him at the moored merchantmen. So helpless. He replied quietly, 'You just murdered mine.'

9

'. . . And Don't Look Back'

At a steady, economical speed the U-Boat thrust her way through the dark water, white feathers of spray bursting occasionally from her raked stem to drift over the bridge like rain. It was cold, but not uncomfortably so, and after what they had been used to there had been few grumbles from the crew. The stores loaded at their new French base had been far more plentiful than usual, and baskets of apples had been wedged anywhere throughout the hull where there was still space.

The ocean had its usual impressive swell, but the tight knot of lookouts stationed around the bridge found it easy to keep their balance. In the forepart of the bridge the officer-of-the-watch levelled his glasses and hunted for the horizon. But it was an hour until dawn, and there was still nothing to betray it.

He could picture it in his mind, the endless expanse of ocean with no land beyond those sharp bows but the southern-most tip of Greenland, four hundred miles away. He was not new to this part of the Western Ocean, and often thought how aptly named that hostile wedge of land had become. Cape Farewell. It had certainly been the last sighting for many an unfortunate mariner.

The officer listened to the powerful throb of diesel engines vibrating through the narrow conning-tower while they sucked down the air from above to charge the batteries.

They would have to dive before too long, and rely solely on the electric motors to carry them as close as possible to the enemy.

He felt the usual tightening of his stomach muscles; one never really got used to it. Nobody who had been aboard during that last attack would forget. The sudden explosion of a faulty torpedo, the boat going into a crash dive as the destroyer had stripped them naked with a starshell. The depth-charges which had gone on and on. Afterwards they had stared at one another with dazed disbelief. They had survived – once again luck had stayed with them. He thought of the captain. Not even a blink. As cool as spring water.

He felt the sailor nearest to him stiffen slightly and knew the man who held all their destinies in his eye and brain was coming up.

Kleiber took several deep breaths to clear his throat and insides from the stench of diesel, boiled cabbage and sweat. It clung to his hair and body; it was like a scar, a mark of their profession.

He had been studying the chart, calculating, and trying to guess exactly when it would happen.

A convoy was heading towards them from Halifax, or should be if the codebreakers at U-Boat HQ were proved right. At least thirty ships, over half of them tankers: a twelve-knot convoy.

How did they know, *really* know, he wondered. Their own agents in Nova Scotia, perhaps? Or had this vital intelligence been transmitted by wireless? Information of such importance was usually sent direct by submarine cable laid on the seabed, which could not be tampered with. Maybe that had been too busy at the time, and some senior officer had decided to risk a coded signal.

Kleiber looked at the sky and thought of the chart again. They were heading north-west, crossing the longitude of forty degrees west. Beyond that the convoy would have no air cover from land-based American or Canadian patrols. The gap, which reached as far east as longitude twenty, *was* the killing-ground. Only an aircraft carrier would suffice, and the allies reserved those to protect their capital ships, or their operations in the Pacific.

He thought suddenly of his mother during that last, unexpected leave. She had wanted to know about the war. A mild, gentle lady who had aged considerably; probably because of the scattered air raids and shortages, he thought. She loved and admired him, proud to a point of embarrassment, and always had a big photograph of him on display for the neighbours' benefit, the one of him shaking hands with the Führer after being awarded his second Iron Cross.

She had been proud too of his young brother Willi, the first one in the family to enter university. She had asked Kleiber repeatedly during his leave how *it* could have happened. A cheeky youth with bad eyesight and student's cap, who had been doing so well with his work. His tutors had told her as much. Then, out of the blue he had been told, along with several other students, that he was required for duty in the Wehrmacht.

Kleiber thought he knew the reason but could not allow himself to believe it. Willi talked too much; but then so did a lot of students. They did not have the discipline and purpose of the armed services to restrain their high spirits. But Willi as a soldier? It was ludicrous.

He lifted his powerful Zeiss night-glasses from the cover of his oilskin and trained them abeam. But it was a fish, leaping from another predator. He readjusted the glasses and stared hard into the darkness. Seven hundred miles abeam lay the coast of Newfoundland, the home of some of the greatest fishermen in the world. The convoy must have wended its way around that coast after leaving Halifax astern to the south-west. Getting the feel of one another, zig-zagging and changing formation until the escort commanders were as satisfied as they could be. A few days later and the watchful anti-submarine aircraft would dwindle in the distance. The convoy would stand alone.

He peered at his watch. Not long now. He remarked as much to the watch officer who repeated his instructions down the voicepipe.

The lieutenant beside him smelt of cigars; probably some he had come by in France. It made Kleiber think of his father, and he knew he had been avoiding that too. His mind had to be empty of everything but the work in hand. His eyes and brain had to be clearer than any prismatic gunsight. He moved away from the others and listened to the thud of diesels dying away to be replaced instantly by the electric motors.

His father had been little more than a motor-mechanic before, but his skills had soon been recognised when the full demands of war were made evident. As the pace had mounted, so his position had expanded and improved. His mother had been pleased; there had never been much money to spare before the war.

Now he was in charge of a whole factory, not a large one, but one involved in manufacturing small, intricate machine parts for tanks and half-tracks.

He had seemed much troubled this time and Kleiber had watched him lighting a cheroot, one of a box he had given him as a present.

Eventually, after taking him to one side, he had explained that he had become unhappy with the way he was expected to work. There were some kind of official supervisors who came and went with lists and demands, longer working hours – in fact a twenty-four-hour rota system was now in force. Kleiber had tried to pull him out of his depression, and told him they never stopped for a minute in the Atlantic. But it had been no use.

His father had stared at him anxiously and had spoken about the people who were being brought to work as unskilled labour, under the supervision of the SS, a unit of which was always at the factory.

Kleiber found himself recalling that conversation over and over now, when all he wanted was to prepare himself for action.

His father had described them as prisoners, civilians for the most part, women as well as men. Half-starved and frightened.

Kleiber bit his lip. The work to support the armed services must go on, no matter what else was happening. Prisoners took no risks, and if they were criminals it was only right they should do something useful to help.

The lieutenant let out a quick breath and Kleiber moved swiftly to join him again. The sky was lightening. There was an horizon of sorts, and he could even see the U-Boat's bows, the saw-like net-cutter rising above it like a scythe.

The dawn strengthened, and although the light was approaching from the east, the sky was so clear that he could see the stain above the horizon. The telltale mark of drifting smoke. In such a vast span of open sea it could mean only one thing. Ships, and many of them.

He called down the voicepipe and guessed he was the first of sixteen U-Boats to make the sighting report. The others, as yet unseen and unheard, were stretched out on either beam. They could muster nearly one hundred torpedoes in the first salvoes.

He saw his men leaping for the oval hatch, leaving him alone on the narrow bridge. It was always the most exhilarating moment. The thought of standing here, doing nothing but wait for the sea to come roaring over the lip of the conning-tower, riding the boat down like some armoured monster until he could feel no more. He snapped down the voicepipe and sealed it by turning the small cock. Then, without haste, he pressed the klaxon alarm before lowering himself through the upper hatch and dragging it down with a thud over his head. The boat was already going into a dive, the water surging into the saddle-tanks to force her under.

Checks completed, the boat glided up again to periscope depth. Kleiber signalled for it to be raised and knelt down to catch it even as it cut above the surface.

There they were, dark flaws against the pale horizon, moving diagonally; slow, tired, already doomed.

The exact moment of truth, the click of cranks which made the final settings to the torpedoes; the sudden chilling stillness.

The periscope hissed down.

'Feueraubis!'

'Fächer eins! . . . *Los!*'

'Fächer zwei! . . . *Los!*'

There was little more than a slight thud as each torpedo started up and flashed from its tube. Kleiber nodded to his engineer and felt the deck begin to tilt down again.

The attack had begun. It would not end until all the tubes were empty, or the boat was scattered across the bottom of this pitiless ocean.

'Signal from commodore, sir! *Alter course in succession, steer zero-five-zero!*'

Howard swung away as another explosion tore the morning apart, and was in time to see the tall white columns falling with deceptive slowness even as the ship began to veer out of formation, smoke and flames spurting through her side and upper deck.

Treherne called, 'Starboard ten! *Steady!* Steer zero-five-zero!'

Gladiator was at the rear of the starboard column and must turn earlier than the others to retain the protective shield on the convoy.

Howard had known it would be today; some of the others had had the same feeling, he thought. It had all started too well; the ships in the convoy were all veterans of the Atlantic and were quick to respond to the signals of the commodore and escort commander alike.

Thirty-two ships, over half of them deep-laden tankers, with four destroyers, six corvettes and an elderly sloop like Ayres's old patrol vessel to protect them. But no air cover, not even for such a vital list of cargoes. The first victim had been one of the tankers, a fairly new vessel which had protested to the commodore when the overall speed was further reduced to eight knots because of a freighter's engine-failure. She had been carrying high-octane aircraft fuel and had exploded in one tremendous fireball, fragments of metal and flaming debris scattering over and around the other ships, the heat so fierce that Howard imagined he could feel it against his face.

Three of the corvettes were working up to full speed as they charged to the attack, their progress marked across the grey sea by towering geysers of water as their depth-charges thundered down. Again and again, the sea's face was littered with stunned or gutted fish which floated through leaking oil, upturned lifeboats and meaningless human remains. Two more explosions on the far side of the convoy, and immediately two more, so that the roar blended together like thunder over the hills.

The yeoman of signals said harshly, 'There's another one, the poor buggers!'

The ship in question was already turning slowly onto her beam, steam shooting from her shattered engine room where her people must have died in the worst known manner.

Crated cargo, dismantled aircraft lined up like unfinished toys, were tumbling into the sea, and one of the lifeboats hurled its occupants down to join them as flames burned through the boat's falls before it could reach the water.

'*Redwing*'s calling up the commodore, sir! Requests permission to pick up survivors.'

Howard turned to watch some men floundering in the sea, staring up at *Gladiator* as she surged past, their cries and screams lost in the thunder of depth-charges and the roar of fans.

'Permission denied.'

The yeoman glanced at his young signalman. 'Don't gape at *me*, watch the bloody commodore!'

It was getting to him. Tommy Tucker, the hard yeoman who saw and heard everything that went on in his bridge but kept it to himself; a man who had seen sailors die horribly in the blaze of a convoy battle, or quietly and without dignity in the freezing water.

Howard heard the brittle edge to his voice. Just how much could a man take, and still be made to watch helpless sailors blown to pieces?

'Signal, sir. *Increase to thirteen knots.*'

The last ship to go had been the offending freighter with engine trouble. She would never delay another convoy.

One more oiler was to explode before a lull fell over the heaving water. Once again the elderly sloop *Redwing* requested permission to search for survivors with the same response. It was the nightmare all over again. *Do not stop; close up the gaps.*

Howard massaged his eyes with his fingers. They should add: *and don't look back!*

He turned deliberately and trained his glasses astern. It was as if the convoy itself was bleeding to death as he watched. Two ships gone completely, four more either burning fiercely or with their decks already awash, their sacrifice marked by a bright sheen of oil as wide as the whole convoy. Boats, wreckage, and men who could only stare with stunned disbelief as the formation headed away.

Howard said, 'It's a pity they can't see this at home, Number One. The black marketeers, the people who brag about getting petrol for their cars despite the rationing.' He turned from the pitiful scene and added with bitterness, '*God damn them all!*'

Howard saw Ayres staring at him from the compass platform, the others around him, moulded together more than ever because of the horror they shared, the apparent helplessness which rendered them impotent while so many died. And tonight the U-Boats would rise like evil sharks to the surface to give chase with greater speed afforded by their diesels. The Admiralty had said there were ten U-Boats in the vicinity. How had they come here? Where did they get this information? Tomorrow would begin like this one. And the next, and the next.

There was a dull boom astern and he heard the Asdic report, 'Ship breaking up, sir!'

Treherne acknowledged it, his features like stone while he lifted his glasses to watch the remaining hulks falling further and further astern. The corvettes closed around their charges again, and Howard imagined their hands working feverishly to reload the depth-charge racks and prepare for the next encounter.

He said, 'See if you can drum up something hot for the lads to drink. The sandwiches are already done in the galley, though God knows the bread will be like asbestos after all this time!'

Treherne passed his instructions to the boatswain's mate and said, 'You knew, didn't you, sir?' It all added up. Howard's lack of surprise, his instructions about there being plenty of sandwiches well in advance.

Howard raised his glasses again as a diamond-bright light winked across the convoy. It was Captain Vickers's *Kinsale* at the head of the port column from where he controlled the escort and gauged the commodore's next move. He seemed to have that uncanny knack of guessing each manoeuvre, and had proved his skill as well as his worth from the moment they had left Halifax.

The yeoman said, '*Kinsale*'s got a contact, sir!' He almost yelled aloud, 'Black pendant's gone up! He's signalled*Ganymede* to assist!'

Stiffly, like old men, the gun-crews and damage control parties crowded around their stations to watch as the big destroyer with the leader's black band on her squat funnel appeared to leap away from the convoy. The bow-wave mounted around her raked stem so that she seemed to dig her stern deeper into the sea to thrust her forward, while tiny figures ran to the quarterdeck to set the charges for the first pattern.

Angled towards her at ninety degrees, *Gladiator*'s sister-ship was swaying in a welter of yellow foam as Colvin brought her hard round, ready to surge across his leader's wake with his own set of charges.

'There she goes!'

There was a ragged cheer as the first charges exploded and hurled spray in the air like something solid. Then another pattern, and as the black pendant vanished at the destroyer's yard, *Ganymede* increased speed to pass across the area where the sea still boiled in torment.

The yeoman called, 'From *Kinsale*, sir. *Join the party!*'

'Starboard fifteen! Full ahead together!'

Howard lowered his eye to the compass. '*Steady!* Steer zero-eight-zero!' Over his shoulder he added, 'Warn Bizley, Number One. Full pattern!' It was like a touch on the shoulder, a chill breeze on the skin. He was almost surprised to hear himself say, 'Belay that, Number One. Tell Guns. Prepare to engage!'

He saw the boy Milvain swaying at the bridge gate, a huge fanny of steaming tea dragging at one arm.

Treherne passed his order and stared across at his captain by the compass. More charges roared down as *Kinsale* thrashed back along the same track.

Howard was aware of so many things at once. The new multiple pom-poms training soundlessly round to starboard, the main armament following suit as if they were about to engage the other destroyers. He also saw the old sloop *Redwing* blowing out smoke as she increased speed to fill *Gladiator's* gap in the defences.

More charges. He was even able to picture them, falling so slowly, down and down to detonate like savage eyes around the submarine's blurred outline.

He rarely thought of the men who served in them. The U-Boat was weapon and crew all in one. A mind of its own. The hunter.

'From *Kinsale*, sir! *Remain on station. I have another contact at three-five-zero!*'

There was something like a groan of disappointment as *Ganymede* heeled over, showing her bilge as she turned steeply to follow the leader once more.

The yeoman exclaimed angrily, 'Lost the bastard!'

Howard said sharply, 'Look!' He raised his glasses and stared at the great surge of bubbles and oil which rose to the surface and rolled swiftly away into the troughs. Then, like an obscene monster, the U-Boat began to break surface, bows first until something brought her under control and she came down fully and untidily on the broken water.

Men appeared just as suddenly on the casing, flowing down the side of the conning-tower, their features lost in distance.

The boatswain's mate gasped, 'The buggers are goin' to surrender!' He was almost incoherent with wild excitement.

The yeoman rasped, 'Are they fuckin' hell!'

Howard shouted, '*Open fire!*' He stared at the surfaced U-Boat as it lay pitching in the disturbance of its own making. She had been damaged by the charges; there were jagged marks on the casing. But the U-Boat's long gun, larger than any of *Gladiator*'s, was already pivotting round until he was looking straight down its muzzle.

'*Hard a-port!*' That would give Finlay a chance to use all his armament, even though the move made *Gladiator* a larger target.

He saw the flash of the U-Boat's gun and heard the shell scream overhead before exploding far abeam. Then the air was ripped apart by the clattering pom-poms and the sharper crash of the four-point-sevens. Water-spouts fell near the submarine's hull and burst in the sea beyond it. Tracer clawed over the water and struck fire from the casing and conning-tower where some madman had managed to run up the German ensign.

The rapid fire of the lighter weapons cut down the U-Boat's gun crew like bloodied rag dolls, but even when the order to cease fire was repeated one Oerlikon gunner continued to rake the enemy's deck until his magazine was empty, and there were only jerking corpses to be seen.

Howard shouted, 'Continue firing! Tell Guns I want to be certain this time.'

Holes appeared in the U-Boat's saddle-tank, and he noticed for the first time that its hull was covered in slime and weed. It had probably been at sea for weeks, maybe refuelled in these same waters by one of their big supply boats, the 'milch-cows'.

He watched more shells burst alongside and found that he could do it without compassion. Even when some small figures appeared on the conning-tower only to be cut down by Finlay's withering fire, he felt nothing but the need to destroy this thing and all that it had come to mean to him.

Treherne said, 'Never thought I'd see the day!'

Howard did not reply but watched intently as the slime-covered hull began to lift into the air bows-first, smoke pumping from the shattered conning-tower. He steadied his glasses with great care and saw some small designs painted on the punctured steel plates below the periscope standards. Ships sunk. Men killed. A record of murder.

Two figures were in the sea, although it was not possible to know how they had survived.

'She's going!'

There was no cheering this time. Just the cold satisfaction of victory after so many, *too* many failures.

The U-Boat dived and Howard called, 'Take her alongside those men in the water, Number One.'

He saw Treherne's surprise and hurt. Because of all the men they had left to die back there. And now they were stopping for two of their attackers. Howard shook his head. 'They are not survivors. To me, they are nothing more than trophies. Evidence of a kill. It's not much, but – '

He ran to the side as a lookout shouted, 'Torpedo running to starboard, sir!' Just for a second or so he saw the steely line as it tore through the water and cut across the bows. If *Gladiator* had not reduced speed to wait for the two Germans, she would have taken the torpedo amidships. It must have been fired at extreme range, perhaps on the off chance of a hit after the first bloody and successful attack. They were lucky.

He felt the shock of the explosion and turned with sudden dismay as the little sloop *Redwing* began to settle down, the sea already surging through the great hole in her side. *Redwing* was on *Gladiator*'s proper station. Again he felt the chill breeze on his skin. *Either way it was meant for us.*

'Slow ahead together. Stand by to go alongside portside-to. Tell the Buffer to have all the hammocks brought up to cushion the two hulls as we come together. Yeoman, call up *Redwing* and tell them to hold on.' He thought suddenly of his ship's motto. *With a strong hand.* It was all he could offer now.

He watched the narrowing gap, saw the chaos where fittings had been flung to the deck, blood running on the steel plates as men had been crushed and broken. A ship dying.

'Stop engines.' He added to the voicepipe, 'Ease her in, Cox'n. We haven't got a lot of time.' Another quick glance. Perhaps even now a U-Boat's crosswires were holding *Gladiator* and her sinking consort like victims in a web. No, this torpedo had come a long way, otherwise either *Kinsale* or *Ganymede* would have made contact.

'Slow astern starboard. *Stop.*'

Treherne stood high above the screen to watch the Buffer and his men reaching out to seize the first staggering figures from the other vessel. Sub-Lieutenant Bizley was taking charge, and he saw Lawford the doctor waiting by the guardrails with his SBA.

Treherne said urgently, 'She's going under, sir!' There was a curtain of steam hissing above the sloop's thin funnel and Howard wondered if any of the stokers had managed to get out.

The last one to be pulled roughly from the tilting deck was the *Redwing*'s captain, a bearded RNR officer, a bit like Treherne.

'Cast off! Slow astern starboard! Stand by with fenders!'

Howard watched the captain's despair. It was physical. Like an unhealable wound. *How I would feel if* Gladiator *went down, and I was left behind.*

'Pass the word to bring him to the bridge.' Howard lowered his eye to the compass again. 'Half ahead together.' When he looked again, *Redwing* was gone, leaving just the usual whirl-pool, the rubbish and the oil. The commodore would likely give him a blast for stopping. 'What the hell – who cares anyway!' He saw some of the sailors grinning at him and realised he had spoken aloud. He felt a sudden warmth for these men, who trusted him, and who could still find a smile somewhere even when others had died. Not unknown merchant sailors this time but men like themselves. The same uniforms and badges, the same backgrounds and grumbles.

Treherne said, 'Steady on zero-five-zero, sir, revolutions one-one-zero.' He eyed Howard, the question still unasked.

Howard thought of the two Germans he had been about to take from the sea when the torpedo had suddenly appeared. He said quietly, 'What Germans?' He turned as the other command-ing officer was helped up the bridge ladder.

The man stared uncertainly at the interlaced gold stripes on Treherne's jacket which matched his own, and then allowed

Howard to guide him to the bridge chair by the screen, not so very different from the one he had just left.

Howard stood beside him and began to fill his pipe. There was nothing he could say to this man. The right words eluded him; the wrong ones would be an insult.

Redwing's captain touched his arm but stared ahead at the approaching convoy. 'Thanks.'

Perhaps there were no words.

Someone said, ''Ere comes the mungie! 'Bout time too!' as the sandwiches were brought through the bridge gate.

Gladiator seemed to shake herself. Once again routine was taking over.

On a grey blustery morning HMS *Gladiator* said goodbye to the convoy and with the other escorts headed for the docks.

Howard sat on the bridge chair and stared through the smeared glass screen while Treherne handed him a cup of steaming tea. Afterwards he knew he must have fallen asleep where he sat, and that Treherne had shaken his arm to wake him.

He shivered. It was cold on the open bridge, more like winter than autumn, but he knew it was not just the weather. He felt utterly drained, and was unable to share the relief of many of his men, the luxury of returning to Liverpool when others had died.

They had lost eleven ships from the convoy, five of them tankers, left astern like drifting pyres to mark their hopeless fight. But for a completely unexpected Force Nine westerly gale which had scattered the U-Boat pack, but had helped rather than hampered the remaining merchantmen, the losses would have been twice as many. From the eleven ships there were barely more than thirty survivors.

Howard swallowed the tea and watched the familiar silhouette of the Crosby Light Vessel as *Gladiator* made another turn and followed the *Kinsale* up-river to the docks.

They had already been ordered to proceed directly to Gladstone Dock and refuel. They would be told eventually when the next convoy was ready for another long haul to Canadian waters. Howard tried to shut it from his mind. *Then back again.* The picture refused to budge. Men in the water calling for help.

Ships sinking and on fire, the roar of torpedoes in the night. He even thought of the two survivors from the U-Boat they had sent to the bottom. With disgust sometimes, because he had been glad to leave them to die. To discover how it felt.

He slid from the chair and picked up his binoculars. 'I'll take over, Number One. You'd better get up forrard for entering dock.'

Treherne hesitated and glanced at the others. Ayres was bending over the ready-use chart-table, but was probably worrying about his brother, and if there was any more news. Finlay, who was the OOW, was looking at the shore, ready to remind the signalmen if there were any lights or flags which they should have seen. Tucker the yeoman was also watching, making certain that Finlay would not catch his team at a loss.

He said, 'Remember, sir, we got a U-Boat.' He forced a grin. 'After our chums blew it to the surface for us! That's a bonus surely?'

Howard bent over the voicepipe. 'Starboard ten. *Steady.* Steer for the mark, Cox'n.' He heard Sweeney's rumbled acknowledgement. How many orders had he passed down this voicepipe? Changes of speed and helm, emergency turns, and desperate zigzags to avoid drifting merchantmen or lifeboats. No wonder the wheelhouse always seemed such a haven of peace in harbour.

He replied, 'A drop in the bucket.' He tried to shake himself out of it. Like the hand on the shoulder again. 'But our people did well, especially when you consider most of them were at school a short while back.' He raised his glasses to look at the birds on the top of the Liver Buildings. It was not really home, but at this moment it felt like it.

The yeoman called, 'From *Kinsale*, sir. *Captain repair on board when convenient.*'

Howard nodded. 'Acknowledge.' He saw the question in Treherne's eyes and said wearily, 'I'm about to get a bottle for going alongside *Redwing*, I expect!'

'Well, if that's all the thanks you get for . . .'

Howard waved to a small tug which was heading down-river, her crew lounging on deck like a bunch of old salts. He turned to answer but Treherne had gone. Seething, no doubt, in defence of his captain.

When convenient was a way of saying he should get shaved and changed before presenting himself in front of Captain Vickers. Maybe the commodore had made an official complaint about his act of mercy. Perhaps it was merely to decide who would take the credit for sinking the German submarine!

In fact it was neither.

As soon as *Gladiator* had secured alongside the oiler in Gladstone Dock, Howard walked across to board the big K-Class destroyer. He felt vaguely embarrassed in his best Number Fives, the gold lace very different from the tarnished, almost brown rings on his sea-going jacket.

Men were at work everywhere, washing down the decks and superstructure to wipe away the stains of battle. Others were dragging sacks of expended cannon shells, which would end up somewhere being made into fresh ammunition. A few would find their way to the stokers' messdeck to be fashioned into ash-trays and paperweights.

The *Kinsale*'s first lieutenant greeted him with a smart salute. 'Bad trip, sir.' He looked at the shore. 'Even this place looks good to me now!'

Howard eyed him gravely. First lieutenants as a breed knew everything, or should do. 'What's all this about, Number One?'

He shrugged. 'In God's name, sir, I really don't know. All I *do* know is that an admiral, no less, is with the captain right now.' He glanced at his watch. 'You're to go down as soon as you arrive.'

Howard could feel him staring after him, probably wondering if he was seeing the next candidate for a court martial.

A white-jacketed steward opened the door for him, but looked away when Howard was about to speak.

Captain Vickers greeted him with a firm handshake and smiled. 'Bloody good show, David!' But the smile did not touch his eyes.

Howard saw a tall rear-admiral standing by an open scuttle drinking coffee. He looked young for his rank, keen-eyed and alert like Vickers.

Vickers began, 'This is Rear-Admiral Lanyon, David. It's all very difficult – ' The admiral put down his cup and looked at Howard very directly.

'Lieutenant-Commander Howard is a good officer, so I'll

come straight to the point. I was asked to come and see you myself, by my daughter actually. I understand that she came to visit you.'

Howard did not know what to say. He had never heard of Lanyon, and his daughter did not make any sense. Lanyon continued, 'You knew her as Kirke, her married name.'

Howard stared at him. That was why they had not known her at Portsmouth; she was using her maiden name.

'So when I heard your ETA at Liverpool I drove up.' He tried to smile, like Vickers, but it would not come. 'As ordered!'

'What is it, sir? Has something happened?' The hand on the shoulder. He should have known.

Lanyon said quietly, 'There was an air raid five days ago. I'm afraid your father was killed. A direct hit on the house.'

Howard walked to an open scuttle and stared out blindly. It was not happening. For an instant he had imagined something was wrong with the girl, then in the same split second he had thought of his brother. Even though he was on a course, things like that did happen. *But not the Guvnor . . .*

He heard himself ask, 'Was it – I mean did he . . .' He could not go on.

Lanyon said, 'My daughter could tell you. She went there afterwards, to find out. It was all over in an instant, I understand. He could have felt nothing. It's not much help, but it's better to know he didn't suffer.'

Captain Vickers asked, 'Drink, David?' He eyed him with concern. 'I'm damn sorry, I really am.'

Howard shook his head. Needing to be alone; not knowing what to do. 'No, I must get back aboard. We're alongside the oiler.'

Vickers said, 'Let your Number One take charge. Do him bloody good!'

The admiral looked at the clock. 'I'm to see the C-in-C very shortly.' He glanced at Howard. 'I'll run you down to Hampshire in my car when you're ready. Suit you?'

Howard nodded. *Suit you?* How he had put it to Bizley about his DSC.

'What about my ship, sir?'

'We'll manage.' The admiral held out his hand for his oak-leaved cap. 'There'll be things you'll want to do, I expect. Your brother's been a tower of strength.'

'I'll see you over the side, sir.' Vickers looked at Howard. 'You stay here, David. Long as you like, right?'

The cabin was suddenly empty and quiet, with only the murmur of a generator and muffled shipboard noises to remind him where he was.

All those miles and all those ships and men. And now this. The Guvnor. He buried his face in his hands to stifle his emotion. What a thing to come home to. Except like the coxswain and Stoker Marshall, he no longer had a home.

There was a discreet tap at the door and the captain's steward padded into the cabin, a glass, filled almost to the brim, balanced on his tray.

He said, 'My old chum, Percy Vallance, told me just how you like it, sir, so I fixed you a big 'un.' He watched him take the glass. 'Sorry about your spot of news, sir.'

'Do they know aboard my ship already?' He pictured them in his mind. Curiosity and sympathy. *See how the Old Man can handle this one.*

The steward shrugged. 'Well, you know the *Andrew*, sir, nothing secret for long in this regiment. It happened to me last year. It's something you don't forget.'

Howard stared at him. Just an ordinary man, who was serving as a steward probably because he could get nothing better. And yet one who had taken it on himself to go over to *Gladiator* and ask his chum how his skipper liked his Horse's Neck.

'Bombing, was it?'

The steward looked into the far distance. 'No, sir. My dad was a merchant seaman. Found dead with some of his mates in an open boat after they was tin-fished in the Atlantic. I've thought of him a few times these last weeks, I can tell you.'

Howard thought of that other drifting boat and its silent crew; Ayres overcoming his fear and horror; the girl's photograph found with one of the ragged corpses.

'Thank you for telling me.' He put down the glass, surprised that it was empty. 'I needed that.'

The steward smiled, knowing that Howard was not referring to the drink. He followed him to the door and said in parting, 'Well, sir, as *I* see it, it's what it's all about.'

The *Kinsale*'s first lieutenant saw him to the brow and saluted again. 'Sorry about your news, sir.'

Howard returned his salute. *Nothing secret for long in this regiment.*

He found Treherne waiting for him but before he could speak said, 'I'm going south for a couple of days, Number One. Look after her for me, and make certain the lads get as much shore leave as you can manage.'

'I just heard, sir. If there's anything I can do . . . but then, you know that by now, I hope?'

Howard met his gaze and thought of how he had nearly broken down, but for an unknown man's simple kindness. 'I may have to hold you to that one day – and yes, I've always known that.'

He looked along the ship's deserted decks. The hands were below in the messes reading their letters, getting ready to go ashore.

Treherne watched him grimly, knowing what he was thinking. *Welcome home.*

10

Every Time You Say Goodbye

The man Howard had known all his life simply as Mister Mills placed two mugs of tea on his scrubbed table and studied the young officer opposite him. 'I've laced it with some rum, David. Do you good. Besides, it's going to be a cold 'un tonight.'

Howard nodded and warmed his hands around the mug. Mister Mills was older, but did not seem to have changed all that much. The same shabby sports jacket, and the beret he always wore indoors and out, pulled tightly down over his ears like a lid. His house was as he remembered, filled with odds and ends, furniture too, which Mister Mills sold when he had the mind to. Some described him as a junk-man, but in these hard times of shortages and rationing, he had come into his own again. He bought bits and pieces from bombed buildings, found furniture for people intending to get married and to hell with the war; like his battered old van, he was a familiar sight around Hampshire.

Howard shivered and thought of the long, fast drive from Liverpool. It had been spent mostly in silence, with Rear-Admiral Lanyon apparently content to leave him to his thoughts while he went through endless clips of signals.

Of the war the rear-admiral had said very little except, 'Your fight in the Atlantic is the essential one. Things must turn the corner soon.' But he was unprepared to enlarge on that flash of optimism.

He had mentioned his daughter only briefly. How she had held up after her pilot husband had been killed in Howard's convoy to Murmansk. Even through the grip of his own worries

Howard had sensed, strangely, that Lanyon had not really approved of Jamie Kirke. He had called him a hero, but it had sounded like a mark of distaste.

He tried not to think of the house he had just left. The stench of wet ash left by the AFS hoses which would cling until the place was rebuilt. Two walls, a solitary chimney-stack standing like a crude monument, all the rest a shambles of broken glass and brickwork, and a hole that covered half the site where the bomb had come screaming down.

Mister Mills had explained how it had happened. A sneak daytime raid intended for the dockyard again, but the enemy aircraft had been confronted by the whole weight of Portsmouth's defences, from the ships in harbour to land-mounted batteries. Their attack had been further snared by the new ranks of barrage-balloons, which had forced the bombers to swerve aside and be caught by the onslaught of combined anti-aircraft fire, 'Like a Brock's benefit', he had described it.

Mister Mills watched him now thoughtfully. 'I've salvaged some of his gear, of course. You'll be coming back here one day, eh?'

Howard heard himself reply without hesitation. 'It's still my home.' The rum-laced tea was helping and he said, 'Where's the grave?'

Mister Mills looked at the window, darker even earlier this evening. 'Other end of the village.' He looked at his companion again, perhaps seeing his dead friend as he had once been before Zeebrugge. 'It was a nice service. There were six killed that day, David.' He let out a long sigh. Remembering. 'A hell of a lot in a place this size. But the pub was saved – that was one blessing, I suppose.'

'Could you tell me again, please?' He watched him pour two more mugs and wondered why he had to know.

'There was an air-raid warning, nothing unusual, even in daylight. The gunfire got so loud I said, we're in for it this time, never guessing the bastards would jettison their bombs over here. So we went out to the little shelter at the back of the house, but the dog was frightened.'

Howard nodded and thought of the dog he had never seen. 'She would be. Her own home was bombed earlier.'

'Just as we reached the shelter, the poor old thing broke away and ran back to the house. Like a shot he was after her, telling me to get down.' He gave a sad smile. 'Well, you know what he was like.'

There was silence and Howard heard a car clattering along the lane. Mister Mills had heard the bomb coming; he was sure he had seen the blur of it a split-second before it struck.

He said, 'They were killed together. I was knocked out myself. When I came to, old Tom the gamekeeper and a special constable were bending over me, and everything seemed to be on fire. I was a bit concussed, *they* said.' He added with his old contempt, 'What the hell do they know?'

Killed together. He thought of the girl with green eyes. She would blame herself for that too.

Mister Mills went on, 'Your brother and his wife were here for the funeral – even the two Eye-tie gardeners came along.' He looked at Howard with sudden interest. 'That young Wren girl was here as well. Real upset, she was.'

The bombs had devastated one complete side of the little lane. The victims shared a grave together, as they had shared their lives in this quiet corner of England.

Mister Mills cocked his head as another car slowed to a halt outside. The rear-admiral had even organised that for him. Mister Mills offered, 'You can stay here if you like.' He tried to shrug it off. 'It's a bit quiet now.'

Howard shook his head. 'I've things to do, but thanks – for everything you did for the Guvnor. I'll not forget. Ever.'

Mister Mills shuffled after him to the garden with its sagging gate. He touched it and said half to himself, 'Must fix it. One day.'

Howard waved to the khaki staff car. 'I'll be in Portsmouth if you need me. And then . . .'

Mister Mills nodded. *And then*. How many times had he pondered over it in his own war? 'Back to the Atlantic, David?'

'Yes.'

They shook hands in silence. Two wars apart, but linked by what they had both lost.

As the big Humber swung on to the main road, Howard turned and gazed at the shabby little figure staring after him.

The driver remarked, 'God, that's a bad mess, sir.'

Howard said, 'It's my home.'

The car wavered and the man said awkwardly, 'I'm sorry, sir, nobody told me.'

Howard stared at the blur of passing fields and hedges, the trees stark and bare of leaves. Another winter drawing near. More convoys. Then what?

Later, as Howard sat in a corner of the large barracks wardroom where he had been booked in by the rear-admiral's flag-lieutenant, he stared at the fire and tried to put together all he had seen and heard.

He toyed with the idea of phoning the girl and wondered if her father had already warned her off, or even if she needed to be dissuaded.

There was a great gust of singing and several of the more senior officers got up and departed with obvious irritation.

Howard glanced across to the activity at the long bar and saw some half-dozen sub-lieutenants, each with pilots' wings displayed above their wavy stripes, and guessed they must just have 'passed out' and were about to join their various squadrons. If they lived long enough, their role might be crucial in the months ahead.

He half-listened to their roar of voices as they kept time to the mess piano, the tune that of 'The Dying Lancer', and thought suddenly of the girl's dead husband.

> Take the cylinder out of my kidneys,
> The connecting rod out of my brain,
> The cam box from under my backbone,
> And assemble the engine again!

Howard stood up and strode to the door. He did not even see one of the bright new subbies nudge a companion. *Look at him. Another one who's bomb-happy!*

All three telephone boxes were occupied and he hesitated, wondering what she might say. If she would pretend she wasn't there and have someone else put him off. In the meantime the next verse had struck up, louder than ever.

> When the court of enquiry assembles,
> Please tell them the reason I died,
> Was because I forgot twice iota,
> Was the minimum angle of glide!

A plump paymaster-commander eased himself from one of the phone boxes and growled, 'They'll soon change their bloody tune when – '

Howard did not hear him finish, and the confined box seemed suddenly private and safe.

It took the best part of ten minutes while he checked the various numbers and extensions and endured the usual questioning and clicks from service telephone operators. And then, all of a sudden, he was through.

He asked carefully, 'Could I speak to Second Officer Lanyon, please.'

He waited for the rebuff, the curt disclaimer; all the while he could feel his heart pounding faster. *I must be really mad. Round the bend.*

'Putting you through, sir.'

She sounded cool and distant. 'Hello, who is that?'

He replied, 'David Howard, you remember when I – ' He stopped, already lost.

She asked, 'Where are you?' She had changed, her voice very low. 'Have you been to the house?'

He nodded, as if he expected her to see him. 'Yes. I'm at RNB. Just for a day or so.' The words were tumbling out as if he feared they would be cut off. 'Your father arranged it. I – I didn't know what had happened 'til he told me.'

She said quietly, 'I know. It was the least we could do. We heard about the convoy, what you went through.' The line clicked but there was no interruption. Maybe you did not break into a call, even one which mentioned naval operations, if the one concerned was a rear-admiral's daughter. She said quickly, 'There's a pub, this side of Gosport – *The Volunteer*.' When he said nothing she said, 'It's quiet, not used much by our people or HMS *Collingwood*.'

He said, 'I shall be there within an hour.' He could not believe what was happening. 'I'll find a friendly driver. I just want to tell you . . .'

A man's voice interrupted patiently, 'You've been disconnected, sir.'

'But I was just speaking to . . .'

'Sorry, sir.' Then what might have been a chuckle. 'It's the war, you know.'

Howard slammed down the telephone and hurried from the box. He almost knocked over a lieutenant who was about to leave the wardroom. They stared at one another and the lieutenant grinned.

'Sinclair, sir.' The grin widened. 'I was a CW candidate in your ship, the *Winsby* – you won't remember me.'

Howard's mind was still reeling, but suddenly a young, eager face formed in his memory. One of the many. He said, 'You wanted to go into submarines when you were commissioned, right?'

The lieutenant stared. '*Right*, sir! Matter of fact, I've a boat coming to collect me right now to take me back to the base at *Dolphin*. What about letting me show you off to my friends, sir?'

Howard's mind was suddenly clear again. 'HMS *Dolphin* – then you probably know a pub called *The Volunteer*?'

'Yes, I know it, sir. Bit too quiet for me though.' His eyes sharpened as he sensed the urgency of the question. 'I can get you there easy enough. I'm duty-boy at *Dolphin* at the moment, just came over with a message for the commodore here.'

Howard took his arm. 'Then lead on. I'll have that drink later, if I may!'

He turned to collect his cap from the table outside the wardroom and the young lieutenant who was serving in submarines, and who had once been a nervous CW candidate in Howard's first command, thought he heard him say just one word. *Fate*.

Howard pushed through the door and parted the heavy blackout curtains, which smelled of tobacco and dust. It was a cosy enough little pub, but after the darkness outside even the dim lighting seemed too bright. There was a fire in the grate where two farm labourers were sipping their pints, a large dog snoozing between them.

There were a few servicemen in the adjoining bar, but thankfully nobody he knew. He had never felt less like talking just for the sake of it. As the lieutenant named Sinclair had described it, *The Volunteer* was pretty quiet. It was hardly surprising, he thought. Sea-going sailors liked something a bit more lively after the strain of watch-keeping and staying alive, while shore-based ones preferred the plentiful if unimaginative food of the various barracks and establishments.

'Evenin', sir.' The landlord wiped an imaginary stain off the bar with his cloth while he watched the newcomer, his eyes moving professionally from Howard's two-and-a-half stripes to his DSC ribbon when he removed his raincoat.

'Horse's Neck, please.' He smiled to break the tension he felt. 'If you can still manage it?'

The man grinned. 'Ah, but if you'd asked for Scotch, that'd be different. I'd have called the police or the Home Guard in case you were a Nazi parachutist! Not had any Scotch for a year!'

Howard took his glass to a corner table while the landlord switched on the nine o'clock news.

Howard hardly listened. In any case he had heard the same sort of thing so many times it made little sense any more: 'During the night our bombers raided targets over the Ruhr and the U-Boat bases at Lorient. Seven of our aircraft failed to return.' He saw the landlord staring at the little wireless, his face grim. Maybe he had someone who flew the hazardous raids deep into enemy territory. The newsreader's well-modulated voice shifted its attention to the Russian front. *Stalemate*. The news was little better from the North African theatre, and he thought momentarily of Ayres and his missing brother.

A breeze fanned the curtain, and she was suddenly here. She glanced quickly around, as he had done, probably for the same reason. She sat down opposite him and removed her tricorn hat to shake out her hair. All the time she watched him, searching his face feature by feature.

'I hope you've not been waiting long?'

Howard signalled the landlord, who, like the two men by the fire, had been staring at the girl as if she had just stepped from the moon.

She said, 'A gin would be nice.'

Had she been going to ask for a sherry, but remembered the last time it had happened in the Guvnor's living room?

'Of course.' Howard moved to the bar and then stopped dead. The newsreader was just ending. Just a small item, which in any daily paper would qualify for no more than a couple of lines: 'The Secretary of the Admiralty regrets to announce the loss on active service of HMS *Redwing*. Next of kin have been informed.' He did not remember paying for the drink. Only that he was seated again, the glass gripped in his fingers.

She took it gently, her eyes studying him anxiously. 'What is it?'

'*Redwing*. I saw her go. That last convoy. We managed to lift off some of her people.'

He stared at the wall but saw only the ship settling deeper and deeper alongside. Dazed, bleeding men being dragged roughly to safety. *Redwing*'s captain on the bridge, his eyes blank with shock. He stared at her hand on his wrist but did not feel it.

'Tell me.'

'I must have been at it too long.' He looked at her hand and wanted to hold it, to let it all flood out. But he knew she would pull away, that he would not be able to stop this time. 'But I had this strange feeling – ' He looked directly into her eyes. The colour of the sea. 'It's impossible of course – '

He felt the slightest pressure on his wrist. 'Try me.'

Howard said, 'I think the torpedo was meant for us.'

She smiled and took her hand away as if she had just realised what she had done. 'Well, thank God it missed!' She raised her glass. 'I can't stay long.' She recognised his disappointment. 'My friend Jane is standing in for me. I simply wanted to see you. To make sure you were all right. It must have been hell for you when you got back.'

'I saw what was left of the place. Mister Mills has done his best.' He smiled with sudden affection. 'Bless him.'

'He's very fond of you, isn't he?'

Howard glanced round as the curtain swirled aside again and two soldiers thudded across the floor in their heavy boots, each looking quickly at the girl before discovering the dartboard on the far side of the bar.

She added, 'I met your brother and his wife.'

'What did you think of Robert?'

He saw her start with surprise that he should ask her. But her reply was in her characteristic, direct fashion. 'Well, I can see him as an admiral.' She smiled for the first time. 'He's not in the least like you.'

Howard grimaced. 'I suppose not.' It was strange, but he had never really thought about it. She was right. Robert was all one would expect of a regular officer. Very straight; but inclined to a stiffness their father had never needed.

When he looked again her smile had gone. She said, 'Will you keep the old house?' She saw him nod and added wistfully, 'I came to like it.' Then she seemed impatient, angry that she could not hide her emotion. 'Poor Lucy. But for me —'

Howard pulled the handkerchief from his breast pocket and put it in her fingers. 'Don't even think it. They were together. Each needed the other.'

He knew the landlord and the two men by the fire were watching intently, but did not care. They probably imagined they had met here in secret. Lovers, when neither was free. *Would that we were.* He said nothing while she dabbed her eyes, then studied herself in her compact mirror.

She said, 'I'm a mess!'

He reached between the glasses and took her hand very carefully. As a man will hold a frightened bird, trying to avoid injuring it. 'I'd like to see you again.'

She studied him curiously. 'I can tell you mean it, and not for the reasons I'm offered from time to time. But it wouldn't work.' She smiled, as if to ease the hurt. 'How would we manage? Have you asked yourself that?'

'Others do.' His voice was sharp. He was thinking of men who had tried to win her favours. *The young widow.* It happened often enough in wartime.

'Maybe.' She was still watching his face, looking for something, or someone. 'I know I couldn't. Not again.' She glanced at her watch. 'I must go. Really.'

He held her hand more tightly. 'Don't you understand? I've been thinking about you ever since that day when the Guvnor —' He looked away. 'Sorry, I didn't mean to drag it all up again.'

Then they were both standing, and in the small bar he could hear the clock ticking.

'It's my fault.' She freed her hand very gently. 'Anyway, what should I do? Every time you say goodbye, it breaks your heart — didn't you know? That's why I'm soldiering on. I want to do something useful. Like you, and all the other people out there who are trying to win this damnable war!' She looked around at the intent faces with a kind of defiance which only made her appear more vulnerable. 'We shall probably bump into one another from time to time. My friend Jane and I are being transferred to Operations.' She hesitated, seeing the dying hope in his eyes. 'Western Approaches, in fact.'

He stared at her. 'Liverpool!'

She replaced her hat, then turned to face him. 'Well, it's not too big a place, is it?'

He would have followed her but she said, 'I've got my bike outside. You stay and have your drink. You've not touched it.' Then she said, 'I shall miss your father, and if you're interested, I think you're exactly like him.' With the same touch of defiance she held up her cheek, and for those few unreal seconds Howard tasted her skin and the gentle fragrance of her hair.

He heard the outside door slam, the far-off wail of an air-raid warning, and pictured her cycling through the darkness to the air station at Lee-on-Solent. He downed the drink in one swallow and picked up his cap.

The landlord nodded as he put the glass on the bar. They were in short supply too. Most of the pubs had the rule, 'no glass no drink', so that customers would refrain from gathering a little hoard of them at every visit.

'Nice lady, sir.' His eyes were full of questions. 'Not married, I see?'

Howard wanted to leave, to think alone. He replied brutally, 'She was. He was killed.'

Outside he paused to look at some searchlight beams wavering across the sky and to get his bearings. As he walked along the darkened road he was torn between despair and a lingering hope. Which, like the horizon and the night sky, had no clear division.

Howard returned to Liverpool after four days, during which time he visited the family solicitor, and spent a whole afternoon signing papers. Even in war there was apparently a lot to do when someone died.

He visited the communal grave, a sad little plot as yet without a proper stone to mark the remains of the six people who lay there. There were a few dead flowers and a fresh bunch of chrysanthemums in a stone pot. There was a card, too, with her name on it. She must have gone there without telling him before she left for a few days' transfer leave. Mister Mills had told him that she had made him promise to keep flowers there until the stone was properly installed; that was something else Howard had signed at the solicitors.

At Liverpool it was raining when he arrived, and by the time he had been aboard *Gladiator* for an hour it was almost as if he had never been away.

Lieutenant Treherne had told him that the group was expected to sail in three more days, or that was the latest buzz. He also told the story of Bizley, who with his second stripe and promised decoration was becoming unbearable. There was also a new navigating officer, Sub-Lieutenant Brian Rooke, one of those rare junior officers from the lower deck who sought and won promotion by way of a scholarship. Most of the other lower deck officers were much like old Arthur Pym: years and years of service from boy seaman, up and up via the Petty Officers' mess and eventually to wardroom with just a thin half-stripe to show for the long, hard slog.

Howard saw Rooke in his quarters, a tough, round-faced man of twenty-four, with a blue chin which apparently defied the sharpest razor. He had a brusque, business-like manner, and his personal report left Howard in no doubt that Treherne's replacement would prove an excellent navigator, if they could hang on to him.

But he had one failing, a chip on his shoulder a mile wide. As Treherne had said with gleeful relish, 'He thinks we're all turning up our noses at a poor ex-matelot!' Treherne had been thinking of Joyce at the time, and all her ideas of *posh officers*.

It was just November when the group left Liverpool to shadow a large westbound convoy which was to be met by Canadian escorts in the usual way. The convoy was attacked by long-range reconnaissance bombers, then U-Boats for much of the way; but using more aggressive tactics than before, Captain Vickers threw his group into the attack again and again and left the close-escort to the corvettes. They lost just two ships, but severely damaged a U-Boat on the surface one night in mid-Atlantic. It was a probable kill. The return run from Halifax with a fast convoy of modern tankers was mauled once again by a U-Boat pack south of Cape Farewell. Once more Vickers impressed it on his escort captains to follow his tactics whenever possible. Drive the U-Boats under, and keep them there so that they could not overhaul the heavy tankers.

It was a record. When they reached the Mersey they had lost only three tankers. Three out of twenty-seven.

Perhaps it had been sheer luck, or maybe the German HQ had misunderstood the convoy's intentions. They might even have withdrawn some of their powerful force of U-Boats for refitting and repair before winter really hit the Western Ocean.

As *Gladiator* headed slowly upriver towards Gladstone Dock, Howard stood on the gratings beside his chair and stared at the mass of dockyard personnel and servicemen who thronged the jetties and moored vessels to watch their return, and then to his amazement, to cheer as if they were the victors.

Leading the group, Vickers's rakish *Kinsale* was blaring 'D'you Ken John Peel?' on all her speakers, adopted by the rugged captain as their own hunting song. Howard left the ship in Treherne's hands and watched the welcome, very moved by what he saw and heard. It had never happened before.

He heard Rooke say, 'Time to turn, sir.'

Treherne nodded. 'Very good.'

Howard did not even have to look. There had been times when he had barely been able to snatch a catnap at sea. Afraid that a youthful and barely-trained officer on watch would do something stupid, lose the next ship ahead in the dark or ram it up the stern by too many revolutions wrongly applied. Somehow, despite the changes, or because of them, they had become a team, and no matter what happened on the next convoy or the one following that, this delirious welcome was a tonic after what they had seen and done.

As the destroyers made their careful turn, one of the Wrens on the signal station's verandah called, 'They're coming, ma'am!'

Celia Lanyon removed her hat and took the proffered oilskin from a grizzled yeoman of signals; it came down to her ankles, but that did not matter. Out on the windswept verandah, the rain plastering her hair to her face, she felt the new excitement in the place, which she had never shared before. The flags soaring up and down, so bright against the grey sky and sombre town; the clatter of signal lamps; and then more cheers as the destroyer with *H-38* painted on her rust-streaked bow edged into view.

She found that she was waving and cheering too, without understanding it. They had called her a blue-stocking, stand-offish, before Jamie had come into her life. But she had never been like this.

Howard turned to watch the yeoman clattering off yet another acknowledgement, his hard features outwardly unmoved by something he probably thought was empty optimism.

Well, perhaps it was. Howard stiffened. But this time it was different. He raised his glasses and trained them through the diagonal rain towards the signal station.

Even in the bulky oilskin, hatless and with her hair clinging to her face, he saw her immediately. He hesitated, then removed his cap and held it high above his head before waving it slowly from side to side.

Treherne called, 'Stand by wire and fenders.' He glanced up at the captain, and gave a slow grin of understanding. Bloody good luck to him.

Ayres gave a nervous cough and Treherne leaned over the voicepipe.

'*Stop port! Slow astern port!*' Just in bloody time.

Gladiator was back again, and although there would be those who would grieve for the men who had died with the three tankers, others would see this as a small break in the cloud.

Howard watched until the signal station was hidden from view. There was hope after all. Perhaps for them, too.

In the same month of November two other events took place – unconnected, but they would prove more important than any of these men and women could appreciate.

There came to Liverpool a new commander-in-chief for Western Approaches, a tireless, dynamic and forceful admiral named Max Horton. He was neither a patient man, nor one who would accept defeat in any form while the convoys braved the Atlantic in all conditions.

The other event occurred in North Africa beside the Qattara Depression, near a place nobody had ever heard of. It was called El Alamein, where for the last time, at the very gates of Egypt, the battered Eighth Army turned and stood fast. Like the thin red line, some said. The retreat was over.

As Howard had thought. There was hope after all.

PART TWO

1943

I

Victors and Victims

'Starboard watch closed up at defence stations, sir.' Lieutenant Finlay's voice was sharper than usual, a sure sign that he was on edge about something. Lieutenant-Commander David Howard licked his lips and savoured the last cup of coffee until morning. It was midnight, the middle watch standing to their various stations while the destroyer rolled easily from side to side at reduced speed.

Howard looked up at the heavy cloud layer, the rare glimpse of a star. It was mid-April, and already the Atlantic was reluctantly showing its mercy after the winter gales. Around and beneath the gently vibrating chair he could sense his ship's mood and that of her company. Just another year; a few months since his father had been killed in the hit-and-run raid, and yet everything was different. Even the ship was changed in some ways, but that was to be expected, he thought. He was lucky to have held on to Treherne as his Number One, and of course, the ship's core, Evan Price, the chief.

But he would soon be losing Finlay, although the gunnery officer had as yet not mentioned he was seeking a transfer to another ship. It was largely due to the bad feeling between him and Bizley, who after receiving his coveted DSC had used every opportunity to cross swords with Finlay, so that Treherne had been forced to stand between them on too many occasions. The wardroom was predominantly a young one still. Old Pym had gone at last to a shore job at HMS *Vernon*, the torpedo school, and was probably boring his recruits to death with his well-worn tales of Jutland. He had quit *Gladiator* as he had served her, a complaint on his tight mouth, a scowl for the growing intake of green and untried sailors. He was not missed. The new Gunner (T), only recently promoted from chief torpedo gunner's mate, was a different sort entirely. Bill Willis was round and jovial, and had a fund of yarns which had even forced Bizley to silence.

Midshipman Esmonde had left to be promoted to sub-lieutenant, although Howard found it hard to imagine him in any sort of real crisis where people would be looking to him for leadership. Treherne had described him as 'a squeaker'. A squeaker he would probably remain. His replacement was a midshipman of a very different kind. His name was Ross, a pale-faced youth who kept very much to himself in spite of their enforced mingling. Howard had spoken to Midshipman Ross when he had come aboard and had decided it would take more than a few months to make him relax. He rarely slept below when the ship was at sea, even in the worst weather, and at action stations he was usually the first at his station on the bridge. He had been serving in a big fleet destroyer called *Lithgow*, a powerful class of vessel much the same type as Captain Vickers's *Kinsale*. The ship had been in the Mediterranean, trying to force the convoys through to beleaguered Malta. A lucky ship, they had said. Until the day she had been attacked by a dozen aircraft all at once. When a rescue vessel had been sent to assist there had been just seven survivors on a Carley float, surrounded by oil and flotsam. Ross had been the only officer out of a company of over two hundred. But he was good at his work and eager to learn; together they probably served as his lifeline. How long, only time would tell.

Gladiator had also got rid of her doctor, much to most people's relief. The newly appointed surgeon-lieutenant, John Moffatt, a Dorset man born and bred, looked every inch a countryman, with rosy cheeks and what Treherne described as a turnip haircut. He was already very popular, and many swore he had once been a vet.

Howard stifled a yawn and thought of the two-month course they had been ordered to complete to their masters' satisfaction by the end of March, only days ago.

Howard had never believed they could have achieved so much or had so much to learn. It had been like going to school all over again. Tactical training ashore in class rooms, and periods at sea which had made the war almost preferable by comparison.

Admiral Max Horton, the new C-in-C Western Approaches, not only lived up to but surpassed all the stories previously told about him. In a few months the whole command was feeling his personal drive and demanding enthusiasm. He soon made it known that he believed in co-ordination, and the use of long-range aircraft with both the Navy and the RAF playing a full role. With extra fuel tanks they narrowed the Atlantic gap even more, and many U-Boats had been forced to run deep when they had discovered hostile aircraft where once the ocean had been theirs alone.

The active and aggressive use of hunter-killer groups was the basis of all new training, and *Gladiator*, with her consorts, had been in the thick of it. With a couple of elderly submarines playing at Germans they had evolved an entirely new method of attack. No longer used only as close escorts for the desperately needed convoys, they worked independently in small groups, sent to seek out the enemy in advance of any convoy due in any area, before a U-Boat pack could be mustered to attack and slaughter it as so many had been.

In some ways, at the beginning, it had been humiliating, and Howard had found himself resenting the bland instructions, the ruthless criticism after an exercise had gone wrong.

Slowly but surely, their instructors had won them round. The U-Boat, after all, had the whole ocean in which to hide. The old method of using depth-charges which took so long to sink and explode at the required depth was not enough. New ahead-throwing mortars with three barrels on each mounting, code-named Squid, were being developed and installed as fast as possible. The new pattern produced meant that the attacking warship could shadow a submerged submarine and still not lose contact if a salvo failed to encircle the enemy. Destroyers and frigates had previously lost vital minutes after they had dropped the old-style pattern over the stern, and had to turn as fast as possible to make another strike.

Until Max Horton's appearance at Western Approaches the theory on sinking submarines had changed little since peacetime, but the effect of the old-style depth-charges had been wrongly estimated. With the German hulls now being constructed of welded pressured steel, it was necessary to get a charge closer than sixty feet to do any lasting damage.

On *Gladiator*'s bridge one day after a fruitless attack, the tall, severe-looking commander who had been Howard's referee had remarked calmly, 'You see, old chap, Jerry's got six hundred feet to play with whenever he feels things are getting too hot.'

Howard had conned his ship slowly round for another attack, remembering all the other times – the lost echoes, the depth-charges killing nothing but fish. His tormentor had added, 'Remember, at four knots a U-Boat can *travel* six hundred feet while the charges are falling.' He had smiled at Howard's resentment. 'Now let's have another go, eh?'

Howard slid from his chair and crossed to the ready-use chart table. It seemed quiet enough. He smiled. *Spring in the air.* As he leaned over the chart and switched on the tiny shaded light he thought he heard Sub-Lieutenant Ayres humming to himself by the magnetic compass. He had been paired off with Finlay for watchkeeping duties, mainly so the first lieutenant could keep an eye on all of them. A sort of trouble-shooter, allowing his captain to keep his distance.

Ayres had certainly changed for the better. Like the news from North Africa, it was not just the continued advance of the Eighth Army against Rommel's invincible Afrika Korps. In their retreat the Germans had allowed one of their prison cages to be overrun. Ayres's brother had been found in it, wounded and still in a state of shock, but alive. The Red Cross had sent word to Ayres's home as soon as they knew.

Howard forgot him as he studied the worn chart, the one with a dark ring left by a cocoa mug like an ancient compass-rose in the corner.

One hundred miles south-south-west of Ireland's Bantry Bay and a convoy would be due to enter St George's Channel in two days' time. All being well. There had been many losses on the Atlantic run, but the deployment of new escort groups had managed to stop the score from rising like last year's brutal testimony.

He could picture the rest of the small group clearly in his mind, as if it was broad daylight. Three other destroyers, all veterans like *Gladiator*, steaming abeam in the new strategy to cover as much sea as possible with both radar and Asdic. One ship to the north of *Gladiator*, the other two equally spaced to the southward.

He was surprised that he could feel so relaxed. It was the first time he had been back in the field since their training had begun, and apart from exercising with the whole group they had covered just one small convoy until it had been met by other escorts from Gibraltar.

The training was over. He had to make certain that nobody forgot, even for a second.

They would patrol their beat, one giant rectangle, until the next convoy was safely passed through their area, unless they were required to offer support to another group or assist the air patrols. It was that flexible.

There was growing speculation about the new 'pocket' air-craft-carriers now being built. Tiny compared to a fleet carrier, they were converted merchantmen with wooden flight decks, from which pilots were expected to take off and land-on in any conditions. If it was true and it worked, the air gap would be closed for good. Convoys would sail with air cover from shore to shore, and no U-Boat would be safe to seek and attack them while on the surface. Like the sudden change of fortune in North Africa, it had once been a despairing dream. Now when the people at home listened eagerly to the news bulletins they could find hope instead of disappointment or fear.

All the way from Alex, household names which had changed hands so many times when the Eighth Army had been in retreat, would now be read out in the reverse order. Tobruk, Benghazi, Sirte and on to Tripoli, the ultimate goals being Tunis and Bone, Rommel's final toehold in Africa. A far cry from the crushing defeats and reverses of just a year ago. He sighed, and knew that Ayres had instantly stopped humming to listen.

What a pity the Guvnor had missed the change of luck. He switched off the light and stood up. *Luck?* Hardly that with all the ships sunk; all the men who had died at sea and on land, or had been hammered out of the sky. Hardly luck.

'Increase to half-speed, Guns. The others in the group will be checking the time and watching us on the radar. We don't want to hang about now and wake up some sleepy U-Boat before we can hit the bugger, do we?'

A shadowy figure moved across the bridge, a steaming fanny of kye swinging to the ship's motion.

Ordinary Seaman Andrew Milvain stopped dead as Howard said, 'We're losing you after this patrol, I believe?' He made it sound friendly and casual, as if he had not already written a good report for the young seaman, who was leaving to attend *King Alfred*, the officers' training establishment at Hove. There, all wartime RNVR officers cut their teeth and swotted to become midshipmen like Ross or subbies like Ayres.

'Yes, sir.' He stammered, 'I – I shall do my best, sir.' He glanced around him in the darkness, his shyness suddenly held at bay. 'But I'll miss the ship, and everyone . . .' His voice tailed away.

I would feel the same. But he said, 'You've made a lot of friends. Just mind you remember them when you get your little bit of gold, eh?' He turned as the wheelhouse acknowledged the increased speed and the bridge began to vibrate more insistently, and the slow roll departed in *Gladiator*'s ruler-sharp wake.

'I'm going to my hutch, Guns.'

'Aye, aye, sir.'

Howard lowered himself to the next deck, past the stammer of morse and murmuring voices in the wheelhouse, on into his tiny sea cabin.

He sat down on the bunk and massaged his eyes. Just a few moments alone to think. He reached out and opened the thermos of tea he knew Vallance would leave for him and tried not to dwell on the girl who came and went with his thoughts like the sun and the moon.

He had seen her only once after the triumphant return to Liverpool. It had been unsatisfactory again, because of the brevity and also because she had had her friend, Jane, with her. *Holding him at arm's length.* When he had been enduring the frustration and demands of the training course with the group, she had also been away with some senior officer on some special assignment. Or so her friend had said when he had telephoned. The one called Jane had left him in little doubt that she was more than willing to stand in for Celia if he gave the word. He had not, and was strangely glad about his decision.

He swallowed the over-sweet tea and took the telephone from its hook.

Finlay responded at once. 'Forebridge, sir?'

'All quiet, Guns?' He had come to rely on most of them more than he could believe. He remembered his first command, the little V & W Class destroyer *Winsby*, a wardroom of recalled old salts or complete amateurs. It all seemed a long, long time ago.

He looked at his new perk, the small radar-repeater on the bulkhead, the light revolving steadily to pick out the little blips on either side. A *long time ago*. Now Howard as a young lieutenant-commander was the senior officer of the group, that was, until they rejoined the others, or whatever else Admiral Horton decided.

Finlay said, 'Passed three sweepers two miles abeam, sir. Making for base.'

Howard nodded. Minesweeping: the most demanding job of all. Day in, day out, every channel must be swept. Just to be sure, for this was one of the main fairways of Western Approaches, with convoys putting out to sea – or making the last miles into harbour, and safety. Until the next time. The men who worked the minesweepers complained it was boring rather than dangerous. But their casualty lists were unmatched.

'Buzz me in an hour, Guns, unless . . .'

He heard his dry chuckle. 'Aye, sir. Unless I need you.'

Howard laid back on the bunk and watched the revolving radar beam until it made him drowsy. He felt the ship lift and plunge beneath him and pictured his men trying to sleep in their messes or huddled at their stations, peering out at the black water.

Gladiator was feeling the change too. No longer a helpless escort, watching while others died. She was her proper self again. A destroyer.

His head lolled and he was instantly asleep.

The dream was rising to a frenzied climax, in which Howard was unable to speak or make himself understood. She was in his arms, watching his mouth, waiting for him to explain with just the hint of a smile on her lips. Despite her nearness, the touch of her body in his hands, Howard was aware only of danger, the need to protect her.

The background was so bright and empty he could barely

look at it, and when she twisted round in his arms he saw another figure standing quite still, his back turned towards them, his arms hanging by his sides.

Even in the whirlpool of his thoughts he knew who it was, why he had come. He was dressed in a leather flying-jacket and fleecy boots. It was something Howard simply knew although he did not see them.

She laughed and ran from his outstretched arms towards the solitary figure, without another glance or any sign that she understood.

She held out her hands and the airman turned to look at her for the first time. But there was no face, just burned flesh and two angry red eyes. Her scream seemed to sear his brain like fire, but still he could not move.

Howard woke up, sweating and gasping even as the scream extended into the piercing call of the telephone.

He managed to speak. 'Captain?'

There was a pause. Like a question mark, he thought later. 'This is Treherne, sir.'

Thoughts burst through his mind and then slowly settled like spray after an exploding depth-charge.

The first lieutenant was on the bridge, but it was still the middle watch. He peered at the bulkhead clock. It was barely three-quarters of an hour since he had lain down. It had felt like an eternity, like torture. The ship was quiet apart from the engines' pulsing beat, and the occasional sluice of water alongside. No action stations, and yet . . .

'Are you all right, sir?'

Howard swallowed. 'Yes. What is it?'

Treherne seemed to turn away, to speak on another telephone perhaps, or to ponder on the captain's state of mind. 'Is your radar-repeater switched on, sir?'

'Yes.' Howard turned and peered at it, her scream still probing his mind. It was only a dream. He gritted his teeth. A bloody nightmare, more likely.

Treherne said evenly, 'Probably nothing, sir. But look at one-five-oh degrees, about ten thousand yards beyond *Hector*. Could that be an echo?'

Howard stared, watching the bright little blobs glow and then fade as the radar beam passed over them. Steering west, all on station, in line abeam. *Hector*, a pre-war destroyer which had seen plenty of action at Dunkirk and off Norway before coming to the Atlantic, was the wing ship. There it was. He felt his body tense on the edge of the bunk, the dream refusing to leave him. It was a very small echo, but it was still there when the radar beam passed over it again.

'Why haven't the other ships reported it?'

Treherne weighed his words with care. 'The conditions tonight might make a difference, sir. I've spoken with Lyons. He's known it before, where one ship can pick up on an echo at a greater range than others. Sometimes it's the set, but this time he thinks it's the heavy cloud.'

Howard thought about it while he watched the repeater. Five miles was the kind of range for radar to pick up a surfaced U-Boat if that was what it was. *Hector* and her nearest consort *Belleisle* were nearer, but they had not so far reported anything.

'I'll come up.' He waited, knowing Treherne was still there. 'And thanks, Number One.'

It was cold on the upper bridge after his brief stay in the sea cabin. There were no stars at all now, the clouds almost as dark as the water.

'Call up *Hector*, Number One. Ask them if they've seen anything.' He studied the bridge repeater while Treherne called up the wing ship on the short wave intercom.

The little blip was still there. There were no patrols out here, or they would have been told. If it was a small Irish vessel she'd be showing lights. But then, if they had any sense they would be snug in port somewhere.

'Negative, sir. But *Hector* is keeping a good lookout.'

'What's the range now?'

'From us, sir?' That was Finlay.

'Of *course*!' He regretted the sharpness in his tone.

Finlay reported stiffly, 'Nineteen thousand yards, sir.'

Howard took the intercom telephone from Treherne and spoke to each captain separately. The result was the same. *Gladiator* was the only one in contact. Unless, of course, her set was faulty.

Howard spoke to the radar office. 'What's it doing now, Lyons?'

Lyons had no doubts. 'Its speed is much like ours, sir. I think it's stalking *us*.'

Howard considered it. 'Tell the other ships to reduce speed to nine knots.' He was thinking aloud. 'If that bastard thought we were four powerful destroyers we wouldn't see his arse for sauerkraut. I think,' he nodded firmly as if to convince himself, 'I *think* he believes we're part of a convoy. After all, they did change the sailing time of one a few days ago, right?' He saw them watching him in the darkness, as if he had suddenly become dangerous.

'We will continue at this reduced speed, course two-five-zero.' He heard Treherne repeating his instructions quietly over the intercom. When Howard had taken his first command to war there had been no such luxury as an intercom which could not be detected. No radar; few fully automatic anti-aircraft guns; and senior officers who for the most part had trained all their lives to believe in the Empire, on which the sun never set. Some of the new escorts coming off the stocks were even more effective and sophisticated.

Treherne called, '*Hector* has the contact, sir. Requests permission to attack.'

'Denied.' Howard looked over his shoulder. 'Sound action stations. Have the Gunner (T) check all watertight doors himself.' He could almost feel Treherne's surprise and added, 'Remember, Number One, he's new in this ship. I'm more concerned with staying in one piece than ruffling his feathers!' He added sharply, 'Or anyone else's for that matter!'

They were steaming almost parallel with the target, for that was what it had become. When the time was right, the four destroyers would pivot to port and in line abreast would charge down on the enemy at full speed.

He said to the bridge at large, 'Well, after this we might know if all that training and sweat did us any good!' It was a relief that somebody laughed. He tried to place the sound in the darkness. Of course, it was Richie, the new one-badge petty officer and yeoman of signals.

Poor Tommy Tucker the original yeoman had finally cracked. For him it could not have come at a worse time. His wife had gone off with a Yank airman when *Gladiator* was on her last convoy, and he must have been brooding about it during the group training. One of the admiral's instructors had tackled him on the bridge about some obscure signals procedure, but Tucker, who had seen every horror the war could throw his way, who had nursed his newly trained bunting-tossers until they could do almost anything, had taken enough.

'What the hell do you know, *sir*? The war looks pretty good to you, I expect, sitting on your fucking arse while others are getting theirs shot off!'

Howard had appealed on his behalf, but Tucker had been sent ashore under guard.

The authorities had two choices for Tucker. A mental ward at a naval hospital and perhaps a discharge, or a court martial and an eventual return to the Atlantic.

Tucker had rejected both options. With his usual hard efficiency he had found a tree and hanged himself.

Howard shivered. But he was still here, in his rightful place, on the bridge.

'Call up the group. We will attack when the target is due south of us.'

'Radar – bridge?'

Treherne was there. 'Bridge?'

'Target bears one-six-five, ten thousand yards!'

Howard stood up behind the forward screen. 'Tell the group. *Execute*, speed fifteen knots!' He sensed the sudden excitement crowding around him. 'Port twenty!' He heard Sweeney's hoarse acknowledgement. He wondered what the coxswain thought about Tucker. Changes in the small petty officers' mess were never welcome, especially for a reason like that.

'Midships! *Meet her*!' He swore to himself. He had allowed his mind to stray. 'Steer one-eight-zero!'

Hidden from one another in the darkness, controlled only by their radar and churning screws, the four destroyers had wheeled round to head at right-angles towards the target. The single ship, the *Blackwall*, on *Gladiator*'s starboard beam would be at the end of the sweep, like the edge of a door while the others swung round on an invisible hinge.

'From *Hector*, sir! *Lost contact!*'

Treherne said, 'Jerry got the message at long last, and dived.'

'From *Blackwall*, sir. *Have Asdic contact at one-seven-zero degrees, one thousand yards!*'

Howard said, 'Tell him, *Tally Ho!*'

'From *Blackwall*, sir. *Am attacking!*'

While the destroyer charged into the attack, the others took up their allotted stations for a five-mile box search. But it was not necessary. *Blackwall* was fitted with the squid mortars as well as her conventional depth-charges, and by the time *Gladiator* had completed her turn, the sea was already stinking of oil.

'Slow ahead together.'

With the ships spread out in the new formation it was unlikely that any other U-Boat could get close enough undetected to carry out an attack.

'Ship breaking up, sir.'

There was a ragged cheer from somewhere aft.

Howard leaned over the screen and peered at the heaving water. Another kill. It had gone like a clock. As all those brasshats had promised it would.

The port lookout called, 'Someone's got out, sir!'

Above the rumble of screws Howard could hear the coughing and retching. God alone knew how they had escaped.

'Lost contact, sir. Target is now on the bottom.'

Howard looked at Treherne's shadowy outline against the grey paint. Imagination, or was it getting lighter already?

'Away sea-boat's crew, Number One, two extra hands to help with possible survivors.'

'Aye, *aye*, sir!'

Within minutes the whaler was hoisted out, lowered and then dropped into the sea to be carried clear by the boat-rope.

The Buffer appeared on the bridge, banging his gloved hands together as he always did when he was pleased about something. 'I've told 'em not to 'ang about, sir.' His teeth were white through the shadows. 'I'll bet that Jerry commander didn't know whether to 'ave a shit or an 'aircut, when 'e saw us comin' at 'im!'

They were all grinning at each other like schoolboys.

Howard thought of the past three years and sighed. *No wonder.*

Treherne said, 'I cleared the after-guns for the whaler, sir. Lieutenant Bizley volunteered to take charge.'

Howard ignored the sting of bitterness in his voice. 'Fall out action stations.' Howard trained his night glasses. 'Whaler's coming back. Have the falls manned. As the Buffer said, we don't want to hang about!' Almost before the boat had been hooked on and run up to the davit-heads, Howard knew something had gone wrong.

There were two Germans only, although neither might live after what they had gone through.

'Slow ahead together. Bring her round, Pilot.' Behind his chair he could hear Bizley panting, as if he had been running.

'It wasn't my fault, sir!'

'I shall decide that. Just tell me, right?'

'I had two hands in the bows, sir. But after we hauled the first German on board, the other started to drift away. He was calling out, choking on oil. One of the bowmen went over the side with a line and put it round the other German. Then – then . . .' He sounded dazed and lost, 'He just vanished under the boat. He never broke surface again.'

A massive figure in oilskin and lifejacket loomed through the bridge gate. It was Leading Seaman Fernie, who had been the whaler's coxswain.

He said harshly, 'It was the kid, sir. Young Andy Milvain from my mess.'

Bizley seemed to regain his composure. 'Go aft, Fernie, I'll deal with you later!'

Howard found that he had pulled out his empty pipe, remembering his brief words to the boy who had wanted to be an officer.

Fernie stood his ground. 'I don't care what *you* do, Mister Bizley! You ordered him over the side, an' I'll say as much if I'm asked!' He swung away as if he had lost his way.

'Steady on one-four-five, sir, one-one-oh revolutions.' A voice from the other world.

'Is that true, Bizley? *Did* you order him over the side?'

'Certainly not, sir. He was over-eager, always wanted to impress . . . you know, sir.'

'Yes. I think I do. Now get about your duties. I shall want a full report before we return to base.'

Treherne said in a hoarse whisper as Bizley's head and shoulders vanished down a bridge ladder, 'What a bloody awful thing to happen! What will his folks think? First one son, then the other. Who'll tell them, for God's sake?'

'I will, Number One.'

He turned as a muffled figure entered the bridge with a fresh fanny of tea. But Howard saw only the bright-eyed youth, Ordinary Seaman Andrew Milvain. His voice hardened. 'So take it off your back, Number One. It *happens*. All we can do is try and pick up the pieces!'

They both knew it was a lie, and when Howard looked again Finlay had resumed his watch, and the first lieutenant had disappeared.

Milvain's father was a major-general so was probably away somewhere. It would not be much of a home for his mother any more.

But in a few weeks or months when the boy's replacement had been settled in, he would soon be just another missing face, and his name would rarely be mentioned. Except by Leading Seaman Fernie perhaps. When one of his mess asked, 'D'you remember that posh kid, Hookey?' He would crush him.

Howard blinked his sore eyes as the morning watch clattered up ladders or slithered behind the gunshields to await the first light of another day.

Treherne came up to take over the morning watch and stood in silence beside his chair while the various voicepipes and telephones reported that they had relieved the others.

Then very soon *Blackwall* showed herself, throwing up spray and not a little smoke as she plunged over some short, steep rollers. When it was light enough Howard studied the other ship through his glasses. The victor. All grins on the upper bridge; a team job, but she had been the one to make it all work and leave the enemy in their tomb on the seabed. Howard had filled his pipe but did not remember doing so. He gripped it with his teeth and tried to strike a match below the shelter of the glass screen. He tried several times and then stared with shock as his hand began to shake uncontrollably.

'Light, sir?' Treherne did not raise his voice. Then he took Howard's wrist in his grasp and held a match to the bowl while their eyes met through the drifting smoke.

Howard exclaimed harshly, 'Christ, what's the *matter* with me?'

'Nothing.' Treherne tossed the match downwind. 'I asked for

that last night. You'd just about had enough. I should have seen, understood.'

Howard removed his battered cap and shook his head in the wet breeze. 'I'll bet you wish you were back with your other ships, Number One?' He could feel the man's strength, the bond which linked them and perhaps always had. Like the thaw after frost; a first warmth.

Treherne bared his teeth through his beard. 'Well, bananas were a lot less trouble to deal with, sir, I'll not deny that!'

Howard watched the other ships taking shape against the endless pattern of whitecaps which had come with a freshening wind.

The hunt goes on. 'I'll make out a suitable signal for the C-in-C, Gordon. He'll be pleased. Another kill so soon – it must mean something.'

Behind his back he imagined he could hear Petty Officer Tucker's ironic laughter.

Sub-Lieutenant Brian Rooke stood by the chart table and watched Treherne as he checked over his calculations. It was stuffy and dark in the chart-room because the ship was preparing for her last night at sea. The remainder of the patrol had passed without incident, and hardly an hour had gone by, or so it seemed, without a signal of congratulations being received. Another escort group had sunk two U-Boats in as many days, so if any proof had been needed about the admiral's strategy they had got it loud and clear.

Treherne said, 'We shall have to stand off until first light, Pilot.' He still found it strange to hear someone else called that. 'I don't reckon on the Old Man dicing with all the local traffic *en route* for Gladstone Dock,' He thought of the strain Howard had shown, the way he always seemed to force himself out of it. 'Shan't be sorry to stretch my legs ashore.' He thought of Joyce waiting to welcome him. 'That was quite a patrol.'

Rooke regarded him warily, as if he suspected that Treherne was about to find fault with his chartwork. 'Is it always like that?'

The door of the W/T office slid open and Hyslop the PO telegraphist, a pencil behind one ear, looked across at them.

'First Lieutenant, sir? I've got something for the captain.'

'What is it?'

'Big raid on Liverpool, sir.' He glanced at his pad. 'Meant for the docks but the flak was too heavy apparently. They knocked down a few streets though. All incoming escorts are to land their medical officers to assist.'

Treherne kept his voice level. 'Birkenhead?'

The PO looked at his pad again in case he had missed something. 'No, sir.'

'I'll tell him.'

He found Howard in his usual place on the port side of the bridge, his glasses hanging loosely around his neck.

Howard did not move as Treherne read him the lengthy signal and the first lieutenant imagined he was thinking about his father, comparing the raids which had been caused by the heavy resistance of AA batteries which covered the real targets. Instead Howard asked, 'Were *our* people all right?'

Treherne looked at him curiously. 'I think so, sir. No reports of any damage to ships and docks.'

Howard stood up and moved about the bridge, his hands touching various pieces of gear and instruments as if he had not seen them before. He asked, 'What's our ETA?'

Treherne replied, 'Well, five o'clock in the morning, sir. But as I said to Pilot you'll not want to . . .'

Howard said, 'Make a signal to give our time of arrival *as calculated*, Number One. Is the raid still going on?'

'No, sir.' He looked at the sky as if he expected to see the glow of fires. He had seen The Pool like that often enough.

Howard nodded. 'Get on with it then. I shall speak to the other captains. It's my responsibility.'

Treherne hurried down the ladder again. Was he still thinking of his father, or was he brooding about the boy who had been drowned? *He takes everything on his shoulders.* He recalled how Marrack had wanted his own command more than anything. Well, he was welcome to it!

Howard replaced the intercom handset and tried to think clearly. There were raids every day; people died, but others managed to soldier on. He turned away. *What she had said.* It couldn't be. Not her. She might not even have been there.

'Permission to step aboard, sir?'

Howard turned. It was Moffatt the new doctor. Wrapped in

a duffel coat, his cap jammed on his head like a pie-crust to keep it from blowing away, he looked more like a proper seadog than a medical man.

'Of course, Doc.' A thought flashed through his mind. 'Did Number One ask you to come, by the way?'

'No, sir. Although he did tell me about the air raid. I've got my gear all ready.'

'I'll be going ashore.' It came out too easily. 'You come with me.'

Moffatt asked quietly, 'Have you got someone there, sir?'

'Why does everyone *keep asking questions?*' He saw a lookout glance round and gripped the doctor's arm. 'Sorry, Doc. Not fair to pull rank. Yes, there is somebody I care about. Very much, although she doesn't know it.'

Moffatt regarded his profile thoughtfully. All bottled up. A man could take just so much. Howard's sudden confidence had touched him. He had always imagined a captain like Howard had no feelings other than for the job in hand. Not because he wanted it like that, but because it was his only way of staying outwardly sane.

Moffatt had got to know his fellow officers and many of the ship's company in his short time aboard. It was odd that nobody had let drop some hint about the captain's private life. After all, he had soon learned that there were no secrets in this *regiment*, as the sailors called it.

'Can't you take a nap, sir? Might help.'

'No. I shall more likely ask you for one of your pills to keep me on my feet.'

Bizley, who was OOW, said, 'Time to make the signal to the group, sir.'

'Do it then.'

Moffatt asked, 'What now?'

'We form line ahead before entering the final approach. There may be sweepers about, even a coastal convoy, although I don't know of any. But the raid may have delayed everything.'

He listened to Bizley's precise tones on the intercom. He was sullen rather than subdued, he thought. Perhaps it had been what he said; an accident. When he made his report, the chief-of-staff would very likely want to interview Bizley, as well as some of the whaler's crew.

He tried not to think of the young seaman. So eager, but he was dead, and a drunken lout like Bully Bishop was still alive.

As *Gladiator* and her consorts passed the Skerries and the northern coast of Anglesey the usual mood of apprehension closed over them for the men who had relatives and friends in the city. Treherne and the coxswain made all the arrangements for local leave for those concerned, and for once there was no idle chatter about the possibilities of 'a good run ashore'.

As the middle watch drew to a close and the ships headed due east towards the mouth of the Mersey the evidence of the raid hung on the air like something physical. There were few fires, but that did not mean much. Howard raised his glasses as the new yeoman of signals triggered off an acknowledgement to a guard boat's challenge. But of course, there would *not* be many fires, Howard thought. The raid had been intended for the ships and docks; the aircraft would be carrying high-explosive bombs, not incendiaries.

He thought of that other return, such a short while ago. The cheering, people thronging the waterfront to wave at them. The girl on the signal station verandah, waving with the rest, oblivious to the rain, her hair plastered across her face.

Shaded lights guided them through the entrance where the stench of charred wood reached everywhere. Torches glinted on the forecastle and he saw the first heaving line snake across, the eye of a wire hawser bobbing after it like some endless snake.

'*Stop port!*' Howard leaned out and saw some men standing by the guardrails staring into the first grey light of dawn. 'Slow astern port!' More wires, the sudden squeak of fenders as the hull came alongside the cats.

The engines quivered into silence and other sounds intruded. Ambulance and fire-engine gongs, the rumble of falling bricks as a bulldozer began to clear a road beyond the docks.

The officer-of-the-guard stepped aboard just as Howard climbed down from the bridge and saluted despite the early hour. Howard saw Moffatt hurrying after him and asked, 'Many casualties?'

The lieutenant was looking at the two German prisoners, one being carried on a stretcher. He replied, 'They're still coming in. Not really sure. Safe enough here though. I've never seen so much flak.'

Howard heard the coxswain bawling names selected for local leave and said, 'But none of *our* people?'

'Only up at the temporary planning room. Some Wrens were killed. Four, I believe.' He was still staring at the Germans, doubtless the first he had seen of the enemy, like most of them. He realised Howard was waiting and added, 'One was an officer. Poor girl had only recently transferred from down south.'

Moffatt was listening and said, 'I've told my SBA to wait with the Jerries. The first lieutenant has sent for the provost people.' He watched Howard's face. Like a man at the foot of the gallows. He snapped, 'Where did they take them – the Wrens, I mean?'

'Brought them down here, with the wounded ones. The sickbay is over . . .'

Moffatt retorted, 'I *know* where it is.' To Howard he added, 'I'll go.'

Howard walked past the quartermaster and sentry and down the brow, which had not even been properly secured yet. He did not see the curious faces, the orderly bustle of ambulances and helmeted police, their uniforms covered with dust.

'And where are *you* going, then?' It was a surgeon-lieutenant, a white coat slung over one arm.

'I'm *Gladiator*'s commanding officer.' He saw the man flinch as if he had sworn at him. 'I want to know about the Wren officer, so *don't waste my time!*'

The lieutenant glanced at Moffatt who gave him a quick nod, then said, 'One was killed, outright I should think; her friend was badly shocked, but she should be OK.'

Howard pushed past another white coat and opened the door. There were two girls lying on beds covered with blankets, their eyes closed, probably drugged.

The young second officer was sitting on a wooden bench, her head lowered, her coat and hair covered with flakes of plaster and paint.

When she looked up Howard almost cried out, as if she were also badly hurt. Her shirt was soaked in blood, her hands and wrists too.

She stared at him for a long moment, her green eyes very bright in the hard glare of sickbay lighting. Then she began to shake, her whole body quivering, yet she made no sound. Moffatt watched, holding the door with his shoulder as the captain raised her to her feet and then very carefully pulled her against him.

'Celia, it's me. Don't be afraid. Everything will be all right now.' Useless, mindless words.

Then she looked up at him again, and there were tears cutting through the grime on her cheeks.

She spoke in a small halting voice, like a child trying to explain something she did not understand. 'We were just sitting there. Jane had told me about the signal, about you and your group. The submarine.' She frowned, trying to remember. 'The teleprinters were making such a din. We knew about the raid, but there was going to be a flap on. The work was nearly done anyway.' She began to shake more violently. 'I – I think we both heard it coming. There was no sound afterwards. I suppose I was deaf or something. Then the emergency lighting came on and I tried to help poor Jane. She had no legs, and she was staring at me. I tried to help, but she was dead.'

'Over here, my dear.' Moffatt waited for Howard to guide her to another bed where she collapsed like a broken puppet.

Howard sat beside her, conscious of her bloodied fingers, which were entwined with his so tightly that he could barely feel them.

She looked at Moffatt for the first time, her eyes moving to the scarlet cloth between his two wavy stripes. 'Doctor.' One word.

'Yes, that's me.' Together they raised her and removed her jacket. The sight of it must have brought back the horror of her friend's death.

'*Hold her!*' Moffatt took her arm, seeing the blood, imagining what it must have been like, and thinking too of the German survivors who had been so grateful to him, and to some of the seamen who had brought them rum and cigarettes. The same men who had been trying to kill each other. It made no sense. 'She'll sleep now.'

Moffatt turned as two nurses came through the door. They both looked worn out but the older one managed to say, 'Thank God, the Navy's here!' To Moffatt she added, 'We'll take care of her. We can get her cleaned up in a moment.'

They all looked at Howard as he asked, 'Does her father know yet?'

The older nurse said sharply, 'We *have* been a bit busy here!'

Howard nodded. 'Can I use a telephone, please?'

Moffatt watched the other nurse as she took Howard to the door and pointed along the corridor. 'Just tell them I said it was okay!'

Moffatt said, 'I have been instructed to stay and give you a hand, Sister. I've brought my bag of tricks with me.'

'What was all *that* about, Doctor?'

Moffatt looked at the girl's upturned face. 'I'm not sure. But I think it was some kind of miracle.'

2

Moment of Peace

After a slow journey from Waterloo, stopping at every station, the train finally came to a halt at Hampton Court, the end of the line. Howard recalled very clearly the instructions he had received over the telephone when he had called to ask about Celia Lanyon. It had been her mother, and Howard was still uncertain whether the welcome had been genuine or if the admiral's lady had been unable to think of a way of putting him off. As he left the station and began to walk across the bridge over the Thames he was conscious of his uncertainty, which even the ageless view of Hampton Court Palace could not dispel.

He had travelled down from London after staying at the naval club, membership of which the Guvnor had insisted on for both his sons. *You never know when you might need a bed.* He had been right about that too. Most of the hotels seemed to be either full of Americans or prosperous-looking business men to whom the war had obviously been kind.

He paused in the dead centre of the bridge and stared along the river. It was easy to put the war aside when you took in this view, he thought. The pleasure boats were covered with awnings for the duration, and anything larger or more powerful than little punts and motor-cruisers had been commandeered long since by the Navy. But there were swans drifting by the banks, and only a few far-off barrage balloons marred the picture of tranquillity. He leaned on the warm stone balustrade and felt the sun on his neck.

He had written too many letters in the past to parents and wives when a loved one had been killed or lost at sea, but only when you came face to face with it did you understand the true shock of war.

He had visited Ordinary Seaman Milvain's family the previous day after telephoning Celia's home number. He knew that if he had done the visit first he would probably never have made the phone call to the house, which, if he remembered the directions correctly, he would be seeing for himself in about fifteen minutes.

Milvain's house had been very different from this riverside with its ancient trees and weathered buildings. It had been in a quiet, expensive street in the centre of Mayfair which had miraculously escaped any really serious bombing. One of the tall, elegant houses had been destroyed, but the site had been tidied up, leaving a neat gap in the street like missing teeth.

Howard had been unable to pay his visit before the news had arrived there in the usual fashion: *Missing and must be presumed dead*. God, it was common enough, but not easy to see for yourself.

In the high-ceilinged drawing room with the curtains half-closed Milvain's mother had listened in silence while he had tried to describe what had happened. She was a severe-looking woman, worn down by her latest loss, and not yet recovered from her other son's death. From a highly-polished table the two silver-framed photographs had regarded Howard as he told her of young Milvain's disappearance. His photograph had shown him as a very new recruit at HMS *Ganges*, a young open face, lacking the later intensity he was to gain at sea. The other was of a serious-eyed two-ringer, the one who had been Bizley's CO.

The only relief had been Milvain's sister, Sarah, a lively, bright-eyed girl who had confided that she hoped to be accepted for the Wrens. Howard noticed the hurt look her mother had given, the bitterness in her tone when she had finally spoken. 'It was to rescue some Germans, you say, Commander Howard?'

In that quiet room, London's traffic muffled by the curtains and the deserted street, Howard imagined he heard Bizley's voice, as if he had been there with him. '*It wasn't my fault, sir!*'

Howard had tried not to think of a memorial he had seen while attending a naval funeral. How long ago? It seemed like a hundred years.

When you stand there, think of us and say, for our tomorrow you gave your today. The Guvnor's war.

Milvain's father, a major-general, was up north; it was not explained what he was doing or how he had accepted the terrible news. Howard was ashamed, but he had been glad to leave the house in Mayfair, especially after Milvain's mother said in the same flat voice, 'He was just a *young boy*. Surely he should not have been given a man's job to do?'

He had recalled a signalman on *Winsby*'s bridge, cut down by machine-gun bullets from a Stuka dive-bomber. They had been going to the assistance of the crew of the East Dudgeon Light Vessel, which the aircraft had been attacking; still a mercifully rare occurrence despite the war's new height of savagery. The signalman had fallen at Howard's feet, his eyes losing focus even as he cried, '*Why me?*' His last words on earth.

Howard could share Milvain's mother's grief, and understand her sense of loss; nevertheless her words had seemed to follow him up the street like an accusation.

He paused now and looked along the tow-path, at Hampton Court Palace drowsing in the sunlight. He was out of breath already. Too many days and nights on an open bridge, too many vivid dreams when he finally got an opportunity to sleep.

Two sailors passed him and saluted smartly. Probably on leave, he thought as he returned the salute. Sailors would be rare around here unless they were free from the sea for awhile. He saw one of them glance quickly at his DSC ribbon; sensed the comradeship you usually felt when you saw the familiar uniform, so out of place inland.

He strode on, trying to recall what the girl's mother had said about their real house being used as a recuperation hospital for officers somewhere. He wondered if she had told him to put him in his place, to imply, without describing it, that their home was rather grand.

For some reason he recalled the way Celia had described his brother. The future admiral. He smiled grimly. It was equally possible to see Lilian, his brother's wife, as *the admiral's lady*.

He saw a man in Home Guard battledress reading a newspaper's glaring headlines, his eyes very intent through some ancient steel-rimmed glasses. Howard wondered if the news had been confirmed. Another setback at this stage would be disastrous.

The headline seemed to shout at him. *Rommel quits North Africa, Germans on the run.*

It was difficult to accept it, let alone take it as gospel truth. He had heard all about it at Liverpool while he had been fretting and waiting to see Celia before she was sent on sick leave.

Hitler had recalled the Desert Fox and left the final retreat of the Afrika Korps to General von Arnim. Nothing could stop the Eighth Army now. For once, the Germans were pinned in a corner of Tunisia, with only the sea at their backs. Without Rommel's inspiration, the general who had been admired by friend and foe alike, it seemed only a matter of days before the remaining troops surrendered, while others were forced to run the gauntlet of Allied submarines and aircraft.

While the U-Boat had gone to the bottom, and Milvain had been taken by the Atlantic as part payment, all this had been happening. Months, years of it, and it had suddenly burst out like a flower on a fast camera lens.

He stopped, breathing hard while he looked up at the imposing house which stood behind an equally old wall. It was hardly any sort of demotion, he decided.

Maybe he should go, now. Catch the next train up to Waterloo before he made a bigger fool of himself . . .

'You must be Commander Howard?'

He saw a tall, slender woman shading her eyes with a rough garden glove, while she held a basket of assorted tools in the other hand.

She put down the basket and tugged off a glove. 'I'm Margaret Lanyon. How do you do?' She shook his hand warmly. 'Come around the side gate and through the garden, will you? We don't use the front entrance much. The Americans camped in Bushy Park keep coming over to ask if the house is open to the public! If it wasn't for their lordships of Admiralty I could make quite a killing as a guide!'

Inside the pleasant, walled garden she paused and studied him, and he thought he could see her daughter somewhere in the scrutiny.

'I cannot thank you enough for what you did.' She smiled.

'May I call you David? I get quite enough spit and polish down at Pompey!'

'I wish I had been there sooner.'

She walked slowly amongst some roses and peered at the buds. 'Early this year.' Then she said, 'You saved her sanity, I really believe that. Her friend, poor Jane — well, it must have been terrible, for those other girls too. Jane was good for my daughter in her funny way. My husband thought she was a bit flighty, but I told him not to be so stuffy. They are young; there just happens to be a war on, but you can't expect people to toss their youth away because of it. They give enough as it is. Now she's dead. Celia insisted on going to the funeral. I went with her . . . it was quite awful, but I expect you know a lot about that aspect?'

Howard smiled and thought of Milvain's mother. 'A bit.' No, she was not like anyone he had expected.

'I just wanted to say something before you meet her. Be gentle with her. She's all we've got, you know.' She lightened it by adding, 'I think George wanted a son so much that Celia joined the Wrens just to please *him*!'

Howard faced her. 'I promise.' He thought he heard footsteps on flagstones and said quickly, 'May I ask you something?' He saw her nod and thought she already knew the question.

'Was she very much in love with her late husband?'

She did not answer directly. 'She told me what happened, that you saw him crash into the sea. I was shocked that she called on you, to ask you about it. And then your poor father — ' She seemed to shake herself mentally, before continuing, 'Jamie was in love. With himself. That is all I *can* say.' Then she said, 'Here she is! The one you really came to see.'

Howard turned and saw her looking at him, not in that direct fashion he had been expecting, but with an expression of shyness. She was dressed in a plain jumper and skirt, and afterwards Howard could not remember even the colour of them. It was as if everything was faded out, with only her face and eyes clear and distinct.

He took her hands in his and said, 'Celia, you look wonderful.'

She studied his face; remembering what, he wondered. That first sight of him in the sickbay, or did it spark off the horror when the emergency lighting had brutally laid bare her friend's injuries?

'How long have you got?'

He smiled. First things first. 'I was just telling your mother . . .' But when he glanced round they had the walled garden to themselves. 'We shook up our Asdic dome a bit. The ship has to be docked so the boffins can have a look at it.' He saw her eyes cloud as he added, 'I have to start back tonight, I'm afraid.'

She turned and slipped her hand through his arm as if it was the most natural thing in the world. 'All that way, just to see me. I had secretly hoped you might. Pity Daddy is at work. He was very touched when you phoned him about me.' He felt the pressure on his arm. 'So was I, afterwards. I must have made a terrible scene.'

He could feel her body trembling and knew that if he tried to comfort her it would get worse.

She said, 'Dear Jane. At the funeral they all looked at me. As if to ask, why Jane and not her?'

She was crying now; Howard felt her forcing out her words, controlling the sobs which were making her shake so violently. She said, 'I'm bad luck; you know that, don't you?'

'*No.*' He felt her turn and stare up at him but kept his eyes on the flowers, the blue sky above the old wall which must have been here when England had waited for Napoleon to invade, and long before that. 'I *don't* know.' He could feel her slipping away. He ought to have known it was hopeless. It had been her mother's way of warning him what to expect.

Then he felt her fingers reach up and touch one of his sideburns, heard her say in barely a whisper, 'It's a little bit grey, David.' She sounded suddenly angry, bitter. 'What are they *doing* to you?'

He thought of Treherne grasping his wrist to light his pipe when he had been incapable of it. How many times had he nearly split apart? And the next time – then what?

He replied, 'Never mind that.' He turned and held her at arms' length. 'Can't you see, girl? I'm in love with you.'

He waited, but she stood quite motionless in his grip, as if she had not heard him properly.

Then she asked quietly, 'Bad luck and everything? No reservations, just like that?'

Her mother appeared at the top of some stone steps that led from the rear of the house.

'I just heard the news, you two! The Germans have surrendered in North Africa!' She closed the door quietly and re-entered the house.

A tabby cat was dozing against the sun-warmed glass of a window and she paused to stroke it, to rouse a protective purr.

She murmured, 'They didn't hear a thing, Stripey. May God protect both of them.'

Captain Ernle Vickers stood, arms folded, while with several other officers he studied the new arrival at Liverpool.

'Well, gentlemen, she may not win any beauty contests, but in her and others to follow I think we will turn the battle of the Atlantic in our favour.'

Howard examined the escort-carrier moored on the opposite side of the dock. Her flight-deck was alive with activity, with figures crawling around and under the neat line of Swordfish torpedo bombers which had been flown-on at sea. The Swordfish, with its fixed undercarriage and open cockpits, looked like something from the Western Front, but it was an endurable and tough aircraft, and its relative slow speed and short take-off made it ideal for depth-charging submarines, and for reconnaissance far out in the Atlantic where no air-cover had been possible before.

Compared with the more majestic fleet carrier she was small – about half her bigger sister's size – but in the dock she seemed like a leviathan, squat and outwardly top-heavy.

Howard said, 'So we and the Americans are going to close the gap quite soon then, sir?'

Captain Vickers took out his pipe and rubbed it against the side of his broken nose, so that flesh seemed to move across his face unhindered. He looked at him searchingly, secretly surprised that Howard looked so fresh. He had been down south and back again within three days; that was something, with wartime train hold-ups. Word had reached him that Howard was badly shaken-up by almost continuous duty in the Atlantic. If it was true, he seemed to have overcome it.

'Next week, in fact.'

Vickers looked at the resting escorts, their hulls showing rust and scrapes from too many miles, too long at sea.

'The cargoes are going to get more valuable, David. More men for the next phase of the war. Troop convoys from Canada and the USA, from New Zealand and Australia. The South Africans have been in the desert all the time, so they at least should get there safely.'

'*Where*, sir?'

Vickers laughed loudly. 'Anyone's guess. But it's no secret that we'll get nowhere in stalemate. You always need the infantryman with his boots firmly planted on enemy soil before you can start thinking in terms of victory. That's where we come in, where most of you have been since the first weeks of war.'

They fell into step together. Howard was quite tall, but beside the broad-shouldered ex-rugger player he felt like a boy. *Kinsale* must have a larger bunk in her sea cabin than any he had seen.

Treherne was waiting with a tubby little man in overalls, who was wearing a bowler hat.

He saluted and said, 'Trouble, I'm afraid, sir.'

Vickers must have ears everywhere. 'The Asdic, Mr Robbins?'

The bowler hat nodded sadly. 'Big job, sir.'

Vickers regarded him coldly. 'I want *Gladiator* ready to sail with the group. You've got twenty-four hours. God, that should be enough!'

'Well, I expect the union will have a moan about it, sir.'

Vickers gave a fierce grin. 'Well, the *union* isn't putting to sea, is it?'

'I'll do what I can, Captain Vickers.' He added gloomily, 'It's asking a lot, you know.'

Vickers winked over his shoulder at Howard. 'Shouldn't have joined!'

He took Howard aside and added, 'That spot of bother over the seaman who was drowned last trip.' His eyes were very steady. 'Bad luck, David. But set against what your team achieved, and the sinking of another U-Boat — well, it's not worth stirring up the mud at some enquiry or other. The group has got a good name already; morale is higher than it ever was in the past, eh? Give the lieutenant a bottle and leave it at that. I'll keep out of it.'

Howard thought of Leading Seaman Fernie's anger and contempt for Bizley. 'I'll do what I can, sir.'

'You do that. I'll see you in *Blackwall* this evening. Gin-pendant's going up. Celebrating the kill.' He strode away, touching his oak-leaved peak with his pipe-stem as he returned a seaman's salute.

Howard shook his head. If Vickers was ever troubled he never showed it. Like the admiral, he had once said, 'I want results, not excuses. And it starts right here with me!'

He walked along the side of the dock looking down at his ship, trying not to think of what might happen next.

She had walked with him to the station at Hampton Court. They had spoken very little and had paused in the centre of the bridge as he had done to look at the swans, the fiery sunset on the palace's historic windows. A moment of peace. Probably the first each of them had known for a long, long time.

She had said quietly, 'Take care of yourself when you cross London. There's bound to be a raid tonight.' She had shivered. 'A bomber's moon.'

They had stood side by side staring at the ticket barrier, the rear end of the train with many of its doors open as passengers climbed aboard. Mostly servicemen, Howard had noticed. Khaki and air-force blue. Cheerful grins, set against tears and clasped hands. Two redcaps stood beside the ticket inspector, running their eyes over the servicemen, always suspicious; looking for a deserter, a drunk, anything to break the monotony.

But the crowd was getting smaller, and the doors were slamming shut, while the guard unrolled his green flag and eyed the station clock.

So much to say. And there was no more time. Perhaps there never was.

She had said, 'You'd better go. You've got two minutes.' She had turned suddenly and looked up at him, her eyes pleading. 'What you asked, what you said . . .' She put her arms round him and somewhere a passenger gave a shrill wolf-whistle, finding safety in anonymity.

Howard answered, 'I told you. I'm in love with you. There's been nobody else. There couldn't be now.'

She had nodded. 'I shall see you very soon. I'm all right now.' She had smiled, and he was reminded instantly of the terrible dream. '*Really*.'

Then they had kissed. It was not an excuse, a last opportunity; it was simply something which seemed to happen, a natural response. The same way she had taken his arm in the walled garden.

'Come along, sir.' The ticket inspector had smiled. 'If it was *me*, I'd stay!'

Howard had hurried away and got into a compartment. When he leaned out of the window the train was already gathering speed; he waved until they passed the level-crossing and the station was out of sight.

Here, in the midst of a noisy dockyard it was still so hard to believe that it had really happened. When she returned to Liverpool might it all come back to haunt her?

He thought too of her dead husband, her mother's words. *Jamie was in love. With himself.* It was still no answer to his question, or what that last quarrel had been about.

Treherne watched him from the brow. He had also noticed the difference. The missing lines at each corner of his mouth, no quick impatient gestures when things went wrong. The new doctor had told him nothing, but he could put most of it together for himself. A woman then. One of the Wrens.

Treherne saw someone hovering by the lobby door. It was Vallance, a tray still in his hand, which was unusual to say the least. Treherne had often thought that the PO steward would make a perfect valet, a gentleman's gentleman.

'Something wrong, PO?' He kept his voice low in order that the captain should be at peace for awhile longer.

'Yessir.' He glanced over his shoulder. 'It's not my place, sir . . .'

Then it was trouble. Mess bills unpaid; wardroom silver, what there was left of it, stolen to be made into brooches by the engine room staff.

'Spit it out.'

Vallance took a deep breath and said in a quietly outraged voice, 'The gunnery officer, Mister Finlay, just piped up that he's got engaged, sir.' He screwed up his eyes to remember it as it had happened in *his* wardroom. 'Mister Bizley was, sort of out of it, y'see. Sir.'

Treherne nodded. 'Go on.'

Vallance said, 'So Mister Bizley calls out, who would want to marry *you?*'

'My God.'

'So with that the gunnery officer snaps back, "At least I don't go round getting our own people killed!"' Vallance went on unhappily, 'They stood shoutin' at one another, and then Mister Bizley aimed a punch at him. Guns, I – I mean Mister Finlay threw a glass of Plymouth gin over him by return.'

Treherne tried to smile. 'I'm glad you noted the brand, Vallance.' But it was not a laughing matter. 'Who else was there?'

'Everyone, sir, 'cept the Gunner (T).'

Treherne felt the anger boiling up like thunder. In the merchant service it was very different. He had known boat-swains and several bully-boy mates who would use their fists rather than make a big yawn out of it. This was not the merchant service however, and *Gladiator* needed her internal unity as much as her weaponry and engines if she was to beat the Atlantic.

Finlay was a fine gunnery officer, but nobody was worth that much. As for bloody Bizley, the *hero*, he knew what he would like to do with him.

The quartermaster, his eyes popping from what he had seen and heard, whispered, 'Cap'n's comin' aboard, sir.'

'Thanks, Laird.'

He met him at the top of the brow and saluted.

Howard glanced along the deck, deserted now but for a couple of electricians and a man with a teapot.

'Trouble, eh?'

Treherne stared at him. 'I was just going to deal with it.'

Howard gestured to the dockside. The wardroom scuttles were open. 'I'd have thought they could hear the row in Birkenhead!' Surprisingly he reached out and touched his sleeve. 'Not your fault, Number One. It's been coming, and like you, I had hoped it would sort itself out.' He nodded to Vallance. 'Bring me a drink aft, will you?'

'How was London, sir?' Vallance was so relieved to see him he could not restrain himself. 'Still showin' the flag, sir?'

Howard thought of the great open spaces outside Waterloo Station where there had once been many streets of little back-to-back houses; a market too, where even in wartime you could get almost anything from a tin of fruit to a puppy. All gone. Wiped out, not even the rubble left, only the kerb stones which marked where people had once played and lived, brought up kids, just so this would happen to them.

'Several flags, I should think.' He turned and looked at Treherne. 'I'll not throw away all that we've learned and endured because of childish behaviour from those who should know better. I'll see both of them. Informally, for the moment anyway, Guns first.'

It was not a happy few minutes which he gave to Finlay.

'I have seen you on my own so that I can speak my mind.' He did not ask the lieutenant to sit down. Very deliberately he took a swallow of Vallance's Horse's Neck, in his special glass. That had been another thing to fan his anger. Vallance had been embarrassed, ashamed even, when others in his position would have hidden their grins until later.

'You have become a very good gunnery officer in this ship. You can be proud of the way you have pulled your department together. Amateurs for the most part, and you have turned them into gunners. That is all I need from you, except your loyalty, see?'

Finlay exclaimed, 'It's not that, sir – he got under my skin . . .'

'And you forgot that you are one of my senior officers. Your childish behaviour comes back to *my* door, or don't you care any more?'

'Care, sir?'

'Well, you *are* applying for a transfer, I believe?'

Finlay's accent had become suddenly more pronounced. 'It's nothing definite, sir.'

Howard did not raise his voice; he did not have to. 'And you call that loyalty, do you? It's not what most people would term it. I know it's been hard for everyone, not just you – and it will get tougher, I shouldn't wonder. So if you're not prepared to show the responsibility you received with your commission, then by God I'll see you *are* replaced, and you can forget the transfer! I would make certain that you never trod the deck of any ship where you would abuse that responsibility! Now *get out*!'

Treherne entered and looked at him admiringly. 'I could see the steam under the door, sir!'

Howard ran his fingers through his hair. '*And* I forgot to congratulate him on his engagement.'

Treherne watched him, waiting to see the strain returning.

'I have to ask before you speak to Bizley – and I know it's a liberty – but what's she like?'

Howard eyed him severely and then smiled. 'I love her.' So simply said.

'Told her, sir?'

'Yes.' He looked at the empty glass and said, 'Tell Vallance.' He let out a great sigh. 'Then send in *Mister* Bizley. It's high time he was told a few home truths.'

Lieutenant Treherne clattered up a bridge ladder and paused to stare across the spray-dappled screen. Two days out from Liverpool, with the ocean reaching away like a shark-blue desert. No land in sight, no ships either. In spite of all Vickers's threats and persuasion the work-force had not completed the repairs on time, and there had been other delays while *Gladiator* had been refloated and prepared for sea.

Thirty-six hours behind schedule they had steamed down St George's Channel and then west into the Atlantic, the Irish coastline a mere purple blur lost in distance.

Treherne had been right round the ship, checking all the departments against the new watchbills and duty rotas he and the coxswain had prepared to make allowances for promotions and replacements.

Lieutenant Finlay was OOW, standing with his booted feet apart, his cap set at a perfect angle. Treherne smiled to himself. The parade ground. Sub-Lieutenant Rooke's buttocks were protruding from the chart table, and the yeoman was giving instruction to a pair of young signalmen. Like the captain, Treherne half-expected to see the taciturn Tucker in his place.

He crossed to the gyro-repeater as Finlay said, 'Steady on two-nine-zero, Number One.' He was still very hang-dog after the interview he had had with the captain.

Treherne nodded. Bizley would be relieving the watch. It was interesting to see the way he and Finlay managed to perform their duties correctly without seeming to notice one another.

Treherne polished his binoculars with a scrap of tissue. 'Are you getting spliced soon, or waiting until after the war, Guns?'

Finlay took it as a fish will snap at bait. 'It'll be soon, Number One, I hope. The war might last forever.'

Treherne grinned. 'Or you might go for a Burton beforehand!'

Finlay grimaced. 'That's a mite cheerless!' He darted a quick glance at the other watchkeepers. 'The Old Man . . .'

'What about him?' Treherne knew exactly what was coming.

'Has he said any more about me leaving the ship?'

Treherne regarded him calmly. 'Not to me.'

'God, he gave me such a bollocking, Number One. After that party in *Blackwall* I *did* apologise. I don't know if it made any difference.'

Treherne said in a fierce whisper, 'What did you expect, you idiot, a fucking medal?'

'I don't see there's any cause to . . .'

'Oh, don't you. Well, even a thick-headed gunnery type should be able to remember what this ship was once like. Nobody could stand a watch without bleating either to the Old Man or Marrack. He carried the lot of us – you seem to have a very convenient memory! Most of the new gun crews couldn't hit a bloody cliff at forty paces! Well that's over now. The skipper's got enough work on his plate, and the pace isn't getting any slower. You had it in for Bizley when he came aboard – now, with an extra bit of gold, he's trying to even the score. I'll be frank with you, Neil – I don't like him either, never have. But if all the people I've disliked since I went to sea as an apprentice were put in Trafalgar Square, there'd be no damn room for the pigeons!'

'Point taken, Number One. I suppose we've all been a bit on edge.'

The navigating officer ducked out of the screened chart table. 'We should rendezvous with the group the day after tomorrow, sir.'

His chin was as blue as ever, Treherne thought. He should cover it with a beard.

The day after tomorrow they would find Vickers, unless new

orders had sent him off somewhere. Ready for another crack at any submarines that were making for some invisible point on this ocean, to meet and await the next convoy. The Jerries might get more than they bargained for this time. The new escort-carrier he had seen in Liverpool had already sailed even before the group, and there was said to be another one already on station. He thought of Joyce in her little flat in Birkenhead, the passion and pleasure they had shared until they could offer and receive no more. He had given her a ring as he had promised. She hadn't had an easy life, especially with her lout of a husband, but it had been the first time he had seen her really cry.

When he had tried to calm her she had sobbed, 'You care, Gordon! You *really do care*!' She had been stark naked on the bed at the time and he had gently smacked her buttocks and replied, 'Just want to make an honest woman of you!'

Now as he stared out at the dark-sided troughs of the Atlantic he was glad he had done it. Legally it meant nothing. But to her, and anyone else who tried to interfere, it meant everything in the world.

A boatswain's mate in a watch-coat turned aside from a voicepipe and looked at him. 'W/T office, sir.'

Treherne bent over the voicepipe. 'First Lieutenant?'

'Ship in distress, sir. Signal from Admiralty.'

Treherne said, 'Send it up.' To Finlay he added, 'Ship in distress? That's not exactly rare around here, surely?'

Finlay grinned. Treherne's rough attitude to discipline and most things naval had driven some of his anxieties away. For the moment.

As he spoke on the telephone Treherne could picture the captain in his 'hutch', as he called it. Thinking of his girl, probably. Good luck to them both, whoever she was. He was pretty certain he knew her now. At the noisy party aboard *Blackwall* before the rest of the group had departed, he had seen a young third officer, one of her wrists in a bandage, who had been in the building next to where the other girls had been killed and injured.

He had seen Howard's face as he had turned to listen to something she had said about another Wren's dead husband, a

RAF pilot who had gone down in a Russian convoy. It didn't need detective work to calculate the rest.

The third officer had probably had too much to drink. At one point she had elaborated to say, 'They were *madly* in love of course – '

Howard had said to him, 'I have to get back to the ship, Number One.' He had gone without another word.

It had been just after that when Finlay had tried to apologise to him for his own behaviour in the wardroom. Treherne shook his head. Poor old Guns. It must have been like playing hopscotch in a minefield.

'Captain?'

'Number One here, sir. Signal from Admiralty. A ship in distress somewhere.' He was relieved to hear a wry chuckle. The magic was still working.

'I'll come up. What's it like?'

'Nor' easterly, but not too bad.' He replaced the receiver and nodded with satisfaction. He could not remember him ever asking that before. He had always known, been down there listening, fretting. Not today, anyway. Howard appeared in a new, clean duffel coat. Probably one of Joyce's, Treherne thought.

The boatswain's mate pulled the little brass tube up the pipe from the W/T office and handed the enclosed signal to him.

Howard glanced at the blue-chinned navigator. 'Work this out on the chart, Pilot. It's only an approximate position, I expect, but in this weather it might not make it too difficult.' He took Treherne to one side. 'The ship was abandoned from the last eastbound convoy. After the other ships had left her astern a U-Boat surfaced and opened fire on the lifeboats.'

'Christ, what sort of people are they?'

Howard waited. He knew that Treherne was seeing himself out there, helpless in a lifeboat. A civilian at war. 'It seems that one of the boats played dead and waited for the sub to make off after the convoy. Then the poor fellows boarded their old ship and managed to get off this signal. There's been nothing further.'

Treherne clenched his fists. 'You should *never* leave your ship, not 'til there's no hope for her.'

Howard said quietly, 'I'm not so certain of that. This one is an ammunition ship, loaded to the gills with every sort of explosive you can think of. She may have gone down, in which case . . .' He walked to the chart and studied it for a full minute. 'Good work, Pilot, that was quick.'

Treherne saw a spark of pleasure in the navigator's eyes. A pretty rare sight, he thought. But the skipper always found time, no matter how steamed-up he might be.

'Look.' Howard probed the chart with some dividers. 'The next big convoy is expected to pass through that very area at night. No stars, remember?' He thought of that other time, her hand on his arm as she had whispered to him, 'A bomber's moon.'

Treherne rubbed his chin. 'There'll be bother enough for the convoy without having a giant bomb passing amongst them.'

'We shall get there first. Tell the Chief he can forget fuel economy for a bit. I want eighteen knots. That should do it. It will give the Gunner (T) something to do if we have to torpedo the wreck.'

Treherne strode to the other telephone, his mind clinging to those few men who had gone back to their ship despite the danger, rather than die like beasts under the U-Boat's machine guns.

'Asdic – Bridge?'

Howard lowered his mouth. 'Captain speaking. Is that Whitelaw?'

'Aye, sir.'

Howard pictured his face, younger than he looked because he had gone almost bald very early. Before 1940 he had been an ice-cream salesman at Worthing in the summers, and in the Odeon cinema for the winters. Now he was in charge of one of *Gladiator*'s most vital weapons.

'Well, have I got to guess?' If it was an echo it was both early and unexpected.

'The set's on the blink, sir.' He sounded despairing, angry. 'It's worse than it was before they fixed it in dock!'

Howard covered the voicepipe with his hand. 'Go and see, Number One. We're losing the Asdic.'

Treherne and the others stared at him. Then Finlay said flatly, 'We'll have to make a signal, give our ETA for returning to Liverpool.'

Howard thought of the old Gunner (T), the unloved Arthur

Pym, when he had once said so scathingly, *In my day we didn't 'ave no bloody Asdic nor radar neither.*

Marrack had answered with his usual cool brevity, 'Unfortunately, bows and arrows have now been banned by the Geneva Convention.'

Surprisingly, that one tiny incident among so many helped to steady him, when seconds earlier he had been stunned into disbelief.

The man in the bowler hat had said, 'The union will have a moan about it.' More than a moan apparently.

The new midshipman, Ross, had appeared on the bridge and was waiting to see if Rooke needed any new charts. He must have heard everything, and was staring out at the great, endless expanse of ocean as if he could see his own fate.

Howard watched him. In war, casualties came in all disguises. He said, 'We're not going back. It should be obvious why.'

It seemed an eternity before Treherne returned to the upper bridge; in fact it was seven minutes.

He said, 'I've had a good look, and the Chief sent a couple of tiffies to give a hand.' He shook his head. 'It's gone completely now. Not even a white walking stick.' Nobody laughed, and the midshipman was gripping a stanchion as if the ship was already heeling over.

Howard heard her voice again. *I'm all right now. Really!* Was anyone?

'Very well.' He glanced at his watch. 'Eighteen knots, remember? Pilot, course to steer, *chop-chop!*' He looked at Treherne's grim features. 'Go round the ship again. Damage control especially. Take the Buffer and the Gunner (T) – he's a good seaman, I'm told.'

Treherne nodded. Boats, bulkheads, watertight doors, the lot. He knew the drill.

Howard glanced away. 'Have W/T code up a signal and pass them our estimated position every half-hour. So if the balloon goes up, we shall at least be able to tell the boss where we are.'

Treherne lowered his voice. 'If anything happens to me . . .' He shook his head stubbornly. 'No, let me finish, sir. There's somebody in Birkenhead. I've left a package for her at the base. But if you make it and I don't, I'd take it as a real favour . . .' He did not go on.

Howard thought of the woman's voice when he had telephoned about Marrack. He was moved. Was that still possible, after all they had seen and done?

He said, 'You can do the same for me, except she'll likely know before anybody.' He shook himself. 'We'll get through.'

Treherne hesitated. 'I think you're doing the right thing anyway, if that matters, sir.'

Howard stared after his broad departing form and said, partly to himself, 'You'll never know how much.'

Then he turned to look for the midshipman. 'Now let's have a look at the chart, shall we? I think we could manage a clean one. Help Pilot as much as you can, eh?'

He saw Rooke about to protest that he could manage on his own and added, 'It's good experience.'

Rooke nodded, understanding. 'Come on, Toby lad. Lesson one, sharpen all the pencils!'

A moment later, her bow-wave rising and tearing apart like a huge moustache, HM Destroyer *Gladiator* altered course and increased speed towards Rooke's little cross on the clean, new chart.

Howard could almost hear the music: 'D'you Ken John Peel?'

He saw a small figure, covered in an oilskin with a woolly hat pulled down over his ears, dragging a large fanny of tea through the bridge gate. He thought of the silent house in Mayfair. *He was just a young boy.* So were we all. Once. When he looked again the figure had gone. Perhaps it was a ghost after all.

When Treherne returned, the watch had changed and Bizley stood on the opposite side of the bridge to Howard's chair.

Howard said, 'We will stand-to at dusk. The hands will have to be fed at action stations. Speak to the PO chef about it.'

Treherne glanced at Bizley's profile. Still smouldering. At least Finlay had got over it. A bottle was a bottle. You took it and let it ride. Grudges were unwanted passengers in any warship.

He thought of what Howard had just said. It did not need spelling out. Howard wanted everyone possible on deck, with all watertight doors shut and secured in case the worst happened. They still had the radar but he thought of that last time, when a U-Boat had been stalking *them* instead of the other way round.

On his way to the galley Treherne met the chief boatswain's

mate, Knocker White, who was supervising the laying-out of an extra scrambling-net near the midships pom-pom mounting.

'We're not goin' back in then, sir?'

'Did you think we would, Buffer?'

The little petty officer showed his uneven teeth. 'Nah, not really, sir.' He stared reflectively abeam. 'When I was an AB in the old *Revenge*, a right pusser ship *she* was, we 'ad a Jimmy-th'-One in 'er 'oo could make yer 'air curl with 'is language — but a real toff of course, in them days.'

Treherne smiled. 'Of *course*.'

'Old Jimmy-th'-One used to say, no matter 'ow bad things get, they can't put you in th' family way in this 'ere mob, so that was a bit of a comfort!' He was still chuckling as Treherne walked away.

The momentary despair had released its hold. Treherne could even smile now. With men like the Buffer, how could they fail?

3

Something Worthwhile

The U-Boat was making good barely three knots as it pushed through the powerful undulating swell of mid-ocean. Steam rose from her casing-deck and conning-tower as the sun, which was directly overhead, gave an illusion of warmth.

All lookouts were in position, and the officer-of-the watch heard the search periscope move its standard; more eyes were busy from beneath his feet.

It was safe enough out here, but you never took unnecessary risks anywhere. Occasionally the lieutenant leaned over the side of the conning-tower to see how one of the seamen was getting on with his quick-dry paint and stencil as he adorned the grey steel with another kill, an American ship which must have been loaded with heavy metal. It had broken its back and gone down after just one torpedo amidships. An American escort had carried out several attacks, but the Yanks lacked the experience of the Tommies, and they had been able to run deep and slip away undamaged. Five other crewmen were lounging on the deck, their bodies naked to the sun, a luxury for their pallid skins and shadowed eyes. The captain allowed five at a time, to smoke, to stare at the sea instead of the curved interior of their boat when they waited to attack or endure a depth-charge bombardment.

One of the men below the conning-tower was playing a sentimental tune on his harmonica while the others listened in silence, or gazed at the vastness of the Atlantic, thinking of home, of that other impossible world.

The lieutenant sighed and straightened his back as the captain climbed swiftly to the bridge. The lieutenant admired and respected his captain; they all did. They depended on his skill and cunning for their very lives. But even in the confines of the boat it seemed impossible to know him, *really* know him. It was like having someone constantly present and yet separated by a thick plate of glass. And he was quite tireless. Each attack was fought as if it was the first one, nothing left to chance, no cutting corners because of all the other encounters, the strain and the anxiety.

Kleiber knew what the other officer was thinking but it did not bother him.

He was tired but would never show it, and his skin felt clammy with sweat beneath his sea-going clothing.

At least today, if things worked properly, some of their discomfort would be eased. One of the big supply submarines was due to rendezvous, part of the chain of *milchküh* boats as they were called, which met the U-Boats at special points, like one giant grid; if you missed one, there was another chance later on. The plan had trebled the sea-time of almost every ocean-going submarine. No longer did they have to abandon a patrol in order to return to base or lose time when making for their allotted area. It meant more strain on every crew, but it kept the boats at sea to attack and destroy as Donitz had planned.

This *milchküh* was new, and their boat was the first on its list. They might get a better choice from this huge travelling victualler's yard and machine shop rolled into one. Fuel, fresh water, food supplies, letters from home, newspapers; even the luxury of proper soap instead of the stuff which felt like slate after a few frugal washes.

Ammunition too, and perhaps they might replace the torpedo which had disgraced itself after one of their attacks on a small convoy. It had started to lose compressed air so that bubbles had surged from a bow-cap, a real gift to any keen-eyed observer in a reconnaissance bomber.

Kleiber would have to fill in a report when he eventually returned to their French lair. But nobody would dare to reprimand him now. There had been too many inexplicable losses amongst the U-Boat fleet of late. Good experienced commanders for the most part, not ones just out of tactical school.

There was also a leak in the forward periscope gland, which

they might or might not be able to fix. But they could manage if it got no worse.

He ticked off the points in his mind like a written list.

Engines and motors, good. Results poor, but they had been homed on to a convoy which had been heavily defended for its small size, and they had managed to obtain just one hit.

He glanced at his watch. *Soon now*. He nodded to the lieutenant who spoke rapidly into the voicepipe. There was no risk of hostile aircraft out here, and the weather was fair for the Atlantic. They would have to open the big forehatch to take on stores, something which no commander wanted to do.

Kleiber had done it often enough to know the risks. He would wait until the actual rendezvous. The lieutenant had merely warned the deck party to be ready.

He tried not to let his mind dwell on the news from North Africa. It had to be faced. It was a reverse, but it would benefit the land-based forces in Europe and on the Russian front. Perhaps there would be a letter from his parents about Willi. The thaw would have come to Russia; the icy holes where the Army had fought and held the line would become slush and mud again. Poor Willi; his ideals had cost him dear. Kleiber glanced over the screen at the men on deck. Willi would be better off here, with him. He studied each man carefully. They looked undernourished, starved of fresh air and clean clothing. Worn, bearded faces, and yet there were few older than the mid-twenties down in the boat itself.

What would the Tommies and their allies do next? Attack through Greece, even after their disastrous lesson at Crete? France perhaps? He dismissed it instantly. He had seen some of the impregnable defences of the Führer's Western Wall for himself. Italy then?

His thoughts returned to Willi. Suppose the high command were already negotiating peace with the allies, to join together and smash into Russia, finish Ivan once and for all.

The lieutenant saw his mouth lift in a small smile and imagined Kleiber was thinking of home; a girl maybe.

Kleiber was picturing the high command on one side and Winston Churchill on the other. He could see no unity there.

A man shouted and he heard the offending periscope squeak in its standard. In the far distance there was a huge disturbance as slowly at first, and then more violently, the big supply-boat heaved itself to the surface, small figures spilling over the conning-tower like a team of athletes. One of Kleiber's men flashed off the recognition signal in response to the usual challenge. The supply-boat was already turning to make a lee for them to move closer alongside.

The supply-boat had surfaced too soon, and too far, he thought, and would waste valuable time with this manoeuvre. Which was why they had not detected its approach. A new milchküh; so maybe an inexperienced commander?

The man with the pot of paint grasped a safety rail and leaned back to study his work. There were over sixty such trophies painted there. Each one a blow for the Fatherland. He grinned at the solemnity of his thought and turned to shade his eyes to look at the other submarine. They might even have some special sausage, like that he had known as a boy in Minden.

He could not see the supply-boat because of the conning-tower. But he saw the captain's white cap, heard him speaking to the control room; one of the lookouts was waving, looking the wrong way.

The man turned and stared out to sea. The reflection was so hard it seemed to drain the sky of colour, but it deepened the grey-blue of the ocean. He blinked. It was impossible. He had been staring too long. Like pieces of glass against the horizon, a ship's bridge caught the sunlight. No; there was more than one, moving across the water faster than any ship. He heard himself cry out, the sudden scuffle on the bridge, and then the scream of a klaxon.

The seaman made to climb up the ladder but he had forgotten the lifeline, always insisted upon when working near the saddle-tanks. From the other side he heard men gasping as they ran frantically for the ladder, and then for the first time, the far-off drone of aircraft engines. *It was impossible*. He struggled, but the line had caught fast. There was a brief shadow and he looked up to see the captain watching him. A glance, nothing more, but the man knew what was happening. He heard the thud of the hatch, the sudden roar of vents as the sea thundered into the tanks to force the U-Boat down into a crash-dive. The man was still screaming as the first depth-charges exploded around the surfaced supply-boat, which with the forward hatch wide open was already doomed.

Then his scream was gone, and the little painted trophies were the last things he ever saw.

Kleiber waited for twenty minutes and then went up to periscope depth. He had heard the depth-charges, dropped from the low-flying biplanes which could only have come from a carrier. He swung the periscope in a complete circle and heard one last muffled explosion, which must have been caused when the supply-boat hit the bottom.

There was nothing, not even one of the strange-looking aircraft which he knew to be Swordfish. He could not even see any oil. It was as if nothing had happened.

He loosened his grasp on the handles; they felt wet, but it had nothing to do with a leaking gland this time.

Something scraped against the hull and he saw a petty officer staring at the curving steel as if he expected to see an intruder. The drowned seaman was still dragging there, his boots scraping against the saddle-tank in the undertow.

He felt he should explain. What was one life when set against so many? At night they would surface and cut the body free.

He leaned on the gently shaking chart table and stared at the wavering calculations.

He did not need to explain anything. He commanded, they did not.

He looked at the palm of his hand where there was sweat, when before there had been none.

The price of vigilance. *Survival*.

'Radar — Bridge. Ship now bears three-three-zero, range ten thousand yards.'

Howard stooped down and peered at the radar-repeater. Like something underwater, he thought, shimmering shapes before the revolving beam passed over the solitary blip.

He asked, 'Anything else, Whitelaw?'

'No, sir.' Whitelaw was probably surprised that he should ask. He would have told him had there been something.

'Revolutions for twelve knots, Number One.' He heard Treherne stir himself, the muffled response from the wheelhouse. 'Steer three-one-five.' It would be dawn soon; there was no point in displaying the ship's complete silhouette against a brightening horizon.

'Steady on three-one-five, sir.' Treherne sounded tense. With no Asdic, a submarine could be right underneath the keel and they would not know. It had been a long two days searching for this ship, and the next large convoy would be passing through this point to pick up additional escorts for the run home. It did not allow for any errors. A large convoy at night was bad anyway, especially as they had heard it had already been attacked and had lost three ships.

Bizley was OOW to help ease the work on the others, and because he was unable to control either his squid or ordinary depth-charges without the Asdic's eye to guide him.

He said to the bridge at large, 'I thought the long-range recce bombers could reach this far out.' Nobody spoke and he added irritably, 'Just one bomb would have put paid to that hulk, surely?'

Howard spoke over his shoulder. 'There are men on that *hulk* – there were, anyway.'

Treherne exclaimed, 'They've suffered enough, I'd have thought?'

Bizley stooped over the gyro. It was to conceal his smile rather than to check the ship's head. It was always easy to bait the first lieutenant into an argument. What the hell did they really care? They had left enough men to die in the sea before; a handful more made little difference.

He saw Treherne and the captain with their heads together, while the navigating officer was hidden inside the canvas hood, busy with his chart with the new midshipman hovering nearby. Signalmen, lookouts, and just below the bridge the Oerlikon gunners moving their slender barrels from side to side, mistrusting every feather of spray, each sudden surge of water.

He thought of the girl he had telephoned before they had left Liverpool. Milvain's sister Sarah had sounded subdued to begin with, but had seemed to brighten up after a few moments, when she had realised who it was. She had told him about Howard's brief visit and had hinted at her mother's coolness towards him. It had been far better than Bizley had dared to hope. He could picture her as he had seen her in the photograph Milvain carried in his wallet. A good family too. It was strange that his CO,

Milvain's brother, had not boasted about it. Father a general, their home a fine house in Mayfair. The things which rated very high in Bizley's suburban background. He had suggested they might meet when he was next on leave. To his surprise, she had sounded genuinely delighted. One hint of caution, however, when she had said that she would have to ask her mother.

Bizley had played his trump card. 'It's my decoration, you see. I feel it was really *because* of your brother – not what I did. I just wanted you to see it, share it.'

He glanced at the others around him. *I'll bloody well show you.*

Leading Seaman Fernie's anger was still a problem, but not as much as he had first thought. He had discovered that Fernie was sweating on getting made-up to petty officer. With promotion almost within his grasp he would be careful not to confront an officer with all the possible consequences of a court of enquiry. Bizley was still shaken by the captain's contemptuous reprimand – he had never had such a strip torn off him. It was so unfair; Milvain's drowning had been an accident, just as he had described in his report. He might have misunderstood when he had been ordered to assist the exhausted German on board. It was certainly not *his* fault. It was probably the youth's eagerness to please his lieutenant that had been the main cause of his accidental death. He smiled to himself. A kind of hero-worship. Milvain's sister would like to hear about that too, he thought.

'Range now five thousand yards. Vessel has turned end-on.'

Treherne muttered, 'Still adrift then.'

Howard thought of the ship beneath him. His men wondering what might happen. Each one of them would be fully aware that all the rafts and Carley floats had been loosened, ready to let go, and the davits turned out so that the whaler and motor boat were free to be lowered with minimum delay. And all the depth-charges were set to safe, so even if a U-Boat was careless enough to surface right beside them it would take too long to release the charges.

Finlay's gun crews were all standing by, ready-use ammunition set to be slammed into every breech, while full magazines were prepared for reloading the pom-poms and Oerlikons.

'Here we go!' That was the yeoman of signals. The horizon

was making its first appearance, caught by a thin rippling line like beaten pewter, below which the sea was as black as ink.

'Is the torpedo gunner's mate all clewed up, Number One?'

'Aye, sir. The Gunner (T) has told him what's expected of him.'

Gladiator's twin quadruple mountings for the twenty-one inch torpedoes had never been used in the war except to put down damaged warships which were beyond recovery, and battered stragglers from convoys. Originally, the peacetime minds which had planned and designed a navy of the future had imagined only a faster war than the previous one. The same line of battle, with the destroyers, the fleet's greyhounds, waiting to dash against the enemy formations under smokescreens if need be and deliver a lethal blow with their torpedoes. The mentality of Jutland, Dogger Bank and the Falklands. Most senior officers had been selected originally from the gunnery branch; submariners and people who believed that the future fleet should be built around aircraft-carriers had often been seen as cranks.

The horrific losses at sea, both in merchant ship tonnage, and the proud names like *Hood* and *Repulse*, *Royal Oak*, *Barham* and the rest had revealed the folly for what it was.

Howard was thinking about it, not for the first time, as he heard one of the torpedo tube mountings squeaking slightly as it was trained abeam.

In today's frantic shipbuilding programme, to equal if not beat the continued list of sinkings, torpedo tubes were considered more as useless top-hamper than truly dangerous weapons. For the anti-submarine war now being waged the deck space was better served by having more types of depth-charge mortars and dual-purpose light guns. Like his brother's newly formed escort group. All new frigates, some as large as *Gladiator*, and not a torpedo amongst them.

But even as he thought it, Howard knew that he had started as a destroyer man, and as an old hand he would so remain if he was given the chance.

'Smoke, sir!'

As the sky continued to brighten, to spill over the horizon and give the ocean its first hint of blue, they saw the great, low-lying pall drifting slowly in the light north-easterly wind.

Treherne said, 'Didn't realise she was burning, sir.'

Howard did not answer. It made the danger impossible to measure; the very real risk of a U-Boat stalking them was almost secondary.

There was probably enough explosive of one kind or another on board that ship to knock down a city the size of Liverpool.

'Doctor requests permission to come to the bridge, sir.'

That was Ayres, tense and brittle as the thing spread itself across the sky like one gigantic stain.

Howard said, 'Yes. All right.' He had barely heard the question. Surely if the fire was really dangerous the ship would have blown up days ago. He heard the doctor arrive in the bridge, but forgot him as he levelled his powerful glasses on the given bearing and saw the ammunition ship for the first time. A great wedge of a vessel, bows deep in the water, smoke coming from several places at once. No flames. Howard found he was biting his lower lip. But between decks it would only take a spark. Even at this range they would feel it.

He strode across the bridge to the opposite side, vague figures moving hastily out of his way.

He leaned over the side and saw the four torpedo tubes, the TGM's crew clustered behind them in their duffel coats, the distance making them look like attentive monks.

Finlay was covering the scene with his own team and said over the gunnery speaker, 'On this course, sir, you will be in position in seven minutes.'

'Thank you.' It was just an equation to Finlay, an exercise in which he would be an onlooker for once.

Howard glanced over at Treherne, his face regaining shape and personality out of the retreating shadows.

'Sir!' The yeoman was peering through his glasses. 'Signal!'

Howard let his glasses fall to his chest. He did not need to watch for more than a few seconds. It was S-O-S, slowly but distinctly spelled out by a powerful torch.

His mouth had gone quite dry. So there were survivors still on board.

Treherne said quietly, 'They've seen us.'

The doctor said, 'Maybe they've still got a boat, sir?'

He watched the captain, the way he was staring at the smoke as if he could neither think or move. It brought back the stark picture of the girl in the sickbay, her shirt and hands soaked in blood, her shock and disbelief as Howard had taken her in his arms.

Howard stepped from the gratings and said, 'Call them up, Yeo. *Slowly*, so they can read you.' He rubbed his eyes, seeing the other vessel as she would appear in the torpedo sights. It would be so easy. Who would blame him? He continued, 'Ask them to abandon ship if they can. We will pick them up.'

The light clattered, the sound incredibly loud in the bridge's tense interior. Glasses were levelled on the eventual response, the blinking light their only, frail contact.

The yeoman was moving his lips as he read the careful signal. '*Unable – to – abandon.*'

Bizley swore. 'What the hell's the matter with them?'

A lookout murmured under his breath, 'Can't imagine!'

The yeoman lowered his glasses. 'They have seven wounded, two badly.'

Howard looked at their faces. Understanding, pity, anxiety. It was all there.

'Bring her round, Pilot, course to close with the ship. Tell W/T to prepare the signal. *Am in contact with ammunition ship. Will attempt to remove survivors from same.*'

Rooke called, 'Steady on three-five-five.'

Howard made himself climb into the tall chair. 'Increase to twenty knots.'

Treherne stood beside him, saying nothing, and he knew that some of the others must be stunned by his decision; hating him for it.

He said, 'What else can I do?' He turned and looked at Treherne. 'In God's name, what do they expect?'

'I've a suggestion, sir.' He watched him steadily, knowing that the wrong word could wreck everything. 'I'll take the whaler, and a crew of volunteers.'

'Just forget it, Number One. I know you mean well, but . . .' He swung round as more smoke belched over the other ship's shattered bridge.

Treherne shook his head. 'If you lay this ship alongside her in that state, we'll all be done for. I've seen plenty of fires at sea, and so have you. She'll be like a bloody furnace. Neither them nor us would stand a chance.'

217

Howard lowered his head. He could smell the fire now, like something alive.

Treherne said, 'Anyway, I'm more used to merchant ships than anyone else.'

Howard lifted his head and studied him intently. 'You really mean it, don't you? You're not just trying to save my neck.'

Treherne replied, 'If you work up to wind'rd, I'll get the boat ready.'

Moffatt the doctor had moved closer. 'I'd like to go with you, Number One.'

Treherne forced a grin. 'There – piece of cake!' He became serious again. 'At least we'll have had a damn good try, sir.'

Howard felt in his pocket but forgot his pipe as he said, 'She might go up at any minute, or she might burn for days, something we must not allow. There's also the real possibility that even now, while we discuss the value of human life, a U-Boat may be homing on to this smoke. Either way, if you're still aboard . . .' He reached over and gripped his arm. 'Well, I won't order you to go.'

Treherne nodded. 'I know. But it just happens to be part of the job I know something about.' He made an attempt at nonchalance. 'Remember what I said about the package.' Then, 'Come on, Doc, let's go and ask for some jolly jacks!'

At the bridge gate he stopped and looked back at Howard on his chair. He did not speak, but his eyes said all that was needed. Then he was gone.

Howard said, 'Slow ahead, together. Starboard fifteen.' He watched the great pall of smoke leaning over as if to engulf them in its stench of burned paint and seared metal.

He must show no doubt or apprehension. There were too many depending on him now.

'Midships.'

He watched the ticking gyro-repeater but saw only Treherne's face.

'Steady.'

'Steady, sir. Course zero-eight-zero, both engines slow ahead.'

'Hold her like that, Swain.' He made himself watch the drifting ship. Upwind of her, the damage was more clearly visible, the list more pronounced. The stern was in the best condition; he could even see her name, *Ohio Star*, but her port of registry had been seared off by the heat as Treherne had described.

He looked across at Ayres. 'Go down and take charge of the lowering party, Sub. Can you manage it?'

Ayres looked at him desperately, his face all eyes. 'Aye, aye, sir.'

'I'll call down when to drop the whaler.'

The yeoman said, 'Boat's already manned, sir.' He looked at one of his signalmen. 'You know what they say about a volunteer in this regiment, my son – he's a bloke who's misunderstood the question!'

Howard looked away. It was all the same pretence. He seemed to hear her voice, her anger when she had exclaimed, 'What are they *doing* to you?'

Then he was off his chair and standing aft by the bridge searchlight and its painted canvas screen.

The whaler was lowered and he could see its shadow moving beneath the keel while the crew waited to man their oars.

'*Slip!*'

The boat veered away and Howard saw the doctor clinging on to his cap. He turned toward Bizley and said, 'Take her round again, but stay upwind. Same revolutions. No sense in charging about the ocean.'

The yeoman said, 'Whaler's lost in the smoke, sir.'

Howard jammed his unlit pipe between his teeth. 'Tell W/T to make the signal now.' *If that lot goes up we'll not get a chance to tell anyone.* But he kept the thought to himself.

Surgeon-Lieutenant Moffatt peered apprehensively at the huge overhang of the *Ohio Star*'s poop. *Gladiator* was not a large warship but the whaler's twenty-seven feet made him feel like a survivor himself.

Leading Seaman Fernie was the coxswain, the tiller-bar grasped in one gloved fist, and beside him, Treherne, already soaked from head to toe, gave the impression of unyielding determination. The volunteers for the boarding party were some of the *Gladiator*'s hard men. Like Bully Bishop the ex-chief quartermaster, and 'Wally' Patch, a pug-faced able seaman who was usually more in trouble than out of it. His friend, Tim Hardy, another AB, was no stranger to the naval glasshouse – a good hand at sea, but ashore he was known to drink and fight in equal proportion.

Moffatt enjoyed his middle-of-the-road status in the destroyer. Dressed like an officer except for the scarlet cloth between his stripes, he could nevertheless feel almost equally at home with the lower deck. In fact he knew some of them better than they realised, as Moffatt had been given the task of censoring their letters in the hunt for careless talk. He had discovered no secrets, but some of the more passionate letters had made even him blush.

But this was very different. The open boat rising and falling between the waves, the five oarsmen concentrating on the stroke and on Fernie's quick warnings and instructions. Moffatt had no idea how they were going to board the badly damaged ship. One false move and they would collide with her, or be capsized by some of the trailing wreckage alongside.

He heard Treherne exclaim, '*There*, Cox'n!' He sounded relieved as he gestured towards a dangling ladder. Moffatt wondered if Treherne had been as confident as his bearded countenance suggested.

There were two extra hands in the bows; Fernie was probably thinking of that other time when one of them had been the boy, Milvain.

'Hold water, port!' Fernie judged it with a skill Moffatt could only guess at. 'Ready, forrard!'

Treherne said, 'This must have been where they re-boarded the ship, Doc!' He had to shout, for the sea under the vessel's stern was like the tide in a cave. 'God knows what happened to their lifeboat. Either broke adrift, or was too badly holed by machine-gun fire!'

A voice called, 'This way, lads!'

Bully Bishop heaved back on his loom and snarled, 'Wot, no tea an' biscuits?'

Fernie snapped, 'Stow it!'

Treherne saw a man staring down from the rail. He was so filthy he could have been anyone.

'Three men will stay in the boat – keep her fended off, but make certain the bow-rope holds fast. I don't want the bloody thing stove in!'

One at a time, waiting for the whaler to lift against the ladder for a second or two, they scrabbled their way up towards the watching face, rung by painful rung.

Treherne was last. 'Up you go, Doc.' He gripped him as Moffatt's cap finally blew from his head and floated away along the side. 'I'll buy you another one if we pull this off!'

The man in the filthy dungarees stared at them, his eyes almost starting from his head. 'You came for us.'

Fernie said thickly, 'Looks that way, mate.'

The man said, 'If that murdering bastard comes back we'd be done for.' He rubbed his smoke-reddened eyes as *Gladiator*'s pale shape glided through the smoke and then vanished again. 'But your skipper'll be listening for those buggers, eh?'

Treherne glanced at the doctor. There was no point in telling him about the Asdic. There could be fifty U-Boats out there for all they knew.

'Lead the way. We'll have to get a move on.' They followed him to a great empty store which must have been the boat-swain's place for stacking all the spare timber and cordage. That had been used for shoring up those bulkheads closest to the explosions. The second torpedo had flooded the first hold, and the weight of water had helped to steady the hull as well as covering the crates of explosives before the fires could reach them.

Treherne found the survivors huddled with their wounded, the only light below coming from holes in the deck overhead.

He made a quick count, fifteen in all, one of whom he realised was the ship's master. He lay propped against some rope fenders, breathing heavily while a youth held his hand and watched over him.

Moffatt said, 'Move along, Sonny. Let me have a look.'

The slight figure turned and stared at him. It was a Chinese girl, her fine features starkly beautiful in this terrible place.

The master said hoarsely, 'My wife, Anna.' He stared at the doctor's hands as he opened his bag and cut away the dirty bandage. 'A bullet, or piece of one.' He groaned as Moffatt probed around his bruised flesh. 'Just cruised past us and strafed the boats as he went, the bastard. He killed both the mates. Christ knows what happened to the rest. I thought he was going to stop and give us our position, a course for land or the shipping lanes. But he just stood there watching while his guns raked the lifeboats.' He had a Welsh lilt to his voice, very like the chief's.

Treherne asked quietly, 'Has that happened before?'

The ship's master peered at the faded lace on Treherne's sleeve. 'One of our mob, eh?' He frowned, trying to remember the question. 'I've been tin-fished twice before. The first submarine commander handed down smokes and some brandy before he shoved off.' He gasped with pain and added between his teeth, 'But that was in the early days. You know . . .'

'Yes, I know.'

Fernie called, 'This one's done for, sir.'

The master turned his head to listen. He said, 'Bulkhead's holding. We did get a pump going for a bit until it packed up. Now there's no power on anything. Just a matter of time.' He flopped back as Moffatt removed the needle from his arm.

'You can start moving him, Number One.' Moffatt, usually so gentle and curious about everything, was suddenly in charge. 'I'm afraid about this other chap.' He watched as Bully Bishop used his razor sharp pusser's dirk to slit open the man's bloodied trousers. He looked grimly at Treherne. 'It's got to come off. May be too late anyway.' He glanced around at the smoke-stains and the crouching, frightened figures. 'It's not exactly Harley Street, is it?'

The young Chinese woman was still beside him. 'It's all right, my dear, your husband will be well again when we can get him to the ship.'

She shook her head, her black hair shining in the smoky air. 'I stay with you. I help. I nurse in Hong Kong.'

Treherne looked at her. There was a story in her, he thought. Perhaps the captain, who must be well over twice her age, had got her away before the Japs had marched in.

Fernie held the badly injured man and caught his breath as the doctor pulled on his gloves and opened what the SBA called Moffatt's tool kit. He tried to imagine what Bizley would have done if he had been in charge. He realised the man was staring at him, his eyes flickering as the drug moved through him.

'Not me *leg*! For God's sake, *not that*!'

The girl dabbed his forehead, her eyes impassive as Moffatt made his first incision.

Treherne watched the big bearded leading hand. Like a gentle bear unless he was roused. Which was why Treherne knew Bizley had lied; just as he understood why the matter had been dropped.

He said, 'The first time I see you with crossed hooks on your sleeve, Fernie, I'll set up the pints until you're awash!'

Fernie saw the girl wrap the amputated leg in some canvas and carry it away. He murmured, 'A girl like that'd never let you down.'

He spoke so vehemently that Treherne guessed there had been someone special in Fernie's life too. *Had been.*

He thought of Joyce and knew he must see her again, even though he had been quite certain he was going to be killed.

Now he stared around, seeing the deck's steep angle, hearing the slosh of the sea between decks. A ship which refused to die, waiting perhaps to take others with her.

Wally Patch called, 'Just the wounded now, sir!'

Treherne touched Fernie's shoulder. 'Can you manage?'

The big man got to his feet, his eyes troubled. 'Yeah, I can manage, sir.' He spread his gloved hands. 'I'll be as quick as I can.'

'Don't worry. The Old Man will come closer when he sees the whaler.'

Fernie walked carefully up the tilting deck. 'Be seeing you.' He grinned. 'Sir.'

It was suddenly very quiet in the dismal place. Just the painful, regular coughing of one of the men who had swallowed too much fuel when he had dived to escape the machine-guns.

Moffatt looked at the girl, 'Go now. And thanks.'

She smiled briefly and went with Fernie.

Moffatt exclaimed, 'No use, can't stop the bleeding. His pulse is going.' Then he lowered his face and said brokenly, 'What a bloody awful way to die!'

One of the other injured men croaked, 'Never you mind, Doc, you done yer best. 'Is number was on it this time, that's all!' He fell back, exhausted.

Moffatt blew his nose. 'How do they stand it? Again and again?'

'I've often wondered.'

It seemed an age before the whaler returned and Fernie explained that the dangling ladder was almost out of reach.

That meant that the ship had gone over still further, and might even capsize.

'It's going to be a rough ride.' Treherne watched Fernie and Patch tying bowlines around the helpless survivors. 'It's better than dying . . .' He broke off, startled, as a loud cracking sound seemed to come straight through the soles of his sea-boots.

Moffatt gasped, 'What was *that*?'

'Bulkhead.' He pushed him with the wounded towards the opening. 'Fast as you like, lads! The old girl's trying to take us with her!'

A man screamed in agony as he sprawled across the whaler's gunwale before being dragged to safety. More smoke exploded into the air, pressurised like steam from within so that Treherne was vaguely reminded of the geysers he had seen in Iceland.

He twisted his head and saw the destroyer swinging round, the sunlight flashing across the bridge screen where Howard would be watching, conning his ship to complete the impossible.

Treherne took a last glance behind him, the two corpses, the bloody parcel beside them. *So this is what it feels like.*

The deck gave a violent lurch and he heard the sudden roar of water, loud cracks as steel plates parted like plywood to the tremendous pressure.

When he climbed down the ladder he had to drop the last few feet into the sea. He clung to the whaler's gunwale as the oarsmen backed water away from the sinking ship. Treherne could see the hull rising over him and wondered if he had left it too late after all; overhead there was a glint of bronze from a motionless screw, which would never come alive again to the clang of the bridge telegraph.

Fernie waited for a seaman to put a bowline around the first lieutenant's shoulders and bellowed, 'Give way, starboard! Back water, port!' He glanced at the towering mass of burned metal as it started to dip deeper by the bows. There the inner fires had been so hot that the hull was black and shimmering from some isolated blaze.

Miracles did happen sometimes. Oil tankers which did not catch fire when torpedoed or bombed; or old veterans like the *Ohio Star* which had spared a few of her people, perhaps to tell the tale of her lonely fight with the Atlantic. An American name, a Welsh master and his lovely Chinese wife.

Treherne felt the bowman dragging at his arm but did not want to miss the moment, to leave without sharing it. 'There she goes!'

One of the less badly wounded clambered to the side and stared as the old ship suddenly lifted her stern and dived.

Treherne turned his head and saw that the unknown seaman was weeping, as if he had lost a friend. Perhaps he had.

The whaler rocked and plunged in the whirlpool that surged around the place where the ship had gone down – Treherne felt it pulling at his legs like something evil, trying to suck him away to follow the ship down and down, so many hundreds of fathoms where there was lasting peace.

He remembered very little after that except for the push and scramble of getting aboard *Gladiator*, with scrambling nets, by brute force, anything.

Faces, wild-eyed, stared at him, while others manned the falls and ran the whaler up to the davit-heads, the boat's usually neat interior slopping with water and bloody dressings.

The bells rang from the bridge, and *Gladiator*'s screws began to thrash the water into a mounting froth as she gathered speed. Men peered at one another, grinned or puffed out their cheeks with relief. The old girl was moving again. Hands reached out to touch Treherne's sodden jacket as he climbed heavily to the bridge.

He saw Howard standing away from the voicepipes as he finished putting his ship on course. He also saw Vallance with a mug in his hand. He had almost never seen the PO steward on the bridge before – Vallance was full of surprises these days.

Howard said quietly, 'It's rum, Number One. I know you don't usually go in for it, but it's the best I can manage at short notice.' He waited while Treherne took a great swallow. 'I'm damned glad to have you back!'

Treherne took another great swallow. 'The Doc did very well.'

'So did you.' He tried to make light of it. 'We even saved their lordships the price of a torpedo.'

Treherne said, 'In all this bloody war, I think that was one of the most worthwhile things we've done together.'

Then he fell silent again, thinking of the master who had now been sunk three times, and who would go back when there was a ship for him. And the girl who would be with him. That was the real difference.

He said, 'I'll go and freshen up, sir.'

Howard handed him his own duffel coat. 'Put this on. Please.' He had seen the sudden exhaustion, emotional and physical; it had been like that for him when Treherne had helped him when he had needed it most. 'It'll be okay.'

But Treherne hadn't moved. He was staring at the sea, and seemed to be grappling for something. Eventually he said, 'All these years, and this is the first time I've known what it's like to have a ship go down under you.' He looked at him, his eyes bleak. 'It's like death.'

4

Distinguished Service

The headquarters of Western Approaches was situated in a massive bomb- and gas-proof citadel beneath the rambling building called Derby House in the city of Liverpool. Concrete and armour plate had changed it from a big basement complex to the Navy's own command-post for the Atlantic battle, and had been its nerve-centre since completion in 1941.

No longer were the various sections scattered along the coast or in other ports; each part contained everything and was readily accessible to the boss, in this case Admiral Max Horton. Minesweeping, convoy plots, enemy activities and RAF Coastal Command; all could be contacted without delay by lifting a telephone, the secret information immediately sifted through a scrambler line. If not, the C-in-C would want to know why, and who was responsible. Its core was of course the operations room, one complete wall of which was covered by a giant chart of the battleground, in some places three times as high as the Wrens and operations team who controlled it. They climbed on sliding ladders to move the many coloured markers representing convoys, escort groups, known information about U-Boat packs and the tell-tale recordings of ship losses. There was another large map on an adjoining wall for the Irish Sea and local coastal convoys. It was fully staffed around the clock, so that what happened in the city above and around it ceased to have any meaning or reality. Only the great ocean and the ceaseless battle for supremacy between enemy and ally made any sense.

A youthful lieutenant regarded Captain Ernle Vickers with due deference. 'Captain Naish can see you now, sir.'

He held open a door labelled *Assistant to Chief of Staff*, and stood slightly to one side as if to hint that the interview would be a short one. But the tall captain who got up from his desk to shake Vickers's hand gave a broad grin. He and Vickers had been midshipmen together and were of about the same seniority.

'Good to see you, Ernle!' He glanced at the hovering lieutenant and added, 'No calls.' The lieutenant fled.

Naish seated his friend and produced a decanter and some glasses from a filing cabinet marked *Pending*, and poured two generous measures. He chuckled, 'I know you're not putting to sea, so you can enjoy some decent Scotch for a change. You can't see the boss – he's playing golf, can you believe? Like Drake and his bowls. This evening the Prime Minister is coming up specially to see him.'

Vickers tasted the Scotch, but refrained from asking his friend where he had obtained it. Naish would tell him in his own good time, if he wanted to. He watched Naish's hand moving a signal clip to examine some files underneath.

'I've just finished reading the report about *Gladiator*'s effort with the *Ohio Star*. Bloody good show, I think.'

'Howard's my best skipper.' Vickers waited. They were both too busy to waste time on a casual interview.

'Yes. He has a fine record. I see that his brother has just completed working-up his own escort group.' He got to the point. 'I've put forward the suggestion that Howard be recommended for the Distinguished Service Order, with a gong of some sort for his Number One. God, I think the whole ship's company should be decorated for the risk they took.'

Vickers had been there when the survivors had been landed; the Chinese girl had been wearing a petty officer's reefer jacket, and had brought cheers from the onlookers and ambulance men.

'That would be just fine. Howard deserves it.'

Naish gave a dry smile. 'I understand that you want him to be made up to acting-commander, so you'll have a proper brasshat as your right-hand man. A bit young, but it would look good when he gets a new ship.'

Vickers grinned broadly. 'The day you prize Howard away from his precious *Gladiator* will be *the day*!'

He watched the man's hands tug at the other file, as if he was reluctant to spoil his news.

'Something rather awkward had turned up.' He opened the papers and Vickers saw the familiar stamp of Admiralty, and the words *Top Secret* in red.

Naish continued, 'An able seaman serving in Light Coastal Forces was killed in the North Sea a little time ago. His name was Hinton, not that it matters. After he was buried, an envelope was sent to C-in-C, the Nore – he was a Chatham rating, you see. Almost like a dying confession – he'd written it himself about a year ago.'

Vickers watched his friend's discomfort, a kind of distaste as he added, 'This chap made certain it would be handed to the proper authority in the event of his death.'

'That's a rum sort of thing to do, Geoffrey.'

Naish looked at him steadily. 'There's an officer in Howard's ship who was awarded the DSC for courage under fire when his MGB was sunk by enemy vessels. Not that far from where this poor chap was killed, curiously enough.'

'Lieutenant Bizley.' He could pick out the face quite easily. A competent enough officer, Howard had said. But a bit too clever for his own good.

'Yes, that's the name . . . It's probably all a waste of time – something that might bring a lot of unhappiness to others, a slur on the name of honour. This rating alleged that Bizley made no attempt to save the wounded, and the captain was still on the bridge, badly shot up when Bizley gave the order to bale-out. There were some others still trapped below, if that wasn't bad enough.' He leaned over with the decanter. 'I think we can do with another tot.'

'But if nobody knows for certain . . .'

Naish glanced at him angrily. 'Too many people know already. The admiral at Chatham, the Admiralty, and now the Special Branch chaps at Bath.'

'So the rubber-heel squad are already involved?'

'I'm afraid so. There was another survivor who got a Mention-in-Despatches. He is being traced. If he backs up this written testimony the whole rotten business will be out in the open.'

'Unlikely, I'd have thought. The other seaman would be in the muck up to his neck!'

'I read Howard's report on the drowning, that rating who was the brother of Bizley's late commanding officer. God knows what the family will have to say about that. Maybe it was only a coincidence. We'll just have to wait and see.'

'*I* knew about that, of course.' Vickers frowned. 'My ships and their morale are more important right now than anything.'

'I agree. But if Bizley lied to play the hero there is no way I can put the lid on it. The boss would have my guts for garters!'

'Shall I have a word with Howard?'

'No. This is between us for the moment. You might mention the possibility of a DSO. I think he's more than earned it.'

They both relaxed and sipped their drinks. The worst had been faced up to. The machine would take over from now on.

'Can we expect anything new in the near future?' It felt cleaner to get back to the war.

Naish pressed his fingertips together. 'A lot of troop convoys. The really precious cargoes. It will be all or nothing this year, I think, both here in the Atlantic and in the Med. The allies will have to make a stab at an invasion down there – to do that they need troops from everywhere. The Germans will know that too unfortunately – so it's business as usual, only more so!'

Just yards away in one corner of the large operations room, Second Officer Celia Lanyon was being shown over the layout by another Wren officer. Her name was Evelyn Major, a rather plain girl who had been a teacher at a fashionable girls' school in Sussex. She even referred to her Wren ratings as 'chaps' when she spoke to them, and Celia could well imagine her waving a lacrosse stick and calling 'Play up, you chaps!' But she certainly took her job at naval operations very seriously. Celia stared at the busy girls on the moving ladders, others sorting the great clips of signals that continually came and went to the hundreds of ships out on the Atlantic at any given time. Her glance lingered on an RAF squadron leader and the other girl said quietly, 'He's married. Anyway he's only a Met officer.' She flushed and exclaimed, 'What a twit I am – your husband was a flier, wasn't he?'

Celia walked to another table where the little pointers were marked with the various warship names, anything from a battle-cruiser to a lowly Asdic trawler. She touched the one now shown to be in port. *Gladiator.*

Evelyn did not miss it. 'You know her captain, don't you?' She smiled. 'Dishy.'

Celia stared at her. 'What do you mean by that?'

'Well, he's such a nice bloke, a lot of my chaps get hot pants when he calls in for something. We heard he came to see you when Jane bought it.'

Celia relaxed slightly. Maybe she was right. Maybe it was better so. Too much grief could tear you apart.

'Yes, he did.' She lifted her chin with something like her old defiance. 'As a matter of fact he telephoned me when the ship got in. To see if I was back from leave.' She hesitated, knowing what Evelyn might think. 'We're going out to dinner this evening.'

'You know you've been put into my quarters to share the place?' She saw her nod and wondered if she should continue. 'It's hard to be alone up here. I don't mind of course, can't see the point really. But should you want . . .' She looked embarrassed. 'Well, I can always clear off for the night.'

'It's not like that.'

'Look, I know what you've been through, but I think you're exactly what he needs. There was some talk . . .'

'Talk? What about?'

'You must have seen it with the Fleet Air Arm boys. Full of bluster and dash, but shit-scared underneath. Round-the-bend, because there's nobody who cares enough to listen.'

'Afternoon, ladies!' Captain Vickers strode past, towering over both of them and leaving a tang of Scotch in his wake.

It gave Celia time to recover herself. She asked, 'Commander Howard, you mean? Tell me – I must know.'

The girl called Evelyn touched her sleeve. 'He's nearly cracked up more than once. Just take a glance at the wall-chart. Every one of those crosses is a ship on the bottom. Can you imagine what it's like out there, month in month out? Holding on, existing while others are being slaughtered?'

Celia stared at the solitary name *Ohio Star.* He had been so casual about it on the telephone, and then she had seen the news report in the paper. Not just obscure names any more. Not this time. Names she knew, names he had mentioned. His most of all.

'Thank you for telling me. I've been too busy feeling sorry for myself. And yes, I do want to share your billet.'

'If you feel it coming on again, my girl, just spill it all to your Auntie Evelyn!' She glared at a small Wren who was staring at her uncertainly. 'What is it, old chap?'

'We thought you should know, ma'am. The C-in-C has just left Hoylake golf course and is on his way.'

'Thanks.' She grinned at Celia. 'You'd better escape while you can. See you here tomorrow. *Sharp*.' She watched Celia walk away, then pause momentarily to glance up at the huge wall-chart, her lips slightly parted as if she were seeing something evil.

Second Officer Major said briskly, 'Come on, chaps, no time for slacking, eh?'

But the mood eluded her, and all she could think about was those two lonely people. Together.

At such short notice the small restaurant, in what had once been one of the port's famous hotels, was not quite what Howard would have liked. One wing of the hotel had been burned out in an incendiary raid, and the empty, blackened windows greeted new arrivals like melancholy eyes. Once it thrived on the great ships which plied the Atlantic between England and the Americas, but now, like so many of the servicemen who stayed or visited there, neither the hotel nor life as it had been lived in those pre-war days, would ever be the same again.

But the food was good, the fish especially fresh and well-cooked, although it was hard not to think of the trawler-men who still plied the sea, with far worse now than the weather to worry about.

Howard watched the girl, who sat directly opposite him, and wished they were quite alone. But the place was almost full, mostly naval officers with their female companions. It was fairly easy to distinguish between the wives and the lovers, and he wondered if Treherne ever came here.

She said, 'I *am* enjoying myself.' She studied his face gravely. 'It was good of you to ask me.' Then she smiled and he felt his heart leap. 'Oh, come on, David – we're behaving like school children! I was so nervous when you rang I almost made some stupid excuse not to come.'

He laughed. 'I was feeling like a junior midshipman!'

She asked, 'What about now?'

He reached across the table and took her hand in his. He saw a few heads turn at nearby tables, but for once, did not care.

'I've thought about you a hell of a lot, Celia.' He saw her eyes widen at the easy use of her name. 'Kept me going when . . .' He shrugged. 'Well, when things got a bit grim.'

'It *was* bad, wasn't it?' She could hear her new friend's voice. *Because nobody cares enough to listen.* 'Tell me. I want to be part of it, try to help.'

His voice was almost distant. 'You need a break from it sometimes – but you can never have it. Every month you give to the Atlantic is more experience, more understanding of the enemy you hardly ever see . . . It gets to you, and sometimes you want to give up.' He raised his eyes and looked directly into hers. 'I expect you've seen the plot, the wall-charts, and all the other exhibits here. But they're ships you see being moved all over the place, ships with men, flesh and blood, who have to take everything the enemy can pitch at them. The skipper of the ammunition ship, for instance.'

She glanced down as his fingers tightened around hers and knew he was back there, reliving it.

He said, 'Tough as old boots. Just a handful of his men and his pretty Chinese wife floating on a mountain of explosives! But he'll be back at sea soon, you'll see.'

She said, 'If I had known, if I had only understood how bad it was. You might have all been killed.'

He smiled. 'As it turned out, the blessed ship went down all on her own. I doubt if the convoy knew anything about it when it passed safely through.'

An elderly waiter came to the table. 'Will you try the sweet, sir?' His tired eyes moved between them and he wondered if he should offer them the room with the double bed and the coal fire, for an hour or so.

She shook her head. 'No, thanks. But I should like some coffee.'

The waiter sniffed. 'It's not *proper* coffee, like the old days, miss.'

As he shuffled away she said, 'I wonder what they think *we* get?'

She realised that he was still holding her hand and when she looked at him she was startled to see the bright intensity in his eyes. 'What is it? Tell me.'

He replied quietly, 'We're friends, Celia, and I want it to be something much more than that.'

He expected her to pull away but she said steadily, 'I'm still here, David.'

'When you came to see me – that first time, remember? I knew you were so unhappy, and my father said that you blamed yourself for what had happened. I don't see you could be blamed for anything like that. I was there, I saw it. It's something you have to harden your soul to, otherwise I, for one, would be useless.'

The coffee came and they did not see it.

Then she said, 'There was a big scene on the last night when I was with him.'

Her lip quivered and Howard said, 'Don't talk about it if it troubles you so much. Nothing is worth that.'

She faced him in her direct way and said, 'Well, I think it is. You see, I have always been a bit – sheltered, isn't that what they say of girls who won't play games? I went to an expensive school where about the only men I ever saw were a clergyman and the gardeners.' She shook her head with something like disbelief. 'How I ever got the nerve to apply for the WRNS I'll never know. Dormitories packed with young girls all trying to outdo each other with their so-called adventures. A lot of them knew my father was a rear-admiral – well, he was a captain then – and they used to pull my leg about it. Was it just a game to me, they used to ask. I was never more serious about anything. I got my commission and went on attachment to the Fleet Air Arm . . . that was where I met Jamie. He seemed to be so full of life – nothing ever appeared to trouble him. I knew he had an eye for the girls – I think everyone knew. More than an eye in a few cases. Because I didn't "join in", and maybe because I was an admiral's daughter . . . I seemed to attract him. It was a kind of madness. *I* was envied for once, admired even for the way I handled it. I don't know if it would ever have worked out. He got very depressed when they told him he was to be grounded. Flying was his life, I should have realised that sooner. Flying, and all the adoration that went with it.'

The waiter's shadow was across the table. 'Would you like the bill, sir?' *She* would go to the ladies' to powder her nose as they always did. Then he would put it to the young lieutenant-commander about the empty bedroom.

Howard said, 'Two brandies.' He saw her start to protest and added, 'Large ones.' He faced her again and said, 'Sorry about that.' He waited, knowing that she was fighting it again.

She said, 'He was seeing some girl, one he'd known at his old airfield. We had a blazing row about it, and he told me about the job he had volunteered for. I asked him not to do it. He'd risked his life countless times. Luck can't last forever.'

She broke off and asked abruptly, 'Do you have a cigarette?'

He shook his head. 'Sorry, I'm a pipe man, but I'll get the old retainer to find some.'

She shook her head so that her hair fell across her forehead, and Howard could easily picture her as a schoolgirl. 'I don't smoke, David. I just thought this might be the time to begin.'

She watched the waiter place the glasses carefully on the table and said, 'This will do, though.'

Howard watched; she was unused to brandy too, he thought. It was best not to recall Vallance's Horse's Necks, which had grown larger and larger over the past months.

She faced him calmly. 'He stormed out of the house, telling me I'd do what he liked, and no stuck-up bitch would change him.' She swallowed some more brandy and looked at him, her eyes very green in the reflected lights. 'He came back that night so drunk he could barely walk. A different man, like somebody else – a stranger. Do you want me to continue?'

Howard said nothing. She was going to tell him anyway, no matter what it might do to her.

She said, 'He wanted me. He kept pulling at me, telling me I'd soon be rid of him. I tried to calm him, to find the man I had married – in the end I was fighting him off.' She gripped his wrist until her nails broke the skin. 'He hit me in the face and threw me on the bed.' Her eyes were quite level and unmoving. 'Then he raped me.'

'Dear God!' Howard pictured it as it must have been. Lust, anger, madness. And she had been made to submit to that and to the memory which had tormented her until now.

She said simply, 'The rest you know. He was killed shortly afterwards.'

Howard said quietly, 'If he hadn't been I think I would have done it for him.'

She released her hand very gently and said, 'The waiter is coming back. I'm told he makes "arrangements" for certain officers and their girlfriends.' She looked for her bag. 'So if I was ever in a position like that, I'm not sure I could . . .' She broke off as the waiter put down the bill on a dented tray.

'Everything all right, miss?'

Her voice was surprisingly calm. 'A very nice meal, thank you.'

To Howard she said, 'Take me home will you, please? I'll show you where I live.' As they walked to the door several heads turned to watch them, something which Howard resented more than he would have believed possible. She said, 'That will give the old goat something to ponder on!'

But Howard knew it was to cover what she had been trying to tell him. That she might never be able to make love again.

As they walked through the darkened streets and watched the first searchlights criss-crossing the sky she said, 'You see, David, I *do* care. Very much. I never thought I would again. Perhaps I didn't even know what I wanted.'

He turned her lightly in his arms. It was not happening. Another dream. 'I love you, Celia. I'll not change.' He held her, and they kissed gently, as if they were meeting for the first time. 'I'd never do or say anything to hurt you.'

Her hands were gripping his jacket as if she would not let him go, and at the same time knew that she must.

She said, 'I know that, David. That's why I want it to be *right*.'

They stood apart as two policemen walked past, their steel helmets shining in the faint searchlights.

All right for some, they would say.

Howard said, 'I'd like to see you again as soon as we get back.'

'Get back?'

'Well, you'll know soon enough when you go to your new job in ops. We're off again now that the maintenance commander

236

has put a rocket under the Asdic people. Don't worry – we're getting pretty good at it now.'

'I'll be watching and thinking about you.' She lifted her head and looked at his outline in the darkness. 'I'm glad I told you about . . .'

He kissed her lightly on the mouth. 'Come on, I'll walk you the rest of the way.'

The smouldering ammunition ship, the inability to listen for U-Boats, even the next convoy; they were all far away.

This was now; and David Howard was young again.

'There's a sight for sore eyes, sir!' Treherne levelled his binoculars and studied the convoy, which was making a wide turn, hard sunlight flashing from tiers of scuttles and across the spacious bridge of the leading ship. Three ocean liners, well known on pre-war cruising posters, none of them a stranger to the Atlantic for those lucky enough in the Depression to be able to afford such luxury. Even their dull grey paint could not disguise their majestic lines, and even as the signal lamps began to blink between Vickers's group and the convoy's own close escort, it was possible to see that the leading ship's upper decks were packed with soldiers. They were mostly American, and had been handed over to their new escort in mid-Atlantic.

Howard loosened his coat; it was surprisingly hot in the open bridge, and he tried to estimate how many troops were crammed into each liner. All bound for Britain, and then after further training, to some point where an invasion must be launched.

'Port fifteen.' Howard glanced at the gyro-repeater. Like the other commanding officers in the group, he knew what to do. Half of them would sweep astern of the convoy's close escort; the rest would take station further to the south. The original escorts must have had their work cut out to keep pace with those powerful ships, he thought; it had made re-fuelling for the destroyers doubly difficult at sea because the liners stopped for nobody.

'Midships . . . Steady.'

'Steady, sir. Course zero-four-zero.' Howard smiled. The right direction anyway. They would be back in port in a couple of days if this weather held.

'Aircraft, sir. Bearing Green four-five. Angle of sight two-oh!'

'Disregard.' Treherne lowered his glasses. Even that was different now. The chill of despair when you sighted any aircraft was less evident. This one was a big Sunderland flying boat, crossing the convoy while the soldiers stared up at its great whale-shape and waved their caps.

Howard heard the clatter of feet on a ladder and knew Bizley had arrived to relieve Treherne for the afternoon watch. Was it noon already?

Bizley seemed to have recovered his old self-confidence, Howard thought. He was discussing course and speed and the air recognition signals as if he had been doing it all his life. At least he and Finlay were avoiding another clash, so Vallance's wardroom would be more peaceful.

Howard climbed onto his chair and thought of the girl he had walked home to her billet, the one she shared with the second officer they called 'Auntie'. It was still hard to believe it had happened, or how it had begun. She was shy; probably still very shocked by what she had told him. But it meant more than that to Howard. She had trusted him. He would never repay it with some clumsy attempt at love. But as he had held her outside the darkened doorway he had felt her pressed against him, and had known then how much he had wanted her.

Sub-Lieutenant Rooke called, 'From *Kinsale*, sir.' He held out the intercom handset, while Howard stared across the screen as if he still expected to see the leader. But she and the others were already out of sight, lost in a rippling mist created by the hard sunshine.

Vickers sounded as if he was on another planet, or was speaking through water.

'Received a signal from the Sunderland, David. Thinks they may have sighted a submarine, submerged and well astern of the convoy. They'll make sure she doesn't surface to try and catch up.' He gave a hollow chuckle. 'No chance of that, eh?'

Howard peered at his little radar-repeater. How huge the troopers' blips looked, the escorts – all destroyers for no corvette would ever keep pace with them – spread around them, a sure shield. *The most precious cargo of of all.*

Vickers added, 'I've detached *Ganymede* to support. You remain on station, just in case.'

Howard relayed the information to Treherne, who was still on the bridge.

He said, 'They'll keep the bastard down. I don't expect the Jerry commander even realised the Sunderland had spotted him. Like a shadow in the water, I suppose.'

The yeoman of signals said, 'There goes *Ganymede*!'

Howard watched their sister-ship angling away towards the opposite horizon where another destroyer, Tail-end Charlie, was signalling to the flying boat as it cruised sedately overhead.

Howard thought of his friend Spike Colvin on *Ganymede*'s bridge, sporting one of the famous brightly-coloured scarves he had worn at sea even as a subbie. He lowered his face to the radar-repeater again. He saw the blip made by the destroyer, a big modern one named *Mediator* over five miles astern. Then *Ganymede*, bustling through the revolving radar beam as if drawn on a wire.

It was a marvel Colvin had ever made command, he thought. He had committed every sort of prank imaginable. He had painted their class number on the grass with weed-killer when they were about to pass out from *Excellent*, the gunnery school. But it had rained unexpectedly and the enormous figures had appeared even as the captain had been about to conduct the passing-out parade. Colvin had confessed. He always had. Another time, at a Christmas party, he had loaded and fired a brass cannon outside the Devonport Barracks wardroom. It had, unfortunately, blown out most of the windows in the commodore's house.

The three troopships were completing another zig-zag, lights flashing to the close escort commander as they wheeled in perfect unison. No chances with this lot, Howard thought.

'Starboard ten. Midships. Steer zero-eight-zero.' He raised his glasses but it was difficult to see *Ganymede* now, and anyway one of the wing escorts blocked the lenses while she, too, made a rapid change of course.

Rooke still held the handset and shouted, 'From *Kinsale*, sir! Sunderland reports torpedoes . . .'

But Howard had already seen the flash, and then a second one. Against the eye-searing sunshine it was little more than a blink. By contrast, when it reached them, the double explosion was like a thunderclap; Howard felt the bridge quiver beneath his sea-boots as if they had run across a sandbar.

Treherne snapped, 'Where the *hell* was that?'

Howard was watching the blip which was furthest astern. It had to be the *Mediator*. There was nothing else that far out.

The Sunderland was already swooping down over the sea's glittering face, depth-charges ready to drop if it sighted anything. That was exactly what the second U-Boat had been depending on.

There was a double flash and even above the mist Howard saw the tall water-spouts shooting skyward, followed instantly by a great plume of black smoke.

'Captain Vickers – for you, sir.'

Howard did not need to be told. The second salvo from a different bearing had hit *Ganymede*.

'Sunderland's dropping floats, David. Take your section to assist.'

'Hard a-starboard. Full ahead together. Steer two-five-zero. Yeoman, make to *Blackwall* and *Belleisle*: *Take station for search on me.*'

Treherne watched him grimly. He knew exactly what Howard was thinking. He had mentioned it several times; what a senior officer had once said to him. *When they start going for the escorts instead of the convoy, you'll know you're winning the battle.*

A powerful blast echoed across the sea, loud enough to muffle *Gladiator*'s racing screws as she worked up to maximum revolutions. A ship blowing up? It would not be depth-charges; the Sunderland would not dare with so many men fighting for their lives in the water. The enemy would know that too. In no time a second Sunderland joined in the patrol, but the U-Boats had gone deep and headed away from danger.

When *Gladiator* and her two consorts reached the scene *Mediator* had already vanished. She had been a big destroyer, newer and more powerful than Vickers's *Kinsale*. She carried about two hundred in her company. Of their sister-ship only the forward portion remained afloat. The torpedoes must have hit her amidships and blown her in half, the engine room exploding like a huge bomb.

Amidst the usual slick of oil and bobbing flotsam Howard could see a few struggling figures; not many.

'Action stations, sir?' Bizley sounded stiff and unreal, as if he did not believe what had happened.

'No. But clear the lower deck, and turn out the boats. Tell Ayres to stand by the Carley floats and scrambling nets.'

Treherne said, 'They're already dealing with it, sir.'

He trained his glasses on the *Ganymede*'s uplifted bows, and wondered how many might be trapped inside. He could see two tiny figures clinging to the port anchor, another trying to pull someone on to a waterlogged float.

'Slow ahead.' Howard heard the motor boat's engine cough into life as it was lowered down alongside. '*Stop engines!*' The moment of risk. He felt suddenly sick, as if nothing would stop him vomiting in front of them all.

'Boats away, sir!'

Blackwall was already lowering her two boats near where the other warship had gone down, while *Belleisle* continued to circle round the scene, her Asdic listening for any tell-tale echo. But in his heart Howard knew there would be none. Two destroyers gone within thirty seconds. They had made their point.

When Howard eventually recalled the boats, and one solitary swimmer was hauled gasping and sobbing up a scrambling net, he had to report to Vickers that only fifty survivors had been rescued between them. Spike Colvin had not been found.

As the whaler was hoisted again, *Ganymede* released a great gout of filthy bubbles and vanished. The whaler's crew had managed to save the two men from her anchor. They had been lucky.

'Increase revolutions to resume patrol, Pilot.' Howard looked at Treherne, his eyes empty of expression. 'How does it feel to be winning, Number One?'

It took several hours to catch up with the convoy, and by then it was near dusk. Howard looked at the tall-sided liners and wondered if any of the troops realised what had happened, and would remember this day when their own time came to risk their lives.

He thought of their other sister-ship, *Garnet*, which was up there with Vickers's section. Her captain, Tom Woodhouse, had been at Dartmouth with him, another irrepressible joker – he and Colvin had been pretty close, too. Might he be thinking the same now? *Who's next?*

He pictured the girl in Liverpool, probably watching the plot right now as the two ships were reported lost. *Next of kin have been informed.* She must not go through all that again.

Later, as he sat in his chair and watched the first stars appear, he thought about it again. Perhaps like a ship's course on the ocean, their fate was already decided.

5

No Greater Love

Another full pattern of depth-charges exploded like distant thunder, but still close enough to shake the submarine from bow to stern. The men at their various stations stared unblinking at the curved hull, their eyes very white in the dimmed lighting.

It had been going on for an hour, even longer when you counted their failed attack on the small, fast convoy.

Standing by the periscope well, Kapitänleutnant Manfred Kleiber shifted his glance from the clock to the depth gauges. There was only one hunter up there now. That same single-screwed engine beat of a corvette, one of the convoy's escort. Perhaps they would give up eventually and hurry away to rejoin the others. He watched some of the men nearest to him, those at the hydroplane controls, the helmsman, the navigating officer. Their hair and shoulders were speckled with the cork-filled paint which had fallen like snowflakes from the deckhead during the last onslaught of depth-charges. Their faces were grey, pallid, even in the warm glow of the control room lighting. Dirty clothes; unshaven sunken faces. *The Grey Wolves*, as one patriotic newspaper had described them.

Those bastards should be here with us, he thought bitterly.

He could guess what most of his men were thinking, that they would soon have to break off the patrol and return to base. It had to be *his* decision. They had already passed the rendezvous time for the final meeting with a supply submarine. Surely they had not lost yet another one? Kleiber knew all about the new tactics, the hunter-killer groups which searched for U-Boats like professional assassins. Three of his own wolf-pack had failed to make contact, so they must have been destroyed. He thought of the base in France. It was high summer now – green fields, sunshine, good food. No wonder his men looked so desperate. He had addressed all of them when he had received the signal from HQ. The Tommies and their allies had made their first move since North Africa, and had succeeded in launching an invasion into Sicily. Not Greece after all, as his group commander had predicted, but they would be driven off or captured. Just like Crete.

His lip curled with contempt. What did he know? The allies were not only still there, but all resistance had ceased. Italy next – it had to be. The Italians had always been the weak link. Despite their outward belief in Fascism, they had proved to be jackals, an army that ran rather than fought to the death.

He saw the hydrophone operator's quick glance, and gave his orders: increase the depth by thirty metres, alter course ninety degrees yet again.

Kleiber was too experienced to need a headset. The thrum-thrum-thrum of the corvette's screw was like an express train. She had turned and was coming on another sweep.

Someone tip-toed through an emergency door, a rag covering his mouth and nose. Kleiber thought of the man who had died, after being hit by a piece of shell splinter on that other occasion when they had approached a convoy on the surface, working into a suitable position to attack. It had been a random shot from an escort, a ship they had not even seen. Just bad luck, for him. With the aid of a medical handbook Kleiber had amputated the man's arm himself when gangrene with its disgusting stench had pervaded the whole boat. He had died under drugs without knowing anything about it. His comrades had been sorry for him; he had been a popular crewman. Now, without exception, they had come to hate him, waiting only to rid themselves of the corpse and its constant reminder of death.

The hull shook wildly as another full pattern roared down. Several lights shattered, and a man cried out, his face cut by flying glass.

The corvette's engine faded again, but the hydrophone operator shook his head. The enemy commander was slowing down – a listening game, or perhaps pausing to await more support.

How much could the hull stand? Kleiber could feel them watching him. Looking for hope, despair, weakness.

He moved to the chart table and studied the pencilled parallelogram which showed the extent of the *milchküh* operational zone. It was no use. She must have gone down. With aircraft more and more in evidence across the once-safe area, they were prime targets, too big and too vulnerable to escape a sudden attack.

All at once, he was desperate to leave; to get back to base, to find out what was happening. Some of his fellow U-Boat commanders had been in the Mediterranean and had been employed against the supply train for the allied invasion. He thought bitterly of the last brief letter he had received from his brother in Russia. He was a fool to write as he did; if his letter had been opened he might have been punished for defeatist talk. But in it he had described the appalling food and shortages of medical supplies, ammunition and just about everything on the Russian front. Kleiber tried not think of what the enemy troops would be eating and drinking in Sicily. He had boarded British supply vessels before sinking them, in the rosier times, and knew well enough how well they lived. He made up his mind. He would tell his men, it would raise their spirits to head for base. A man could survive these conditions for just so long. The alternative could not even be entertained.

But first . . . He gave his orders without even raising his voice. He was not being callous; and if he was, it was the Atlantic's responsibility. There were two torpedoes left, and with only three hits and no definite kills throughout the whole patrol, Kleiber had felt disillusioned and frustrated by the latest setback of the supply-boat.

He heard the thud of watertight doors closing and could picture his men peering at one another as each door opened and shut on their private, sealed compartments. How would the dead man's relatives behave if they knew the last move he would make for the Fatherland?

The corvette was on the move again, her engine's thrashing beat fading as she prepared for a change of bearing, which at any time might bring her detection gear tapping at the submerged hull like a blind man's stick. A light flickered on the control panel. It was ready. The corpse was in an empty torpedo tube complete with any litter which the seamen had been able to gather. The engineer officer would supply some oil, but not much. Without the supply-boat it would be a long, painful haul back to France.

She was coming in to the attack; the loud cracks against the hull were the worst so far. She must have got a contact.

He snapped his order and saw the light flicker as the tube disgorged its contents into the sea. Kleiber could feel cold sweat beneath the rim of his soiled white cap. Like ice rime while he counted seconds and imagined the spread-eagled corpse, dressed in proper waterproof clothing, floating up to the sunshine, surrounded with odds and ends from the rubbish bins, and a quick discharge of oil. He felt his mouth tightening with the insane desire to laugh. It was to be hoped the Tommies didn't notice that their 'volunteer' had only one arm! Then he controlled his thoughts with cold determination; such hysteria was dangerous, destructive.

They were staring at the hull again, listening; straining every muscle for a sign.

Very slowly and carefully Kleiber brought his command round in a wide arc, the motors so reduced they were barely audible.

Round and further still, until the hydrophone operator reported that the corvette was stopping, and then that all hydrophone effects had ceased. Kleiber frowned, gauging where the sun would be when he went to periscope depth. He could see it all as if he were there. A boat being lowered to gather the evidence of a kill. If anything went wrong now the enemy commander would have no more doubts – he would *know* there was a submarine here. He might even have called for air support.

Kleiber nodded to his first officer and bent right down almost to his knees as the air was forced into the ballast tanks, the hydroplanes moving like fins to make the boat's movements slow and stealthy. At forty metres Kleiber ordered the attack periscope to be raised again, so slowly that he could hear the mechanic's rough breathing as he controlled it.

Faint green light, then purplish-blue as the lens cut above the surface. Kleiber saw the motionless corvette framed in the crosswires, her boat probably lowered on the opposite side to retrieve the grisly evidence of their 'kill'.

Kleiber did not linger long. Just enough to note the corvette's number: HMS *Malva*. Probably of all the warships in the Atlantic these stocky little vessels had been the U-Boat's greatest enemy.

The hull jerked twice and the periscope hissed down into its well as the boat gathered speed and swung away, the water roaring into her tanks again to carry her down deep.

A petty officer by the plot pressed his stop-watch and gasped as the exploding torpedoes threw the hull over, the sound sighing across and past them to be lost in the vastness of the ocean.

Moments later they heard the grinding echo of tearing steel, as the corvette began to break up on her way to the bottom.

Kleiber walked to the chart, shutting his ears to the crazed cheers and insane laughter which passed through the U-Boat like echoes from Bedlam. If the grand admiral ordered him to attack escorts as a priority, that he would do without question.

He must stop thinking of his brother and his starving comrades in Russia, and of the richly loaded food ships which he might lose because of this new instruction.

Above them, and falling further and further astern, the corvette's survivors floated in their lifejackets or struggled through the oil slick in search of a raft or some piece of wood to keep them afloat. There had been no time to make a distress signal; no time for anything; and most if not all of these men would die before anyone came to search for them.

Among the gasping, struggling survivors, the dead German floated indifferently, unaware of what he had done, without even the satisfaction of revenge. In the Atlantic there was no such luxury.

The main operations room at Liverpool seemed even busier than usual. Second Officer Celia Lanyon shared a desk with her roommate, Evelyn Major, and together they were sorting through the latest signals which had been gathered by the SDO along another corridor in the citadel.

It was late afternoon, in the month of September, and all day the place had been buzzing with the news of the follow-up to the invasion of the Italian mainland. Wherever possible the Italians were throwing down their arms, offering their services to the allies, when earlier they had been sworn enemies. The complete collapse of Germany's strongest partner had been settled when the Italian flagship had led the main part of their fleet under the guns of Malta, that bombed and battered island which had once been one of Mussolini's hoped-for prizes.

Every day they had expected a reverse, another of the disappointments which had been their lot in the past years. But apart from the arrival of early rain in southern Italy, which had clogged down the movement of tanks and supplies, there was no sign of impending difficulty. There had been losses on the beaches when the Allied armies had first stormed ashore, while at sea the covering warships and bombardment squadron had been introduced to Germany's latest secret weapon: a glider-bomb which could be directed onto a floating target, and which had brought fresh problems to the fleet's gunnery officers. The flagship *Warspite* had been hit, and several major warships, including the US cruiser *Savannah*, had suffered heavy damage and casualties.

But down here in operations, despite the heartening news from the Mediterranean, defeat and victory remained strangely remote, like the city overhead. At this particular moment two major convoys were at sea, an eastbound and a westbound, which should be passing overnight some ninety miles apart.

The eastbound convoy was from Halifax, and included two large troopships as well as several freighters carrying vehicles and crated aircraft. As Celia checked the columns of names against the duty operations officer's list she thought of *Gladiator*, somewhere out there with the escort group under Captain Vickers's control. She had met Howard only three times since he had taken her back to the billet from the hotel – the group had been operating for much of the time from Iceland, to make certain that the flow of troopships reached port unscathed.

She remembered so clearly the moment when she had seen the two ships marked as lost on the plot. *Mediator*, and the one commanded by his friend, *Ganymede*. Just fifty survivors between them. It had torn at her heart like claws when he had told her. Even that he had been reluctant to do. As if he wanted to shield her from the true horror of the life they were sharing.

The enemy attacks on escort vessels were not coincidental; other ships had been mauled both by submarines and aircraft, with several new crosses on the plot to give grim evidence of this new phase of war.

The duty operations officer sauntered over to their table and nodded. 'Take a break. I have a feeling things will hot up shortly. The boss is here already, usually a bad omen.'

The tiny room where the officers could have tea or relax with a smoke was almost humid – the summer had been a long one.

Evelyn brought two cups of tea and one spoon. 'All there are left.' She sat down untidily and thrust out her legs like a man.

Celia thought of the way he had held her, how she had realised he had wanted her so desperately. She did not know, could not tell . . .

She looked up, startled, as the other Wren said, 'Auntie time, old chap. Isn't it about the right moment to spill the beans? If you don't, you'll drive yourself crazy. You've lost weight – something you never needed, not like *me*!' She became serious again. 'What does *he* think?'

Perhaps she was right. That it might help to talk. 'He loves me.' It sounded so empty that she said, '*Really* loves me. God knows, I'm bad luck – I told him that too.' She stood up suddenly and walked across the room. 'I'm afraid. I want him to love me.'

'And you think that you might not be able to give it in return? That he'll be hurt, get tired of waiting, something like that?'

She sat down again and gave a small smile. 'Very like that.'

'I think I know you pretty well, Celia. I know you're not the type to leap into bed with anyone you take a fancy to, and from what you've told me he certainly doesn't sound the type either. Otherwise you'd never have opened up to him about what happened with Jamie.'

Celia sighed. 'I do seem to tell you rather a lot, don't I?'

'Not much else to do up here.' She watched her warily. 'I have a cousin who's got a cottage up in the Lake District. I could easily fix it, next time you can both snatch some leave.'

Celia stared at her. 'What, a secret place, you mean? Just like that? A little black nightie and some perfume?'

Evelyn smiled. 'Has he ever suggested anything of the kind?'

Celia said nothing. Howard had told her about the girl he had once known, and, she suspected, had loved. He had just received his first command and had gone straight into the thick of it when, she guessed, he had won his DSC. The girl had not waited for him, and Celia wondered how it had affected him. She had been shocked when they had last met in that same shabby restaurant before he had sailed again for Iceland. He had seemed empty, utterly drained; even the news of his proposed DSO had had no effect.

'I would give myself to him tomorrow if I thought it would help. Give him something to – to hold on to.' She hesitated, remembering what he had said. *Can't you see, girl? I'm in love with you!* 'I wouldn't want to with anyone else.'

Evelyn said kindly, in her brisk, no-nonsense manner, 'Sounds suspiciously like love to me, Celia.'

She barely heard, remembering the flecks of grey in his hair, the lines at his mouth; the way he clung to her hand, like a lifeline.

'What shall I say? What must I do?'

They returned to the desk and she saw the chief of staff's assistant in deep conference with the other heads of department.

A Wren petty officer with a coder's badge on her sleeve bent down by their desk.

'The eastbound's in a spot of bother, ma'am. Their escort carrier has engine trouble and will return to Halifax. The westbound has another carrier, the *Seeker* – she will supply air cover from tomorrow.'

'Thanks.' Evelyn leafed expertly through her file and then handed the relevant flimsy to a messenger. Between her teeth she said, 'The carrier breakdown has delayed our eastbound.' She squinted at the plot. Almost too casually she added, 'The thirty-second escort group has been redirected. Two hundred miles. Should be all right according to the Met report.'

Celia watched the little counters appear for the first time: Captain Vickers's *Kinsale*, and then some twenty miles distant, the half-leader, H-38. There was a gap this time. Poor *Ganymede*.

And so it went on. Signals in and out, senior officers speaking to their various subordinates. The Wrens up and down the ladders, moving ships, marking some losses in a coastal convoy, with the RAF Coastal Command people listening to the latest Met reports, the availability of their new long-range aircraft from Northern Ireland, Iceland and Newfoundland.

The duty operations officer, an RNVR lieutenant-commander, said, 'One of the additional escorts has made a distress signal, sir.'

The assistant to the chief-of-staff folded his arms while the others around him poised themselves as they had done so many times.

Captain Naish stared hard at the plot. 'Make a signal to the thirty-second group – Captain Vickers will act on this. He must be the closest.' He waited for the telephones to click into action. 'How bad is it?'

'One torpedo, sir. Down by the bows. Requires assistance.'

'With this convoy coming through I can't spare any other escorts, Tim. The half-leader will be the most available – ask Vickers to detach *Gladiator*. She was the last to refuel.'

A door opened and without looking the girl knew it was the boss.

He asked, 'Which escort?'

'The corvette *Tacitus*, sir. Lieutenant-Commander Marrack.'

'Keep me informed.' The door closed again.

The two Wren officers looked at each other and Celia said quietly, 'Why can't they send someone else?'

Evelyn watched her unhappily, not understanding.

She said, 'He's often spoken of Marrack. *They* were friends too.' She pushed her knuckles into her mouth and then said in a small voice, 'Don't you see? After *Ganymede* and everything else . . .' She could not go on.

'I *do* see.' Evelyn stared at the plot but saw only the little marker, where a solitary escort lay at the mercy of the sea and the enemy. *Gladiator* would be on her way by now, and should reach the torpedoed vessel by dawn. Marrack's ship must have helped escort the carrier to safety and been trying to return to the convoy. She glanced at the two RAF officers. But there *should* be long-range air cover, even at that distance, when daylight found them.

Beside her Celia took the latest pad of signals from a messenger and waited for her vision to clear.

To herself she whispered, *Oh, David, I do love you so.*

The duty officer rapped out more figures and the ladders began to move again. 'To commodore. *There are now twenty-plus U-Boats in your vicinity.*'

Naish patted his pockets but had forgotten his cigarettes. He pictured his tall friend directing his killer-group to the eastbound convoy: *D'you Ken John Peel?* It was very apt. His glance fell on the latest female addition to the ops room. Rear-Admiral Lanyon's daughter. She would be a real catch for some lucky chap. But she looked strained and pale, and he suddenly remembered a rumour he had picked up at the club. As she stared at the small isolated counter, *H-38*, Captain Naish knew that it was no longer just a rumour.

Howard slid open the chart-room door and stared at Treherne and Rooke, who were busy with their calculations. It was all but dark beyond the ship, with thick cloud and the hint of rain. He should never have allowed himself to lie down in his sea cabin; it was always worse this way, the sudden shrill of the telephone, all his instincts forcing sleep and escape into the background.

'No further signals, Number One?'

'None, sir.' Treherne watched him, saw the battle Howard was already fighting.

Howard looked at Rooke. 'Well, *come on*, man, I'm not a bloody mind-reader!'

Rooke pointed with his dividers. 'Twenty-five degrees west, fifty-five north, sir.'

'I'm going up top.' Howard fastened his duffel coat, the one he had once offered to Treherne. 'By the time I get there I want the course-to-steer, and the ETA. I shall have a word with the Chief.'

He pulled the door behind him and for just a few moments stood with his back against the damp steel while he calmed his breathing.

On the other side of the door Treherne said quietly, 'Take it off your back, Pilot. He didn't mean to bite your head off. *Tacitus*'s skipper used to be Number One here. A pal of his.' He smiled sadly. 'One of the family, so to speak.'

Rooke sighed. 'In that case . . .'

Treherne made for the door. 'In that case, *get it right*!'

On the upper bridge Howard replaced the engine room telephone and listened to the regular beat of engines.

He heard Rooke and Treherne speaking by the ready-use

chart-table, transferring the calculations which the navigator had just completed.

Rooke said, 'Course-to-steer is two-four-five, sir.'

Howard glanced at Treherne's shaggy silhouette. 'Bring her round. Revs for twenty knots. With the sea fairly calm, we shouldn't shake about too much, but better warn the watch below.'

'Aye, aye, sir.' They would be having their supper when *Gladiator* worked up to that sort of speed, big, sickening swoops across the unbroken swell. It was to be hoped the PO chef had not produced anything too greasy.

He heard Rooke say carefully, 'Estimated time of arrival will be six o'clock onwards, sir. Daylight if the visibility's good.'

'Right.' Howard could sense Rooke's resentment, but it did not seem to matter. Once he would have apologised instantly for unfairly berating a subordinate. Those days had gone somewhere out here in the Atlantic. Tomorrow there might be air cover, or there might not. Two large convoys passing, vital supplies, and more troops to extend the victories in Italy, and elsewhere.

But at this moment there were only two ships he cared about, and Marrack would be desperate. His first command. What he had always wanted. Even the corvette's reported position was too vague for complete accuracy. There was never enough time when hell burst in on you.

He watched the sea creaming away from either bow, the spray starting to drift over the bridge or beat against the glass screen. Lucky they had been the last to take on fuel from a fleet tanker; otherwise, someone else would be heading for that tiny pencilled cross down to south-west-by-south. The telephone in his sea cabin had torn him from another terrible dream. He had been helplessly watching her being raped by the man in the flying-suit; holding her down and laughing, laughing.

Treherne rejoined him. 'No more from W/T, sir. Keeping the air clear for the strategists.' He said it without bitterness, but Howard could feel the hurt he was sharing with him.

Treherne said unexpectedly, 'Had a bit of good news when we were in last, sir. My girl's husband got himself killed.' He chuckled in the darkness. 'He was pissed apparently, and got run over by an armoured car!'

They both laughed like schoolboys, and then Howard stared at him, knowing they were both going quite mad; there was no other explanation. 'Are you going to get married now?'

'Not sure, sir. My old lady walked out on me. I shall have to look into the legal thing when I get a chance.' He added sharply, 'If that bastard had laid a hand on her again, I would have done him in myself!'

Howard thought of what he had said to the girl in the restaurant. 'It must be catching.'

He leaned his head on his arms and felt the desire to sleep clouding his mind. But he knew that if he did, the terrible dream would be waiting to mock and torment him.

Instead he said, 'See if you can rustle up something hot to drink. It's going to be a long night.'

Howard buttoned up the collar of his oilskin as the rain slashed diagonally across the open bridge. It was heavy and surprisingly cold, a reminder, if anyone should need it, that autumn and winter came early to the Western Ocean. The lookouts were changed yet again to prevent them becoming dulled by the regular plunging motion, when they might miss something. The monotonous ping of the Asdic, the occasional shuffle of feet from the crew of B-gun below the bridge, all told of nervous readiness. If there was a battle going on in one or other of the big convoys, it was too far away to concern them. Everybody in *Gladiator*'s company would also be aware that they were drawing further and further from aid with each swing of the propellers.

Howard peered through the screen and saw the sea surging alongside. Beyond the curling bow-wave there was just the merest glimpse of the nearest troughs, riding past like heaving black oil.

Treherne was beside him again, trying to make sure he had forgotten nothing.

Howard said, 'We shall stay at defence stations, Number One, but I want both watches on deck, the hull sealed like a sardine tin. I've told Guns that he is excused watchkeeping – I want his control position manned and ready in case we need a starshell or something more lethal. He also knows that the short-range weapons will remain closed-up.' He mopped his face with a towel, but that was already sodden. 'This will play hell with visibility.'

'I've warned radar and Asdic, sir.' Treherne hesitated, unwilling to say it. 'We must expect the worst to have happened, sir.'

'Yes.' He sounded very quiet, his voice almost lost in the surge and spray of the old enemy. 'I realise that. But Marrack won't use his W/T any more. If there's still a U-Boat about, and we have to face that, it might pick up his signals.'

He heard the midshipman burst into a fit of nervous coughing. It often happened, and had got worse since the loss of *Ganymede* and *Mediator*. He had spoken to Moffatt about it, and the doctor had said angrily, 'I'll have a word if you like, sir. Some fool at the hospital must have been deaf and blind to send a kid like him back to sea so soon after losing his ship – he's a nervous wreck.'

Howard called across the bridge. 'Come here, Mid!'

Ross felt his way over the slippery decking and waited, mute in the darkness.

'I need all my most experienced officers up here. I've sent Mister Ayres down aft with the Buffer's party. You go and assist.' He looked away, thinking of the corvette. If the weather worsened they might not even find her unless they got help from a recce aircraft. 'And, Ross – I think you should have advice ashore. You've had a bad time.'

Treherne popped a piece of chocolate into his mouth and marvelled that Howard could adjust his mind to something so obscure.

The midshipman seemed to shake his head. 'I'd rather not, sir.' When Howard said nothing he added tightly, 'You know what they'll say, sir. They'll probably discharge me.'

Howard could feel his desperation. They probably would too, he thought. *It'll be my turn if I'm not careful.*

'All right. We'll see. Now you go and help Ayres.'

He listened to him groping down the ladder, his coughs beginning again. How old was he – eighteen? He was like one of the Great War people Howard had seen as a child. Still shell-shocked, reliving the hell which Mister Mills had sometimes described.

He wondered how the rebuilding of the house in Hampshire was progressing. It would give Mister Mills something to supervise; an occupation he badly needed now that the Guvnor had gone.

Howard's brother had wanted nothing to do with it. He already had a home of his own, although God alone knew how he was paying for such a grand place. But his wife Lilian had money, and knew exactly what she wanted for Robert and her own future.

Rain dashed over his oilskin and made his face feel raw. *Future* – how could anyone know?

'Time?'

Rooke called out, 'Five-thirty, sir.' He sounded unhappy, as if wondering whether he would be blamed if they failed to make contact.

Treherne picked his teeth free of chocolate. He usually saved his nutty ration for Joyce, but just this once he needed the energy they said it gave you. Joyce . . . She had been good about the telegram from the War Office. It had been followed by a letter from her husband's CO. He must have been drunk when he'd written it, he thought. It had made the man's death sound like a national disaster.

He said, 'Should get a bit brighter soon.'

'Convince me.'

Treherne tightened his collar but felt the rain running down his spine. 'Well, it says . . .'

'Radar – Bridge!'

'Forebridge?'

'Getting a faint effect at two-six-zero, about twelve thousand yards.' He fell silent as if, unheard, he were swearing to himself. 'Sorry, sir. Thought I'd lost it again.'

Treherne was peering at the radar-repeater. 'Nothing.'

Howard asked, 'What do you think, Lyons?' He was passing the buck, but he knew the man well. Someone who would appreciate the trust.

'Small vessel, sir. Appears to be stationary.'

Howard turned away, his blood suddenly tingling. 'Found him!' He walked to the compass. 'Starboard ten – Midships – Steady!'

'Steady, sir.' Sweeney was there without being called. 'On two-six-six.'

'Steer two-six-zero.' He groped for the engine room handset.

'Chief? This is the captain.' He stared at the darkness but saw Evan Price vividly in his mind's eye, down below the waterline with his racing machinery and steamy, tropical warmth. 'I think we've found her. But I want you to reduce to half-speed. Full revs or dead stop if I say so, right?'

He thought he heard Price chuckle. 'Isn't that what the bridge always wants, sir?'

Treherne watched him moving restlessly this way and that, and heard him say, 'Tell Guns what's happening.'

There was something unusual about him. An edginess which, if he felt it, he always managed to conceal. Except that once. Treherne wiped his binoculars; that memory always touched him. Like sharing something very private.

Bizley climbed into the bridge. 'Sir?'

Howard did not turn. 'Yes. I want you here, with me. Take over the con. Pilot will fill you in.'

Howard turned towards Treherne, and was surprised that he could suddenly see his bearded face and the battered cap he always wore on watch. A different badge now, but Howard knew it was one of his old company caps. A talisman maybe.

'Daylight, at last!'

It was little more than a grey blur, beyond which the sea and horizon were still one.

Howard said, 'I wonder if their radar is still working?'

Treherne said nothing. The blip on the radar might be something else. Or they might all be dead.

Sub-Lieutenant Rooke offered, 'I served in her class of corvettes, sir. The radar was always very reliable.'

'Thanks.' Howard laid out his busy thoughts. It could have been destroyed in the explosion. Anything might have happened.

Treherne tugged his beard as the radar operator reported no change, other than the range had fallen to ten thousand yards.

Howard said, 'Slow ahead together.' The motion seemed to become more violent immediately, loose equipment and metal mugs adding to the clatter of ship noises.

'Revolutions seven-zero, sir.'

Treherne remarked, 'We could fire a rocket, sir. We'd know for sure then.' Why were they slowing down? Prolonging the uncertainty, even the risk, if there was some survivors up there, five miles beyond the dark arrowhead of *Gladiator's* bows . . .

Howard faced him and Treherne was stunned by the intensity of his stare. 'What is it, sir? Can I do something?'

Howard brushed against a stiff-backed lookout as he pulled Treherne to the port corner. 'You'll think me mad, Gordon.'

Treherne waited, holding his breath. He had noticed that Howard had often called him by his first name, even on the bridge in front of the others. It had pleased him, until now. Something was badly wrong.

'Tell me, sir.'

Howard lowered his voice, feeling his stomach contract to the savage motion. Or was it just that? 'I think there's a bloody U-Boat up there.'

Treherne felt the water on his spine change to ice. He was afraid to speak.

'It'll be submerged, otherwise Lyons would have picked it up by now.' His mind switched like lightning. 'Tell Asdic to cease tracking.'

He removed his cap and pushed his fingers through his hair. *What is the matter with me?*

Or was it some kind of instinct, living so long with this danger that he could sense the submarine, lying there like a shark, waiting for any rescuer who was coming to the corvette's assistance? To make the score two instead of one.

'Tell Ayres to prepare a full pattern, Number One.' His voice was clipped and formal again. 'Squid too.' He added with sudden vehemence, 'I'm going to get that bastard!'

A signalman whispered to his yeoman, '*What* bastard, Yeo?'

'Christ if I know, my son.'

The gunnery speaker squeaked into life. 'No target, sir.'

Radar next. 'Range now eight thousand yards, sir.'

'*Ship*, sir! Starboard bow!'

The light was spreading through the thick clouds to light up the sea's face in small glittering patches. Howard steadied his elbows on the wet steel and moved his glasses very slowly across the bearing.

Treherne said hoarsely, 'Corvette! It's her all right!'

Howard held his glasses with care as he examined the tiny picture, which grew and faded as the clouds bellied above it.

Her bows were very low in the water, and it was a wonder the bulkheads had not collapsed altogether. There was no smoke, just a barely perceptible roll as she drifted through the troughs.

Treherne asked quietly, 'What d'you reckon now, sir?'

'They must have sighted us.' He could see it in his mind. The despair giving way to hope. Alone no more. And a ship they would know well coming to the rescue. Howard shook his head as if he were arguing with someone visible only to himself.

'Call her up, Yeoman. Make our number.'

Bizley said sulkily, 'They must be blind!' He was suddenly remembering the sharpness of Marrack's tongue.

The light clattered noisily while everyone on the bridge peered at the little ship's dark outline, afraid they might miss something.

The yeoman of signals licked his lips and said, 'At last!' He watched the slow blink of *Tacitus*'s lamp then exclaimed, '*Contact at three-three-zero!*' He swallowed hard and stared at Howard. 'Then, *God bless you!*'

Howard flung himself forward. 'Full ahead together! Starboard fifteen! Steer three-one-zero!' He glanced at Treherne as the bells rang like mad things. 'Start the attack! Get on to Asdic and tell him — ' The roar of the explosion was deafening, and as Howard jumped on to a grating to clear his vision he saw the cascades of water still falling like an unwilling curtain, the sea's dark face pockmarked with a thousand falling fragments.

'Asdic reports, no contact, sir.'

'Tell them to *keep searching!*' He felt the sea roaring past the hull, but all he could see was the widening whirlpool of oil and other flotsam. Marrack had known the U-Boat was there, and had tried to warn him, even though he had known the price. *God bless you.* It was like hearing his voice.

Gladiator made two extensive sweeps but there was no contact. The U-Boat commander might have used a stern-tube for the final shot; either way there was nothing. When they returned to the place where Marrack's command had gone down they found only two survivors. Marrack would have had all his people on deck, gathered well away from the submerged bow section. It was not war. It was cold-blooded murder. A broken ship, like a tethered goat waiting for the tiger.

At noon a huge, four-engined Liberator found them and carried on with the search. There was no result.

Howard climbed into his chair as his ship began to reduce speed. It was one thing to die; another entirely to make the gesture which Marrack had known was taking away his company's last chance of survival. But for it, *Gladiator* would be down there with them.

He began to shake very badly and found he was helpless to prevent it.

Treherne moved beside him as the doctor appeared on the bridge. '*Well?*' He saw Moffatt glance at the captain but shook his head angrily. 'Leave it, Doc!'

Moffatt stared out at the brightening sea. 'One survivor was a signalman. Just a kid.'

Treherne glanced at their own signalmen, shocked and still looking at each other like strangers. 'Aren't they all?' he said savagely.

Howard seemed to rise from his own despair. 'A signalman? Did he say anything?' He would have been there on Marrack's bridge. The bunting-tossers, as they were nicknamed, saw everything.

Moffatt replied, 'They were trying to get back to the convoy after seeing the damaged escort-carrier into safety. Then after the explosion the U-Boat surfaced and opened fire with her deck gun. The corvette lost her W/T, and was barely able to stay afloat. The Germans must have realised or detected the SOS . . . they just stood off and waited. There were a lot of injured men after the first torpedo. Now they're all gone.'

Howard asked, 'What else did he say?' He knew there was more.

Moffatt sighed. 'When he saw your signal the captain called out, "My old ship. I knew it would be her!"' He watched Howard as if uncertain whether or not to continue. 'Then he told the signalman to reply to you — the senior one was wounded. Then he said, "I've done for the lot of us." There might have been more, but the lad doesn't remember — he was in the sea being sucked down when he came to. Didn't even recall the explosion.'

Treherne remarked, 'It's often like that, Doc.' It was just something to say to break the tension.

Howard said, 'Course and speed to rejoin the group.' He twisted round in his chair and said, 'It's all right, Doc, I'm not ready for the men in white coats yet.' He strained his eyes, but there was nothing. Not even a wisp of smoke.

'Write this down, Yeoman, and pass it to W/T. *To Admiralty, repeated C-in-C Western Approaches. Tacitus sunk by second torpedo. No contact. Two survivors.* Get their names before you send it.'

Moffatt said dully, 'Just the one, Yeoman. The second man died.'

He heard Rooke speak into the voicepipe. 'Steer zero-nine-zero. Revolutions one-one-zero.'

Then Sweeney's thick voice. 'One-one-zero revs replied, sir.'

Howard watched the great curving wake as *Gladiator* came under command on her new course.

When he looked again Moffatt had gone. He said, 'Get the people fed, will you, Gordon. Go round the ship yourself. You know what to do.'

Treherne was about to leave but something made him return to the tall chair.

Howard stared at him, and there were real tears in his eyes as he said in a whisper, ' "*I've done for the lot of us.*" What a bloody way to be remembered, eh?'

Treherne touched his oilskin and said roughly, 'Well, you damned well saved all of *us* – and begging your pardon, sir, don't you ever bloody well forget it!'

Howard nodded very slowly. 'Thanks.' He studied him for several seconds, as if he were looking for something and, perhaps, finding it. Then he said, 'I'll speak to the lads over the tannoy presently.' He stared emptily at the ocean. 'But now I need to . . .'

'I know.' Treherne backed away. He had never spoken like that to any captain. He could not get over it. Like that other time – Howard had *known*. Most skippers would have gone charging to the rescue, eyes for nothing but the torpedoed ship. It might have been too late for all of them. To Bizley he said harshly, 'See that the Old Man's not disturbed, right?'

The lieutenant looked at him blandly. 'Something wrong, Number One?'

Treherne glanced at the oilskinned figure leaning against the side and dropped his voice. 'Just remember, *laddie*, but for him you'd have had your arse blown off just now.' He saw the sudden fear in Bizley's eyes. 'So shove that in your pipe and smoke it!'

Surgeon-Lieutenant Moffatt was seated comfortably in the wardroom that evening when Treherne entered, shaking water off his clothing like a great dog. 'I was thinking about our midshipman, Number One. He might beat this thing yet without being put ashore.' He looked up from an old magazine. 'What's wrong?'

'You can forget about Midshipman Ross, Doc.' He glared at the pantry hatch. 'Could I use a bloody drink just now? Trouble is, I don't think I'd stop, and it's still three days to the Liverpool Bar.' He saw down heavily. 'I've been all over the ship, Doc. He's not aboard.' He saw the shocked surprise on Moffatt's face. 'No point in going back to look for him. Anyway, we're ordered to rejoin the group at first light.'

'Have you told the Captain?'

'I'm about to.' He stared at the deckhead as if he could see the bridge from here. 'That's just about all he needs!'

'Why did he do it? Suicide?' Moffatt's mind was rushing through the medical books. 'Afraid of fighting it?'

The sea broke over the quarterdeck and sluiced away across the opposite side in a noisy torrent.

'Hear it, Doc? He lost the will to fight *that* anymore!' He slammed out of the wardroom and thought suddenly of Howard's words. What a bloody way to be remembered.

Next of kin have been informed.

6

Nine Days

David Howard turned up the collar of his greatcoat and walked uncertainly out of the small railway station. The train had been unheated, and it seemed to have taken him all day to travel the sixty-odd miles north from Liverpool.

It was already dark and utterly alien, with a tangy edge to the air which he guessed came from the big lake.

He had no sense of place or direction, which was hardly surprising, and every muscle and bone was making a separate protest. Now that he was here he was not at all sure he was doing the right thing; maybe she had suggested it because she was sorry for him and nothing more.

He thought of the meeting he had had with Captain Vickers on the group's return from sea; the stern gravity in his tone which was new to Howard.

'You can't take everything on yourself, David. It has an effect on you, naturally, but I simply can't afford a weak link in my chain of command. You are my best commanding officer, your record second to none, and I'll make no secret of the fact I've suggested you soon get a lift up the ladder, a brass-hat, even if the war ends before you can confirm it. The fact is, David, it *happens*. It might be any one of us next time – you of all people should know that!'

Howard's mind had strayed to the song he had heard a seaman murmuring to himself. *We're here today and gone tomorrow.*

He had answered, 'I'm all right, sir. I won't let you down.'

'I'm depending on it.'

Had Vickers really understood, or would he insist on a transfer, or worse a shore job? Another bomb-happy veteran to flash his gongs at green recruits.

Vickers had continued relentlessly, 'I was going to suggest a bit of leave and put another commanding officer in your place.' He had held up a big hand to stifle his protest, '*Temporarily.* I knew you wouldn't care too much for that idea, eh?'

'She's my ship, sir.' He had even been surprised by the desperation in his own voice. 'I'd not leave her like that.'

Vickers had nodded and relit his huge briar pipe. 'I understand. I was like that myself. Once. Fact is, *Kinsale* is due for boiler-clean and radar check, I've already discussed it with the chief of staff.' His eyes had burned through the pipe-smoke. 'Would you trust your own Captain (D) in your place for say, ten days?'

Even as he had said it, Howard had known that the suggestion had no alternative which would leave him in command.

'Besides which, it might do your people good to be senior ship for the time being.' So it was settled.

He had telephoned Celia from the yard and had been astonished when she had mentioned the cottage owned by her friend's cousin. Her voice had been almost breathless, and it had been a bad line anyway. She had left him little time to discuss it, so intent was she on explaining about food rations, the destination, and how to get there.

She had ended by saying, 'I do so want to see you. I nearly made myself sick, thinking about you. And don't worry about anything – just come to the cottage. I'll be there, waiting.'

He had wanted to protest, to remind her what people would think and say. She must have known his very thoughts. 'Look, David, I don't care about anyone else. I just want us to be together, away from all the . . .' He had heard her catch her breath, 'From all the waste.'

But that had been then. Maybe she was not so certain now.

Two shaded headlights came on from the car park and an ancient Wolseley rolled forward into the forecourt. A gangling figure in a loose raincoat climbed out and shook his hand.

'My name's Major, Tom Major. My cousin told me to brighten the place up a bit for you.' He heaved Howard's case and respirator into the boot and added, 'It's a mite cold for

October, but you'll be snug enough. I use the place, or did, for the summers up here.' He turned and looked at Howard in the dim glow of the headlamps. 'Welcome to Windermere.'

Howard wondered just how many other people knew. More nudges and winks. He settled in the seat and as an army car passed them he saw a sticker on the Wolseley's windscreen silhouetted in the headlights. *Doctor*. At best it explained where he got his petrol; at worst it sounded like some kind of plot, with Celia being used as the innocent instrument.

'Not far, bit off the beaten track. Where are you from – um, David?'

'Hampshire.'

The man grinned. 'Naval family. It would be.'

Howard watched the black trees skimming past. No place for the amateur driver.

'Been at sea lately?'

Howard tried to relax. His cousin had not told him much then.

He answered, 'Yes. Convoys mostly.' He didn't want to be drawn into conversation about it, but knew that the man was only trying to be friendly.

He said, 'So you're a doctor?'

'At the moment I'm *the* doctor! The others are either in the forces or helping out at the hospitals. This suits me. Doesn't give me too much time to think.' He pulled over and stopped suddenly, the engine thrumming quietly in the darkness. 'My brother was shot down over Germany, and now my young son can't wait to join up, as he puts it, *before the war's over*.' He turned and looked at him, but his face was hidden in shadow. 'Tell me something. Is it all worth it? *Are* we going to win?'

Howard tried to smile, but thought of the one survivor from Marrack's ship, the one Moffatt had described as just a kid. 'We have to.'

He wound down the window and felt the damp air on his face. Not the bitter touch of the North Atlantic with its tang of salt and fuel oil; a gentle, fresh breeze. No wonder the doctor loved the place. 'Otherwise all this is finished. It will never be the same again, but at least it will be *ours*.'

His companion jammed the car in gear and drove onto the

lane again; it was even narrower than the one in Hampshire where the bombs had come screaming down.

Eventually he said, 'If you need me, my number's by the phone. I gather you've both been through it.' He shook his head. 'I'm not prying, but I'm here if you want me.'

'Thanks. I'm sorry I've been a bit screwed-up.' He thought of Treherne on the bridge after Marrack's ship had vanished. *Don't you ever bloody well forget it!* He found time to wonder how he and Vickers would hit it off.

'Here it is. Watch out for the puddles. The lake's over there. You can see it in the daylight.'

They stood side by side looking at the cottage's square silhouette. There would be a moon soon, and Howard thought he saw smoke from the squat chimney stack.

Then the doctor held out his hand. 'I can't lend you the car, but there are some old bikes in the shed.'

Howard watched him drive away, then turned and walked slowly towards the front door.

It opened wide even before he reached it and she was in his arms, her hair pressed against his cheek while she hugged him. Then she took his hand and helped him in with his case.

She had a great log fire roaring in the hearth, and the place had been made to look lived-in, pleased with itself, as the shadows danced and flickered around the room.

Howard slipped out of his greatcoat and tossed his cap on to a chair.

'Let me look at you.' She was dressed in a white, roll-necked sweater and a pair of sailor's bell-bottoms. He held her again and then they kissed for the first time. 'I never thought it could happen. I shall probably find it's all a dream.'

She pinched his arm gently and said, 'See? I'm real!'

Her eyes were very bright, her cheeks flushed, and not merely from the fire. He noticed too that she was wearing her wedding ring. She saw his glance and removed it – like a guilty child, he thought. But there was nothing childish in her voice as she looked at him and said, 'I borrowed this one. It's not his. It's just that I've done a bit of shopping, and some of the people round here are – well, you know . . .' She held him again, but would not look at him. 'We are alone here. This is our place for . . .'

'Nine whole days.' He tried not to think of *Gladiator* leaving harbour without him. Vickers on his chair; the old destroyer hand. Probably he'd be loving every minute, he thought; Vickers made no secret of the fact he regarded the more modern destroyers as a collection of gimmicks.

She led him to the table; even that she had decorated with some sort of autumnal fern. 'Wine on ice – champagne, in fact ...' She saw his disbelief. 'There is *some* use in being an admiral's daughter!'

They embraced again, uncertainly, as if they did not know what was happening.

She said softly, 'You can have a bath – it's all a bit Heath Robinson, but it works – then get out of uniform, and I'll give you a meal to remember.' She held him at arms' length, smiling at him; her heart was almost breaking at his expression. It was something like gratitude. Then she said, 'Stop worrying about me for once, and think of yourself. I said I was bad luck for you, that I'd never go through all that again ... I'm still not sure if I'll be able – '

He touched her mouth. 'Don't, Celia. I love you. I *want* you, all for myself – no matter what.' She tried to release his grip but he said, 'Just be with me.'

'I must put a log on the fire.' As she stooped down, her hair falling over her forehead, she said quietly, 'You see, David, it came to me quite suddenly, that day when everything was so terrible for you and we were so far apart. I *want* you to love me. I don't think it's wicked or pointless because of the war – it's something I must have known since that day when I made you talk about Jamie, with never a thought for what you had just been through.'

He knelt behind her and put his arms around her waist while they both stared into the blaze.

'I don't know what I'd have done if you hadn't come.'

He caressed her and felt her muscles tense. 'I'd never hurt you.'

She stood up and watched him as he took off his jacket and tossed it on to another chair.

She said, 'You're not very tidy, *Commander*.'

Their eyes met, and each knew there was no going back, even if they had wanted to.

She left the door ajar and walked across the adjoining room, her bare feet noiseless on the scattered rugs. Through a window she could see the stark outlines of trees, the bright moonlight making the sky almost white by comparison.

She moved slowly past the table where they had eaten and talked, each trying to find the other. The champagne bottle stood upended in its bucket, the doctor's ice long turned to tepid water. They had left more than they had eaten; nervousness and the need of one another had seen to that. She stood quite still in front of the great fireplace and held out her arms to the fallen embers which had so recently been a roaring mass of flames.

She had been nursing him against her body, calming him, after he had cried out. She had felt the pang of jealousy, until she had remembered that the name he had uttered, Ross, had been that of the missing midshipman and not some other girl's.

Was that what had really become of Jamie? The war already become too much and he had wanted to end it, in the only way he knew. She was surprised that she could think of it now, without guilt any more, without anything more than curiosity.

Jamie had often spoken of his previous squadron commander, an ace, and all that went with it. He had been nicknamed Dicer because of the chances he took, and over the years of fighting he had shot down what must have amounted to a whole enemy squadron. Then, one day, flying alone in his beloved Spit, he had been attacked by a solitary Messerschmitt, and had crashed on a nearby beach. When the salvage team had arrived to clear the wreckage, they had discovered the firing button still at safe, the guns fully loaded. Was that how it happened? Too much flying, sated with all the individual killing. Like Dicer, perhaps Jamie had ended it in the way he had always expected to die, in close combat, but his death arranged by himself.

Without thought she took a shawl from the sofa and walked to the window and looked out at the arctic landscape. She could even see the same moonlight glittering on the lake through the trees.

She shivered as a vixen gave her shrill bark amongst the undergrowth, and pulled the shawl closer over her shoulders.

Then, trying to keep her mind clear, she thought of what had happened to her. Jamie had always been eager, even violent, needing to conquer rather than seduce her. She thought suddenly of her dead friend Jane, who had said more than once that the climax was the true delight of making love. The complete giving of one to the other. No wonder Daddy had thought of her as flighty.

Celia had never experienced it. Not even tonight when he had held her and touched her, and then entered her. David had been gentle and caring, as she had known he would be, but there had been some pain, and she had clenched her fists over his shoulders so that he should not know, or blame himself. It had been such a long while since . . .

She touched her breasts through her nightdress, as he had done, her thighs and the smooth skin where she had sensed him preparing her for that dreamed-of and feared moment when she would feel him come into her. He had fallen asleep almost immediately, and for hours she had held him, soothing his nightmares, praying that he would have no regrets when he remembered.

She found she was still shivering, and yet her limbs felt no chill. It was like hearing a voice, feeling hands gripping her arms.

She walked to the table and groped in the shadows for the brandy she had left untouched.

Like the time in the restaurant when she had secretly wished that the old waiter *had* offered the room; that they had taken it no matter what people had thought, or if her parents had got to know about it.

The brandy was like fire on her tongue. She tossed the shawl aside and the invisible hands propelled her forward again.

The room was full of moonlight, and on the opposite side of the bed she saw herself reflected in the old-fashioned wardrobe's mirror where their discarded uniforms hung together like interlopers.

She heard him stir, his breathing quicken, but she kept her eyes on her reflection as with slow deliberation she pulled up her nightdress, over her head, before throwing it towards a chair.

In the cold light her naked body, her fine uplifted breasts seemed to shine like sculptured marble. She said, 'You're my man, David.' She knelt on the heavy feather-bedded mattress and took his hand in hers. 'And I will be yours for as long as you want.' His face was in shadow but she could sense his desire for her as she pulled his hand to where he had touched her, roused her, entered her. Then she had been passive and frightened. Now she knew her passion for him had over-ridden everything.

They lay in each other's arms, her leg thrown across his body, prolonging it with their caresses and kisses. Quite suddenly she exclaimed, 'Take me, David. All you know, all you've wanted to do . . .' The rest was lost as he turned her carefully on to her back.

Outside, the vixen's cry went unheard.

A million miles away from that isolated cottage, Lieutenant Lionel Bizley pushed past two naval ratings and closed the telephone booth behind him.

Gladiator was getting under way in less than an hour, and if the formidable Captain (D) discovered what he was doing things would get nasty. But there had been talk of leave, two weeks at least, after this next operation, whatever it was. He had to let Sarah Milvain know about it. With luck he might be able to stay at their Mayfair house, provided her mother, who sounded a bit of a battleaxe, would allow it.

A house in Mayfair. In Bizley's suburban mind it was something between high society and Hollywood.

He had already revamped his own background, to make it suitable for Sarah's parents, especially the general if he happened to be there. He would describe his father as being in banking, maybe in the City. People were always impressed by finance. It was a joke when you thought about it. The dingy little high street bank in Horsham, where his father had been for most of his life. And his mother, who was undoubtedly proud of her son's becoming 'a real officer', as she had put it, more so since his DSC – she would be amazed when he told them where he had been and stayed, and about the girl he had met.

Through the glass he saw *Gladiator*'s chief quartermaster walking slowly back towards Gladstone Dock, an empty mail sack over one arm. It gave Bizley a sense of nervous urgency and he cursed impatiently as the telephone rattled and clicked in his grasp. 'Come on, *damn you!*'

Then he heard her voice. It was a relief to find it was not her mother, with so little time left to talk.

'It's me! Lionel!' He glanced at the queue outside the booth. 'Don't say anything, Sarah, we might get cut off.'

She sounded faraway, surprised. 'I hoped you would call.'

Bizley studied himself in the little mirror below the printed notice which said WHAT TO DO IN AN AIR RAID. Some wag had scrawled, *Try not to shit yourself!*

'Fact is, I may get some leave shortly. I was wondering . . .' She must have moved away to close a door somewhere. He flushed at the thought of their privacy.

'Sorry, Lionel, I'm back.' She cleared her throat. 'Leave, you say? That will be nice for you.'

It was not quite what he had expected. *Nice.* How his mother would have described it.

'Is something wrong? Are you all right?'

She said, 'I was listening for Mother. She's a bit upset.'

'I'm sorry. Give her my love. Tell her I'm still in one piece. I'm *longing* to meet her.'

'There was a man here to see her.' His lie seemed to have gone unnoticed.

'Man? What man?'

Somebody unseen rapped on the glass with some pennies but Bizley glared out, shaking his head.

He repeated the question and she replied, 'She won't say, but he was an official of some kind. I let him in. He was from the Admiralty. Mother got very upset. He apparently asked her a lot of questions about Greg – his death, things like that.' There was a sob in her voice. 'Why can't they leave things alone? He even mentioned poor Andy.'

Somewhere an air raid warning wailed dismally. It was strange to think it was all that way away, in London.

Bizley stared at the mirror at his own eyes, which were suddenly wide with shocked disbelief.

'Maybe he was just doing it for the records, you know.' But his mind seemed to scream at him. *They suspect something!* All this time, and somebody had probed what had happened.

He said, 'I'll ring again. Must go. Take care . . .'

'But it *is* all right, isn't it, Lionel? They're not keeping something secret from us – *you* would know, surely?' She was still speaking when he carefully replaced the telephone and pushed out into the shadows.

There was nothing to worry about. They had quite rightly accepted his report. And the two other survivors would know better than to interfere.

By the time he reached *Gladiator*'s brow he was sweating badly, as if he had been running all the way.

The duty quartermaster and gangway sentry were lounging by the lobby desk, and Bizley shouted, '*Stand up!* Smarten yourselves, or I'll have you in front of the first lieutenant!' But even that gave him no satisfaction.

The quartermaster adjusted his cap and muttered, 'I'd been 'opin' he might drop dead, Bill.'

The sentry grinned. 'Probably caught the boat up. I'm real sorry for the prostitute!' They both laughed.

In his small cabin Bizley knelt down and took a bottle of vodka from his locker. He had been given it on the North Russian run. He disliked it, but had been told it did not lie on your breath. He tossed some water out of his tooth-glass and poured until it was half-full.

It seemed to work.

Don't be such a bloody fool. Nobody knows. He touched the blue and white ribbon on his jacket and took another swallow. *Just keep your nerve.*

Over the tannoy the voice called, 'Special sea dutymen to your stations! All the port watch! First part forrard, second part aft, stand by for leaving harbour!'

Bizley stood up. That was more like it. Routine and duty. He would show them all!

David Howard lay on his back and stared at the ceiling. There was a smell of woodsmoke, mingled with another, of bacon. He had slept well, a night devoid of pressure and guilt, and he had awakened with her in his arms, wrapped around each other, and at peace. They made love with fierceness and sometimes in slow harmony, neither willing to think of the hours or the days. There was just four more left.

The door opened and she stood there looking at him. She was wearing his pyjama jacket and nothing more, not even slippers while she had been preparing breakfast, or perhaps it was lunch.

'We'll have another lovely walk today.' She moved to the bed and watched him with a tenderness she had never known. 'But first we eat. It's egg day today, a ration not to be missed!'

He rolled over and held her, then slipped his hand beneath the pyjama jacket and stroked her buttocks. 'You are quite shameless.' He pulled her down on to the bed. 'And I love you.'

She watched his eyes as he unbuttoned the jacket and touched her, his hand moving as if independent of its owner to explore and arouse her again. He had confided a lot about his war, and the more he had talked while they had sat by the fire each evening after their walks, their simple adventures, the calmer he had become. She had tried not to think of their eventual parting. In a matter of weeks it would be Christmas; the Atlantic at its worst. *This* would have to last.

She said, 'If you keep touching me there I shall forget about the eggs!'

He had not even blurted out his doubts again. The way he had blamed himself for not understanding what the midshipman might do, how he should perhaps have reacted differently to his friend Marrack's ordeal. Once in the night he had sat up staring at her, but she had known he was asleep. 'He just sat there waiting to die, and it was all because of me!' In the morning he had not remembered it, nor had he mentioned it since.

She felt his fingers move down across her stomach and gave up the battle. Afterwards they lay together and watched the cold sunlight lance across the room.

She said, 'I can still feel you, David. So deep. So much love.'

He raised himself on one elbow. 'We don't talk about it, Celia, but it's still there.' He touched her hair, and saw her watching him. 'I'd like to know – do you think you might change your mind?'

She stared at him, her eyes very green in the smoky sunshine. 'About us?'

He held her hand tightly in his. 'Would you marry me?'

'Hold me.' She buried her face on his shoulder. 'Is it wrong to want someone so much? To put *us* first, instead of the bloody war?'

He stroked her bare back. He had never heard her swear before. 'That's settled then.'

They both stiffened as the telephone shattered the peace and the stillness like an alarm bell.

She walked naked to the table and lifted the telephone to her ear, watching his face the whole time.

She said, 'I thought you might. Yes, I'll tell him. Bless you.'

She replaced the receiver and picked up the pyjama jacket.

'Who was that?' Just for an instant he had felt the same old dread.

'It was Mummy.' She regarded him gravely. 'We always tell each other where we are. You never know, these days.'

'You *told* her?' He reached out as she brushed against the bed. 'About us?'

She smiled down at him. 'I think she's always known.' She stepped back out of reach. 'Eggs first.' She wiped her eyes with the pyjama sleeve. 'No walk today. Let's keep this world to ourselves.'

7

Turning the Corner

Despite the powerful fans at either end of the huge U-Boat pens, the damp air was acrid with diesel as one of a pair of boats made ready to depart stern-first.

On the bridge of his own boat Kleiber watched with professional interest as more smoke puffed over the pier-like jetty which separated them, and forced several of the line-handling party into a fit of coughing. He knew the other boat's commanding officer, and they had been together for most of the war. It went no further than that. Korvettenkapitän Otto Schneider was the propaganda department's dream; either that, or he had some very good friends there. His rugged grin had appeared many times on newsreels and in the daily press. Usually seen with someone senior and important, either from the naval staff or a well-known party member. His conning-tower was covered with the record of his kills and the boat's insignia, a grinning shark in a horned helmet.

In Kleiber's view he was a boaster, a man who would snap at the most insignificant targets merely to add to his score. There was envy of course; Kleiber could accept that too. Schneider had bagged some important targets as well as the little fish, and was probably the most decorated U-Boat captain who was still alive.

Before leaving this French base today, for instance, he had been bragging about a British corvette named *Tacitus* which he had put down some time ago; of how he had cruised around and waited for a second kill, the destroyer which had been despatched to search for her. He had known of Kleiber's interest in the British destroyer *Gladiator*; nearly all the veterans here did. Schneider had banged him on the back, laughing, as he had described the change of luck, when survivors on the stopped and torpedoed corvette had sent out a warning in time for the destroyer to start her attack. So the *Tacitus* had been sunk, and Kleiber could see the fresh little painting below all the rest to mark her destruction.

Schneider was waving to him now, as his submarine began to move slowly astern towards the harbour. Kleiber tossed a curt salute. Schneider was, after all, his superior.

How different it had been this time, he thought. Not even the staff officers had been able to reassure him that another supply-submarine would be on its proper station when he needed to restock and refuel. There had been some news from home, but the letters had shown a different address. The house had been evacuated after a tremendous air raid which had knocked down most of the streets he had known as a boy. His parents were all right, but his father's news was brief and uninformative where his work was concerned, as if he were now afraid that some official might open and read it.

There was no further contact with Willi, and the next winter had already come to the Russian front. How could he manage – survive?

A voicepipe chattered and was answered instantly by a petty officer.

Kleiber spoke to the control room and watched his men on the forecasing deck singling up the wires even as the great diesels coughed into life.

There had been another serious reverse last month, news of which had only recently been released to the public. The mighty battleship *Tirpitz*, the most powerful in the world, had been seriously crippled by a midget submarine attack in her Norwegian fjord. Nobody knew or would say how long it might take to repair this great ship, or how serious the damage was. But apart from the famous and successful battle-cruiser *Scharnhorst*, she was the last of their major warships still operational. It might mean that the enemy convoys to Russia would be able to increase without fear of attack by *Tirpitz*. Again, he thought of his young brother. Ivan would be strengthened by all this foreign aid and weapons; things might even deteriorate again on that terrible front, despite the sacrifices of the Wehrmacht.

The U-Boat service was the most dangerous in the whole Navy, but at least it was commanded by Admiral Donitz, who really knew and understood the men he directed and inspired. A successful submariner himself in the Great War, he was always ready to listen to his commanding officers on their return from patrols.

The battle over the Atlantic *had* to be won, and both sides were well aware of this. Survival, determination and courage rated as highly as new weapons and better equipment.

That had been another difference on his return to base. Some of the machine parts and replacements were from Kiel and other yards, spares taken from battered hulls too badly damaged to be repaired.

Kleiber stamped his fleece-lined boots and considered what lay ahead. It was October, and outside this massively constructed bunker it was said to be snowing. They would have to be extra careful when cruising on the surface in Biscay. A radar-carrying aircraft could detect them even through snow, when they would be badly hampered by it.

He thought again of Schneider's jibe about the *Gladiator*, and wondered what sort of man commanded her. But she had probably had several; it was well known that the British had been so unprepared for war that commands had been handed out to anyone with even basic experience. It would be interesting to know, all the same. At the same time he was angry with himself for even considering it. War was not a game, not something for individual contests as Schneider seemed to think. It was for a perfectly co-ordinated machine, with one mind and one aim to control it.

There was something else which troubled him. This time he had not made the long journey to see his parents. Instead he had shared any such freedom with Ingrid. She was not German but Austrian, a nursing orderly in the naval hospital at nearby Lorient. He had first met her when visiting a wounded brother-officer there. She was dark, and when he had first seen her, her skin had been brown from the summer sunshine. Her hair was jet-black; she had told him her mother was Belgian. At first, whenever they had accidentally met, Kleiber had been attracted to her although he had told himself it was totally wrong, as well as irrational, to become involved. He had seen what it had done to others: a wife in Germany, a mistress in France or any one of the many countries where the swastika flew in conquest.

She, on the other hand, had seemed nervous of him, as if he had carried some scent of danger. But this time it had changed, and they had become intimate. It still unsettled him. He was out of his depth with her passion, her wanton abandon when they had intercourse. It was not love; so what might it be, and could it ever distract him from his demanding profession? If Schneider knew about that, the whole base would soon be made aware of it.

The conning-tower was vibrating less jerkily now as the engines settled down, and the reports of readiness in all sections were just being completed. If it were not snowing Ingrid might have been watching. You could see the Bay from the hospital. What did it matter? There would be another in her bed once he was gone. But it *did* matter, and it troubled him. Small hips and large inviting breasts, and a darting tongue which had at first embarrassed him and then goaded him to a madness he had not known before.

Bells clanged, and the last line was lifted from a bollard and hauled across to the casing to be stowed away until . . . When would that be? Very smoothly, the submarine began to thrust astern, the diesel fumes drifting over the bridge where the red ensign with its black cross and swastika hung limply against its staff. *When would that be?*

At the end of the last pier, his commanding officer stood gravely watching the dark, shining hull sliding out towards the thickening snow. Kleiber threw up another salute and guessed that the man was probably contemplating the empty berths, and wondering if they would ever be occupied again.

They followed a little launch with a shaded light until Kleiber was satisfied. A check with the control room; a last look around, although it was already quite dark, with the snow falling across the glistening hull like an impenetrable curtain.

Once out in open water it would be miserable for the watchkeepers under these conditions. But they would be changed regularly and could not complain. Kleiber felt something of his old confidence. For their captain would be here all the time until the first test-dive.

He and Schneider would remain in company in case of air attack while they were surfaced. Their combined firepower might be able to deal with the slower, heavier air patrols, although he preferred vigilance to a senseless duel which could soon be ended when reinforcements arrived.

The men stooping and crouching on the foredeck, struggling with the wires and fenders, glanced into the snow as the guide-boat gave a cheerful toot on its whistle.

They stared at its fading shadow with something like contempt. How much did a whistle cost, compared with what they were going to do over the next weeks?

Kleiber wiped his powerful Zeiss glasses and hung them carefully beneath his coat. Men moved past and vanished into the comparative warmth of the hull, and soon he felt the deck lift lazily to the first challenge of the Atlantic.

A petty officer hauled down the sodden ensign and folded it away, his eyes searching for the land. But there was only snow.

He had seen a choir of school children practising their carols for Christmas. They had fallen silent when they had seen him stop to listen.

He glanced at the captain's back. They would not return in time for Christmas; perhaps they would never return. He thought of one little French girl in that choir. About the same age as his own daughter, whom he had not seen for a year. She had looked straight into his eyes. He had never seen such hatred in anyone, in all his life.

Howard thrust his head and shoulders underneath the water-proof hood and switched on the light. He could feel the sleety rain hammering his oilskin and legs while he peered at the chart and compared Rooke's calculations with the latest information from the Admiralty.

He stood away from the table and felt the rain return to the attack. The snow had been bad enough, like driving blind through a fog. But at least he had been able to stay dry.

He pictured their companions, *Blackwall* to port and *Belleisle* to starboard, keeping in company as much by guesswork as by radar.

Treherne was waiting for him.

Howard gripped a stanchion as the bridge dipped over steeply and another big roller cruised against the hull.

He said, 'Convoy's all right apparently. No further attacks anyway. But one of the big tankers hit earlier is in trouble — even so, Captain Vickers and his section might be able to cope. He's with the air support group. *Seeker* will be able to provide air cover as soon as the weather improves.' He could see it all. The big convoy of thirty heavily loaded merchantmen, but, unlike the early days, with an impressive US and Canadian escort, now within five hundred miles of the Irish coast. They had lost two ships, and the tanker, one of the largest in the Atlantic, had somehow survived a torpedo without either blowing up or sinking. The convoy could not hang about for one ship, no matter how valuable. This was where the independent escort-attack groups could prove their worth. Vickers was out there somewhere, and the tough little escort-carrier might make all the difference. Howard added, 'They've sent the ocean salvage tug *Tiberius* from Plymouth. That great lump could bash through a hurricane if need be!'

He thought of Vickers's obvious pleasure when he had returned from his leave. 'You've done wonders with this ship, David! God, I'm almost sorry to be going back to *Kinsale*!'

They had sailed from Liverpool as a group almost immediately. Intelligence had warned of a buildup of U-Boats which were expected to go for the convoy like terriers. To lose only two ships from it was nothing less than a miracle. If they could still save the tanker it might give the enemy something to brood over.

There was another escort group to the north of the convoy, and a cruiser squadron on stand-by. The slackening of naval action in the Mediterranean had released more warships than anyone had believed possible.

'Take over, Number One. I'm going down for a dry towel.'

Treherne watched him leave. Was it the same man who had nearly broken down on this very bridge? It was as if he had been taken over by something even more powerful than fear and despair.

He heard Rooke passing his instructions to the wheelhouse, his body shining in the steady downpour. November already. Another year. He pictured their position, three destroyers, all veterans, some two hundred miles south-west of Land's End, and about the same westwards from Ushant. The enemy. Well within range of German aircraft, and yet it no longer felt so critical. The arrival of the little escort-carriers had changed everything. They were nicknamed Woolworths Carriers, or 'banana boats' by the lads — although here on the bridge they had refrained from the latter, he had noticed, for his benefit.

He thought of Joyce when he had told her about the solicitor's confidence that his first marriage could be proved null and void. Apparently desertion for whatever reason still counted for a lot.

She had been overwhelmed. '*Marriage*, you mean, Gordon?' Her eyes had shone with tears of happiness. So perhaps she had inwardly doubted his final intentions. 'I'll see you never regret it!' It had been a wild two days in her little flat.

He had been doubly glad to see Howard back in his chair. He had half-dreaded that he might be grounded for medical reasons; many commanding officers had gone under with less cause. The other reason for his relief had been the departure of Captain Vickers. It had been rather like having God on the bridge, and even for such a short time he had made his considerable presence felt. Treherne was not used to close contact with a senior, four-ringed captain, and had known that Finlay and some of the others had been amused at his efforts not to show it.

He peered at his watch. 'Midnight soon, Pilot. Have you sent a bosun's mate to rouse the starboard watch?'

Rooke said, 'Five minutes ago, Number One.' Even he seemed more at ease with Howard back in the saddle.

'Good.' He pictured Howard with his girl. What had they done? Where had they been, he wondered? He tried to think of them behaving like Joyce and himself, but was not so certain about that.

Rooke lurched across the bridge as the sea boomed against the side and flung a towering mass of water along the iron deck so that the superstructure seemed to shake from the weight of it.

'Think we'll be in for Christmas, Number One?'

'That would be nice.' He thought of Joyce, who would get all embarrassed when he suggested she came to a wardroom party. 'It would be my first in this bloody war, if so!'

A signalman groped towards them. 'From W/T, sir. *Two U-Boats destroyed by convoy's close escort.*'

The officers stared at each other in the drenching darkness. 'By God, Pilot, that evens the score a bit, eh?'

Howard had not mentioned Marrack again; nor would he. In most escort vessels and other small ships on active service it was the same. Gone but not forgotten. Anyone new and green who broke the rule would be met with chilling stares. He thought too of Midshipman Ross. How could he have done it? Just step off the ship into the darkness, to break surface in time to see *Gladiator*'s wake and nothing more. With luck he might have thrown himself over the side if he had to do it. The great screws would suck him into their embrace with only a split-second of agony.

Ross had not been replaced as yet. It was to be hoped that the next one had a better deal.

He heard Bizley's affected drawl on the ladder and steeled himself. He was definitely going round the bend, Treherne thought. Always asking questions about naval procedures, the various departments at the Admiralty, until the Chief had asked wryly, 'Are you thinking of asking for a shore job, then? Be an *admiral* next, see?'

The bridge messenger called above the noise of sea and rain, 'W/T, sir!'

Treherne moved to the voicepipe, his old sea-boots slithering the last few feet.

'First Lieutenant!'

It was the petty officer telegraphist himself, even at this hour. He had complained about stomach pains to Moffatt. Ulcers probably. Anyway they might lose him when they got back. It was a pity. He was the best.

Hyslop spoke distinctly up the voicepipe. 'From Admiralty, sir. *There are two U-Boats to the north of your position. Reported by RAF Coastal Command. Said to be heading north-west. Ends.*'

Treherne muttered, 'Thanks, it's enough as far as I'm concerned.' He looked at Rooke. 'Prepare the plot, old son. Two subs, hundred miles to the north. God knows where they are now. Too late for the convoy, I'd have thought.'

Reluctantly he picked up the solitary telephone by the bridge chair. 'Captain, sir?'

Howard stepped into the chart-room and watched Rooke busy with his dividers and parallel rulers.

He had been massaging his face and throat with a clean dry towel, thinking of the girl, *his* girl now, of their last embraces before they had parted, looking back at the doctor's holiday cottage as if they were leaving part of themselves behind. They had barely spoken when the doctor had called to drive them to the station. Wrapped in their individual thoughts, their hearts and bodies too aware of one another for words.

Howard had last seen her at the headquarters complex when he had attended a brief conference held for the various escort groups being deployed for the big eastbound convoy.

She had been standing by a noisy teleprinter which was churning out paper as if it would never stop. She had formed his name with her lips, and the three words, *I love you*, before they had been sent packing to their various commands.

If only he could have held her just once more. Felt her body against his, her hair brushing his mouth. In the same breath he knew it would have made their parting far worse.

'Two U-Boats, then.' He lit his pipe and marvelled it was such a luxury after the pitching, open bridge.

Rooke said warily, 'About here, sir.'

'I don't see why the RAF didn't give them a pasting, sir.' Treherne tried not to stare at Howard's relaxed grip on his pipe. Even his eyes seemed more interested than anxious as he studied the pencilled lines and bearings.

Howard said, 'Look at the time of origin, Number One. Not too much light when the Coastal Command people made the sighting. The Germans may or may not have seen the plane. It doesn't help us much.' He made up his mind. 'Give me those dividers, Pilot.' He felt them watching as he leaned over the table, gauging his own movements against the sickening lurch of the sealed chart-room.

'The Germans knew all about the convoy. It is an important one. A bit of face-saving will be called for.' He tossed down the dividers. 'Their high command is almost interchangeable with the Admiralty, you know.' He smiled briefly. 'Find that signal about the salvage tug, will you?'

Rooke hurried away and Treherne said, 'After the *Tiberius*?'

Howard looked at his disbelief. 'Why not? Without the tug, the tanker will be forced to remain at the mercy of the sea and the enemy. You can't expect either the convoy commodore or the escort-carrier to hang about forever.'

Rooke returned and handed him the pad. Howard nodded, his eyes suddenly very bright.

'It must be that. These two beauties might well have a crack at the tanker themselves. A couple of days. Right up their street.' He picked up the dividers and waited for the deck to surge upright again. 'Lay off a course to intercept. To make good three-five-zero. I'll have a word with our two chums and put them in the picture.' He faced Treherne as Rooke hurried for the bridge ladder. 'It would be nice if we could stalk *them* for a change!'

Treherne swallowed hard. 'Very.' Could ten days really do that for anyone?

Howard heard somebody coughing in the wheelhouse but then it changed into a loud sneeze. For just a few seconds he had thought of Midshipman Ross. If only there had been more time to know him – to help him, perhaps. He listened to the boom of the sea and the great sluice of it alongside, and pictured him falling, his scream lost in the ocean's triumph. Out here, there was never enough time.

Howard said, 'I'll go up. Then, when I've spoken to *Blackwall* and *Belleisle*, I think I might have a catnap in the hutch. See that I'm called when the morning watch is closed up. It seems pretty quiet in this neck of the woods.' He hesitated before sliding the door open, remembering the time when he had turned on Rooke, and had been forced to crouch outside this same place while he fought his own destruction.

He said, 'So they bagged two more U-Boats, eh?' His eyes were almost boyish. Almost. 'Well, we'll make it three, Number One – at least!'

Treherne said, 'I did hear a buzz that you're getting a leg up, sir. If so, congratulations. There's nobody better. Will it mean leaving *Gladiator*?'

Howard sat on a locker and watched his sea-boot swinging to the savage motion.

'No secrets, eh? I thought it was just a suggestion!' He became serious at the sight of Treherne's anxiety. 'Leave this ship? Not now, not after all that we've done together. A brass-hat ... Well, we shall have to see.' He touched the damp grey steel of the side. 'Leave you, old girl? To hell with that!'

The door closed and Treherne smiled to himself. Then he looked at the gyro-repeater as it ticked lazily back and forth and with a curse snatched up the bridge handset.

He heard Bizley's voice. 'Officer-of-the-Watch?'

'What the *bloody hell's* the matter with you, man?' He heard him snort. 'Check the helm — we're wandering about the ocean like a whore at a wedding! The Old Man's on his way up, so *jump about*, laddie!'

He waited for his anger to disperse and grinned.

He would have to watch Mister high-and-mighty Bizley. Something must have happened recently to make him so careless. Well, he could take a long walk on a short pier any time he liked; but when everybody else's arse was in danger it was no longer a joke.

Treherne looked at the chart. Two submarines — going for a kill, then on to another more valuable one. He heard the muffled clang of bells and the instant response from the engine room. By daylight *Gladiator* and her consorts would be close enough to the course taken by the big salvage tug.

He leaned on the chart and compressed the estimated positions between his large hands.

He thought of Howard's assessment, of his complete self-control. His beard parted in a smile. 'Here we go, then. Tally-bloody-ho!'

Howard swallowed the last of his scalding coffee and relished it as the heat roused his body. It was five-fifteen in the morning, but apart from an occasional greyness to starboard there was little hint of a new day. He handed the mug to a messenger and tried to settle himself more comfortably in his tall chair. He could feel the hard pressure of metal on his ribs through the layers of protective clothing, first one side, then the other as *Gladiator* plunged over serried lines of sharp rollers. It was raining, but impossible to distinguish it from spray flung back from the stem; it all tasted of salt.

The ship had been at action stations for half an hour after the latest signal from the Admiralty. Another aircraft of Coastal Command had reported seeing two tiny plumes of smoke when there had been a brief moment of good visibility. It was just luck; in such a vast area it might easily have gone unseen. It could only mean that the two U-Boats were still heading on the same course as before and were being forced to charge their batteries while still submerged. With growing air cover and the use of small escort-carriers, the enemy submarines were finding it less and less easy to surface and run on their diesels while charging batteries. Most of the submarines had been fitted with a breathing pipe which stood vertical with the periscopes when in use. The *schnorchel*, as it was called, had to be used with skill and great care. If the boat 'porpoised' with it raised, it would automatically close itself against an inrush of water. Unless the electric motors were brought into play instantly the interior of the hull would become a vacuum, the air sucked into the diesels to leave the crewmen gasping out their lives while the boat plunged to the bottom.

There had been reports of several of the big supply-submarines being caught on the surface with their hatches open while they prepared to service an operational U-Boat. Maybe these two U-Boats had been charging batteries while they still had a chance, in case their own rendezvous had been made useless.

As Treherne had remarked, 'It made a nice change!'

The Coastal Command aircraft had been at the end of its patrol, and had already dropped most of its depth-charges to help out a small westbound convoy. Aiming for the nearest little plume of smoke it had dived and released the last two charges. When the pilot had completed a turn around the area both U-Boats had dived, and there had been no sign of oil or wreckage. It must have given them a bloody headache all the same, Howard thought.

More air support had been promised when visibility improved, and the escort-carrier *Seeker* might be near enough to scramble her own Swordfish torpedo bombers.

The Admiralty had also advised that the ocean-going salvage tug was still on course. They had said little else in case the signal was intercepted and the code broken again.

Howard raised his glasses to peer abeam for *Blackwall*, but could see nothing but an occasional welter of heavy spray as her bows crashed down into the sea.

Treherne waited beside his chair, mopping his face and cursing the rain.

'They may split up when they realise we're on to them, sir.'

'Could be. *Belleisle* will remain on standby just in case that happens.'

Treherne fell silent again, seeing the ship as he had when the hands had gone to action stations. Main armament already angled out to cover both sides, the short-range weapons stripped and ready, spare magazines and trailing belts of heavy-calibre bullets prepared and unrestricted. Ayres was in charge of the depth-charges; Howard had decided it would give him more experience, while Bizley was right here on the bridge, still sulking from the bottle he had rightly given him.

He thought of the engine room and boiler room staff, being tossed about in the din of roaring fans and thrashing screws. One false step and a stoker could end up as a part of the machinery. And in the centre of his noisy, glistening world, Taff Price would be watching everything and everybody. Down there, *he* was captain and engineer all rolled into one.

'Call up the others, Number One. *Time to begin. Reduce to half-speed as arranged. Commence the sweep.* Pilot, warn Asdic and radar.' He held the luminous dial of his watch just an inch from his eyes before more spray dashed over him. 'Pass the word to the wheelhouse!'

He heard Bizley snapping his orders down the voicepipe and felt the heavy throb of engines drop slightly, although in the bruising motion it was hard to see much difference.

He watched his radar-repeater and saw the two blips of the other destroyers start to angle out slightly, so that the final formation became like the prongs of a giant trident.

If only the weather would clear, or the sullen clouds would allow some daylight to show the way.

Howard thought suddenly of the girl in that big operations room, watching, checking; a part of their team.

'Asdic – Bridge?'

Howard snatched up the handset. 'Captain!'

'Contact, sir – echo bears zero-two-zero, moving right.'

Howard stared at Treherne. 'One of the bastards is doubling

back. Maybe he's twigged us. Go and check the Asdic team. This has got to be just right!' Over his shoulder he called, 'Signal the contact to *Belleisle*. Repeat to *Blackwall*, but she needs to stay where she is in case the other bugger shows up!' He bent over the voicepipe. 'Starboard ten!' He watched the gyro-repeater begin to tick round as the wheel went over, boots slipping and men clutching for handholds everywhere in the ship. 'Midships – *Steady*!'

'Steady, sir! Zero-one-zero.'

Howard smiled to himself. You could never disturb the coxswain.

'Very well. Steer zero-two-zero.' He saw the compass settle again and thought of the tense little group in the wheelhouse beneath his feet. Bob Sweeney, the quartermasters working the telegraphs and revolutions control on either side of him. The navigator's yeoman in his little allotted space with the plot-table, and a boatswain's mate at the voicepipes.

Howard added, 'We're after a sub, by the way.'

Sweeney gave a chuckle. 'Thought we might be, sir.'

'Asdic – Bridge.' It was Treherne's voice. 'Target still moving right, sir. Very slow, same bearing.'

Howard rubbed his chin. Suppose that aircraft *had* damaged one of them? This U-Boat would be off like a rabbit otherwise; they must have picked up the HE of at least one of the destroyers by now. Another trap then? He dismissed it instantly. The stakes were too high this time.

Treherne sounded as if he was concentrating every nerve. 'As before, sir. Moving right, but almost stopped.'

Bizley found that despite the streaming bridge he was still able to sweat. He stared through the gloom at Howard's motionless figure, perched on the edge of his chair where he could see and reach all that he needed.

'Aircraft, sir!'

Bizley gave a tense laugh. '*Where*, man?'

It roared directly overhead and moments later a recognition pattern of flares drifted through the rain.

Rooke said, 'It's getting brighter, sir!'

Howard nodded. A thread of silver had appeared beneath some of the clouds beyond the bows. A quick glance at the radar-repeater; both of the others were on station, *Blackwall* hanging back, ready to charge in to the attack if the manoeuvre they had trained and practised for so wearily began to go wrong.

He heard the murmur of commands over the intercom and guessed that Finlay was preparing his main armament. Just in case.

'Target seems to have stopped, sir.'

Howard looked at the radar again. Nothing. To the bridge at large he said, 'He's either shamming or damaged.' He took the intercom from Rooke and spoke briefly to the other captains. 'I'm going in. Widen your sweep for number two.' He put it down and blinked as a shaft of watery light clouded the caked salt on the glass screen. 'Captain Vickers would love this!'

He heard the snap of clips, as the yeoman bent the black flag on to the halliards.

'Come back to me, Number One.' He felt the deck shivering. Like a beast smelling something injured. 'Make to Admiralty, repeated C-in-C Western Approaches. *Am in firm contact with submarine in position whatever . . .*' He saw Rooke scribbling on a signal pad. '*Am attacking.*'

A great shadow passed overhead, the engines' roar seeming to reach them long afterwards. If the second U-Boat was still hanging about it was unlikely it would risk coming to periscope depth. It was a great comfort. Treherne was back, his eyes on the compass as *Gladiator* followed Howard's instructions.

'Steady on zero-five-zero, sir.'

'Asdic – Bridge. Target stationary, sir. Same bearing.'

Howard snapped, 'He's going to fire blind.' He leaned forward. 'Full ahead together! Stand by depth-charges and mortars!'

Up, forward, and down deep, into each rearing trough, so that the ship shook violently from truck to keel as if she were ploughing over sandbars.

'Continuous echo, sir!'

Seconds later the sea erupted astern and on either beam, and torrents of water thundered down again even as *Gladiator* made a sweeping turn to loose off her squid mortars. More violent explosions which cracked against the bilges like shellfire. Howard bent over the compass again. '*Second attack!*'

Bizley said, 'Depth-charge party not yet reported, sir.'

Even amidst this uncertainty and danger Howard wondered

why Bizley had bothered to mention it. They had not yet completed their turn, and Ayres had the best team anyone could ask for. It was probably to suggest that the young sub-lieutenant did not have the skill Bizley himself had displayed when he had been in charge down aft.

Howard put his eye to the ticking compass and gritted his teeth. *I must be getting like Number One where Bizley's concerned!*

'Steady on two-two-oh, sir!'

'Very well. Half ahead together.' He glanced through the screen in time to see *Belleisle*'s murky outline heading away, or so it appeared, as they lined up on the new course.

He saw Treherne glance at him. 'What is it, Number One?'

Treherne coughed. 'I thought I heard you say *softly, softly*?'

Howard smiled. 'Did I?' He tensed as the Asdic reported that the target was on the move again but still at reduced speed.

'Make to *Blackwall*! Attack!'

The other destroyer was thrusting over the waves, smoke trailing from her twin funnels as her revolutions mounted.

Her depth-charges seemed muffled, but Howard saw the sea churned up into tall pillars, as once again the surface seethed with the impact of the explosions.

'Stand by, Guns!'

'Asdic – Bridge. Bad interference – target's probably surfacing!'

'A- and B-guns, semi-armour piercing, load, load, load!'

Treherne was on tip-toe even though he was the tallest man in the bridge. 'Where *is* the bastard?'

The aircraft, a twin-engined Hudson bomber, roared throatily above the masthead, waggling its wings, glad to be making it a combined operation.

'*U-Boat surfacing! Starboard bow!*'

Howard flung up his glasses as the submarine's raked stem began to rise above the crests. 'Oh no, you bloody don't!' He reached for the handset. '*Open fire!*'

The two forward guns recoiled instantly, one shell exploding directly alongside the hull, the other throwing up a sheet of spray far abeam.

'Layer on! Trainer on! *Shoot!*'

The U-Boat had floundered to the surface and through his

glasses Howard could see the deep scars on the conning-tower, some broken plates where a depth-charge had made its mark.

Treherne yelled, '*Got him!*'

Howard settled his glasses on the boat's conning-tower and felt a chill run through him. The grinning shark emblem in its horned helmet seemed to be staring directly at him. Almost to himself he said, 'That's Otto Schneider's boat, Gordon. My God, we've done for one of their aces!'

Two more shells exploded against the slime-covered hull, and it gave a violent lurch and began to settle down by the bows, the cigar-shaped stern section rising from the sea to reveal the motionless screws. Nobody had appeared on the conning-tower, and when the sea reached the foot of the narrow structure which had been witness to so many sinkings, Howard saw the long columns of trophies, the one at the end being that of a corvette. Somehow he knew it was Marrack's.

He heard Treherne say thickly, 'That was the bastard who machine-gunned the lifeboats. I'd forgotten it. One of the survivors told me about the shark on the conning-tower. Sorry, sir, I just – forgot.'

'You were busy at the time.' Howard tested his own reactions but he felt neither elation nor pity. There was smoke now, probably from an electrical fire deep inside the hull. From a deadly weapon, something feared and hated, it had become a rigid coffin for Schneider and all his men.

Oily bubbles, obscene and horrific, surrounded the angled hull. The stern rose higher and higher, until it seemed to stand upright like some kind of marker, a memorial perhaps to all those this thing had killed and maimed.

Howard leaned over the voicepipe. '*Stop engines!*' He sensed the sudden confusion as the others dragged their eyes from the dying U-Boat to stare at him.

Treherne knew; or thought he did. 'Sir?'

The Hudson bomber was streaking back along its original course, a signal lamp blinking so rapidly even the yeoman could barely read it.

'*Torpedo approaching to starboard!*'

The U-Boat was about to make the final dive when the torpedo struck it and blasted the hull into great fragments, some of which were hurled high into the air by the force of the explosion.

Treherne watched the spreading arena of oil, the bubbles and the drifting pall of smoke. Far away he heard the old Hudson dropping her own charges where the other U-Boat must have been, while *Belleisle* increased speed to join in the search.

'You knew, didn't you, sir? Like that other time?'

Howard looked at him, suddenly drained when before he had felt nothing but the driving urge to find and kill the enemy.

'It was too far away. So it *had* to be an acoustic torpedo. I stopped our engines so it had nothing to home on to. Schneider's boat was the nearest thing.' He shrugged and even that made his shoulders ache. 'Someone up there likes us quite a lot, Number One.' He turned as the *Blackwall* split the morning apart with her shrill whistle. 'Slow ahead together. Signal the others to take station as before.'

Treherne gripped his hand. 'I'd never have believed it if anyone had told me!'

Howard watched Rooke laying off a new course, his fingers deftly working with ruler and pencil, but his mind still ringing to that last moment of triumph. He had probably not even thought of how near they had all been to joining Schneider's coffin on the bottom.

Schneider had been one of a few U-Boat commanders who had risen above their secret, faceless existence. Theirs was a dangerous war, and many more would pay with their lives for trying to reach just one target too many. But Schneider's reputation had been more than that of courage and success. It had created fear. He had even put down neutral ships, when there had been any neutrals left in this war, and was said to be dedicated, as if it was some private mission.

Howard walked to the rear of the bridge and stared down at the narrow shining deck, where Ayres and his men were all laughing and slapping each other on the back while they reloaded their racks. As well they might, he thought with sudden pride. Schoolboys and tradesmen against one of Hitler's crack commanders.

Treherne watched him light his pipe, saw the way his fingers were quite firm as he tamped down the tobacco and watched the smoke streaming over the bridge ladder.

'Fall out action stations, Number One. Our old Hudson will be sniffing around until it's relieved . . . I don't think even that bloody kraut will risk another attack.'

'You think it was the same one that almost got us before, don't you, sir?'

'Maybe.' He rubbed his eyes. 'See if you can rustle up some sandwiches, will you?'

He thought of Treherne's question and knew he had deliberately avoided it. Such things did not happen in wartime. He thought suddenly of Marrack and his little ship.

He said quietly, 'It was just for you, *Number One*.'

In spite of all the buzzes and informed sources, HM Destroyer *Gladiator* did not return to Liverpool in time for Christmas; nor did she remain in Gladstone Dock long enough to welcome the New Year. But not to celebrate their brief return and all they had achieved was out of the question, so a wardroom party was hastily arranged to fall somewhere in between.

Howard had no idea just how many people had been invited, nor did he expect *Gladiator*'s wardroom to be able to cope. A mass of figures, some from the other ships in the group, friends from Western Approaches HQ, and many more who had worked on their behalf in the bitter months and years of the same endless battle.

The boss did not come himself although he had sent for Howard personally to congratulate him on his success as Vickers's second-in-command, and particularly his attack on Schneider's U-Boat and its destruction. Max Horton made no secret of the fact that it was a perfect example of his own strategy, the true co-operation between air and sea forces, something which had once been virtually unknown. Howard had learned that the salvage tug had finally reached her objective and, with air cover from the carrier *Seeker*, had got the big oil tanker safely into harbour.

Howard pushed his way through the throng, shaking hands, seeing faces he knew well, others he knew not at all. Captain Vickers towered above everybody, and was seen to place each empty glass on the overhead vent trunking. It was to be hoped that Vallance took them down before the ship left harbour again.

Then at long last he saw Celia by the door, Ayres pointing towards him to show her the way.

She gasped, 'Sorry I'm late. Last minute flap.' She removed her hat and shook out her curls. 'What a scrum! "Auntie" will be along later!' She took a glass from a messman's tray and looked at him, her eyes very green. For a few seconds the place was empty but for them, the din around the wardroom no more of an intrusion than the normal sounds of the sea.

She said, 'You look wonderful. I'm selfish – I want you to myself.' She glanced at the nearest guests. 'They like you a lot, David. Auntie's chaps think you're the greatest!' She laughed and held his arm. 'When your signal arrived I just sat there and prayed. I'm so *proud* of you. Of everything about you.' She touched the two ribbons on his jacket. 'I love you so much it hurts!'

She saw Treherne pushing through the crowd with a pretty-looking girl in a brightly coloured dress.

Howard waved to them. 'That's Joyce. They're getting spliced quite soon.'

'Oh, David.' She dropped her eyes. 'I went down to Hampshire while you were away – it was official but I made a detour to see your – ' She hesitated, then faced him again. '*Our* house. Your friend Mister Mills is doing a fine job with the builders.' He felt her grip tighten on his arm as she whispered against his ear, 'We shall make love there!'

He led her across the wardroom until they had reached Vickers.

'Here she is, sir.'

Vickers swooped down and kissed her cheek. 'Lucky devil, David!'

He glanced at Howard's DSO ribbon and said, 'I gather that the official presentation is to be made in the New Year, by HM the K no less.'

The girl said, 'Will you take me, David?'

'Of course he will!' Vickers signalled to Vallance with a glass, mostly to avoid coming eye-to-eye with Lieutenant Bizley. What a bloody difference, he thought. He had been discussing Bizley earlier with his friend, the assistant to the chief of staff. It would be interesting to hear his views when he arrived for the party and saw the lieutenant for himself. Bizley was looking a bit the worse for wear, he thought. His face was red and shining, and Vickers guessed he had been drinking more than he should.

Captain Naish had told him the bones of the Special Branch report on the matter. They had run the other survivor from Bizley's motor gunboat to earth; he had been given a Mention-in-Despatches for his part in the affair. Just as Vickers had suggested when it had first been raised, the man had stuck to his guns, and had backed up Bizley's own account of the sinking, and the deaths of her small company. But he had made one thing very clear. He had been obeying Bizley's orders, and had been too busy lowering the float to see what had happened on the bridge. 'So there's an end to the bloody matter, Ernle. I'm only sorry it took so long!'

Naish had stared at him with amazement when he had retorted, 'Why not ask Bizley himself? I really don't see why we have to build a battleship to sink a ruddy dinghy!'

Vickers said abruptly, 'Maybe Captain Naish can't come, David. Would you like to say your piece before all your guests are awash? A bit of grub might do wonders then!'

Howard looked at the girl beside him. 'Ready, Celia? Can you stand it?'

She smiled and replied nervously, 'I am my father's daughter. We've shared everything since we came together.'

Howard caught Treherne's eye and the bearded lieutenant banged loudly on the pantry counter with a pewter tankard.

Eventually there was silence and Treherne said, 'I'm not one for speeches.' He looked across at them. 'But as Number One of this ship . . .'

Someone called, 'Couldn't they do any better, Gordon?'

Treherne ignored him. 'In a day or so we shall be at sea again, so in a fashion this is our way of welcoming 1944 and the hopes which will come with it. In the last twelve months we've lost a lot of good friends, and seen many a fine ship torn to ribbons out there on the Western Ocean.' He had their full attention now, and Howard saw a young Wren wiping her eyes with her handkerchief. *Part of the team.*

'I've been at sea all my life, and I'm a hell of a lot older than most of you here. I've seen a lot of places, done a lot of things, some of which I'm not too proud of now.' He reached behind his back and took Joyce's hand in his. 'But I'd never been afraid, you see, not really *afraid* until I came to the Atlantic. With respect to senior officers present, never mind what *they* tell us, I think we've turned the corner, and next year the enemy will be on the run!'

He waited for some cheering to die down and added soberly, 'For my part, I owe my sanity and survival to one man, and he's right here with us now.' He raised a big hand. 'I think our captain wishes to say something, for he's the one I referred to. Escort duty is the worst there is, and the Atlantic is a sewer where war is stealth, survival and murder.' He raised a glass steadily and stared at Howard across the others. 'You happen to be the bravest, most decent man I have ever met.' He turned away, unable to continue.

Celia gripped Howard's arm. 'Oh, David, I'm so glad to be here.'

There were claps and cheers as Howard stepped up on to the fireplace.

'Thank you, Number One. I could have made almost the same speech about you.' They raised their glasses to one another and he continued, 'We all know what we have done, what we might be required to do in 1944. Having a command is often, necessarily, a lonely job, so you learn to share your emotions when the pressure is temporarily removed.' He took her hand and helped her up beside him. 'So please share this particular miracle with us. What better place to announce our engagement, what better company too . . .' The rest was drowned by a wave of cheering and stamping feet. It was so loud, in fact, that not even Vallance saw Rooke, who was OOD, signalling frantically from the doorway.

Captain Vickers turned as the din of cheering faded away and saw his friend Captain Naish looking at him with quiet satisfaction.

He was ushered to the fireplace and after shaking hands with Howard and his girl he turned and faced the others; rather like a judge about to make a summing-up, Howard thought.

Naish said, 'Needless to say I add my congratulations to our young captain and his lovely Wren. I'm a bit late, but I didn't want to interrupt what I heard from the passageway.' His eyes settled on Treherne. 'I think you expressed it better than any politician,' he gave a dry cough, 'or *senior officer* for that matter!'

He looked around at their faces, young but old, tired but somehow elated by what they had seen and shared.

'I have to tell you, gentlemen, we have received a signal from Admiral Fraser's flagship *Duke of York*, which reports that yesterday he met with, and after a fierce engagement, destroyed the German battle-cruiser *Scharnhorst* off North Cape.' In the stunned silence he sought out Treherne again and said, 'We have indeed "turned the corner"!'

Vickers remarked, 'North Cape, in winter. The poor devils.'

Naish said coldly, 'Only three were picked up from the *Hood*, remember?'

Howard heard the exchange and wondered. Vickers, the fighting destroyer captain who had been in the thick of it for four years and yet could still find compassion for a brave and determined enemy. Naish, on the other hand, saw nothing but the impossible prize which this victory at sea might offer. Was it because it was harder to send others to fight than to face the immediate brutality of war? He knew he might never understand, and for a moment longer, would not care too much.

There was so much noise now as the stewards and messmen were struggling to lay out great trays of sausage rolls, sandwiches and other goodies, Howard doubted if anyone saw them leave; and together they walked along the deserted iron deck, with the noise of the wardroom party still ringing in their ears.

There was a moon of sorts, playing a will-o'-the-wisp game as it floated from one fast cloud to another. The ship's fittings stood out stark and black against the sky; the whaler's davits, and the rolled scrambling nets where men had clung to be rescued or had drowned within seconds of safety. The guns, covered to hide their smoke-stained muzzles, still reminders of Finlay's action against the last U-Boat.

There was more noise coming aft from the forecastle where they were trying to celebrate Christmas and the New Year all at once.

A gangway sentry straightened his back as he saw them.

Howard paused. 'They looking after you all right, Glossop?' He need not have asked; he could smell the rum at four paces.

The sentry bobbed his head. 'Er, congratulations, sir, an' miss. Just 'eard!'

She touched his arm. 'Thank you.'

They moved on and knew the sentry was staring after them.

They paused again by the guardrails, at the place where Treherne had suggested the midshipman had thrown himself over. Even that no longer seemed real, or relevant. That was his other world.

She was staring at him, her face very pale in the eerie light. 'It's hard to imagine what it's like when . . .' She looked at the motionless guns, the empty mountings. 'So still. At peace.' She faced him again and he could imagine her expression even though the moonlight had gone again.

'Up there.' She looked towards the square, uncompromising shape of the bridge. 'Where you are at sea.' Her voice faltered just once. 'Next time, I'd like to *know*. So that I can be there with you when you reach out for me.'

Together they climbed the icy rungs to the bridge, pausing to look into the gleaming, empty wheelhouse, where men had fought, hated and known fear. The only sound came from the W/T office where a solitary telegraphist was reading a magazine and eating a bun. He did not even see them.

She gripped his shoulders and said, 'All the way. Please?'

It was bitterly cold on the upper bridge, everything damp to the touch. They were lying outboard of two other destroyers, but they could have been deserted as they lay in the silent shadows.

He guided her to the high bridge chair and wiped it with a cloth before lifting her on to it.

She kissed him then, and they clung together for a long time.

Then she allowed him to help her down again and stood for a few more moments looking around at the distorted shapes and reflections, so that she would remember.

She said quietly, 'I shall be here. When you need me. Now that I know.'

They made their way down to the main deck again and she said, 'You'll never be alone again.'

A blacked-out tug surged past and *Gladiator* swayed very slightly against the other vessels.

She put her hand on the guardrail. It was as if the ship was stirring herself. Eager to leave and get back to the only life she knew.

Not yet. Not yet. I've only just found him.

Another year was just over the horizon; nobody could foretell what it might bring, what pain it could offer.

But for the two figures merged together by the guardrail, this was reward enough.

EPILOGUE

1944

Howard lay quite stiff and unmoving on the top of his small bunk as the telephone shattered his dream like an explosion.

It was Finlay, who was OOW. 'Sorry to bother you, sir, but Captain Vickers would like to talk on the intercom.'

'I'll come up.' How many hundreds of times had he said that? He swung his legs from the bunk and stared for a few seconds at the new cap with its bright oak leaves around the peak, which waited to remind him of what had happened. When he caught sight of himself in reflection or a mirror he barely recognised himself. A young face, with a commander's cap. Although he wore his old sea-going jacket the bright new stripes on that, too, seemed to accentuate a complete change. He stared around the tiny sea cabin. Even that thrust at his heart like a knife.

Vickers had been firm about it. 'Things have changed, David. New ships, fresh equipment and still not enough experienced officers to take command. The Navy's your career, and this accelerated promotion can do you nothing but good. You'll be an asset to your next assignment.'

He could still hear his own voice, protesting. 'What about *Gladiator*, sir?'

Just for a moment Vickers's tone had softened. 'With *Garnet*, she's to be cut down to a long-range escort. You know the idea; it's been very useful with some of the older destroyers, the V and W's for instance. *Gladiator* has a lot of good service to offer, but as a destroyer, with a commander on the bridge – well, I'm afraid that's over, or will be after the next convoy.'

Howard made his way to the upper bridge and looked across

at *Kinsale*'s hazy outline. It was strange weather, cold up here, but the air was almost humid when you stood out of the Atlantic wind. It was nearly August, but the ocean was as grey as ever, the great unbroken troughs stretching away into the late afternoon sunlight like moving glass. Where had the last months gone? He thought of the wardroom party; Celia, with his ring on her hand; the moments of peace and happiness.

Then on to more troop convoys, from Canada and the United States, the final build-up which had exploded across the world's headlines on a bitter cold day in June, when the Allied armies had landed in Normandy, the shores of Hitler's West Wall, and were even now fanning across France towards the Low Countries, and south towards the Cherbourg Peninsula. The German High Command would have no choice but to evacuate their Biscay submarine bases, and return once more to their homeland. Otherwise the bases and pens would be cut off by the advancing armies and overwhelmed.

It would be a bitter pill for the U-Boat men to swallow. After all their successes, their near-victory in the Atlantic, they would have to withdraw to the old bases in Germany, with the dreaded Rosegarden to face once again.

Howard picked up the handset and heard Vickers say, 'Did I get you out of bed, David?'

Howard smiled. It was not Vickers's fault. It was nobody's. He glanced around the familiar bridge. So many hours; filthy nights, burning ships, dying sailors.

'What can I do, sir?'

'I've had a top-secret signal from the Admiralty. Two convoys are passing one another tonight, as you know; we shall be standing by to offer extra support. The fortieth escort group and a carrier are doing the same to the north.'

Howard waited. He knew all this. After tomorrow they would be heading back for Liverpool. He felt the catch in his throat. *Gladiator*'s final passage as a true destroyer, and his own last days in command.

Vickers continued, 'You read the reports about the *Burmese Princess* — well, something's gone wrong apparently. She's had a complete power-failure.'

Howard signalled quickly to Finlay for a pad and pulled a pencil from his pocket as Vickers gave him the ship's reported position. He saw that Treherne had arrived on the bridge as if he had sensed something unusual.

Vickers said, 'I hate to send you, but I'm needed here. It'll give them a bit of a boost if you're standing by. Air cover *will* be provided.'

'I'm on my way, sir.' He handed the intercom to Finlay as Treherne asked, 'Trouble, sir?' His eyes were on Howard's new cap as if he did not accept the change either.

'Put this position on the chart. About a hundred miles west of the Irish coast. We're going to offer support.'

Treherne's eyes sharpened as he studied the pad. '*Burmese Princess*. I remember her well. She used to be on the Far East run from Southampton. A cargo-liner – I never liked the mixture!'

'Well, she's not any more, Number One.' He watched him steadily. 'She's a hospital ship now.' She was packed with wounded soldiers, some from the Normandy landings in June, others, more badly injured, from the invasions of Sicily and Italy last year. Her power defect had slowed her passage considerably, and whereas hospital ships were usually left alone by U-Boats, unless escorted, this change of timing might lay her wide open to attack.

Treherne bent over the chart table. 'We should make contact around dawn, sir. No U-Boats reported in that area. All after the two convoys, I expect.'

'Very well, Number One. Course to intercept. Make to *Kinsale, Hate to leave you*.'

The reply winked back across the heaving, shining swell. '*Parting is such sweet sorrow. Good luck*.'

Treherne said, 'At least we might be back in the Pool before the others!'

Howard climbed into his chair and imagined her sitting on it. Holding her in his arms in this place which must have brought home to her his world; the daily acceptance of danger.

They had set the date for their marriage in October, when, Vickers had hinted, there would be some leave going. After that? He touched the rough grey steel. Not back to *Gladiator* again. Not ever.

He thought of the Normandy invasion. Did it mean that this would be the last summer at war? Was that just possible?

'I've been thinking, Number One.' He looked at him gravely. 'If I made a special request through Captain Vickers, would you be prepared to take command of her?'

Treherne saw the pain in his eyes. *He really loves this ship.* Treherne had known that almost from the beginning, but it was still a shock to see it in Howard's face, hear it in his question.

'Well, you know how I feel about a command, sir.'

'But *Gladiator*'s not just any ship.'

'I know it, sir.'

'Then at least think about it before we get in.'

Treherne watched as Bizley climbed into the bridge to relieve the OOW. He looked very strained, but his tone was haughty as ever as he took the con from Finlay.

Vickers had confided in Howard about the enquiries by the Special Branch. 'Would have told you before, but . . .'

That one word *but* counted for such a lot in this Navy, he thought. True or false, it mattered little. If Bizley's story was a lie, nothing could shift him from it now. He would be more insufferable than ever. Even that jolted Howard badly. Bizley would be someone else's responsibility after the next two days or so.

He tried to settle himself more comfortably as Finlay strode from the bridge, after giving Bizley a chilling glance. They would all be split up. Except the Chief, and the Gunner (T). Finlay was going on a long gunnery course, and Ayres to Portland for anti-submarine training. Bizley would probably be advanced to first lieutenant in some other escort, while Treherne . . . Perhaps he might change his mind. Howard looked at the scarred paint, the tarnished instruments nearby. She needed someone who understood.

The ship went to action stations to test guns and prepare for the night, then the starboard watch closed-up for defence stations as was usual. Gallons of tea and cocoa, greasy sausages and tinned potatoes. Men came and went about their duties, the ocean and the radar empty of surprises.

Howard dozed in his chair, awakening occasionally as W/T reported there was fog in their vicinity. But it was patchy, and when they drove through it they saw it clinging to the radar and rigging like ragged spectres.

It was sometime before dawn when the radar picked up the

other ship, adrift, and as they were soon to discover, without lights or power. Usually the sides of hospital ships were brightly lit to display their white hulls and huge red crosses, a protection which, for the most part, had been successful. Hospital ships which had fallen to enemy action had been sunk by aircraft, dive-bombers, where there were only seconds to distinguish the difference.

Howard stood at the forepart of the bridge. 'Slow ahead together. Steer zero-six-zero.' Should be able to see her soon. To the yeoman he added, 'Be ready to call her up.'

Aircraft today, Vickers had said. Then what? A ship the size of the *Burmese Princess* probably carried several hundred wounded men. A tug might be needed.

He called to Treherne, 'Clear lower deck, Number One. Don't worry – I'm not sending you across this time!'

Treherne waited for the order to be piped, the watch below to come bustling on deck. Howard said, 'I could try to take her in tow. But it might be construed as an act of war by the enemy.'

'Ship, sir! Port bow!'

'All right, Yeoman!'

The Aldis lamp clattered noisily, the flash seemingly extra bright in the misty darkness.

A torch flashed back to them and the yeoman muttered, 'God, their power really *is* kaput!'

Howard watched the other ship looming out of the gloom; a cargo-liner as Treherne had described, and now that they were closer he could see the pale hull, ghostly against the moving water. He switched on the loud-hailer, his voice metallic as it boomed against the other ship and back again. '*Burmese Princess* ahoy! This is the destroyer *Gladiator*! What is the trouble?'

The other man sounded miles away, and was probably using a megaphone. 'Generator fault, Captain! It was good of you to come! These poor soldiers are being rolled about with no way on the ship!'

'How many?'

'Five hundred, Captain, bound for Halifax!' He seemed to brighten up and shouted, 'My chief has just reported that he's nearly ready to proceed!'

Rooke said, 'Generators – what a time to happen!'

Treherne retorted coldly, 'She's about twenty-five years old, Pilot! I reckon she's earned a bit of a rest!'

Bizley stood by the compass platform, thinking of his earlier fears. Nothing had happened. It had all been for nothing. When he got shot of this ship he would go and see Sarah. He was in the clear. What did they know about it anyway? He felt his confidence returning like the glow of vodka.

They were almost alongside now, the other ship rising above *Gladiator*'s deck like a cliff. There was a faint sound of machinery, and someone down aft gave a cheer. At any moment the sides would light up again; her errand of mercy would continue.

'Aircraft, sir!'

Three flares dropped from the clouds, and the yeoman triggered off an acknowledgement. A Coastal Command Hudson was circling around, widening its search area as it rumbled away into the distance, satisfied that help was on hand.

'Asdic – Bridge!'

Howard ducked down. 'Captain!'

'Strong contact at one-six-zero, sir. *Closing*!'

Treherne gasped, 'Christ, a sitting duck!'

Howard yelled, 'Full ahead together!' He stared through the screen as the other ship began to slide past. 'Tell W/T! Signal Admiralty, repeated C-in-C!'

'Both engines full ahead, sir. Steady on zero-six-zero!'

'Warn depth-charge party, Number One! Guns, stand by to engage!'

Gladiator was drawing well ahead of the hospital ship when the helm started to go over. Suction from the larger vessel, a mechanical defect – who could tell? Tilting right over, just as the photograph had portrayed her on her first trials, she charged across the *Burmese Princess*'s bows, so close that had the larger ship been under way she would have sliced them in half.

Howard did not hear the torpedo as it hit the forecastle, but he was flung to the deck, buried by tons of water that stank of explosive. He tried to pull himself to his feet but cried out as pain took away his breath and left him too dazed to move. He was aware of lights in the sky, the rising scream of aero engines as the aircraft tore down to the attack. More explosions, bombs or depth-charges he did not know; it could even be beneath him in the hull itself.

Treherne was helping him up, and even as he propped him against the tall chair Howard knew the deck was already at an angle.

'Tell the Chief! Clear the engine room!' He dragged himself to the screen and looked over at the forecastle. There was nothing forward of B-gun. Just jagged metal where the blast had torn it away. Men were calling and running, and Howard remembered that he had cleared the lower deck. *Had he known that too?* Had the ship known, and shown her anger by turning to block the torpedo's path?

Someone shouted, 'They got that bloody U-Boat!' Then he broke off, sobbing, as he cried, 'It's *me*, Tom – speak to me, for Christ's sake!'

'Assess and report damage.'

Treherne stayed with him. 'I'll get the Doc.' Howard shook his head and fought against the pain. He must not faint now. He had trained all his life for this. The one thing that they all hoped would never happen. His mind would not accept it even though he knew *Gladiator* was finished.

'Just my ribs, Gordon . . . Christ, what a mess!'

There was a banshee screech of steam as the chief released the pressure on the boilers. Thank God he was safe. Another dread; it had happened to so many.

'Bulkheads are holding, sir.' Rooke held the telephone to his ear but watched the instruments fall from his table as the list increased.

'Make sure the depth-charges are at safe – pitch the primers over board!'

Finlay had arrived. 'All done. I can't find Ayres though.' He stepped aside as the PO steward ran on to the bridge and helped to support Howard against the chair. 'I've got the photo of yer dad, sir. In the oilskin bag.' He was shivering, talking rapidly to conceal his terror. 'Will we be all right, sir?'

Treherne said, 'Shall I send the confidential books over the side, sir?'

He wanted to shout at Howard. *She's done for, can't you see? You've tried, but there's nothing more we can do except save ourselves.* Instead he said, quite calmly, 'Time to move.'

Howard peered at him. Celia would see it as she had seen all the others. Little black crosses. The secretary of the Admiralty regrets to announce the loss of HMS *Gladiator*. Next of kin have been informed.

Oh God, not for Celia! Not again!

He said between his teeth, 'Muster the hands.' He winced as the aircraft thundered overhead again; he realised that it was getting much brighter, with the hard, pitiless light adding to the shock and destruction.

And the chief was here now, hatless and with grease on his face, his eyes everywhere as if he felt unsafe up here on the bridge.

'Thanks, Chief. I'm glad you got your people out.' He groaned as the deck gave a lurch and something heavy came adrift between decks.

Price said, 'That bulkhead'll not hold, sir. I've had a look. It's weeping water like fury.'

'Very well. Clear the bridge, Number One. You take charge on deck.'

Treherne looked at him grimly. 'Guns can deal with that. I'm staying with you.'

Howard held on to his shoulder and nodded heavily. 'The old firm, eh?'

At the break in the forecastle some of the hands were already preparing to lower the whaler; the motor boat on the opposite side would not budge as the davits had buckled in the blast like cardboard.

The Buffer was striding about and turned as his friend the coxswain, with the wheelhouse party, joined him on the iron deck.

He grinned. 'Finished with engines, 'Swain?'

Sweeney looked at the dark lapping water and sighed. 'Too bloody old for this caper. It's a job in the barracks for me!'

Moffatt was kneeling on the sloping deck, his knees torn on the cracked plating as he knelt over Sub-Lieutenant Ayres.

'Get this officer to a raft, Buffer!'

Knocker White peered down at him. The bandages made it worse, he thought. Ayres had lost an arm and a leg in the explosion. It would be kinder to leave him with the ship. But he shouted, 'Dobson, Bully Bishop, over here at the double!'

Drugged though he was Ayres seemed to know what was happening. '*Help me.* I can't feel anything!' He was still whimpering when they carried him away.

Bizley felt sick, from fear or from shock he did not know. They would be safe, those who had survived. The hospital ship was right here, a helpless spectator, but with boats and men in plenty. When they got back he would make the most of his survivor's leave and then – he clapped his hand to his pocket. *The medal.* His precious DSC was still in his cabin!

'Take charge, Cox'n!' He ran aft up the rising slope; the others did not even see him go.

It was frightening and eerie between decks. All the familiar places and memories. Shattered crockery and a puddle of coffee in the pantry, the wardroom curtains standing out from their rails at stiff, unreal angles. He slithered to a halt by his cabin and stared as Leading Seaman Fernie, carrying a large flashlight, came up the deck towards him.

'What are *you* doing here?'

Fernie faced him wearily. 'What does it look like?'

'When we get back, you'll bloody well regret this! My record is *clean*, do you hear?' He laughed and Fernie smelled the vodka.

He watched Bizley stagger into his cabin and drag at a drawer to find the little box he prized above all else.

Fernie heard the torpedo gunner's mate shout down the hatch. 'Come up from there, Fernie! We're baling out!' His head vanished.

Fernie felt the rage rushing through him, consuming him like blazing fuel on the sea.

With unexpected swiftness he swung the cabin door shut and threw on the emergency clips. He heard the frantic hammering, the faint shouts turn to screams, and then he walked away and up the ladder, sealing that hatch, too, behind him.

The ship shook again, and men huddled together in the inflated life-jackets while the lowered whaler pitched alongside, oars and boathooks ready to fend off the torn metal.

On the bridge Finlay stood against the flag lockers, with their upended bunting strewn around as if there had been a wild party.

'Boat and rafts lowered, sir. I'm afraid we had to bring Dick Ayres back inboard.' He sounded suddenly at a loss. 'He just died. Three more killed, and Lieutenant Bizley is missing.'

Again the bridge seemed to shake itself and Howard said, 'Give us a hand, Gordon.'

Treherne looked at him in the strange light. 'If it's any use, sir . . . I *would* have accepted your offer – as it is – well, she doesn't need any of us any more.'

The three of them followed Vallance down to the side deck where it was almost impossible to stand. The after part must be right out of the water, the screws stopped as Schneider's U-Boat had been.

'*Easy*, sir!' Treherne watched despairingly as Howard tried to turn and look at his ship. At any second that bulkhead would go, but he stopped to listen as Howard said in a whisper, 'You were right, Number One. When you came back from that ammunition ship. It *is* like death.'

The whaler and floats paddled clear of the side while the boat tried to tow clusters of swimmers to safety from the inevitable undertow.

Howard sat propped in a big Carley float, Treherne holding his shoulders, Evan Price supporting him on the other side. The old firm, here to see her go. The last rites.

There was cheering too, waves and waves of it, and Treherne said quietly, 'It's the squaddies on the hospital ship. Look at them. Lining the rails, those who can stand, poor devils. They know she did it for them.'

Price said tersely, 'Oh God, there she goes!'

There was a devastating crack and *Gladiator* began to slide quickly into that churning whirlpool they had witnessed so often.

Then just as quickly, she was gone, with the sea still boiling as if she might yet burst up again with her old defiance.

As if to mark the end, all the hospital ship's lights came on, and after a further hesitation she began to lower her boats to assist.

Did ships really have souls? Was it because of pride that *Gladiator* had acted as she had, rather than face the ignominious saws and torches of some dockyard?

Howard let his head fall back against Treherne's shoulder and stared at the clouds. He would tell Celia all about it. How they had lost the last battle; but had saved so many.

With a strong hand, even to the end.